Hopelessly addicted to esp[...]
Kristine Lynn pens high-s[...]
wee morning hours before [...]
Oregon college. Luckily, the stakes there aren't as
dire. When she's not grading, writing, or searching
for the perfect vanilla latte, she can be found on the
hiking trails behind her home with her daughter and
puppy. She'd love to connect on X, Facebook, or
Instagram.

Louisa Heaton lives on Hayling Island, Hampshire,
with her husband, four children and a small zoo. She
has worked in various roles in the health industry—
most recently four years as a community first
responder, answering 999 calls. When not writing
Louisa enjoys other creative pursuits, including
reading, quilting and patchwork—usually instead of
the things she *ought* to be doing!

WEDDING DATE WITH DR PETRIDES

KRISTINE LYNN

NEW YEAR TO NINE-MONTH SURPRISE

LOUISA HEATON

MILLS & BOON

First published in Great Britain 2025
by Mills & Boon, an imprint of HarperCollins*Publishers* Ltd,
1 London Bridge Street, London, SE1 9GF

www.harpercollins.co.uk

HarperCollins*Publishers* Macken House, 39/40 Mayor Street Upper,
Dublin 1, D01 C9W8, Ireland

Wedding Date with Dr Petrides © 2025 Harlequin Enterprises ULC

New Year to Nine-Month Surprise © 2025 Harlequin Enterprises ULC

Special thanks and acknowledgement are given to
Kristine Lynn and Louisa Heaton for their contributions to
the Royal York Hospital miniseries.

ISBN: 978-0-263-32526-3

12/25

MIX
Paper | Supporting
responsible forestry
FSC™ C007454

This book contains FSC™ certified paper
and other controlled sources to ensure responsible forest management.

For more information visit www.harpercollins.co.uk/green.

Printed and Bound in the UK using 100% Renewable Electricity
at CPI Group (UK) Ltd, Croydon, CR0 4YY

WEDDING DATE WITH DR PETRIDES

KRISTINE LYNN

MILLS & BOON

For J.P.

If we hadn't met, this book would have been written *soooo* much faster ;). But life would also be that much less lovely. You're a good problem to have...

CHAPTER ONE

DR. ARES PETRIDES let the joy of Christmas calm the edge he'd been feeling since that morning. The tree, finally secured in the reception area of the Royal York Hospital, was rewrapped in festive lights, and now had brightly covered presents beneath it for the children in the pediatric ward. The scents of pine, cinnamon and cloves were somehow present, as if the magic of the season could control when and where molecules could travel.

The piano Christmas music piped in through the overhead speakers added to the holiday feel. He might be at work preparing for the unknowns a holiday could bring to the Accident & Emergency department, but it didn't matter. Ares loved Christmas, a time for giving and receiving love, even if what kind of love had transitioned throughout his life.

He traced a thumb over his phone, where he'd received the information that his past was about to collide with his future in a matter of days.

If only his family could understand that just because he didn't want what they wanted for him—namely a wife and kids to carry on his Greek lineage—it didn't mean he lived a loveless life. How else would they describe the very real desire to save lives in the A&E? It was the purest kind of love there was, to give everything of himself to someone from whom he stood to gain nothing.

But that was the rub, wasn't it? He *had* wanted that kind of love, but not if it was going to compete with his actual passion—being a doctor. He also hadn't wanted a family on his parents' terms, which meant Greek babies with a Greek woman…and living in Greece. They even had a woman picked out for him, and he'd gone along with it for as long as he could. Ariadne was a lovely woman, but just not for him. That she'd been collateral damage in the war between what he wanted and what his parents wanted for him was tragic—especially since it caused a rift between their two families, who had been friends for centuries, it seemed.

After the breakup, his parents made it abundantly clear they wanted nothing to do with him if he didn't marry and start making those Greek babies.

So, he'd left.

Which was how he found himself alone or with colleagues every Christmas holiday.

He didn't mind. Especially since things had more or less gone back to normal at the hospital the past few days after the excitement at the beginning of the month.

In fact, the whole festive scene in front of him almost erased the monumental disaster that had preceded the holiday. The irony of a hospital Christmas tree falling on Kyle Windgate—a local celebrity who'd won a national singing competition, the *Great British Sing-Off*—and injuring him wasn't lost on the staff of the Royal York Hospital. It made for interesting drama to joke about with Ruby Phillips, his fellow A&E physician and best friend.

Ares and Ruby had been called to the A&E that night to perform surgery on the tree-falling victim. That he was now famous didn't bode well, but Ares liked the guy. He was kind, funny and played a helluva guitar.

Since the Royal York seemed prone to that kind of drama, the two of them had a running joke about filming a reality television show there. Now that there had been twenty-four-hour film crews posted outside the hospital since December 1, thanks to the Great Christmas Tree Disaster, as they'd dubbed it, the joke had lost a bit of its luster.

Thankfully, he and Ruby didn't let it sway the fun they had together on shift. He still chided her about everything from her snack to television choices. He wasn't so elitist he couldn't enjoy a good romantic comedy from time to time, but those modern dating shows were trash. And the snack cakes she ingested by the handful on busy nights at the A&E? She was a physician and had to know how unhealthy they were.

Not that she was unhealthy in any other way he could see. No, Ruby was that rare kind of woman who looked better without makeup, and somehow made surgical scrubs look as alluring as a cocktail dress. She was stunning, only ten centimeters shy of his two-meter frame, but slim, with a honey-blond bob that framed the creamy skin of her face, and piercing gray eyes that seemed to peer into the soul of whomever she was speaking to. To top it off, she was sweet and caring, not to mention she had a sense of humor that could level him with fits of giggles unbefitting a man of his upbringing.

Which was why he couldn't get over Byron leaving her over something as silly as a busy schedule all those years ago. The loss had rocked her, and from what Ares could tell, she hadn't had a serious boyfriend since, focusing on work instead of the string of bad dates she'd been on. Anyone could see how dedicated Ruby was to helping others, which to him was something that made her more attractive, not less.

Ares swallowed, but his throat was suddenly thick and dry.

No way was it because imagining Ruby in scrubs and other clothing led to thinking of her in no clothing at all.

Theos, he needed to get laid if he'd dipped back into lusting after Ruby territory. It wasn't the first time that'd happened. How could it not, when she was as gorgeous as she was and their friendship had evolved into one of deep, meaningful conversation?

He wasn't uninterested, just…not interested in dating, period. Not anymore. He'd made his choice and his life was good. Fine. Even if he changed his mind, sure, maybe Ruby would be the type of woman he'd be into, but jeopardizing their friendship was a nonnegotiable. She was the best part of his day, and he wouldn't risk that for a chance their chemistry extended to the bedroom.

Though, even his buddies from work, Ryan—the head of midwifery—and Noa—one of Royal York's pediatric docs—questioned their friendship. According to the guys, Ruby and Ares had to have had an illicit affair at some point the way they teased and laughed and shared intimate inside jokes. There was no way two people with a platonic friendship who teased like they did and were single hadn't banged.

Ares smiled, thinking about the last time he and Ruby had joked about that. Maybe one day, they'd mess with their friends and pretend to flirt at the nurses' station, see what rumors they could dredge up. But again, why bother with what anyone else thought? The two of them knew what they were—and what they weren't—and that was all that mattered.

"Penny for your thoughts?" a silky voice interrupted his stroll down memory lane.

"They were about you, actually," he said, nudging Ruby with his hip. Was the star on the top of the tree crooked? He couldn't tell, but he wasn't about to fix it if it was. The tree may have been all but bolted to the floorboards now, but it was a bad-luck omen as far as Ares was concerned.

"Oh yeah? About how amazing and talented and all around awesome I am?"

He turned to face her, and his thoughts got stuck in his throat, which was still dry as the dunes on Lemnos. Maybe he was coming down with something. Or maybe it was because something about Ruby's smile was different. Was she wearing lip gloss? And her eyes... He'd never seen her in the mascara and light eye shadow she wore. The combination made the gray orbs look like oracles.

He had a few questions he'd ask them if he could...

"As a matter of fact, that's exactly what I was thinking. Remember our first Christmas on shift together? You hated me and almost made me rethink the magic of the holiday."

She laughed, and it tickled a place in his chest that made him uncomfortable. For some reason, it made him think of the text his mother had sent earlier, but ultimately, he ignored both.

"Well, you were a jerk who took my surgery."

"I had two more years of experience over you."

"In another hospital. It doesn't count. And I was reeling from a breakup." *Yeah, to a jerk who never deserved you in the first place.* She ripped open a snack cake and he groaned.

"You're kidding, right? It's barely breakfast time. On Christmas Day."

Ruby took a bite.

"What? I don't see what's wrong with cake for break-fast." She smiled, chocolate fudge coating her teeth. He chuckled. "Besides, it's five o'clock somewhere."

"That's for whisky."

She rolled her head, her bob held perfectly in place. Why was he curious to know what she looked like all mussed up after sleep or vigorous exercise? Not exactly best-friend thoughts.

"Fine. Anyway, I forgot my breakfast at home and since everything in York is closed for the holiday, and our hos-pital pastries are at least a week old, I raided my stash. I'm not as bougie as you, Dr. Petrides."

He winced. Anytime anyone mentioned his family's wealth or status, it set him on edge. It wasn't *his* wealth, *his* status. And he'd run from it the first moment he could, hadn't he?

Just not far enough, a voice from his subconscious chimed in. No, as it turned out, there was no place too far for him to run from his heritage and duty. He and Ariadne might be no more than memories, but his parents' wishes haunted him from an ocean away. Soon enough, the ghosts of his past would land on these shores, though.

"So, what's with the new look? You trolling for injured men home from the war to nurse back to health, Florence Nightingale?"

Red painted her cheeks, a constant side effect of his teas-ing. Not exactly a reason he wanted to stop, especially when she looked adorable when she was aggravated with him.

"No. I took new pictures for the app and forgot to wipe it off." She swiped at her eyes, but he grabbed her hand be-fore she could remove any of the makeup.

"Leave it. It's—" *Sexy? Gorgeous?* Neither were adjec-tives he could use with his best friend. His *platonic* best friend. "Nice. Matches the holiday. And who knows, maybe you'll actually meet a young man who's bringing his grandmother in for heart pain."

She giggled, but that thing in his chest, the one he'd ignored? Yeah, it full-on thumped now, imagining Ruby with anyone else. He wasn't sure why—it couldn't be jealousy. He just wanted her to find someone who actually deserved her and wasn't convinced that would come from an algorithm. How could an app show the way her eyes lit up like lightning in a storm cloud when she was excited and how they turned a turbulent gray when she was annoyed?

So, what, she should be with someone like you?

No. Definitely *not* him. He was so far away from that metric, he might as well be back in Greece. He considered himself lucky he even got to be her friend.

"Don't bring innocent grandmothers into my dating life. Sheesh. I'm still getting gifs from Byron's grandmother, and they're worse now that the wedding is so close."

"I forgot about that. I can't believe you're still planning to go." She hadn't said much about the event, but he knew she was struggling with it. Byron had left Ruby six years prior, and she'd been healing until he had the nerve to invite her to the wedding. From what Ares garnered, Ruby had been invited since she was a "friend of the family." Ridiculous. A friend didn't bail on a woman simply because she worked harder than he did.

She shrugged. "Can't back out now. Not without looking like an absolute loser." Another qualifier he wouldn't use to describe her. Ever. "Which I will if 'Nick from Fulford' ghosts me like the last few guys I swiped right for. Honestly, when did that become a thing? Not returning someone's texts all of a sudden just because I suggested our second date would be going to an ex's wedding? What are we, fifteen years old?"

He laughed. No guy in his right mind would say yes to being a wedding date after knowing a woman for a week. Even someone as gorgeous as Ruby. That she didn't see the issue was one more reason he loved this woman.

As a friend, of course.

Her eyes darkened to a stormy gray, which was a tempest the right guy wouldn't mind getting tossed around in.

"This isn't funny, Petrides."

He held his hands up in defeat. "Fine. So why're you back on the apps, anyway?" His favorite subject to tease her about was the frogs she met there. They might have profiles that made them resemble princes, but that luster fell off the minute she met them. "I thought you were 'done with that mess,'" he said, quoting her.

"Well, until I land a date to the wedding, which is just after New Year's, might I remind you, I'll do whatever it takes short of selling myself on the open market. There's not a chance in hell I'm showing up to that wedding alone."

"Can't you tell them you got called into work and not go at all?" It wasn't outside the realm of reality.

Her lips twisted into a scowl. "No. Tried that and my mom read me the riot act. According to her, I need to 'grow up and get over him,' which I have, by the way."

Something in her jaw sharpened when she mentioned her mother. He knew Ruby had her own complicated history with her family—that she never mentioned her father was one sticking point—but Ares never wanted to pry too much, not when it seemed to elicit the kind of emotion flitting over her perfect features like now.

He'd much rather make her laugh.

"I know. It's been six years, right?" And had she really

loved Byron anyway? Ares didn't think so. Her discomfort at going to the wedding seemed to be more about her reputation than any lingering feelings.

"Exactly. Six years single? I'll be labeled as the spinster Byron ruined. No, thanks. I'll go, but I might have to resort to paying someone to pretend to be my date."

Ares wiped an errant dab of chocolate from the corner of her mouth. Heat blossomed on his thumb where it touched her skin, and he pulled back.

"Well, I'm inclined to agree. Someone's got to keep you cleaned up so you don't see your ex for the first time in six years with frosting on your face."

"Ugh. You're the worst friend, you know that, right?" She grabbed her coat and smiled. "And nice sweater, by the way. You'd better change before you get screeched at by Patty."

"I'll take my chances," Ares said. "But I think I win this year, yeah?" He pointed to the embroidered Christmas tree and line beneath it that read *Feliz Navi-Docs.*

"I dunno… I think I did pretty well." She lifted her scrubs and revealed a tight green tee emblazoned with a Santa hat in the corner. The text read, *Two people I never lie to—Santa and an X-ray tech. They can see right through you.*

Ares laughed. "That's pretty good, Phillips. We might have to ask Fran for a weigh-in."

"Done. But you'd better not let Kyle Windgate see yours. He's a little jumpy around Christmas trees these days."

Ares's phone chimed the special ringtone he'd assigned his grandmother. He hadn't responded to their last text, so they were sending in the cavalry, weren't they?

"Hey, not to change the subject, but I've got news for you. My own family drama to help you forget about yours. Call it a Christmas gift. Meet me for lunch and we'll chat?"

"Royal York cafeteria food on Christmas Day?"

"It's better than that trash you're eating," he teased, pointing to the now-empty cake wrapper.

"Maybe. Anyway, lunch sounds good. Spring for a ginger molasses cookie and it's a date. I have a gift for you, too. I'll bring it to lunch." She winked and headed off. "I'll see you back in A&E? Oh, and Merry Christmas, Ares."

"You, too, Rube."

Ruby walked down the hall toward their wing of the hospital.

He gathered the tablet and lab coat from his cubby. The flurry of white outside meant it wasn't likely they'd have a quiet Christmas on shift. Snow mixed with eggnog didn't always bode well for folks. Too bad, since his brain had been whirring since Ruby had said "date" in reference to their lunch meetup.

Still, he was at ease for the first time since he'd received the text from his family. Ruby wasn't the only one slated to attend an event she didn't want to go to. His family was flying into York to celebrate with him on New Year's Eve, a night he usually reserved for a book, whisky and early night in after a long shift. Not only that, but they'd be in town the whole next week, and he didn't have the energy to focus on them and work at the same time. Work had to be his focus. Ariadne wasn't the only one hurt in their breakup. The last time he'd let his family interfere with his job on her behalf, a man had died.

Never again. Even if it made him a pariah to his family.

He considered his own advice to Ruby about ducking out of the family event, but it was more complicated than that. They were coming to him after almost seven years of never visiting once. He had to at least try to make an effort, even if it cost him.

And it would. God knew they weren't just coming to visit for visiting's sake. No, they had an agenda, likely a ploy to trick him into dating a new woman of their choosing, and even more likely she'd be from Greece to convince him to move back home. Hell, if he knew his grandmother, she'd bring the woman along so he couldn't say no.

Please don't let it be Ariadne. They'd all just gotten back on good terms a year ago.

He ran a hand through his hair as the familiar rhythmic pulsing of the life flight helicopter drowned out the Christmas music.

Maybe he should take that advice from Ruby and bring a date to the party so their plan would fall flat. *Hmm.* Who would he bring that wouldn't take the date as anything other than a ploy to thwart his family's agenda? Not any of the women he'd spent company with lately. They'd all wanted more from him, and that wasn't possible. He was fine with female companionship, a mutual sating of need, but that was where the line was drawn.

More was a four-letter word.

Maybe he'd brainstorm with Ruby at lunch if things weren't too busy.

Teasing aside, he had a real gift for her in addition to the gossip he'd planned to share with her about his family descending on his world at the end of the week. The Greek necklace was one he'd been holding on to, a gift from his grandmother for a special woman in his life, and he couldn't think of anyone more special to him than Ruby.

A flutter in his chest stopped him on the way back to A&E. Damn if he didn't have another idea.

It might be the worst one of his life, but if not, it would help out both of them.

Well…maybe.

If it went wrong, it might get in the way of their friend-ship, but they'd been through worse, hadn't they? Besides, as best friends, wasn't helping out one another in times of crises what they were there for?

The tightness in his chest loosened. It might take some convincing on Ruby's end, but he was a 100 percent cer-tain that his harebrained idea was the answer to both their unwanted family events coming up.

The crooked star atop the tree and the bright lights wrapped around it seemed brighter. Christmas was a time of magic, and he just might need a little of his own to pitch his wild idea to his best friend—and hope she didn't land him on a gurney of his own for even suggesting it.

CHAPTER TWO

RUBY PHILLIPS BIT back a grin. Smiling like that—like a girl with a crush—wasn't exactly appropriate in the emergency department of a hospital on Christmas Day. Nor was it appropriate after a conversation with her best friend.

Best friend. A title it would serve her well to remember.

Sure, Ares was handsome as all get out. A Michelangelo statue come to life, with chiseled features and dreamy Mediterranean skin that glistened even in the dullest UK winter light. And his eyes…deep, intense brown that reminded her of smooth leather. He was well-liked by female colleagues and patients alike, and had earned the nickname Greek God for more than one reason. Ruby teased him about his exploits—all with consenting women hoping they'd be the one to turn the doc into a "relationship guy." She considered it retribution for the hell he gave her about being on dating apps.

Ruby chuckled at the chatter in the locker rooms. Not one of the women chasing Ares understood that the man wanted a committed relationship, but never at the expense of his job. And they all wanted him to back off at work and choose them instead.

Which was why she and Ares worked so well together—as friends anyway. They were both chronic overachievers and workaholics but enjoyed the life they'd carved out for themselves. At least, most days she did.

It would be nice to have a relationship, someone whose chest she could melt into at the end of a long day, someone to kiss her senseless and remind her there was more to life than medicine...

But, was there, really? Her father and Byron had cemented the idea that the only person she could really count on at the end of the day was herself, the only constant was medicine. Her dad had kick-started Ruby's general distrust of the opposite sex, first by abandoning her and her brother after divorcing their mom—saying that he needed time to figure out his own career and needs—then by starting a whole new family in Wales in direct opposition to his previous statement not six months later. She got a holiday card from him and his wife each year, showing off their perfect little family, but otherwise they didn't talk.

That, and the way her mother mourned the loss of her husband as if she didn't have two children to raise, determined the course of Ruby's career. Medicine wouldn't leave, wouldn't neglect, wouldn't hurt her. In fact, it gave her a chance to heal others from actual ailments and injuries, taking her mind off her own internal wounds.

It was the perfect distraction.

Of course, her heart had gotten the better of her once, with Byron. She couldn't deny that in spite of the dangers of letting someone into her world, she wanted a person to build a life with. Byron had seemed a good fit...until he wasn't. He eventually capitulated that life as the partner to an A&E doc meant no time for a woman to dote on him.

So once again, Ruby was alone, no one but herself to count on. She wouldn't make the mistake of trusting someone else with that ever again. Not even Ares, who had proved all men weren't selfish creatures, because she wasn't related to or sleeping with him, either.

As if she'd conjured the man, he strode through the A&E doors looking very much like his Greek God nickname. She might have a mild crush on her best friend, but only because look at him—he was a specimen worthy of her medically trained eye.

She shook her head and made her way over to him.

"What's the story? Any cases we should be aware of?" She knew better than to announce how slow it was for a holiday morning. Doing so would jinx the quiet, and they'd be flooded with sliced fingers from ham-carving, broken limbs from ladders and tree-decorating, and the rest of the holiday-related melee that emergency departments saw on Christmas.

"Nothing yet, but I wanted to go through our cases from last night and see how they're faring. Join me on rounds until the rest of the team shows up?"

"Sounds good. Hey, while we're at it, I saw Kyle's name pop up on the outpatient list. Is he finally starting PT?"

"It looks like it. Physio called and he's starting with them this week. It sounds like he's doing well postsurgery, and he could make a full recovery from the injury."

Ruby exhaled. Their job was stressful on a good day— ordinary people with ordinary lives counting on the team of physicians at the Royal York to keep that ordinariness in the face of tragedy and injury. But to have a public figure injured, on the premises no less, meant a different kind of scrutiny.

Thankfully, they were a rock star team. Kyle would be back on the road promoting his newest album soon enough.

Ruby pulled up their first patient's chart before beginning rounds.

"Sara Kennedy, thirty-four years old, was treated for severe preeclampsia last night." She whistled. "Her labs don't look great, but there's been some improvement since last night."

"I don't think she's going to make it until New Year's, though. Looks like she might be our first Christmas mom."

"Not a bad way to ring in the holiday as long as we can keep mom and baby healthy." She read over the chart again, noting the difference between Sara's evening blood pressure and this morning's. Even if she didn't decompensate, she wouldn't hold these numbers long. Time was their enemy most days in the A&E, and holidays didn't change that one simple fact.

"They're going to need to expand the maternity wing with these amazing birth stories," Ares said. "Let's make sure that happens for her." Ruby smiled. Her colleague and best friend might appear to be a workaholic and chronic dater, but his heart was three times the size of anyone else's. His eternal optimism was admirable, if sometimes at odds with what they did for a living.

Still, he was right about the maternity wing.

The Royal York had a world-class birthing ward with state-of-the-art technology to help moms like Sara deliver their babies safely, with minimum risk to themselves. They also boasted a wall of photos of babies born on holidays that mothers came by frequently to add updates to. From time to time, she'd make an excuse to see her midwife friend, Ginger, on the third floor. She'd casually swing by to see the babies and look out over the "wall of life," as she'd dubbed it.

It wasn't that Ruby wished she was up in maternity. She was made for the adrenaline of the accident and emergency department, but there was a part of her that craved love and life over the death and injury they were faced with daily.

Her visits to the birthing center grounded her, reminding her why she fought for the lives of the patients who came into her A&E. They had families and friends who relied on doctors like Ruby and Ares to keep those communities intact.

It was all the more pertinent to know that, save the occasional tourist coming in with a broken bone or heart complication while on vacation, Ruby was helping keep her own York community healthy.

That mattered, and saving Sara and her unborn child was part of the equation.

"What're you thinking? OB is on call but not on-site," she said.

"Why don't you contact the on-call team and make sure Sara's prepped. I'll breeze through the rest of our rounds to make sure everyone is stable and check in with you right after?"

"Sounds like a plan. I'll make sure the nurses draw the labs and get Sara to the operating suite. I'll call the OB to take over, and let you know if there's any hiccups." Her phone buzzed and she glanced at the screen. She scowled. Not related to work. In fact, it was another reminder of why she worked so hard in the first place—her dating life left so much to be desired.

"Everything okay?" Ares asked.

She shook her head. "Here yes, just not outside the hospital walls. Remind me if I ever try and date again that I'm clearly not cut out for it. All my genes appear to have been honed into surgical skills instead of interpersonal."

Nor could the battle of nature or nurture be counted on. Everything she'd learned from her parents screamed that single life was better. When was she going to finally learn that at least alone she couldn't be blindsided?

If she could just get one date to one event, she'd give up the whole idea of dating this time around…

"Lemme guess. Prince Perfect is bailing on your date?" She nodded and bit back at the heat in her throat. This wasn't worth getting worked up over. Not when people's lives were on the line. "Oh, Ruby. Hell, sorry. I was teasing you."

Of course he was. "It's fine." She pasted on a smile. It was the nature of their friendship, the gentle teasing and needling one another about the parts of their lives they kept secret from the rest of the world. Normally she didn't mind, but seeing Sara in that bed, a husband waiting anxiously in the lobby for good news about his wife and child, Ruby's heart ached.

She wasn't asking for that. A family and partner might mean security and being seen beyond the butt of a joke, but it also meant someone to lose at the end of the day when work got busy. Or worse yet, life intervened and injury compounded loss into something unfathomable.

She didn't want that, any of it, but was it too much to ask for a date to her ex's wedding so she could at least pretend she'd done more with her past six years than work?

Ah, but what was the use in pretending? Even if she somehow found a random man from one of her dating sites to bring to Byron's wedding, something her ex had told her six years ago would remain true. Even now, she could still hear the taunt as Byron had walked away.

All you'll ever want is that job, and even if I come second, that's not going to be enough. And it shouldn't be for you, either, Rubes.

Was he really right, after all this time?

"Ruby, you deserve more than being stood up time and time again," Ares said, breaking through her fog of memories. He'd had that ability since they'd met, which was what made him her best friend.

Did she, though? Did she truly deserve to find a willing partner when she could never be one in return?

One thing she was absolutely certain of was how she wished for the gentle teasing instead of the look of pity on Ares's beautiful face. His sad eyes reflected how the rest of the world likely saw her—a workaholic who couldn't sustain anything resembling a relationship outside those she'd formed within the walls of the Royal York.

"Thanks for saying that, Ares. It'll be all right. I mean, worst case, I fake the development of some emergent medical condition no one in Byron's family is going to search for and I skip the wedding. Maybe you're right and there are worse things than being labeled a workaholic when the work we do saves lives. It's not like Byron can say the same about being a day trader."

"True. But listen, I have an idea about how to avoid all of that if you're up for hearing it." Ares bit his bottom lip. In all the years she'd known the man, he'd never appeared as anything other than confident, deserving of his position inside the hospital. So, why then, did he seem nervous?

"I'll take anything you've got, Ares."

He opened his mouth to reply as Carol, a nurse from A&E, waved to them.

"We've got incoming traumas from two in-home accidents," she shouted.

"Um, can we talk about this later? Lunch?"

"Of course. Please don't feel like you have to fix this for me, Ares. You're my friend, sure, but this is my mess, and I need to clean it up."

He frowned. Had she said something wrong?

"But still—if there's anything I can do…"

He trailed off, and the words were on her lips almost fast enough she couldn't stop them from tumbling out. Almost.

Yeah, she almost said. *You can come with me and pretend we're madly in love.*

Thank goodness her prefrontal cortex was sound enough to stop her from saying *that*.

"I'm good, thanks. I'll see you at lunch?"

"You bet." He took off his Christmas sweater, and Ruby made a show of looking away. Though, it was a little difficult to miss the tight white T-shirt he wore under it. Even out of the corner of her eye, she couldn't help notice the way his muscles roped as he strained against the fabric, how his strength didn't stop at his arms, but carried across his broad shoulders and down over his torso.

She swallowed hard, grateful for the harsh hospital lighting that would at least take the lustful edge off her thinking. Why couldn't she have been blessed with a friend who was average looking, moderately skilled at his job and possessed a normal human's income?

Instead, she was best friends with a deliciously handsome, incredibly talented and insanely wealthy Greek playboy.

She bit back a laugh that was highly inappropriate given the austere setting of the emergency front desk.

On paper, Ares was exactly who she *wished* she could bring to the wedding, if only to showcase the fact that she was lucky enough to be his friend, at least. She sobered, her smile falling.

That might be true, but where had the idiotic idea to *actually* bring Ares to the wedding come from? Sure, she and Ares had joked about doing that exact same thing at work—pretending they were dating to tease the rest of the Royal York staff. They were always insinuating that Ares and Ruby had something brewing beneath the surface, so why not give them some ammunition for fun? It's not as if it would be a difficult feat to accomplish; she and Ares had a way about them that made communication effortless. Throw in a glass of wine and subtle touch or two and it would be easy to pretend they were together for a night.

But a joke played on friends was a ruse that had no implications. Bringing her best friend to a wedding that her whole hometown would attend meant she'd need to explain away the reason she and Ares didn't work out each time she visited after the wedding. And that would be impossible if she and Ares were still as close as they were now.

Worse yet was the way her stomach flipped when she thought about what it would be like to have him with her at a wedding. Dancing to the sappy music, Ares's arms around her waist. Forcing herself to gaze into his eyes and pretend he didn't have any effect on her. They'd never actually blurred the lines with their flirtations and teasing, but from time to time, Ruby had left their exchanges feeling…*something*.

Something more than was okay.

Yeah, bringing Ares Petrides to her ex's wedding was a nonstarter. Not only because of the technical challenges of pretending to date her best friend, but because fake dating never worked out for the pretend couple. One of them always caught feelings, at least in the books she read after a long shift.

Too bad, though. Ares was handsome enough he might make Byron regret leaving Ruby behind all those years ago. Not to mention start a few rumors with the bridesmaids.

He folded his sweater and put his scrubs back on, looking every bit the professional she knew him to be. As he turned to go, she called after him.

"Ares?"

Her stomach lurched at the look on his face. She recognized the look, having felt it herself each time she swiped open her dating apps.

Hope.

But what did it mean in this context?

"Thanks for asking. I didn't mean to wave you off—you know I value your input. This is just…well, it's embarrassing. I can't get a single man to go on one simple date with me, which only serves to confirm Byron's assumptions all those years ago. I was rather hoping to show him what a well-rounded person I've become, and I'm just testy that it won't happen now."

A shadow passed over Ares's deep brown eyes. His jaw twitched, and she wished she knew him just well enough to understand what it all meant. But today, he'd been an enigma, a man with more left to discover, she realized.

He leaned over her and she caught the pine and cinnamon scent again. It made her slightly dizzy and there was that something more she always felt when they were this close.

"You know what I hate the most?" he asked. His voice was like his eyes—thick espresso poured over ice. Smooth and viscous. She let it wash over her.

"What's that?" she whispered. When he tucked an errant lock of hair behind her ear, she shivered in spite of the warmth in the room. His gaze remained locked on hers and just like that, the heat in her belly evaporated, the chill rolling through her.

"That Byron, a mid-level trader with no other passions, no work ethic, and to be honest, a physique that tells me he doesn't step foot outside after work, can get to you like that. You, who heals patient after patient efficiently—"

"You always hated that about me. That I'm too quick in

patients' rooms—" He put a finger to her lips to silence her. Why did she feel the desire to suck that finger between her lips all of a sudden?

"You, who is efficient and balances me when I spend far too long chatting up patients, who sees brilliant medical saves where no one else does each time a challenge arises, who curls up to read books that don't at all match her personality, who runs the River Ouse each weekend rain or shine because it 'brings me joy to see the couples on their walks and families enjoying time together.' You, who makes me egg sandwiches even though you think the smell of deviled eggs is what again?"

"Like smelling toots from the geriatric wing," she said, giggling.

"Yes, that. Ruby, you're so much more than pathetic, or a workaholic and that a silly ex-boyfriend couldn't see that only means he's not enough, not you."

Their friendship had weathered some storms, but she'd never doubted that she and Ares understood one another. What she didn't realize was how well the man actually *knew* her. Like, all the small things she'd told him he'd tucked away and brought back just now. It unnerved her.

He took a deep breath that hitched at the end. "The real question is why you think his opinion should matter at all. He never deserved you."

Ruby was frozen to the spot and not even a code blue could have moved her. Where was Ares's gentle chiding? The devilish smile he wore when he was teasing her about her lack of a dating life? *That* Ares she knew what to do with. This one felt…*dangerous*.

Lethal. At least to the way of life she'd cultivated.

"Anyway," he said, clearing his throat. He stepped back and the moment vanished. Had the pulsing energy between them been real, or was it a Christmas-induced fabrication as a result of desperation and too much eggnog the evening before? "Do me a favor and don't cut me out of the process. Let's brainstorm a way out of this at lunch, okay?"

She nodded, and he headed to the next ICU room. Ruby watched him go and her stomach flipped. Lunch suddenly seemed too far away, and at the same time, coming up far too quickly for her to have her feelings in check by then.

What the heck had that exchange been about, and why did she feel like the answer might change *everything*?

CHAPTER THREE

ARES FLIPPED THROUGH the chart on the next patient three times before he could make sense of the results of the CT scan. It wasn't that he couldn't see the tumor sitting on the man's occipital orb as clearly as if it had a sign announcing its presence.

No, uncharacteristically, the rereading of the chart was due solely to him acting like a damned fool with Ruby. The thing was, he couldn't figure out why he'd stepped out of Sara's room and felt different somehow.

Maybe it was seeing a woman about to lose everything that threw things into harsh perspective for him. And on his favorite holiday, no less. He shook his head. That couldn't be it. For crying out loud, he worked in a busy A&E unit at a hospital. He dealt with people on the knife's edge of loss every day, multiple times a day in fact. It's what kept his heart pumping, knowing it was often only him and his team—Ruby included—that stood between the patient and death.

So, then what was different today?

He and Ruby were close friends, best friends actually. He couldn't figure out why he was suddenly overwhelmed with the need to fix her situation for her, and in the least convenient way possible. Sure, it made sense on paper to go with her to the wedding, in part because what he'd ask in return—that she join him for his family's New Year's Eve party as his date—would serve both their interests.

But it also added a level of complication to their friendship he wasn't sure would hold up under the weight. Because lately, he'd been feeling *things*—messy, inconvenient things—when he and Ruby teased one another. Well, not so much then, but definitely when her eyes crinkled in the corners when she'd giggle, or when he'd catch the light snort she gave when she was really laughing. At some point, he'd made it his side job at the hospital to encourage one of those two moments to occur every time they worked a case together. He'd told himself it was because his best friend needed some joy in her life, and he could afford to help give her some.

But now, under the intense glow of the ICU lights that felt as if he was in a confessional, the truth settled around him. He liked making her laugh because of how it made him feel. Like he was the kind of man who was capable enough to make Ruby Phillips smile.

Oof. Like he'd thought earlier, his feelings were inconvenient at best. At least he had some time between now and lunch to work through them.

Hopefully, the morning would ease into things slowly so he could use that time to think.

The doors from A&E blew open and Ares glanced over. He sighed. Saying things were slow at a bar or hospital invoked the curse of cases flooding in, and it looked like that went for merely thinking it, too. Apparently, this time it came with more than just an influx of patients for them to treat.

The new lead flight medic stormed in with wild brown hair dappled in snow. She pushed a kid on a stretcher and maneuvered the thing like she'd worked there ten months, not minutes. Teddy Vaughn, another flight medic at the hospital—who'd lost the lead promotion to her—was at her heels looking less than pleased.

"Teddy, hey," Ares said. "Whatcha got?"

"Kid has a suspected break. Fell down a damned ravine." Ares brought the child into an examination room and confirmed it.

"We need to prepare him for surgery. Nice job getting him here before he froze his bal…" The new flight medic moved in front of Ares and made him feel like she was the one in charge. She'd be good in her position with leadership like that. "Oh hey. I don't think we've met."

He extended his hand and she took it, ignoring the sour look on Teddy's face. He wished Teddy could've held back for a day at least to let Angel settle in. He had no idea what the two were tense about already, but he had a feeling they would be at one another's throats in a while. It had been a close race to see who earned the position of lead flight medic, but Ares had heard from the hiring committee Angel Flores had earned the job with prejudice. Teddy would figure that out himself soon enough. Until then, maybe Ares and Ruby could make a batch of popcorn and watch these two figure out how to work with one another.

"Nice to meet *you*." The way she said, "you" was clearly a pointed jab at Teddy, whom she did not seem pleased to be working with. Teddy frowned. Oh well. His feelings weren't Ares's concern. Making Angel feel comfortable so she did the tough work ahead of her was.

Ares filled Teddy in on Kyle's condition and recovery, watching Angel and Teddy work alongside one another. It was like watching a well-rehearsed dance, and they'd only been on shift together for hours maybe. They'd be a good team eventually.

He finished up with the prep and headed to the nurses' station at the end of the reception area as a page came. Damn. It was a three-car pileup outside the city, and there were multiple crash victims coming in.

Johnson and Petre would have to take over surgery on the kid. He'd do what he could until the other victims arrived, but he had a feeling that with his experience, he'd be needed elsewhere. So much for a lull to think.

That was too much of a Christmas miracle to hope for, it seemed.

Ruby came out of Sara's room, her brow tight with concern.

"Those numbers won't last long. We'll need to get an OB in here pretty soon."

"Agreed. Hartford is on his way. Did you get the page?" he asked.

She nodded and grabbed an elastic from her wrist, tying her hair up in a half ponytail.

"I did. Looks like someone must've jinxed the holiday calm."

He raised his hand sheepishly and she laughed. He tried not to notice the way her updo exposed the side of her slender neck and earlobes, which he just realized had small silver hoops in them, a Christmas tree dangling from the bottoms.

He smiled. Ruby was a secret romantic, wasn't she? For all the efficiency and tough talk she spouted at Royal York, she harbored a softer side he didn't think many people got to see. Had Byron?

For some reason, just thinking the guy's name made Ares's blood boil. Sending Ruby alone and unarmed with a date into the viper's nest that would be Byron's wedding seemed wrong. She could handle herself, sure, but should she have to?

"So how are we dividing this? I think Petre was on his way in. Do you want to partner with him and I'll take Johnson?"

"Nah. They work well together and so do we. Let's team up this morning if you're cool with that."

Ares caught a flash of heat as it spread across Ruby's cheeks. What was that about?

"Unless you'd rather work with Johnson?" he hedged.

Ruby looked at her feet. "It's not that, but you and I have been tag teaming a lot lately. People might get the wrong idea."

Ares rubbed his chest where a knot seemed to have gathered. Robert Johnson had asked Ruby out a few times back when he'd first arrived in York from London. He was everything a surgeon from the city should be—suave, polished and able to separate work from play. The man dated quite a few women from York and its surrounding villages, but kept coming back to Ruby. Whether it was a challenge he never seemed to master or something more, Ares hadn't been able to suss out, but Robert wasn't a fan of Ruby and Ares's friendship, that was for certain.

It's not like Ares didn't agree with Robert. Ruby was amazing. Polished herself, if not suave with all the chocolate cakes she ate and left the wrappers discarded around the bay for him to clean up after. But she was stunning and smart. A catch, if someone could appreciate all of her like she deserved.

She took out her earrings, securing them in a small pouch in her lab coat. Her bare earlobes somehow accentuated the smoothness of her skin. Damn. Why was he suddenly so aware of this woman?

A shiver rippled over Ares's skin. What if he sent Ruby to work with Dr. Johnson and she got to talking about her dateless dilemma? Would he invite himself as a way past her "I don't date" defenses?

Yeah. Not on Ares's watch.

"Actually, you know what?" he said, grabbing his stethoscope. "Scratch that. There's an incoming kid and the three MVCs. Johnson and Petre are good with peds, and we all know you aren't exactly kid-friendly."

Her skin flushed again, and she whacked him playfully on the shoulder.

"I love kids. That's not fair."

"I know," he admitted. In fact, knowing she'd wanted some of her own before Byron unceremoniously dumped her and made her think she didn't have the "mothering gene" as he'd said, was another check in the "Byron's an ass" box. He had a feeling it went deeper than that, maybe all the way back to the reason she never mentioned her father. He'd always been curious about his best friend, but now, a burning need to know *why* she reacted the way she did consumed him. Wrong time and place, though. They could dive into it after the holiday. "But you don't exactly linger in the rooms once they're stable. Peds needs that extra time you don't believe in."

"Very funny, Ares. I prefer to think of myself as efficient, keeping the cogs of this great hospital moving. If we all spent the same amount of time with patients hobnobbing as you do, there'd be a line out the door for our care. I'm just doing my job, which does not include asking patients what their favorite holiday dessert is, thank you very much. In. Out. Save them. Move on. They don't need more than that."

He chuckled, glad for the added levity of the moment. It felt like old times.

"Yeah, sure. Tell that to the kid who wanted you to play the Juliet to his Romeo."

"He was better off with Nurse Tanya. I'm trash at doing voices for puppets. I feel so silly. Anyway, I see your point. Let's take the morning shift together and reassess after lunch."

Why was she working so hard to ditch him? He didn't have time to question it though, as the doors opened, bringing a cacophony of noise and melee to their feet.

"Three MVC victims," a medic shouted, wheeling in a gurney with an unresponsive victim. "First is a female, twenty-four, tachycardic and thready pulse. Where do you want her?"

"Let's get her in room three in case she codes. What else you got?"

The medic rattled off the other two cases, both less severe, including the driver that had caused the wreck, a man who'd apparently already imbibed on festive fizz before ten in the morning.

It was going to be a long Christmas Day if this was any indication. At least he had Ruby by his side to alleviate the frustration that was sure to come when they were exhausted at the end of it.

"Ruby, you're with me." As she slid in beside him, a peace fell over Ares.

He could tackle anything with this woman by his side, a fact he wasn't about to dissect right now. No, it was time to focus and to get to the only other thing that brought him that peace.

"Okay, team. Let's get to work and make some Christmas miracles happen."

CHAPTER FOUR

RUBY MASKED UP and held the scalpel over the taut abdomen of her patient. The procedure would leave a scar that would mar the mid-twenty year old's perfect skin, but if Ruby had anything to say about it, she'd be alive, and that's what mattered.

"Scalpel," she said, taking the instrument given to her and slicing along the sternum of the patient. "Okay, let's see what we can do to save your life, Jane."

She referenced the term they used for female patients without identification, Jane Doe. As far as the medics and police at the scene had observed, the woman hadn't been carrying anything other than a bottle of wine and an apology note, signed "XOXO, Me." It'd been written to a woman named Chelsea, who police had started searching for within the area of the crash.

"I overheard the medics saying she was in her house slippers," Ares said, cracking open the sternum and reaching in to tamp the bleed they were there to fix. This woman had hours to live if they didn't find it. "She just wanted to go see a loved one for the holiday and make amends, and look where that good deed landed her."

"There's a lesson there somewhere," Ruby answered. "Probably to wear winter boots anytime you head out of your house. Cute panties, too." She smiled beneath her mask, but Ares's brows pulled tight.

She'd thought it was funny, a way to lighten the mood while they worked. When Ares's gaze dipped to her hips, however, she was grateful for the mask that hid her blush. Was he imagining the underwear she'd put on that morning? Surely not, or at least she hoped not. At best, he'd be disappointed in the plain black, high-waisted undergarment she wore because she needed it to stay in place while she worked a twelve-hour shift.

Why did she feel a rush of embarrassment at that fact? Like it mattered in the least what Ares Petrides thought of her panties.

"I thought it was a lesson to avoid reconnecting after people have shown who they are."

She murmured something of an agreement, but had to work to steady her hands. Was he talking about her plans to attend Byron's wedding? Or his own family separation? He'd been pretty tight-lipped about the latter, only alluding to enough details that she knew there was a rift that kept him from going back to Greece, even to visit. And as far as she knew, his family had never been here to see where he worked and lived, either.

As much as she knew about her best friend, so much of him remained a mystery to her.

She took the clamp and with her surgical light positioned just so, leaned over the patient to place it where Ares motioned to her.

He was right on one account—they worked well together, regardless. There was a seamless energy they shared, a wordless connection that allowed them to anticipate one another's moves in surgery.

Is that why he'd wanted to work with her that morning?

If she'd been forced at confession to share her real feelings—that she'd seen him balk at Johnson's name—she would say otherwise. Another mystery.

Because Ares shouldn't care what she wore under her scrubs, or who she worked with. He certainly shouldn't have an opinion about who she dated or not. Though, as she imagined those three scenarios in reverse, her skin warmed again, this time the heat traveling over her body like an out-of-control forest blaze.

She'd be fine if Ares worked with that new medic, Angel, and she knew he went out from time to time with women. But imagining what he wore under his blue scrubs, the fabric that clung tight to his hips and…other places?

God, had someone turned up the thermostat?

The heart rate monitor spiked, issuing a shrill alarm that roused her from her very inconvenient—and inappropriate—thoughts of Ares in boxer briefs.

"What do we have?" she asked.

"She's coding. It looks like another bleed, but I can't reach it."

"I've got it." Ruby's hands were already inside the patient's chest, feeling for what they'd missed. It had to be small if it wasn't on the monitor, but big enough that with the other trauma, it was causing the patient's vitals to plummet. "I'm not feeling anything. Push six of adenosine and let's see if we can slow her down while I get this bleed."

"Where do you need me?" Ares asked.

"Can you move the lap pads? I'm worried the bleed is close to the original."

"I didn't feel anything, but yeah, you've got it."

Ruby's own pulse spiked. It wasn't nerves, or even anxiety, but adrenaline. She lived for this challenge, for finding the answer to a problem and fixing it. Who needed a relationship that, in her experience, only created problems rather than offered solutions? Surgery and the fast pace of the A&E was all the lover she needed.

As if the universe agreed with her, her fingers traced the new bleed, just millimeters from the first.

"I've got it."

"I'll clamp it while you prep to tie," Ares told her. She nodded in agreement, releasing her hands and taking the offered suture kit from the scrub nurse. They were a well-oiled machine, and in minutes, they were closing the patient up, her heart rate and other vitals stabilized. She'd live, and barring any unforeseen complications, would fully recover so this was only a bad memory.

Who knew what awaited the woman when she left the Royal York, though. She'd been on her way to apologize to someone, and her holiday had been derailed by a man who'd drunk too much on his way to his own family dinner.

Another reason Ruby worked as hard as she did. She could control what happened inside the walls of the hospital, but outside them? It was chaos, and she'd had enough of that growing up with an absentee father and neglectful mother.

"Good work in there," Ares told her as they scrubbed off. "I almost missed that."

"You wouldn't have. But that's why we're a good team, right?" She needed him to say he wanted to work with her because they partnered well in the OR, not because of any jealousy of who she did or didn't work with.

"It is." He frowned while he brushed between his fingers with the soap. "Hey, did Johnson finally get the message?"

And there it was. The hint of something more, something heavier than the light teasing. Something had shifted today, maybe had been shifting in incremental moments she hadn't noticed until now. But what it all meant, she couldn't be sure. Only that she had a feeling in the pit of her stomach, in the place her intuition helped her make life or death decisions on a moment's notice, that things between her and Ares weren't quite the same.

"He did." What she didn't say? Johnson had backed off because he'd thought she was dating Ares in secret. She hadn't corrected him. "Anyway, what's your take on our next step? The two other arrivals are about the same for triage, and Johnson is still with the kid."

"I want to take the man next. He's older and seemed a little out of it. I'm worried the initial work-up missed something."

"A head injury?"

"Maybe. Or blow to the chest that could exacerbate a heart condition. Did you see his fingertips?"

In truth, she hadn't paid that close attention when he'd arrived. The nurses did the initial work-up since he wasn't in critical condition.

The driver of the car that had caused this whole mess wasn't as high on her priority list as he seemed to be for Ares. Ruby couldn't have cared less what happened to him, as long as she fulfilled her Hippocratic oath to heal and cause no harm. Beyond that, all she saw was a man who'd been selfish enough to ruin his own and two other families' Christmas.

That was the thing about the career they'd taken on. It didn't really matter what they felt about a situation; their sole job was caring for the patient, no matter the fault or circumstances. Sometimes it grated on her, but with colleagues like Ares, it was easier. He took the emotional labor of caring for their patients, leaving her to efficiently provide care and then move on. It was a tag team that worked, even if she didn't understand Ares's positioning. Why would he care about a patient's backstory when they worked in the A&E? A dismal number of patients came to them too late to save, and the rest were transferred to different units once the emergency team stabilized them. They were the "American diner" version of medical care, as her friend, Ginger, had taken to calling them. "Churn and burn 'em," she teased.

Ruby didn't disagree.

"Okay. Let's see what we're working with."

"Ruby?" Ares asked outside the triage room. She stopped and looked up at him expectantly. Too bad the man wasn't interested in dating. The right woman for him could sure get lost in those espresso-colored eyes. "I just wanted to say thanks."

"For what?" Confusion settled around her shoulders, which were tired from the long repair that aortic valve had turned into.

"For working these holidays. I know you and I are, by default, the two always called in, but it's still nice to have working with you to look forward to."

"Of course. This is our tradition. Some people might be fine with turkey and potatoes, but not us," she said. That was their inside joke, starting with "some people" and ending with "but, not us."

He laughed and something loosened in her chest. They were okay.

"No, not us. Anyway, let's go meet Mr. Ramish."

Ruby sighed. She didn't want to meet the man, just treat him, but Ares wouldn't be Ares without overly caring for the people who came through Royal York's doors.

He claimed that to fully heal, they needed more than just good medical care. He thought kindness was just as important as the right medications.

She didn't disagree with that, just whether it was their

role as A&E doctors. It's not like she was ever rude, just…
quick. Efficient. They weren't the long-term care for these
folks. They were the first line of defense. Let the ICU staff
baby them.

The patient didn't meet their gazes when they walked in.

"Hey there, Mr. Ramish. I'm Dr. Petrides, and this is
Dr. Phillips. We're going to assess your injuries and make
sure you're sent to the right places in the hospital, but first,
Merry Christmas."

The man grumbled something unintelligible. Ruby resisted the urge to roll her eyes as she took his pulse. It was
a little uneven for her comfort, but they'd need to do more
of a work-up to see why and make a course of action.

Ares wasn't deterred. "I saw on your intake form that
you'd been driving under the influence. Get started on the
holiday a little early, or is there something more to it we
should know?"

What else could they need to know? The guy had been
drinking and driving and hit two other cars on Christmas
morning.

"Nope. Numbing up for the day, that's all."

Ares checked Mr. Ramish's eyes and noted something on
the tablet. A glance at her own showed he suspected blunt
force trauma to the side of the head where the driver had
hit his head on the window. That was a solid guess and at
a minimum would get them a rush on the tests they'd need
to do a full assessment.

"That a regular thing, or just the holidays?" Ares asked.
She glanced at him. What was he getting at? If the man
was a drunk, the best thing for everyone would be to get
him off the streets. Why did it matter if he was only drunk
some of the time?

Mr. Ramish looked up at Ares, who stopped what he was

doing and sat on the side of the bed. He put his hand on the man's shoulder and to Ruby's shock, tears welled instantly in Mr. Ramish's eyes.

"The holidays are hard, aren't they? Family drama, triggering memories... It can be a lot, can't it?" Mr. Ramish nodded, tears falling on his stained T-shirt. "And I don't think you meant to hurt those people, or even get behind the wheel, did you?"

But he had! Ruby wanted to shout. He had gotten behind the wheel, and that choice had ruined two people's holidays, if not weeks.

"I—" he started. He sniffled and continued. "I didn't think it was a problem. I just wanted to get home before people started travelin' for the holiday."

"You were at a bar?" Ares asked.

Mr. Ramish nodded.

"Same one each year. Usually I stay till I sober up, but I got antsy. I'm so damn sorry. I didn't think it would cause any harm. I was only a few blocks from home. Only drove because of the snow. Weren't expectin' that."

"Us, either. Why do you go to that bar each year?" Ares asked. He still hadn't moved from his spot on the side of the bed. Ruby, meanwhile, was hustling through the workup so they could move on.

"My daughter." He sniffled, but there was fortitude in his voice. "She died three years ago today. She'd just had her own child three months before. I miss her somethin' fierce, but it doesn't mean what I did was right. I'm really sorry."

Ruby froze midway through placing an IV. She bit back shame and swallowed the heat at the back of her throat. The pressure behind her eyes didn't abate, however.

His daughter... She'd died on *Christmas*? How awful. How had he survived that?

Oh, God. She'd made a rash judgment about the man, and it had almost influenced her care of him. Worse, she'd pegged him harshly—and wrongly—as a drunk when he was just a man in the most amount of pain imaginable.

"I'm so sorry," she whispered. Mr. Ramish shook his head.

"I don't deserve your sympathy. I'm thinkin' I owe those other people one of my own. They okay?"

"I'm legally not allowed to share another patient's status with anyone outside their family," Ares said, but at the same time he nodded vigorously. Mr. Ramish smiled. It was thin, but there.

As surprised as she was about the news Mr. Ramish had shared, she was more shocked by the way Ares had gotten through to him so quickly.

Though maybe she shouldn't be. Ares had been this way as long as she'd known him. Sweet, attentive and…present. With everyone in his life. Why wasn't he interested in dating when he had so much interest in other people, especially friends and his patients?

Maybe there was more to Ares than even she'd realized. He'd been calm and kind and found a different type of bleed where she'd only seen a man with no external injuries. If she was honest with herself, she could use some of that to rub off on her.

One thing was for certain. If he was open to it, like really open, she'd ask him to be her date to Byron's wedding.

Maybe time outside the hospital with him, even under false pretenses, would help her get a read on just what was going on with her mysterious best friend.

CHAPTER FIVE

ARES MADE IT to lunch feeling as if a train had run over him, then backed over the carnage. Every muscle ached, and it was barely two in the afternoon. They had a long day ahead of them if this was going to be the pace of things on the holiday.

It wasn't all intense accidents like it'd started out, but rather the usual Christmas melee that poured in. They saw two men who'd fallen off roofs putting up last minute holiday lights despite the turn in weather the day before. There were three minor burns from home chefs attempting to impress visiting family with their culinary skills. And of course, they'd sutured at least three hands, fingers and even one torso for accidents that happened while opening presents or chopping vegetables.

The holidays were dangerous, made all the more so by people dipping into the eggnog early. He had to laugh, especially since all of them would be fine, and make it to dinner with their families.

Only one man had begged for them to hold him a little longer so he didn't have to catch any grief from his wife's parents. Ares could relate, so he'd let the man "wait for tests" in an empty, unused room.

His ability to relate was compounded when his phone buzzed between patients.

His mother. He sighed and flipped it open. She had an uncanny knack for knowing when he was available. Even if, to them, he really wasn't.

Hello, son. He sighed at the formality, the implication of the familial bond, especially in the matriarchal Petrides family. The moniker "son" was at once a biological fact and a reminder of his duties in the role.

Merry Christmas and Kalá Christoúgenna. I'm assuming you're working today since we haven't heard from you. Hopefully, I'm wrong and you're spending time with a woman I hope to meet this weekend.

Ares pinched the bridge of his nose. The passive-aggressive tone dripped from each syllable. She'd not mentioned bringing a potential match for him, unless her words were an intentional ruse designed for him to admit he was coming alone. Who knew what he'd be met with if he did such a thing.

And now he'd gone and checked the text, meaning she'd see it as read. Avoiding her would only mean she'd pass the torch to the next member of his family and he did not want to have to tell his grandmother to leave him alone, and on Christmas Day no less. He could, however, be vague.

Yes, I'm on shift. Kalá Christoúgenna to you all.

We check into the hotel in four days, the party is in six. I can't imagine why you haven't visited us the past few years but I expect you to be there for the party, as we're hosting it to see you and meet the people most important to you.

Meaning, the woman he must have been dating if he hadn't come home. Because a job or magnetic pull to make up for past mistakes wasn't in their wheelhouse of understanding, not when "get married and procreate" was practically the Petrides family motto. Hell, the family crest could be a set of wedding bands and a ball and chain. Maybe it actually was.

I'll be there. I already asked for the time off when I got your first text. He hesitated sending the next part, but the pull of duty overwhelmed him. Ugh. This was why he avoided his family. They meant well, but their need for absolute devotion was dangerous to the other life Ares had built for himself. Anything I can bring or do to help?

The three dots took forever to disappear, and in their wake was his answer.

Yes, actually. We'd love to meet this woman and before the family descends. Let's do cocktails before the event, yes? I'll be in touch soon about the rest.

The rest? And how many of his family were making the trip to York? This was the opposite of a Christmas miracle; he felt as if he'd stepped into a dystopian nightmare.

On one hand, he had to hand it to his mother. He'd never mentioned a woman, but in not mentioning one, she'd made up her mind. She was persistent, per usual.

The only question was what to do about it now. He'd stew about it, maybe risk Ruby teasing him for the easy way his mother had broken down the rock-solid wall he'd built between them and his life and tell her the whole thing at lunch. Or at least he'd try. There was so much he hadn't told her, mostly because he hadn't figured out how in the beginning, not without sounding like a world-class jerk, anyway.

Because to share the bare bones of it—he left his family and fiancée and fortune because of a desire to help people and his family kept wanting *more* from him, including him finding happiness outside work—made him sound ungrateful. And that wasn't the truth of it at all.

He'd have worried about that detail, the "how to tell my best friend a condensed version of my story before my family descends upon us" part, but the weather brought in another round of vehicle collision patients. Thankfully, most of them weren't as traumatic as the first woman who was still waiting for someone to come claim her.

He and Ruby worked quietly through the steady stream of sutures and surgeries and even one coding. Bringing the guy back off the edge of death was a particular kind of high Ares hadn't found a replacement for.

The teasing between him and Ruby fell off with no food or rest to fan the flames. Instead of being awkward, it was kinda…nice. Ares was comfortable with Ruby, and for the first time in his adult life, the shame that followed him about his past, his family money and his biggest mistake didn't seem like insurmountable hurdles if she was there to talk to him about it all.

Maybe that was the real Christmas miracle—that he still had her friendship.

"I need food, stat, or I won't be responsible for what I do next," Ruby said, stripping off her gloves and mask and tossing them.

"Oh, I've seen you hungry and no one wants that. Come on, I'm buying." He held out his arm and instead of linking hers, she tucked against his core and nestled her head in the crook of his shoulder. She wasn't a short woman by traditional standards, but she felt tiny pressed against him. He let his arm fall, and when she let out a deep sigh, the heat from her breath warm on his chest, he squeezed her tighter.

Ruby hummed as they walked, and he could feel the exhaustion in her heavy steps. Not that he cared. He loved that she trusted him to carry her to food. Heck, that she trusted him, period.

"Hey, Rubes," he whispered against her hair when they got to the cafeteria. "What're you having?"

"Can't I just have another cake and call it a day?" she whined. "I don't wanna make any decisions." Her voice broke at the end. Uh-oh. She was fading. He'd seen Ruby in various stages of hunger, and they'd somehow passed hangry and were speeding toward weepy if he didn't feed her fast.

"No. But you sit here and I'll bring you something, okay?"

"Okay." She leaned her head back and shot him a sleepy grin. "Thanks, Ares. You're the literal best."

He tucked the sweet comment into his chest for later and resisted the sudden and pervasive urge to kiss her forehead. Where did that desire come from? Likely his own hunger pains that were making him loopy.

"Sit tight. I'll be back."

Ten minutes later, they each had a plate of roast beef, mashed potato and a salad in front of them, with pie on the way. Sure, it was hospital food, but they were both ravenous enough it seemed like a feast fit for the new King.

"This is the single best meal I've had. Today, at least," Ruby said, wiping her mouth with the back of her hand. For a polished, professional surgeon in the premier A&E ward of York, she was a bit of a mess.

My mess.

Another of those intrusive thoughts. He needed to get

a read on them, and quickly. No way he could pitch what he was about to while he was thinking very inappropriate things about his best friend.

"That's not saying much since you've only had petrol station snacks so far."

"Fair. Thanks for this, anyway. I was three seconds from tears and then I'm hopeless." Maybe that's what was happening. He was feeling the need to help her, and let her help him. The rest was just his mind's way of sifting through that rubble. It's not like he'd trained the muscle about how to react in situations like this. He not only didn't fake date; he didn't date, beyond the casual fling from time to time.

The same moment from his past that had him working overtime to right a mistake was the reason for that, *and* the reason he had become a semiprofessional at dodging his family, too. Unfortunately, they'd seemed to catch on and had backed him into a corner about both. Like it or not, he would be going to the New Year's Eve party his mother and grandmother were throwing—in his city no less. And, if the latest text was to be taken seriously, they expected to "meet a charming woman that must've stolen your heart and time."

He saw it two ways. He could tell them the only mistress he had was the A&E department at the Royal York Hospital—and she was a needy broad who demanded everything he had to give. Or…the idea he'd had earlier came barreling back, knocking him off balance.

Ruby. He'd thought of pitching that he'd be her date to the wedding when they were at lunch. But now his brain went into overdrive, taking that idea further. What if…

What if she joined him in return for his New Year's party? They'd be doing each other a favor…

No. This is a horrible idea…

Or was it? He could fake it and pretend, as Ruby was planning to do, that he had a fulfilling life outside the bustle of the hospital. It might not have worked with him and Ariadne, but he could show them he was still a Petrides, by appearances anyway.

Only one of those choices was going to silence his mother's endless pleas to find a woman, marry her and start making babies. At least she'd relinquished her demand that his bride be Greek as well. Still, marrying wasn't for him. How could he ask another person to wear the chain-mail suit of guilt he donned the last time he chose family over work and lost a patient?

How could he expect anyone to understand the crippling vision that came to him each night when he closed his eyes—of the man's young wife clutching her infant child to her breast as she wailed for the loss of her beloved?

It was strong enough an image he could almost imagine he'd actually been in the room when she'd been told. He should have been, a detail that added a heaviness to the vision.

Ares wasn't such a cynic to believe that he didn't deserve happiness because he'd stripped the woman of hers, but he did feel a pervasive need to right that wrong by dedicating every ounce of his time to saving whoever he could. That meant putting his family on the back burner, and excising the idea of love from his life as if it were an invasive tumor. He and Ariadne were never meant to be, but they hadn't had even a shred of a chance after that. It wouldn't be different for any other woman in his life, ever. He'd made sure of that with the way he'd dedicated himself to work.

At least in his heart. In public, it was more complicated, at least until New Year's Eve.

He cleared his throat. "Speaking of hopeless," he said.

She glanced up at him, a crumb of pie on her bottom lip. He used the pad of his thumb to wipe it away and ignored the heat that spread up his hand from where his skin had touched hers. "I want to talk about your plans for attending Byron's wedding."

"Jeez, thanks, Ares. With friends like you, who needs enemies?"

He let out a nervous bubble of laughter. "Sorry. That's not what I meant. He's hopeless, as is the situation. Not you."

"Whatever. Anyway, I hope you have some brilliant idea tucked away in that cute head of yours." Did she just call him cute? His skin prickled with awareness. "Because right now my plans are to pregame at Mick's before the ceremony and try not to embarrass myself when I show up alone on the dance floor."

"Yeah, that's not happening." Ares might be nervous, but hearing his friend's plan for attending the wedding sobered him up. He was there to help, to fix, to heal. *That* was his lot in life, not preserving the family lineage or wealth. "I do have a better idea, actually, but I need you to let me get all the way through it before you interrupt, okay?"

"I don't interrupt—" she started, then at his smirk, she shrugged. "Fine. Go ahead." She put her fork down on her empty plate, and he couldn't help but be impressed. She'd eaten as much as him. God knew they'd worked up an appetite.

"Here goes." He said that as much to hype himself up. "*I'm* your Christmas present."

His hand reflexively went to the locket in his pocket. Paired with the offer he was about to make, the latter didn't feel appropriate. He'd find another time to give her the more sentimental gift.

When Ruby's eyes went wide, and her cheeks flushed

with heat, he realized how that sounded. But he couldn't stop the image of her actually unwrapping him, and letting him do the same to her. *Kristos*, he needed to get his thoughts out of the gutter. Maybe it was time he got laid so he stopped thinking about having sex with his best friend. Because that was definitely off the table, especially if they went through with what he was about to propose.

"I mean, I'm going to be your date." When the confusion lingered, he clarified, "For the wedding." Her mouth fell open as if in rebuttal, but he shook his head. She closed her mouth and gestured that he continue. "I dress up nicely, I've been properly trained in ballroom so I won't embarrass you on the dance floor, and I'll be the designated driver so you can get absolutely bashed."

She giggled, then covered her mouth. She'd told him once she was always embarrassed of her laugh, but he'd never shared his feelings about her giggles. They were 90 percent of the reason he teased her—so he could keep hearing the sound.

"Did you know I had the same idea earlier, but I thought it was the first sign I needed to eat something?"

He laughed. "It's wild, for sure. But what do you think now that we've both scarfed our meals?"

She shrugged and took the last bite of his pie from his plate. "It's not a terrible plan, but you know the wedding date I need is actually a wedding, rehearsal dinner and winery date. Byron does nothing the easy way, so I get to show up to not one awkward event, but three."

"Three for the price of one? Hmm. Sounds fine to me."

She seemed to assess him. "What do you get out of it, besides a lifetime ability to tease me about it afterward?"

His smile fell. Had he overdone the teasing, perhaps

crossed into playground bully? If that's all she thought of him, he had some repairing to do.

"Not at all. In fact, in return for what I will, indeed, ask in return, I promise never to tease you about being brave enough to go to your ex's wedding. How's that?"

She swallowed hard, her eyes narrowed as if in suspicion. "And what are you asking of me?"

Thank the gods his tanned, Greek skin didn't show emotion near as flagrantly as Ruby's pale UK skin did. Because he felt the sting of desire warm every cell of his body when his brain caught up to what she was asking.

"Not that."

Though...

No, he told his overactive libido. *Not. That.* Not with her. He respected her as a friend, a physician, and thought she was one of the most beautiful people he'd ever met, inside and out. Adding anything else would only complicate things. Bring them too close to dating.

The head of midwifery walked by and waved, on the phone to someone. As he passed, Ares got a hint of something spicy. Something Ryan had brought for lunch judging by the box he carried. He inhaled deeply and shivered. They weren't Greek spices, but they still bore the weight of nostalgia and added to the feeling of unease in Ares's chest.

"I was hoping you'd join me for my mother's New Year's Eve party as my fake date. She might sneak cocktails in there, too, but I'll keep you posted. As I'm sure you're aware, it's been a while since I went home," he said. He fortified himself with a deep breath. She took his hand and his breathing immediately calmed. Ruby'd always had that effect on him.

"In Greece? That's a quick turnaround, Ares, but—"

He shook his head.

The reason for the length between visits was never far from his thoughts, though, and she couldn't always be there to calm him off a ledge. He'd gone to see his family at their insistence, ignoring the pull of his intuition that his patient needed to be closely watched. The man had undergone surgery on a spinal injury and had initial signs of sepsis. But when Ares's family called on him to repair the damage he'd done to Ariadne and her family by leaving so abruptly, calling off their engagement in the process, he felt the biological need to answer.

So, he had. And his patient had died before he even touched down in Greece.

The unknown of what might have been had he stayed to fulfill his duty to his patient, to the hospital, had lived rent-free in Ares's mind every day since. With each patient he saw, each case he took on, he imagined that man's sacrifice. And that grief drove him forward at the cost of everything else in his life.

After all, he'd left his family obligations to pursue medicine, and he'd failed both by leaving that day. Never again, he vowed.

"Not in Greece," he said. "They're coming here, since I apparently took too long to get to them."

Ruby's gray eyes widened enough he could see the hints of baby blue in them. Did she know how expressive her mannerisms were? It was adorable.

"Wow. Your folks are coming to York? That's a big deal. They've never been, right?"

Ares shook his head. "Nope. They assumed I'd be back each year, but after my first visit home, I... I never went back."

Now he wished she knew the whole story so she'd understand why this was such a big deal. But Christmas—at work no less—wasn't the time to get into it.

She squeezed his hand, knowing, if not the gist of the reason he carried a lifetime of guilt around with him, that he was troubled about his relationship with his family.

"Whatever's bothering you, you should know I think you're an amazing person and phenomenal doctor. Whatever they can't see is their blindness, not yours."

Hearing her say it eased his burden a fraction. But not enough.

"Anyway, it's not just my folks. It sounds like the whole Petrides clan is coming, hence the party." His lips twisted into a sardonic smile. "They're expecting to meet the 'reason I haven't been home,' which obviously has to be a woman. God forbid I love my job enough to dedicate myself to it." Ares felt his blood pressure increase. Thankfully, it leveled as he glanced at Ruby.

Her hand shook in his. "Well…" she said. "Um, that's interesting. And you're sure you want to bring me? I mean, I've always been curious about your family, but it seems like they're expecting someone…serious."

Ares waved his free hand behind him. "Do I *have* anyone serious? I mean, by all accounts, you're the most serious person in my life. It's not a complete lie, bringing you in that capacity…"

The truth of that made his skin itch. He'd gone on casual dates, sure, but quit them before they became anything more intense than a way to blow off steam. Because of that, he only went out with women who wanted the same thing.

"Okay. So, walk me through it, Petrides. What do you need from me?"

"Does that mean you're in?"

She shrugged again, but the smile on her face gave him

something he hadn't had since he received the text from his mother—hope.

"I guess, but I don't know that I can promise to be sober for your party. Meeting a bunch of Greek billionaires wasn't on my bingo card this holiday season."

It hadn't been on his, either. "Fair enough. How about I sweeten the deal and be the designated driver for each of the events?"

"Hmm. I think you're right—this is the only answer to both our problems." She held out her free hand and he shook it. "You've got a deal, Dr. Petrides. I hope you're prepared for me to be the best damn fake girlfriend you've ever had."

He couldn't have stopped the grin that erupted on his face, not with a 400-charge from a set of AED paddles.

"You already are. And think of the bonus. If we play our cards right, we can trick the hospital into believing we're dating, too."

"Ha!" She laughed. "We won't have to try too hard to pull off that practical joke. They already think we're dating. This will just have them planning a wedding on our behalf."

"See? This is the gift that will keep on giving. We can fool our families *and* knock out a work-prank we've been teasing about for years."

She laughed and picked up their trays, bringing them to the drop off station closest to their table.

"Oh, boy, Ares. You really know how to make the holidays interesting. But hey, I have a gift for you." She dipped into her lab coat and pulled out a festively wrapped gift.

"If this is another attempt to get me to journal in some hippy notebook—"

"Just open it. I think I did better this year."

He unwrapped the paper carefully and almost choked on his surprise.

"It's *Emma*. Kristos, is this a first edition?" He was close to tears. He'd shared that he loved the story from the time he was forced in secondary school to read it and…she'd remembered it and tracked down a rare copy. "It's…it's perfect, Ruby. Thank you."

His voice was thick with emotion.

"You're welcome. See? I'm already killing it at the fake girlfriend thing."

"You have no idea—"

Their beepers went off simultaneously.

"Dammit. Time to get back to work," he said. "Thank you again, Ruby. Really. This is too much."

She shrugged and pecked his cheek before they strode with purpose back to the A&E department.

Hours later, Ares was exhausted but…fulfilled. Whole. It wasn't a traditional Christmas, not in the least. There'd been no cooking with a house full of guests, no big meal with everyone around the dining room table, no gifts pulled from under the tree to share with loved ones.

Ares smiled as he walked to his car, a light snow falling on the almost-empty parking lot. No, it might not have been the holiday his parents would have wished for him, but he couldn't escape the thought that he'd gotten everything he'd ever wanted.

CHAPTER SIX

RUBY SLIPPED ON the emerald-green cocktail dress over her lacy undergarments and tights. The dress clung to her curves and accentuated parts of her that she'd forgotten existed since she was either in scrubs or sweatpants most of the time.

Heck, when was the last time she even donned jeans for dinner with a friend? It'd been a while, that was for certain.

And now she was bypassing all the normal steps of friendship and letting Ares accompany her to an ex's wedding—or rather the drinks reception before the main event in six days' time, which would be the date to make all other dates pale in comparison. God, New Year's and the wedding that followed couldn't come soon enough. She needed this to be over.

At least this dip into the formal events was a nice teaser. If it went poorly, she could always tell Byron's family, and her own, that Ares had been pulled off for an emergency shift the day of the wedding.

Okay, this would be fine. It had to be; too much was at risk if it wasn't, starting with the most important—her friendship with Ares.

She attempted to sit on the edge of the bed, but the satin gown was too slick against the fabric and she slid to the floor. A shrill giggle escaped her lungs.

Oh, how did I get into this mess?

She blamed the fact that she'd been starving at work on Christmas as the reason for saying yes. Sure, he'd asked her *after* they'd eaten the paltry Christmas dinner, but still, what other reason had she for saying yes to this insane plan of his? Because it wasn't just a single date, either. No, he'd join her for Byron's rehearsal dinner, then wedding, *and* he'd be taking her as his date for his mother's New Year's Eve party.

A party where his whole family would be in attendance.

Ugh. What had she been thinking? The one line she'd been stuck on for three days popped up again, cruel in its persistence.

I'm your Christmas present.

She shivered. The moment he'd said that, she'd had a very visceral response. Her brain had conjured up an image of Ares in a fitted sweater and jeans—a laid-back version of his usual attire. Except in this image, her hands were peeling the clothing off him as if he were, very much in fact, a gift for her to unwrap. Even now, she let the image linger a little longer than was healthy.

Yeah, unfortunately, that was more likely the cause of her saying yes to Ares's asinine plan. Not that she hadn't had the same idea, but he'd certainly raised the stakes with the invitation to his family's party. Not to mention left her pondering what the man would wear to the wedding and whether it would replace the image of her tearing his clothes off him like a wild beast.

Yes, the turn of events was very unfortunate indeed.

Also unfortunate? She'd had to work the rest of the Christmas shift with Ares, and the next two after that. In fact, she didn't have a day scheduled away from the man for over a week since they'd stacked shifts to have their four events off together.

The doorbell rang and she hefted herself off the floor—no small feat with her tall frame wrapped in a fitted gown and high heels to top the whole thing off.

She made her way to the door just as someone knocked again.

"I'm here, jeez," she muttered. Whatever sharp retort she'd had next on her tongue dissolved as she opened the door. Ares stood in front of her, a bouquet of calla lilies in his hands. He fiddled with them, and she took advantage of his distracted gaze to fully appreciate the man in a bespoke suit, the first few buttons of his shirt undone so his impressive, tan chest was on display.

All at once, she was transported to another world, one where her best friend ran a Greek empire worth billions. Where everyone who met him bowed to his every command. Because that's who she saw—a mogul, not an emergency room physician.

A flood of heat rushed to her stomach as she took him in. The black suit jacket was highlighted by a sea-green silk shirt that complemented her dress. An emerald-green-and-turquoise pocket square completed the look and made it appear as if they'd coordinated their attire. All she'd actually done was reply to his text inquiring about her outfit with a photo of it on the hanger.

But then there was the man himself…

His hair was slicked back, his face clean shaven, which exposed an angular jawline that she could have used to slice into skin in surgery. When his gaze rose to meet hers, she noticed small flecks of amber in his eyes, brought out by the colors in his outfit. That's not all she noticed.

He gasped as his gaze slid over her dress, and the smile tugging at the corners of his lips was different from his teasing one. Combined with the intensity of his gaze, it was almost…predatory. Lethal. Like she was the only prey in an open field and he was ravenous.

Surely it was just a trick of the light, of the newness of seeing one another outside the hospital. He didn't really think of her as anything other than his friend and colleague. Besides, even if he did, he didn't want a partner.

She didn't, either, not with any seriousness outside those damned apps. That was in part because of the abject horror dating turned out to be. Each first date was a job interview at best, and even if there was a connection, which she'd only felt a handful of times, then she was forced to retell the same stories and hear someone else's. It all felt so…forced.

It's not like she enjoyed being alone; she craved connection, but between crappy dates and the less-than-lovely example of dating and marriage her parents had provided, what was the point?

Especially when a date would inevitably get bored of her being pulled into work by the hospital? That's what happened with Byron, and she swore she could see the same dull gloss of her dates' eyes when she told them she was an A&E doctor.

Why couldn't it be as easy with other men—available men—as it was with Ares? Ares, who was looking at her the way she'd wanted to be gazed at her whole adult life.

"Wow," was all he said. He cleared his throat and took her hand, spinning her. "Who knew you cleaned up so nice, Phillips?"

She grinned, glad they were back to playful chiding so whatever heat she'd felt building in her stomach, then chest, could dissipate. They were friends. This wasn't a real date. If it were, she wasn't sure she'd want to leave her living room. She could so easily—far too easily—imagine pushing the man onto her couch and kissing him senseless.

He looked good. Better than usual.

Part of that was how relaxed he seemed to be. Good grief, how the man fended off women outside the hospital was surely a feat to behold. No wonder he worked as hard as he did—that was probably easier than avoiding the women who probably flocked to him.

"Back at you, Petrides. I can see why your family wants you to captain their ship, so to speak. You certainly look the part." A flash of that shadow passed over his features before evaporating again.

"Thanks. Someone's got to make sure Byron knows what he gave up and who is appreciating it now. I'm glad this fits the bill." He tugged on the suit jacket and Ruby swallowed hard. Yeah, it did that. And then some. She felt a small measure of glee at how handsome her date was. He continued, pulling a small box out of his breast pocket. "To that end, I brought you something. It's from my grandmother and when you sent the photo of your dress, I figured—"

By then, she'd opened it and gasped. Inside the box was a stunning emerald pendant on a gold chain that looked… Old. Expensive. Rare.

"It's incredible, but do you trust me to wear it tonight and get it back to her safely?"

He frowned. "It's a gift, Ruby, not a loan." Before she could express her appreciation and confusion, he was clasping it around her bare neck. The metal was cool against her flushed skin, but she felt otherwise…

Perfect. Glancing in the mirror, she was forced to see how right he was. The necklace was perfect for this outfit, as was her date.

"Why me?"

He shrugged, his lips pressed in concentration as he straightened it on her neckline.

"It's always been you." She held her breath as his fingers traced the chain along her neckline. Did he see the goose pimples that erupted under his touch? She shivered. "There. It looks like it was meant for you."

"Thank you. It's perfect, Ares. Thank her, too."

"You'll do that next week."

"True. Um, well, shall we?" she asked. Suddenly, she was anxious to get to the wine bar, though not necessarily to get this over with as she imagined she'd feel.

"Just a sec," he said. "I brought you one other thing," he said, reaching into his suit jacket. She held her breath. She hadn't thought to get him a gift and he'd brought two. Was she supposed to give him something, too? Oh, she was woefully out of practice when it came to dating—or fake dating. Or whatever this was.

"Ares, I don't need another thing—"

When he pulled out a wrapped cake that was not only from a petrol station, but smushed from being in his breast pocket, she laughed loudly.

"Never mind. I love it. How did you know?" she asked, taking the treat. As if in answer, her stomach roared.

"You got off shift an hour ago, and I know you take your time decompressing before you eat. I didn't want you dissolving into a puddle at your first glass of malbec, so I thought a pre-party snack was in order."

She wouldn't have been as pleased if he'd shown up with a puppy and keys to a Mediterranean beach home. The man knew her through and through. The odd part of it was, she and Byron had dated for almost two years, and he'd never understood her the way Ares did. Did that make this more of a real date, or signify that she and Byron weren't meant to be?

Or both? Neither?

Confusion swirled in her stomach so she ripped open the cake and took a bite to stave it off.

"Tanks," she said, her mouth full. "We should go."

He nodded and led her to his car. She glanced up at him, and he smiled as he wiped what must have been a crumb from her lips.

"What is this?" she asked, gesturing to the Rolls-Royce Phantom outside her small cottage. She'd lived modestly, despite her decent income, since living alone always made her feel as if she still had too much space, too much…stuff. But this luxury in front of her home made it seem as if she lived in abject poverty.

"It's the one treat I allow myself," he said, grinning. In that moment, no matter how inadequate her satin cocktail dress felt, she appreciated her best friend's taste in vehicles. If she *had* to go to her ex's wedding, on the arm of a handsome billionaire in a car worth more than her home and car combined was one hell of a way to make an entrance…

That proved to be very true as they drove up. Most of the party was out front under a tent that must have been erected for the party. The layout of the tent had the opening facing the driveway and views of the River Ouse.

Which meant all eyes were on them as they pulled up to the event space. Ares put the vehicle in Park and Ruby was a little disappointed the ride was over. A Rolls-Royce, even on her decent pay, wasn't ever going to be in her price range, and it drove like a dream. She was officially ruined when it came to luxury, unfortunately for her Audi.

Ares opened her door and helped her out, and those now-familiar sparks buzzed between their palms. He squeezed her hand, in response to feeling the same pulse of energy, or to calm her, she couldn't be sure. She only knew the latter worked, regardless of the fluttering in her stomach.

"You ready for this?" he asked, leaning in to whisper in her ear. He put a hand affectionately around her waist and kissed her forehead as the valet closed the car door, seemingly just as pleased about the car he got to park.

"As ready as I'll ever be for anything other than being pulled into emergency surgery," she groaned, careful to keep a smile on her face. Ares was playing his part oh-so-well. The rest was up to her to sell, or this entire ruse was for nothing and she may as well have taken on an extra shift.

"You never know. If Byron says even one thing I consider anything other than apologetic and kind toward you, you might get your chance to operate after all."

Ruby laughed and leaned against Ares's chest as they walked. That wasn't even a hard sell, as the pebble walkway didn't lend itself to the mile-high heels she wore. At least the snow had melted out here in the outskirts of York.

"That's not very 'do no harm' of you."

"Oh, Ruby, that suggestion flies out the window if someone interferes with your well-being."

Ruby could have shucked her shawl at the door. She was warm all of a sudden, and they'd only just arrived at the tent.

"Ruby Phillips, as I live and breathe. I didn't think we'd see you tonight," a nasally voice called out from the entrance.

"This is Janet, Byron's mother. She's a pistol, so watch out," Ruby whispered under her breath. Ares gave no sign he'd heard her, save a squeeze of her hip where his hand rested. She trusted him, but it all of a sudden occurred to her that she'd brought her best friend into the lion's den. At least they'd get this all over with before the wedding itself.

"Janet, hello. I RSVP'd that myself and a guest would be here when I got Byron's generous invitation." She pasted a smile on her lips. "I wouldn't miss getting to see him find his happiness. After all, that's why we parted ways as friends—so we could find what, and who, we were meant to be with."

The implication was laid out on the table—*don't say a thing about me coming to the event when your son invited me after breaking my heart six years ago.*

Janet's smile was pinched. It wasn't very kind of Ruby to notice, but Janet hadn't taken very good care of herself since Ruby had stopped helping her with her diabetes after her split from Byron. Maybe Ruby would pull her aside and talk to her later.

"Speaking of, allow me to introduce myself," Ares said, breaking the tension. "I'm the plus-one, Ares. Might I say, you know how to throw a lovely event, Janet. The lighting and decor reminds me of that show in America—the one with the couple in Waco, Texas?"

Janet's whole face shifted into one Ruby had only seen once or twice. If she didn't know any better, she'd say Janet looked *pleased.* Happy, even.

"I *love* that show!" she exclaimed, resting a hand on Ares's forearm. Ruby resisted the urge to roll her eyes.

"Are you kidding?" Ares feigned surprise, his free hand on his chest. "Those two, the way they playfully tease one another but you can tell there's real friendship, real love there? What's not to appreciate? It reminds me of you and I, actually, Ruby."

He leaned down and kissed her cheek, giving her access to the mint on his breath. It made her feel like she'd already imbibed wine. Combined with the sentiment, it was heady. Dizzying.

Well, this sensation is new. Not altogether unwelcome, just…different.

"Do you watch the one where they travel around the world looking for homes?"

"Of course," Ares replied. A server walked by with trays of sparkling white wine, and he grabbed one for Ruby and Janet. "How do you think I found out about York when I was looking to move out of Greece?"

Janet tittered. "Where did you find this one, Ruby? He's surprising."

"That he is," Ruby agreed. The question was, how much of it was real and what was manufactured for appearances? He was a little too good at this fake dating thing. She wasn't sure she could keep up his level of attentiveness when she was his date later in the week.

"You don't strike me as a man who watches reality television, Ares," Janet continued, taking the wine and sipping it while her gaze traveled up and down Ares's frame.

"You don't know what kind of man he is," Ruby mentioned under her breath. Thankfully, only Ares seemed to notice her quip, and he tickled her side right where he knew she was sensitive. She giggled, and Janet's smile widened.

"Well, I'm glad you two made it. Ruby, you look well and thanks for bringing this—" Janet looked at a loss for how to describe Ares. Ruby understood that quandary. "Lovely man with you. I'm not sure where my son is, most likely at the bar with his brothers and father, but enjoy yourselves and I'll let Byron know you're here."

Janet must have gone straight to her son, because not moments later Ruby's past was facing her head-on.

"Byron," she said. "Congratulations. This is a beautiful event. I can't wait to see you finally tie the knot with Krista."

Byron had started dating Krista almost immediately after he'd broken things off with Ruby. At first, Ruby had been crushed all over again by Byron's quick replacement of her, but as life settled and she no longer had to worry about how to appease him with a lighter work schedule, she realized she'd be okay and so would he. That mattered just as much to her, that her ex find someone who made him happy. And he had. Ruby had work and Byron had Krista. Everything was just as it should be.

"Ruby," he replied, a curt nod all he gave her in reply. In fact, he barely made eye contact with her. Instead, his gaze darted back and forth between Ares's hand on her hip and the man himself. "I'm Byron, Ruby's—"

"The groom and lucky man of today's event." Ares cut him off, thankfully before he could finish that sentence at his pre-wedding toast. "I've heard so much about you. As my lovely partner said, congratulations and thank you for inviting us."

Ares leaned in toward Byron. "Thanks for letting this one go, too. She's the best thing that ever happened to me," he whispered, loud enough Ruby heard every word over the acoustic guitar from the band at the front of the tent. Ruby was appreciative of his hand still around her waist, keeping her steady, even if the close contact made her heart race. The juxtaposition of the two men in front of her was almost too much to handle. One of them was pinched and unsmiling and thankfully in her past. The other held her steady and spoke words to her she'd never known she needed to hear. Even if they were disorienting coming from him.

Because he wasn't her future. Just her present, and only a friend at that. Still, Byron couldn't know that, and the look he gave them both was one of disdain and…regret? The wistful way his gaze held Ruby's for a moment made her nostalgic, yes. But also more certain than ever they'd made the right choice in breaking it off.

"It looks like we both are where we're supposed to be," he told her.

"I thought the same thing a moment ago," she agreed, leaning into Ares. She might as well take a page from his fake-dating manual and lean in—literally—to the idea. After all, it's why they were there.

"I hope you're happy, Ruby. It's all I've ever wanted for you." With that, Byron strode off, looking very much as if he'd swallowed an iron pipe that was keeping him rigid.

"Ugh." Ruby grabbed another glass of wine from a passing server. "Did he really just say he broke up with me so I could be happy?"

"He did. And in a way, that's exactly what happened, isn't it? I mean, he's a fool, but he did you a favor, Ruby. I have so many questions about how you stayed with that humorless man for two whole years, but not tonight. Tonight is for celebrating you and all you've done to avoid being the one in the white dress headed toward a future where being Mrs. Byron would mean a life of no laughter, no teasing about eating cake and—"

"Probably no cake at all," she added. Ares laughed and toasted her.

"Regardless, this little date is…interesting. It's like a practice run for dealing with my own family. I'll have to give you the Cliffs Notes after the rehearsal dinner tomorrow."

"It can't be worse than this circus," Ruby teased. She did feel lighter, less plagued by guilt than she had expected.

"Oh, Ruby, my family will make this seem like going on vacation to the Maldives."

Ruby exhaled and swallowed the contents of her glass. "Oh, goody. I'm now supremely glad you're driving tonight, Petrides. I forgot just how trying this family is and if I have

a week more of this, I'm gonna need to be not-sober for it."
She glanced at Byron and his mother, neither looking like
they were at a celebratory event. "But you're right. Maybe
I dodged a bullet."

"You did, for so many reasons."

His thumb still rubbed her hip, and she wasn't sure what
to do about it. On one hand, it felt…good. Natural. But on
the other hand, it made her feel other things that were more
than good.

A temperature read would show how warm the gesture
made her, and heaven forbid a blood pressure cuff be attached. She'd be sent to the A&E as a patient in distress.
Except it wasn't stressful… Not at all. It was lovely.

Still… She couldn't get used to it. It was fake.

A rebuttal formed on her lips but then she spotted a
friendly face.

"Are you up for facing my family now that we've gotten
through the reason we're here?" she whispered. "No teasing allowed, though. My brother will take the bait, and I'll
never hear the end of it." She tipped her glass back and let
the fizzy liquid soothe her frayed nerves. Thank goodness
she'd eaten the cake in the car or she'd feel these effects
even more.

"Of course. I'm looking forward to it." He leaned down
and whispered to her, "And Ruby, I'd never embarrass you.
That's not why I'm here."

She knew why he was, on paper anyway. They were trad-
ing dates to buffer the effects of family.

"Thank you," she said, drawing him into a hug. The
problem she hadn't anticipated was how good it felt to have
him at her side.

*This isn't real. Don't let that feeling percolate. Definitely
don't let it grow roots.*

"Hi, Matthew," Ruby said.

"Hey, Rubes." He hugged his sister and whispered in her ear, "I wasn't sure you'd make it. Glad to see you, though. I forgot how pretentious Byron's family is."

She cleared her throat and forced a smile, gesturing to Ares.

"Matthew, this is my... Ares." They shook hands. "And that's an understatement about Byron's family. They can be intense for sure."

"How'd you do that for two years?" he asked her.

"Who knows. I worked a lot," she laughed. "And mom kept telling me what a great fit we were since our families were friends." That, and she got the feeling that her mom wanted her to find love so she was off the hook, as if to say *I didn't do too much damage to you being an emotionally unavailable parent. Look—you found love, so how bad could your childhood have been?* "Anyway, I'm glad to see you. Sorry I had to work the holiday again. How was dinner with Mom?"

"Fine. She drank too much wine and kept asking when I was going to settle down and have babies. So, par, really."

Par, indeed. Some days, Ruby understood why her father had left and started over. She'd never forgive him for abandoning her and Matthew, but their mother had always erred toward the melodramatic.

It no longer mattered, though. That was the past and she had a good life with friends and a career she loved. She had Ares and her brother.

The music from the event washed over them, and Ruby tried to relax. Maybe she *had* been working too much. Family was a lot to handle, her family especially, but it was also a community that was always there. During the holidays that became even more apparent.

"Sorry I missed it. I'll drop in on her and take the heat off you for a bit. Does she know about Geoff?"

Ruby's brother had been dating Geoff for a year, but their mother still hadn't wrapped her head around the fact that neither of her kids were likely to give her grandchildren.

"I don't want to talk about that tonight. I'd rather get drunk. So, Ares, is it? Tell me some things about my sister. How do you know her?"

"This is Dr. Petrides that I work with," she offered. To say more was to open her own box of questions that couldn't ever be shut again. And she needed it to stay lock tight.

"Wait. I didn't put this together. Are you Ares Petrides, like of the Petrides Global Enterprises family?" Matthew asked.

"One and the same. It's my father's company, but my brother's at the helm now that I've taken a different career path."

To Ares's credit, he didn't flinch, not noticeably to anyone else, that was. However, she knew the man better than she knew herself some days, and his calm, caring exterior always faltered when his family was brought up. In this case, she noticed the small tic in his jaw that broke the veneer of his perfect smile.

"Man, we always thought Ruby was impressive, but landing a guy like you makes me respect my sister so much more." Matthew clapped Ruby on the shoulder playfully, but Ares moved his hand to the spot and rubbed it with his thumb affectionately.

The increase in their physicality she'd expected as part of the ruse they were upholding. What she hadn't anticipated was her body's physiological response to his touch. Her skin blossomed under each graze of his thumb, and each peck of his lips sent her head spinning and heart racing as if she was fifteen and crushing on a schoolmate. She also hadn't anticipated liking those feelings as much as she did.

Dammit, she needed to be careful.

"Your sister is more impressive than any of you realize. Did she tell you she saved a woman's life the other day by catching an aortic bleed all of us missed? She's the real prize." Ares pulled Ruby close and kissed the top of her head. He released a peaceful sigh, and she was pretty sure her heart melted to her rib cage.

Careful, schmareful.

"Thanks, hon." She beamed up at him. She could get used to fake dating the man if it came with perks like this.

When he smiled back at her, her pulse quickened. There was a hint of color on Ares's cheeks and his eyes glittered.

"I mean it, Ruby. You're the best of all of us and always have been. I'm just glad I noticed before I had to be asked to be your maid of honor at your wedding. Don't know I could have handled letting you go."

Ruby was washed with glee as Byron walked by just at the right time for Ares's speech.

However, she knew Ares's intonations—all of them. His teasing voice reserved for Ruby and a few nurses, his friendly, at-work tone used with patients he somehow cajoled into telling far too much about their lives, and even the lilt his flirtatious banter took when he was amping up their friendship to fake out their friends at the hospital.

None of those matched the serious, calm delivery of what was one of the nicest things anyone had ever said about Ruby.

"Damn, sis. I've got to say, we've been worried about you the past few years, but it seems like we didn't have any real reason to be."

"I'll take care of your sister," Ares said, tilting Ruby's

chin up so their gazes met. "I promise," he added, holding her gaze with a matching assurance. "That is, anything she doesn't take care of herself."

"Well, if I know my sister, you'll struggle to find something she can't do. She sing for you yet?"

Ares smiled and Ruby froze. They'd be caught for sure if he answered no. She sang every morning while she got ready for work and at night while she unwound before settling in for a mug of tea and a romance novel.

"You mean her morning serenades? They're the best way to start my day," Ares said. "Her Adele covers are almost better than the original."

"I've told her the same thing. Sis, this one's a keeper. Hey, I'm gonna refill these taster glasses with a Petite Syrah. Get you both one, too?"

Ruby nodded but Ares, true to his word to be her designated driver, shook his head. "I'm going to find Krista to congratulate her, but come find us?" Ruby asked. Matthew said he would.

The three of them parted ways, but not before Matthew tucked Ares into a quick side hug and shoulder pat. The moment was tender and somehow more real than anything in Ruby's life to that point.

"How did you know I sang?" she asked.

He smiled and kissed her hand. No one seemed to be watching, which confused Ruby.

"You sing at work when you're coming off an all-nighter. I'm only admitting to staying late to listen because I am delirious with hunger. I didn't have any of those cakes to soften the blow," he teased.

"Oh no, I should have shared," she lamented, embarrassed by how quickly she'd devoured the dessert in the car. "Let's get you food." She led him toward the table of hors d'oeuvres and made sure they stocked up on crepes and kabobs.

"Not at all. I'm only teasing. Anyway, sometimes, if I've had a long day, I'll stand off to one side of the entrance to the women's locker room and just listen to you sing. It's better than any medicine I've ever tried to stave off the loneliness of this job."

"Oh. Okay. Thank you." Byron had hated her singing, had asked her repeatedly to stop so he could hear himself think. She moved away from yet another juxtaposing thought of the two men since comparing them was fruitless. It's not like Ares was her real new boyfriend. "Thanks for being there for this. You handled them all so well. Also," Ruby said, scanning the crowd so she wasn't surprised by Bryon, "thank you for saying those things about me to Byron and his mother. My brother, too. I don't know why it's important they see me as strong, but it is. Even if it isn't true."

Ares turned her around and the intensity of his gaze unnerved her. "Why do you think you are anything other than the strongest woman we all know?"

"Because I'm exactly what Byron said I am—a person who works, sure. And is damn good at it. But that's it, isn't it?"

Ares's hands wrapped around the base of her skull, drawing her in. She inhaled sharply.

"Ruby, hear this. Every word I said to people tonight is true." He leaned in and tucked her hair behind her ear before his lips grazed the base of her neck. This was too much. And also, somehow not enough. She shivered in his arms while heat flooded her abdomen. "Every. Word."

She thought back to their conversations. Surely not *every* word... What he'd shared, what he'd said...it was so much more than friendly banter, or even the musings of a first date. No, they were the kinds of things someone said when they were dating. In love, even.

She gazed up at him, one of his hands on her hip, the other cupping her jaw. When he leaned down and kissed her in front of most of the people from her past, she couldn't help the aching in her chest from taking over like a raging inferno. Forget being careful, she needed to run from this feeling or risk being a victim of her own poor choices. Because her brain couldn't make sense of this, and until it could, she didn't know what to tell it to listen to—her body or her mind.

Was this man, possibly, a real part of her future?

No. This is a ruse. Finally, something that made sense.

When Matthew showed up with her glass of red wine, she merely held on to it. If she was going to survive this week of fake dating, she'd need to be as aware as possible, in case her libido or heart got the wrong message.

With a man as wonderful as Ares playing this dangerous game with her heart, who knew what kind of damage would happen? Dr. Ruby Phillips might be an expert on the inner workings of the cardio-thoracic system, but when it came to her own heart, experience had shown her it couldn't be trusted.

If she wasn't careful, she'd break her own heart and no one, no matter how competent a doctor, would repair it this time around.

CHAPTER SEVEN

ARES WALKED RUBY along the pathway to her home. Before picking her up that evening, he'd only been there once prior and he'd marveled at how simply *her* the space was. The front garden was no exception. The snow still clung to the bushes and pots, but the stone path was cleared. The night was brisk, but warmer than it had been Christmas Day.

Never before had he been so thankful for a long walk to the front door. The night was almost over, and he found he didn't want it to be. They'd talked the whole drive from the wine bar. They'd discussed their dating histories, ostensibly to "get their stories straight" in case they were questioned, but really, Ares was just horribly curious about all things Ruby Phillips. The men who'd fumbled her included.

He wouldn't admit this out loud, but he kinda wanted to thank every man on the list for messing up so he could be there tonight, as her date.

The thing he wouldn't quite admit, not even to himself? It'd felt more real than he'd intended. In fact, he'd found himself sharing far too many personal thoughts he'd coveted close to his chest for years now. It'd started as a way to make the lie they were selling—that they'd arrived not as dates, but as a couple.

Until it had morphed into him letting out the crush he'd harbored on his best friend like he'd been poked with holes and could no longer contain it. But containing it was imperative; any physician would anticipate the cause of death for friendship if he—a terminal monogamist-turned-bachelor—announced even an innocent crush.

Because where could it go?

"So, let me get this straight," he said, stalling. "Byron dumped you—like an idiot, I might add—and you didn't date for almost a *year*? And when you did, it was with Tony from the *gym*?"

"You make me sound pathetic, Ares. See? This is why I'm giving up dating entirely. It's not worth wading through the frogs."

He pulled her in close and kissed the top of her head. He couldn't keep from pressing his lips to any part of her that she'd let him. They were almost at her door and he felt rushed. As if he were running out of time.

Anxious about what it all meant.

He needed to get back to who Ruby was to him. His friend that he teased. Not the one he couldn't stop kissing and touching. Either way, that part was coming to an end. They were at her door, and behind it was reality. No kissing, no sweet words of affection he hadn't realized he felt as deeply as he did.

Just…friendship.

"You're anything but pathetic, Ruby. And remember, I'm the one who dated the same woman twice and didn't remember until she sprung meeting her parents on me. At a hospital event, no less."

Ruby giggled and a new chamber in his locked heart clicked open. Her laugh was one brand of infectious when he teased her—a large reason why he'd never let up on that account. But when he told self-effacing jokes or retold gossip from the guys' locker room at the hospital?

That laugh was his favorite so far.

"That just might land you at the top of the pile, Petrides."

"I know. And now *you* know why *I* don't date."

She leaned back, and the cool air that took the space she'd occupied felt heavy. Lonely.

"Is that true? Or is it because of what happened before I met you?" He froze. Did she know about the patient he'd lost? "You know, we've never talked about Ariadne."

He exhaled a sigh of relief. He didn't mind talking about his ex, but his wounds and triggers were too much to tackle when he was feeling so many other things for Ruby all of a sudden. All of their patients had families, or most of them, anyway. And they were colleagues in an A&E department; of course they'd incurred their share of loss. But Ares knew this topic would bring him and Ruby closer and he…

He couldn't go there.

He nodded. It might be a cop-out, but it was all he had at the moment and he wasn't saying good-night, either. He was stuck in friendship purgatory with a woman he cared for.

"Ariadne was a family friend and honestly, we would have broken up so much sooner if our parents hadn't egged us on from birth. It was as close to an arranged setup as we have nowadays and I really hurt her—and her family—when I moved here and didn't invite her to make the move with me."

"I'm sorry. Is that why you're not close with your family?"

More tough questions. The thing was, he ached to dive into all of it with her, something he'd never felt with anyone. Which was exactly why he couldn't.

"It's part of it. I think Ariadne showed me that nothing—not family, not a partner, not even my own pervasive loneliness—is worth the guilt on the other side if and when things go south."

That much was true, at least.

Ruby squeezed his hand and like it did every other time he shared a story that was lodged in his heart like a barb, it loosened, then fell off. The way she leaned into him, buried her head where the injury was, acted as a salve, healing the open wound.

But that invited a different problem. Two, actually.

If he went for what he wanted at that moment—a kiss good-night worthy of the date they'd shared—he was putting their friendship on the operating table and the outcome wasn't favorable.

Second, Ruby would be far worse for his attention at the hospital than his family ever was. Who knew what kind of mistakes he'd make if he worried about her safety, her laughter...

Her.

"I know why you believe that, and I'm sorry it's been like that for you. But loss is inevitable, Ares. Pretending it isn't is like tempting the gods. Pretending you have more control than they have is like angering them."

If only she knew how well he knew that.

"I think I angered the gods when I left the family business to pursue my own dreams." It was only a partial joke.

Ruby rubbed his hand in hers. The soft skin against his calluses was like silk covering his rough patches.

"No, Ares. That isn't what happened. You made a choice, and sure, it might have led to an unfavorable outcome for some people, but that doesn't mean it was wrong. First of all, life isn't that simple. I mean, is pleasing your family somehow better than being vulnerable and creating your own life?"

Ares felt as if he'd been punched. "Um, no. But like you said, it's complicated."

"Explain it to me."

She crossed her arms, and in an effort to get them back on track, he started talking.

Risk, be damned.

"My family and I weren't close before. They want more from me than I'm willing to give—"

"Like, they want you married off and producing adorable Greek babies?"

His stoic veneer cracked. "Yeah. Exactly."

"So tell them no."

Ares slumped against the bench at Ruby's door. "I've tried. That's not a word my billionaire parents are used to hearing. My absence says it for me."

"Until they show up at your door."

He gazed up at her, then stood, taking her hands back in his. "What about you? Why are you giving up just because you've run up against some duds?"

Ares watched the color rise up Ruby's chest, painting her in soft pink. Her eyes dipped to their shoes. He'd hit a nerve.

"Because you're right on one account. If I'm going to trade the safety of single life where I can work when and how I want for someone else's needs, I need to know they're not going to be like the rest and leave me when things get tough." Ares's skin prickled with awareness. Isn't that what he'd done with every other thing in his life outside medicine? Run when it got hard? "Anyway, not one of those dates have made me feel as excited as this fake date. Or as calm as you've made me feel. Nor have they made my stomach do that thing where it—well, never mind."

Ares tilted Ruby's chin until her gaze met his.

"Finish that sentence, Ruby." It wasn't a demand, but

the answer mattered to him. From the way the color on her cheeks deepened to red, it mattered to her, too.

"Don't read into it," she warned. *Too late.* He'd already committed the whole list of how this "date" had made her feel to memory. "But I've never felt that thing people talk about in movies. You know, where a person gets that swishy feeling in their belly when they're around someone…in particular."

Special. Someone they cared for. He kept his thoughts to himself in the hopes—worries?—she'd get there herself. Meanwhile, he'd closed the gap between them, and her breath swirled around him like a fog he wouldn't mind being trapped in.

Purgatory was bad, but this was flirting with annihilation.

"You know?" she asked. He nodded. "Have you ever felt that?"

He ran the back of his fingers along her chin, across her cheek, down her neck. At her collarbone, he traced it with the pad of his thumb.

"I have." He swallowed hard, his stomach feeling like a hurricane had erupted in it. "I do."

"So, you see my problem. If I can't muster what I feel for a…*friend* on a date, what hope does it have to turn into anything? I might as well be alone." She sighed into his palm, eyes closed, and he just held her. "If only this were a real date, then—"

Forget a hurricane, his stomach had taken flight, headed straight for his throat.

"Ruby—"

She opened her eyes and pushed back from him. "Sorry, I didn't mean that. I know it isn't. I was just saying that if

it were, this is what I'd want to feel, you know. I mean...
Ugh. Sorry."

Her exposed skin was the color of her name.

"Stop apologizing for being who you are and saying what
you feel, Ruby. That's not who we are. So," he said, "what
would we do?" She gazed up at him, confusion etched in
her arched brows. "If this were a real date, what would
come next?"

The corner of her mouth twitched up, and he knew damn
well what *he'd* do if this were real.

"Um, you'd wait for me to get my keys and..." She trailed
off. He'd never seen Ruby Phillips nervous. Then again,
he'd never felt the intensity of desire pooling in his stomach, either. This was new territory, that was for certain.

"And?"

"And you'd give me a tender hug goodbye before making sure I get in safely."

Ares barked out a laugh. "Bullshit."

A grin spread across her face.

"You know that's not what would happen. Why won't
you talk to me, Ruby? I'm your best friend."

She inhaled sharply.

"I—" She closed her eyes and her lips formed a small
pout. "I suppose you'd kiss me. Soft at first, then with more
passion."

Ares dipped his head and drew her into him. His lips
met hers, and he released the tension in his arm in case she
needed to back away, in case he was reading this all wrong.

Instead, her mouth opened for him.

His tongue traced her lips just as she'd asked. Softly at
first, then with the passion he felt brewing inside him since
he'd opened the door and seen her in that dress. Or maybe
he'd been fooling himself all along and he was kissing her

with longing he'd developed over years of caring for this woman.

They were friends, sure, but there'd always been an undercurrent of...

More.

That current swept him away, had him diving into her as if she was the pool of life, the answer to every question he'd ever had. His tongue tangled with hers as his hands fisted in her hair. They were leaning against the door, her body pressed against his. They had coats on, but still...

He could feel every inch of her tall frame against every inch of his. And the word *more* became kindling to the fire now roaring within him.

"Uh-oh," he whispered. She gazed up at him, and he kissed her again. "This is going to be a problem, isn't it?"

"Only if you let it." With that, she kissed him this time, diving into him with a fervor he'd never expected.

He forced himself to break away, held back a groan when Ruby moaned against his lips.

"Then what?" he whispered, nibbling on her tender earlobe. "What would come next?"

"Then," she said. Her voice was a tremble, and it caused him to drive his hips into hers. Her gasp came with a leg wrapped around his hip, opening up to him more. "Then we'd make out like teenagers before I gazed up at you with a question in my eyes."

He peered into her gray eyes, transfixed at how they shifted under the light they were under.

"Ask it," he demanded. "Tell me what you want, Ruby. Anything, and I'll give it to you."

"Will you come in and stay with me tonight?"

He groaned into her neck, a flash of hunger burning away any possibility of an answer other than "yes."

"Hell yes, I will." With that, he picked her up, surprised that, though she was nearly as tall as him, he could lift her with ease. She giggled and wrapped both legs around him, leaning back to unlock the door.

He didn't put her down when they got inside. "Then what?" he asked again.

"If this were a real date, I'd ask if you want a nightcap, but that's...that's not what I want."

She bit her bottom lip, and he groaned with an ache to take that lip into his mouth and suck on it until she was wet for him. Jeez, this woman had him undone.

"What do you want? I'm in a position to give you whatever you desire, Ruby. And nothing is off-limits." He kissed her. "Nothing."

The pause between his question and her answer was heavy with anticipation. It was the cusp of everything they'd ever been to one another, and if they toppled over the edge, the world would surely shift beneath them and look vastly different afterward.

He didn't care. Hell, he *wanted* the seismic shift. Needed it.

Needed *her*.

"I want you, Ares. In my bed, on top of me, inside me. I want all of you."

That was all the permission he needed.

"Where?" he growled.

She pointed down the hallway and he didn't hesitate. He swiped a pile of dresses she must've gone through onto the floor and laid her down gently.

Her dress hitched up, exposing the tops of her thighs and though he'd secretly wondered what Ruby's body looked like under all those clothes, nothing could have prepared him for her creamy skin beckoning him to taste it.

Every cell of his own skin was on fire, touching her the only way to extinguish the flames.

Aching need coursed through him, but he couldn't rush this. Wouldn't.

He gripped her knees and spread them until he could fit between her legs. Kneeling in front of her, careful to keep eye contact, he slid his hands up her smooth expanse, sated and driven further at the same time. When he reached her hips, he kissed over her cream lace panties. She smelled like roses and the sea. It reminded him of the coast back home in Greece, and for the first time since he'd left, nostalgia hit him with blunt force.

He nuzzled her center, desperate to inhale more of her, to taste her.

"Can I?"

"Please. Yes." She nodded and ran her fingers through his hair, encouraging him. He hooked the lace and pulled them down around her ankles, then dipped into her folds. He could die happy right here—licking and sucking at her core, tasting the brine and sweet floral that was unique to Ruby.

He pulled at her core and she gasped. He held back a smile and watched for her cues. Cupping her backside, he pulled her down to the end of the bed so he could engulf himself in her.

Her lips parted and her back arched. "God, Ares. I mean… Oh, my, *God.*"

She was so responsive, purring under his touch when he reached a place that made her feel good. It was like learning a new surgical technique, seeing the outcome in real time.

It was addictive.

He slid a finger between her folds, doubling his efforts. She cried out and fisted her hands in his hair while he tugged and sucked her to climax. When she screamed his name, he laughed. Forget teasing to get her to smile and giggle. He wanted his name on her lips at the height of pleasure.

That, he'd do anything to re-create.

He pulled the dress over her head and kissed up her stomach, tracing the curve of her breasts after unclasping her bra. He made his way to her taut buds and nibbled on each, noting that her back arched under him again.

He was learning her like he had learned the human body in medical school, but he only wanted to specialize in her, not emergency medicine. No, give him a course in making Ruby moan like she did when he sucked her nipple and teased it with his teeth. Or a residency in the way her breath hitched when he slipped two fingers inside her and pulled toward her core. He'd give anything to be placed, not at a dream A&E research hospital, but at her feet where he could taste her at will.

The curves and peaks and valleys she'd hidden under scrubs were laid out bare in front of him. It was everything he'd wanted and so much he'd never imagined possible. It was safe to say this was the best night of his life. And he'd barely tasted her.

A fact he planned on remedying immediately.

As if she'd read his mind, she pulled him up until their faces were aligned. He kissed her nose, each cheek, then her lips.

"I wasn't done down there," he said. She grinned and ran her hands through his hair.

"And if I wanted you inside me so I could make you come? What would you say to that?"

"Do you have a condom?" he asked. Her laughter was full and light, like Ruby, period.

"I do. Call it wishful thinking, but in that drawer by my bedside."

In seconds he was disrobed, sheathed and standing over her naked body.

Dammit. Had he ever wanted anything so badly, so deeply and completely in his life? Not even medicine came to mind. Ruby's body, pliable and willing, consumed his focus.

"You're beautiful," she whispered. The glittering in her eyes said she believed that, and he had to let her. He'd never had a problem getting dates, had recognized his own masculinity, if not handsomeness. Thanks to his Greek Adonis of a father for those genes. And yet, he'd still never thought of his body as anything other than an extension of his medical instruments.

None of the rest of it mattered before Ruby's assessment of him. She made him feel like a *man*.

If only he could return the favor. "You're everything," he replied. She sighed and spread her legs for him. He propped himself at her entrance. "Are you sure?" he asked. She nodded, lifted her hips to meet his tip. He teased her opening and found her wet and ready for him.

He slid in up to his hilt and groaned. She took him completely. As they rocked, found their rhythm and he learned more of what pleased her, he made sure to etch each one in his memories. All he wanted was to please her.

And that he did until the dawn broke through the drapes.

The morning came quicker than he'd have liked, but seeing her spread across the sheets, every inch of her committed to his memory, he felt…okay. Things had shifted, yes, but nothing bad. If anything, he wanted to hurry to work, to do a damn good job so he could be a man she was proud of, and then hurry home for more of whatever the night before had been.

Hmm. Maybe he'd been wrong about things for some time. At a minimum, he wanted to enjoy her, at least while they continued this ruse the next few days.

When she woke, he forgot that it was still winter outside, that his parents and family were arriving in hours to his town. All he saw was the sun in her eyes and smile.

"Hi, you."

"Ares," she said. Recognition shadowed her features, and she sat up immediately. He braced himself for the regret she might be experiencing. "Last night felt like a dream, but it happened, didn't it?"

He nodded.

Please, he said, echoing a version of a prayer he uttered before each surgery. *Let this be okay.*

"It did. Are you okay with what we did?"

She smiled, then, a wide grin that burned off any doubts.

"I mean, yeah. There were some things we did that will probably make me blush when I think back on them, but I liked all of it."

Ares exhaled a deep breath.

"Thank goodness. I wasn't above begging you to want to do this again, and Ruby, it's not pretty when I'm on my knees."

"I beg to differ." She winked and bit her lip, and it was his turn to laugh. God, she surprised him. She'd been his best friend for years now, his colleague for longer, but only a day as her lover and he was transformed. "But you really want to do this again? Now? Aren't you exhausted?"

He pulled her in and growled as he kissed her deeply. "Woman, I couldn't ever be too tired to do what we just did. But no, I meant after today." He inhaled, refusing to overthink this. "What would you say about seeing how this goes? I mean, worst case scenario, it makes us more believable on our fake dates."

He held his breath again.

"And best case? I mean, you don't want to date."

"Neither do you."

"Touché," she said, kissing his nose. "So where does that leave us? Friends who—"

"No," he said. Friends no longer felt like enough when it came to Ruby. That was the biggest shift of all last night. "At the core, sure, but this week, why don't we see where this goes and we can get back to being friends after the events if this doesn't feel right? I mean, no one knows me better, and Ruby, I don't want to know anyone else the way I got to know you last night. Just you."

"Just me?" Her voice cracked, and he squeezed her tight against him. A deep desire to protect her hurt feelings from past partners and future hurt competed with the desire to love her into submission.

"Just you. What do you say? More than friends this week?"

"Yes," she whispered, rocking into him. "Let's see where this goes at the wedding and New Year's Eve party. We can reassess then?" He nodded. "Okay, then let's see if you meant what you said about not getting too tired for sex." And just like that, the best night of his life turned into the best morning. If only the buzzing phone on the nightstand could be ignored. The outside world would get to them at some point, but for now, Ares was content.

Only a small tingle of worry nagged at him as he thought of how quickly she'd changed his mind about his priorities. But that was a problem for future Ares. This one had a naked woman in bed, and he intended to focus on that and leave the rest for later.

This time, he wouldn't let the consequences touch him and wreck something beautiful. Guilt would have to take a back seat. As he kissed her and slid inside her again, he wondered if he was naive enough to believe that was possible, or if he'd figured out how to actually have it all.

CHAPTER EIGHT

RUBY SMILED AS she pulled on her scrubs and tossed her hair. A hand playfully slapped her on the butt as she bent over her sink to put on a thin layer of mascara. Two more days left of the year and somehow, the whole tone of her year had shifted.

"What's that smile for?" Ares asked.

"I'm just…happy."

"Good. That's the plan, you know. To keep that smile on your face indefinitely." He kissed her forehead and walked out of the bathroom humming the song to something they'd heard in the car on the way home the night before. He'd taken her out to dinner and cocktails and when they'd driven back into her driveway, she'd been shocked to find that four hours had passed. Normally, she counted down the minutes to the end of her dates.

They'd made out to the pop song, and she'd gone to bed draped on Ares's chest feeling like a teenager with a massive crush.

Her smile deepened, and she wasn't sure how she was supposed to pretend things weren't a 100 percent different from the last time she'd stepped through the doors of the Royal York.

How she was supposed to act as if she hadn't slept with

her best friend and in doing so upended every thought she'd had about dating, intimacy and—

Well, she wouldn't go there. Not when the terms of their new...*agreement* were so tenuous. At best they were friends with benefits. At best this ended at the chime of the new year, and they could go back to being friends.

At best, she'd be able to forget the way Ares's hands had wrapped around her stomach, sliding up and cupping her breasts, or how he'd kissed the top of her head just before she fell asleep the past two nights and sighed contentedly. Or how he'd sought her out in the middle of the night, tucking himself against her form and molding to her.

Yeah, forgetting that would be no problem. She released a sigh of her own, far less content than Ares's. New Year's Eve was tomorrow. Time could slow down and she wouldn't mind.

"You ready?" he asked, popping his head into the bathroom.

"Yep." For what, she wasn't sure. But she gathered her things, somewhat less enthusiastic about going to work than she had been.

They'd agreed to walk in separately to work so they didn't draw too much attention to themselves. Funnily, now that there was actually something to tempt the gossip at the hospital, they both felt it was better to keep what they had going on a secret. This wasn't a practical joke, or a joke, period.

And their friends would tease them as if it were if they didn't keep it quiet.

An hour later, she wasn't sure that was possible. She was treating a child with a broken ankle from sliding down the ice and as soon as she left the room after setting the injury, Ares pulled her into an on-call room and kissed her up against the wall.

"What are you doing?" she asked, breathless. He grinned and nibbled on her neck, sending shivers across her skin.

"Kissing my fake girlfriend at work. Mmm," he murmured against her shoulder. "You smell good. Like vanilla."

"Better than antiseptic," she teased. He laughed, the vibration of his lips tickling her. "But we're going to get caught, Ares."

"So what?"

"So, didn't we agree not to let our friends know we're—"

She didn't know how to finish that sentence. Sleeping together? Fake dating? Neither seemed appropriate.

"That doesn't mean we can't steal some moments together and make the most of this time, in my opinion." He bit her earlobe playfully, and she inhaled sharply. "Unless you want me to stop…"

She shook her head as much as she could with a handsome man attached to it.

"No. Don't." That was the problem, as far as she saw it. She didn't want to stop at all. And there was an end date on this. Because she knew her best friend and his determination not to get entangled in a relationship was too strong. Not even good sex had ever jarred him from that singular goal.

"Okay. Well, how about we meet here at lunch and steal a quick nap?"

She laughed. "Is that what we're calling it now? A nap?"

Ares chuckled and pulled her into a kiss. "Whatever gets you back in my arms, Dr. Phillips."

He gave her one more perfunctory kiss and then left the on-call room before her. She was careful to look in each direction before leaving. Angel, the new lead flight medic, was at the end of the hall in a deep discussion with Teddy, both of them looking frustrated with the other. Teddy's hands were dug into the pockets of his flight suit and Angel's were flying around like she was the pilot of the medic helicopter, not the physician on board.

Ruby shook her head. When would those two realize they were on the same team? In another world, one where their fire aimed at the other was tempered into another form, they might even be good together. Hmm. Not her circus, and not anything she felt like meddling with.

But she did take advantage of the distraction to slip from the on-call room unseen. She ran a hand through her hair, taming it, and checked her cell. There were a few texts, one from her mom. She swiped open the chain and frowned.

Hi, hun. Wish I could have made it to Byron's wine bar event, but I had a tough day. You know better than most how hard weddings are for me. I'll do my best to see you at the actual wedding, though, okay? Matthew told me you're bringing a date. Janet texted this morning and loved him. I can't wait to meet this mystery man. Hope you're doing well. XO Mom

It was so like her mother to bail on a family event because she was "having a hard day." As if she was the only woman in the world to have gone through a traumatic divorce and raised two kids. Or let those two kids raise themselves when she couldn't get out of bed. Ruby didn't know how to respond, so she sent a smiley face and quick innocuous text.

See you soon. Love you.

She didn't want to add anything about Ares for two reasons. The first was the same reason they weren't saying anything about the change in terms of their friendship at work. It seemed private, intimate, and sharing it would somehow dilute the preciousness of…whatever this was.

The second was less about her and her feelings and more that by the time she figured out what was going on between her and Ares, there was a strong chance it would be over.

Still, the text from her mother did point out a flaw in her and Ares's plan. Namely how they were supposed to come out of this unscathed and still be friends when they were playing house in front of the people who loved them most.

Explaining that they simply went separate ways wouldn't be enough, would it?

Ruby's pager went off, disrupting her inner spiral.

"Dammit," she whispered. An incoming child with suspected hypothermia. She jogged down to the intake and met the medics. "What's the story?" she asked.

"Kid fell in the River Ouse," Mel, the medic, said. "Was messing around with friends and slipped. Kids ran off and left him so they wouldn't get in trouble. Got a call from a woman reading in her front room and saw the whole thing. Good thing, too. He wouldn't have lasted five more minutes in that water this time of year."

"Good grief. I wish this was the first time I've heard that story. They catch the kids?"

Mel nodded. "Yeah, one of them turned the rest in. Felt bad."

Ruby shook her head. "Thank goodness. What're his vitals?"

"Thready pulse, weak breath sounds. Found unconscious and hasn't come back around."

"Okay. We'll take it from here. I appreciate you, Mel."

Ruby took the gurney and instructed the nurse to get started on an IV and warming blanket. No one else was around. Where was Ares? They'd been working together pretty consistently, and his absence struck her as odd.

"Looks like you're short-staffed today."

"We are," Ruby agreed. "People out for the holidays or picked up some bug from visiting family. The usual." Ruby didn't care—the busier she stayed, the less she thought about Ares or how, for the first time in her adult life, she realized why she'd had that desire to find a partner who understood her love for medicine and the want for someone to share it with. She couldn't imagine the loneliness of her mother's life—having given up on everything and everyone because she'd been hurt before. Sure, that seemed easier on one hand, but wasn't it better to keep trying for a life you wanted?

You just gave up on dating before Ares posed his idea to be each other's dates to the wedding and party, her snarky mind reminded her.

It was right, but Ruby hadn't ever given up permanent hope she'd meet someone. It was just the timeline of needing a man to be by her side at Christmas that had her spinning.

Though, she had been feeling pretty hopeless before Ares's idea. Maybe that's the real reason his attentiveness, his touch and his presence had affected her. She'd been starved and he provided a meal.

He hadn't, however, offered to feed her longer than Byron's wedding a few days after New Year's, so she'd better not get used to these…*tastes*. Soon enough, she'd be providing for herself again.

"Need help? I've still got nursing privileges."

"I'd love that. Just till we get him stable." Ruby loved

Mel. She was another medic who worked the same holidays, same shifts as Ruby and Ares. They'd gotten to know one another over brief cups of coffee on stolen breaks between patients. Like Ruby, Mel's life revolved around the hospital and her career.

The two women worked in silence while they got the patient hooked up to saline and the thawing process started. At first, it seemed like they might have an uncomplicated save as the boy's vitals improved.

Then, his sats devolved and the alarm went off, indicating they'd lost his pulse.

"Dammit. We're losing him," Ruby said. "I'd like to increase his temp a little quicker."

"We don't want to send him into shock," Mel advised. Ruby nodded her agreement.

"We need another pair of hands. Can you ask the charge nurse to page Dr. Petrides?" Mel sprinted out of the room and came back seconds later with Ares in tow.

"Catch me up. What happened?" Ares asked. Mel worked the IVs while Ruby performed CPR and Ares got the AED paddles ready. Ruby filled Ares in on the circumstances of the boy's fall into the river. "Kids can be awful," he said. "Have his parents been notified?"

Mel nodded. "We got ahold of them on the way in. They both work swing shifts, and he was supposed to be at one of the other kids' houses. Luckily, the boy had an unlocked phone or we'd be dealing with an underage John Doe. No ID, no wallet. Just a boy thinking he could mess around with his friends on a day off school. Until the people he trusted turned on him."

Ruby bit her lip, desperate to stave off the flash of heat behind her eyes. She didn't want to be alone, but in the end, weren't they all? Maybe her mom was on to something. When things got tough, people ran. That was the way of it.

She moved away from the boy so Ares could place the paddles on his chest. Ares went back to the device and Ruby took control of the shock to the boy's heart, hoping to jump-start it.

Come on, she thought. *Come back to us.*

"Yes, kids can be awful," she whispered. "Charge me to 200." So could adults. Her mom, hurt from her own absent relationship, had run from her kids rather than face the tough circumstances and rise above them. Byron had done the same. Even her brother had dropped off the radar when he'd met his now-fiancé. Ruby could count on one hand who she could rely on in life.

Mel and her other coworkers.

Ares. But to what end? If this new relationship didn't fizzle as they were hoping it would in the end, and exploded instead, her whole life would be blown up along with it. Their colleagues would be forced to take a side, and she'd be alone at home *and* at work.

What had she been thinking, agreeing to see where things went with Ares? It certainly looked different in the light of day.

Fake dating for an event was one thing—heck, it was just a quick week of events. But they'd upped the ante by exploring the physical thing brewing between them that first night.

Regrets? her subconscious asked. No, she didn't think so. At least not yet. But she'd have to be careful, tread lightly on the shaky ground this fake relationship was built on.

The high-pitched whine of the AED machine was shrill, but welcome.

"Clear," she called, desperate to make this part of her

life—what Ares called "old faithful"—work. This boy had to have a chance to see that not all people abandoned you. That some people dug in when the rest left. She shocked the boy, and his chest rose and fell with the effort. "Push two of epi and let's go to 300."

Another shock and no change.

"Come on," she whispered. "You've got so much time ahead of you. Come back."

"He's not responding," Ares said, putting a hand on her lower back. It centered her, but did nothing to weaken her resolve.

"I want to go again. Charge to 300."

"Ruby—"

She leveled him with a glare. He nodded and charged the machine while Mel resumed compressing the boy's chest. She trusted Ares, but needed to know she'd tried everything.

"Okay, Mel. Clear."

Mel stepped back and Ruby didn't let the tiny lifeless form on the gurney distract her. Nor the man's gentle, stalwart presence behind her.

She placed the paddles on the boy's chest and sent a small prayer to whatever saint looked out over children and adults who'd trusted the wrong person.

Let this boy not pay for that mistake with his life. Please, she added. With that, she hit the button and watched his back arch, his lips part.

And then a steady beep beep beep filled the room, drowned only by the exhales of all three medics.

"You got him back," Ares said, stepping again into the fray and adjusting lines, medicines and the boy's position on the bed. Ruby felt his gaze on her, but couldn't read the emotion behind it. "Damn, that was close, but his other sats are coming back, too. Ruby, I mean, Dr. Phillips, you made the right call."

"Thanks. I was just stubborn, that's all."

Ares stared into her eyes, and she felt torn between looking away and holding him there to figure out why he was looking at her with a question in his eyes.

Ask it, she thought. At the same time, she didn't want to know. Not with Mel here, not at work.

He rubbed Ruby's shoulders, and it snapped her control. She pulled out of his touch under the guise of filling out the tablet with their journey to get the boy back in sinus rhythm.

In real life, before they'd slept together, a simple kind touch like that would have not only been welcome from Ares, but normal. Now, though, she worried the whole world could see through it to what it made her feel.

Feelings she couldn't put words to yet, so better to avoid the confusion.

"Man, that was intense," Mel said, wiping her bangs, damp with sweat, from her eyes. "It kinda makes me want to come back here for a bit instead of being cramped in the rig."

"You should—we could use a good physician's assistant on staff," Ares said. His pager went off, eliciting a frown from him that evaporated the moment he met Ruby's gaze. A small measure of pride that she had that pull on him tugged at her heart. To Ruby, he added, "I've got to take this. As usual, it was good working with you. See you later? Late lunch so we can go over protocol?" The wink he shot her was pure devilishness and more akin to the man she'd known the past few years.

Her stomach answered first, though not in response to the "lunch" he mentioned. All she'd been able to imagine since their hot kiss in the on-call room was the "nap" Ares had mentioned. Now he'd said "protocol," a joke between them since he'd woken her up that morning with a "protocol" that included his tongue in very sensitive places on her body.

Just thinking about it made her stomach flip.

Honestly, she'd never imagined her body could be so responsive to a man. Then again, the one to draw it out of her was her best friend, a man she wasn't allowed to actually catch feelings for, so maybe she should tell her stomach—and heart—to shut up.

"Yeah, see you later." On the way out, Ares pinched her backside the same way he did when they were alone. It had the effect of turning Ruby's skin hot. She was incredibly thankful for the scrubs she wore that hid all manner of sins.

She was also thankful that Mel didn't seem to catch on.

"You have a good holiday?" Mel asked as they filled out the paperwork on the boy.

"We did." She cringed when the word came out. *We*—such a damning word that inspired the kind of hope Ruby wasn't ready to ask for. Mel's brow went up in question. "Dr. Petrides is joining me at a couple events over the holidays so I don't have to go alone."

On paper, that was true, at least.

Mel shrugged. "Ah, I see. Wish I had someone who would do the same for me. It's part of why I work so damn much. I don't want to be stuck at the kids' table yet again."

Ruby forced a smile, but then thought of the event two nights earlier with her brother. Showing up with Ares was the first time anyone had taken her seriously as a physician and honored her choice to work as hard as she did. Why was that a weakness for women, but lauded in men?

"I hear you. How was your holiday? Did you brave the kids' table to see family after work?"

"Not this year. Couldn't do it, especially because my sister got engaged. All the attention will be on her until the second round of drinks when people will zero in on me and my very single status." Again, Ruby understood. Mel grabbed her medic's jacket and stopped at the doorway. "I wish hanging with my family didn't mean doing CPR on someone else's every year. Maybe we should make a new tradition next year and all get together for a meal after work. We're family, in a crazy kind of way."

She shrugged and left Ruby there with her thoughts. On one hand, Mel was right on the money. They *were* all family—a ragtag group of doctors, midwives, medics and nurses. But two things Mel said sat wrong on Ruby's heart.

First, that work was a replacement for other parts of their lives. Had Ruby been hiding out at the hospital as a way to avoid real commitment? Sure, her last few dates hadn't gone well on their own accord, but maybe part of it was her.

Second, Mel mentioned making their own traditions and their own family. While Ruby agreed, the only thing she saw in the back of her mind when Mel said that was Ares.

What that meant for their part-time fling and ruse—and the full-time friendship behind both—Ruby couldn't guess.

Only that extracting themselves from this mess they made wouldn't be as easy as either of them had imagined.

CHAPTER NINE

THREE EVENTS REMAINING. That was all that stood between him and the life he'd carefully cultivated for himself. A few days after New Year's, he could go back to being Ruby's friend, a dedicated physician at Royal York's A&E department, and former Greek heir to a fortune.

Three titles bestowed upon him, only one of which mattered at the moment.

And it wasn't the one he'd been expecting. He'd assumed that he and Ruby would be able to keep their friendship what it was, his family would go home and he'd go right back to being dedicated to work as he'd been before. Work that mattered deeply to him.

Or at least, that was the idea when he'd first set out to play Ruby's boyfriend for the events leading up to his family's New Year's Eve party and Byron's wedding. Now, he wasn't so sure, especially standing at her bedroom door, watching her slip into a black pants suit that stopped his breath.

She hadn't put a shirt on under the jacket. He had seen the style on other women before. But on Ruby? Her gray eyes popped against the midnight-dark fabric, and the deep-V of the suit showed off the tops of breasts he'd just finished sampling.

God, he wanted more. All of her, even if that was the

last thing he should pursue. But it showed no signs of stopping, which was problematic since his parents' New Year's Eve party was tomorrow night, and Byron's wedding only four days away.

Their time was coming to an end.

"So let me get this straight," he said, desperate to find a topic that they could talk about that didn't involve her stripping for him and skipping the event altogether. His addiction to her was quickly moving to an all-consuming one. "The wine bar was a get-to-know-you event, and this is the official engagement party?"

"Not exactly. Tonight is the rehearsal dinner. The engagement party happened four months ago, and I wasn't invited."

"But they sent you an invite to the wedding? What's that about?"

She shrugged, and he tried not to watch how the gesture made her breasts lift in response. Jeez. How was he supposed to get through this event and not ogle her the entire time? He wasn't sure he'd see one centimeter of the venue when his date was as stunning as she was.

"They probably thought I'd be working. It was on a bank holiday, and I never had a single one of those off when Byron and I were together."

Ares thought of a lot of things that were different when Ruby and Byron were together. Ruby's work schedule was certainly one of them, but so was her inability to see what a fool the guy was. If Ares accomplished anything with this fake-dating scheme, he hoped for two things: first, to give Ruby the pleasure and joy she craved, and two, the knowledge that she deserved more than any man could give her—himself included.

"Well, they can suck it. You're amazing, and they're

lucky you're gracing their paltry event with your amaz-
ingness."

"Just call me Princess Kate," she teased back. She put
on a set of earrings, and he resisted the urge to touch where
the metal met her lobes. He smiled, but not even Cathe-
rine, Princess of Wales, would class up the event like Ruby
would. She made everything look good. "And don't waste
your energy caring why Byron's family does anything. You
don't have to have anything to do with him after the wedding."

The problem was simple, scientifically speaking. He'd
changed his mind about his priorities. Or rather, his mind
had been changed for him. Sure, he wanted Ruby—like
deeply, completely wanted her. His skin called out to touch
hers when she was anywhere in the vicinity, a liability given
what they did for a profession.

But his mind and body wanted everything to do with her,
maybe had through their whole friendship. Even if that included her dodgy ex-boyfriend.

There was only one crux. His heart had recently tried
adding something to that conversation, but Ares wasn't
there yet. He didn't know if he ever could be—not with
Ruby or anyone for that matter.

Either way, something about taking on an all-consuming
desire like Ruby had turned off his other one.

Medicine. He still loved his job, but when the chief of
surgery asked him that morning to take on an extra shift,
a shift that would have made him late for Byron's rehearsal
dinner with Ruby, he'd turned it down without a shred of
guilt.

He'd committed to her and that promise mattered.

"You ready?" she asked him. He almost responded "for
what?" but caught himself.

"I sure am. And might I say, Dr. Phillips, you look incredible."

The blush staining her chest and cheeks was the stuff of romance novels.

"You sure can. You don't clean up so bad yourself, Dr. Petrides." Her words were hedged, but he knew the look in her eyes. It was the same as his—lust and desire and the spark ready to be set ablaze when they got home.

"Okay, then," she said, grabbing a small black and pearl clutch, "we should get to the dinner. It starts in fifteen minutes, and not even that rocket ship you call a car will get us through town traffic at supper."

Ares smiled.

"Woman, you have no idea what this car can do." He winked, appreciating the smile it brought to her lips.

They drove in silence, which wasn't awkward or tension-filled at all. In fact, paired with the light piano instrumental music in the background and her holding his hand over the center console, it was peaceful.

He almost didn't want the drive to be over.

"Okay, round two. Thank you again for doing this, Ares. It means so much to me. And sorry we couldn't get together with your mom for drinks."

"It's my pleasure, Ruby." And it was, more than she knew. "Don't worry about my mom. Tomorrow will be plenty with my family, and they understood."

That wasn't entirely true, but best not to worry Ruby with it.

Ruby smiled, but it didn't reach her eyes. Interesting and something to note to come back to later.

"And it was really nice meeting your friends and family. Gives me insight into who you are and why you are the way you are."

"You mean neurotic and unfeeling?"

"Have I ever said anything close to that?" he wondered out loud. Had his teasing been that cruel? God, he hoped not or he'd have to make a massive change, and quickly.

"Not exactly, but you are prone to teasing me about my insecurities, which are largely things others have called neurotic." He cringed. What kind of person could ever say that about Ruby? She was quirky, yes, but those traits made her unique and unforgettable. Perfect.

Tell her that, his subconscious nudged.

No, he couldn't. Not yet. Not without this feeling a bit too much like a real date. Did he care about her? Immensely. Did that mean he could or should push this into dating territory? Not without hurting her, himself, or both of them.

"As for the unfeeling part," she continued, "that's just what you say at work every time I leave a patient's room."

He laughed. "Woman, you act like the patient's chart will self-destruct in five seconds if you don't save the patient, put the chart away and sprint from the room. You called it efficiency, and maybe you're right. It's not my style, but I've never called you unfeeling. In fact, sometimes I'd say the opposite."

She crossed her arms over her chest and even in his peripheral vision, he observed the way the jacket opened, giving access to her in a way he was hoping to exploit that evening.

"Excuse me, it *is* efficient. More than spending an hour chatting up each patient and getting their whole life story. We work in the A&E department, sir. Not maternity or hospice."

He got out and walked over to open her car door.

"Can I tell you a secret?" he whispered in her ear. Her gasp sent a shiver down his spine.

"Yes," she replied. The word was thick with want.

"Two, actually. The first is that you're stunning and the most beautiful woman I've ever been lucky enough to take on a date." She leaned against him and clutched his jacket lapel. If he had any sense, he'd take her right home and make love to her until she forgot everything negative anyone had ever said about her.

"The second?"

He kissed the top of her head. "Spending time with patients means I catch things that might get in the way of their care later on. We need your efficiency to keep beds open, but I like to think my way of listening to what the tests aren't showing us yet helps save lives, too."

She gazed up at him, her lips parted.

"That's what happened with the man on Christmas Day. The driver who lost his daughter."

He nodded. "You handled the medicine that would heal him, and I made sure he got the mental health evaluation that could ensure he moved forward with life after healing physically. We're a good team, Ruby."

"We are. We're different, though, aren't we? I'm a lot, I know."

There was her self-effacing talk again. If only she could view herself through his eyes.

"Sweetheart," he said, noting the way her eyes got big. "You and I couldn't be more different in some ways. But in every way that matters, I see you and wouldn't want you to change a damn thing about yourself. You're perfect."

There. He'd said it. And they were still standing there; the world didn't stop moving. He did feel an infinitesimal shift, but it wasn't uncomfortable. "Also, I'd stomp on anyone who tried to tell you otherwise. Speaking of, shall we get to dinner? Making a fashionable entrance is one thing, but we might be pushing it."

She nodded and he led her into the venue, a stately mansion that had been renovated to accommodate intimate weddings and formal dinners such as this. Byron certainly was making a show of his relationship, wasn't he?

In Ares's experience, the louder people had to be in a public space about how happy they were—alone or coupled—the less true it was.

But what was the difference between that and keeping cards too close to one's chest? Was that problematic, too?

He thought about how he'd played cards with Teddy on a break, walked with Ryan through the halls to process losing a patient, or even assisted Ash with an ortho case and itched to tell them what he'd been feeling with and for Ruby. But he'd not been able to suss out whether he just wanted to gossip, or share what was in his heart, and until he could make heads or tails of his feelings, he'd keep quiet about them.

He was happy, full stop. Well, happy and a little terrified, but that was natural as relationships shifted, wasn't it?

When they were sitting at the table, Ares was pleased to see they'd been placed next to a woman who had to be Ruby's mom. She had the same natural grace and beauty as her daughter, though it seemed as if life had been hard on the woman. She didn't have the same laugh lines as Ruby, nor the light that shone in her gray eyes.

When they embraced, that confirmed his suspicions, even though their hug was stilted as far as he could tell.

"This must be the man I've heard so much about," her mother said. "I'm Eleanor, Ruby's mother."

"I would have guessed sister," Ares said, "but it's a pleasure to meet you. I'm Ares Petrides, a physician at the Royal York and number one fan of your daughter." He wanted to add that he'd heard a lot about the woman, but the truth was, he hadn't. There was so much mystery to Ruby he had yet to discover. He was excited to unearth more about the woman who'd come to be so important to him.

"A charmer, hmm?" Eleanor asked.

"Through and through," Ruby answered, leaning into Ares's chest. He exhaled, peace enveloping him as it always did when she was near. "How are you feeling, Mom?"

Eleanor waved away Ruby's question. "Fine, fine. Much better. In fact, I'm hoping to do some dancing after we eat and drink on Byron's tab. I love Hank and Janet, you know that, but I still can't believe the nerve of that man for leaving you."

Ruby bristled, and Ares rubbed her shoulders in response. She relaxed, but didn't answer. Instead, she took a long sip of the red wine in front of her.

"You and I agree on one thing," Ares said. "Though I kinda want to thank the man for letting her go."

"You know you actually did that the other night?" Ruby asked.

Eleanor laughed. "You didn't!"

Ares shrugged and snatched a sip of Ruby's water. "I guess I did, but what can I say? That guy's loss is 100 percent my gain."

"Aww, Ruby. You didn't tell me how sweet Ares is. Do me a favor, love. Will you grab us drinks at the bar so I can talk to this man more?"

"Sure, Mom." Ruby's tender kiss on her mom's head spoke volumes. His gaze followed her as she moved through the crowd. She could have been in her scrubs and she'd still be the most beautifully captivating woman in the room, including the bride-to-be.

People pulled her into hugs, wrapped her in conversation and made her laugh harder than he'd seen. If he'd ever called her unfeeling, he'd been wrong. So wrong.

He could have watched her all night, but Eleanor pulled him back into conversation.

"You care a lot about her, don't you?" she asked him.

He'd be a fool to deny it, even if the answer made his pulse race.

"I do. Very much."

"And you two started as friends?"

"We did. I actually can't remember a time we weren't close."

Eleanor sipped a drink he hadn't seen her with. So, sending Ruby away was a way to get him alone. Pro move.

"Okay, we can both spend the night telling each other how great my daughter is, but I want to know about you, Ares. Who are you, where did you come from and where is that lovely accent from?"

Normally, Ares despised talking about himself, especially his past, but seeing as how his past was sitting in a hotel a few miles away, maybe it would be good. He told Eleanor how he'd moved from Greece after turning away his family's fortune to pursue medicine. He skipped the part about running from the romantic commitment that his family expected of him, reasoning it wouldn't sit well with his fake-girlfriend's mom.

It also didn't sit well with him—the fake part. He couldn't give Ruby more, but he also wasn't sure how he was supposed to be making these connections between their lives and walk away from her, either.

"Ruby is lucky. You're an amazing man," Eleanor said.

"I'm the lucky one. You've raised two great kids."

"Well, one of them, anyway," Ruby said. Ares hadn't seen her come back, but her voice wrapped around his heart and squeezed. God, this woman had infected him like a virus. "You telling my mom all my secrets?" she asked.

"Nope, just my own."

"Oooh, well, then maybe I should send you up to the dessert table so I can grill my mom for the dirty details." They ate the dinner that arrived, each of them enjoying discussion with each other. Ruby ate off his plate as she usually did at the hospital, and one hand rested on his thigh. It felt...normal. Not scary, not threatening to what they'd had before.

Just *good. Right.*

After dinner she leaned over and kissed his cheek, which had been part of their modus operandi for the holiday parties so far. If they were a couple, they should act like it—at least that had been the original plan until they'd erupted and let their passion consume them after the wine bar.

Things had shifted, in a good way then, at least to Ares. The way he saw it, there were two benefits to them sharing a bed between events that Ares could see: first, it made their ruse so much more believable. Everyone at the wedding events saw them as a united front, and even Byron had greeted him warmly when they arrived. Second, though, was having the events to blow off the steam he felt building between times; they could curl up together and explore this building passion.

Kissing her at work might be verboten, but here, at a wedding rehearsal dinner? Hell, it was expected. He took the opportunity to cup her jaw and bring her in for a passionate kiss he'd wanted to give her since she put on the earrings at her house.

"So, about those secrets," she said, when their plates were cleared.

"You know I'll tell you anything you want to know."

She smiled. "There is one thing..."

Eleanor politely diverted her attention to talk to Byron's future bride about her honeymoon. When the two got up to find Byron, Ares and Ruby were alone in a dark corner of the dining room.

"Oh yeah?" Ares whispered. He slid a hand discreetly between Ruby's jacket and bare skin. He was half hard just imagining getting home and taking off her trousers, then unbuttoning the oversize jacket to reveal the perfect silhouette beneath. "What's that one thing? It might be the same thing I'm hoping for."

He kissed her neck, biting it. Her soft moan turned his erection into something far more potent and hungry. Something not meant for public consumption.

"Oh, you think so?"

His hand slid up until he cupped her breast. He was grateful for the baggy fabric that hid his attempt to get this woman to leave early and let him go down on her in the car. Then again at home…

She cupped her hand over his erection and he growled.

"Yes. I want you, Ruby. I want to bend you over and take you from behind while you wear this jacket. But first, I want to trail my tongue over your center and make you come so I can taste your pleasure."

She moaned, less softly this time. Thankfully, the music had picked up, indicating the party was in full swing.

"Mmm. That sounds nice, but it wasn't what I was thinking."

Her finger crooked under his chin, tilting his gaze until it met hers. The light danced in her irises, the gray with blue flecks like cool pools that washed over his heart and threatened to drown him.

"Then what were you thinking?" Based on the past couple nights, he could only imagine. Ruby was far more sensual and sexual a person than he'd ever expected. Another loss to Byron and a win for Ares.

For a split second, he allowed an unspoken fear in— who would get to experience this woman if he had to set her free? He didn't know if he'd know the man, but Ares already hated him.

Ruby kissed him, bringing him back to the present, where she was still his.

"I want…" she said, as the music behind them reached a crescendo, "to dance with my fake boyfriend."

He barked out a laugh that drew some glances, but thankfully, it also had the effect of tamping his erection.

"You, Dr. Phillips, are surprising. Fun as hell, but you never cease to keep me on my toes."

She pecked him on the cheek, her smile bright. Holding out her hand, she stood. "Good. I'd hate to be one of those boring old couples who can't stand one another and who tell the same stories day after day."

He bristled slightly, but hopefully she missed the way his shoulders tightened with tension. He did his best to release it as he followed her to the dance floor, but the last part of her teasing bothered him. Was she under the impression they were actually a full-blown couple at this point? He understood the confusion, especially since he'd invited in a physical intimacy that muddied the waters.

But, right now at least, he couldn't be her actual boyfriend, no matter how much the idea appealed to him on paper. She was everything he'd want if he were capable of wanting that. But as soon as the idea occurred to him, his patient's wife's face materialized and he was forced to reckon with his mistakes.

Medicine was the only love he could serve, at least to keep his monsters at bay.

You've slept through the night each time you've stayed with Ruby. Could she help with that, too?

If he allowed himself to seek an answer to his subconscious's question, and he lost more patients, more work that mattered, would he ever be okay? The risk was simply too great.

This was fun, easy even, but a cloud hung over Ares's head. His event was next, and he was looking forward to it far less than this. It also was the second-to-last of their string of dates, meaning he only had a few more moments like this, with Ruby curled against his chest.

But a string untied, letting some of the weight fall at his feet. It was also one step closer he'd be to getting himself back to the way things should be—him taking care of patients, and Ruby as his best friend.

As great as this all was, he'd been kidding himself thinking he could bring it further than this week, hadn't he?

When she sighed, his hand reflexively curled at the base of her neck.

God, this was going to kill them both. The question was whether their friendship would survive or be pronounced DOA at the scene.

Two events. Only two more until he got his answer to that question, at least.

CHAPTER TEN

ARES WAS QUIET on the way home. It wasn't the same as the peaceful silence they'd shared on the way to the rehearsal dinner. This was pregnant with tension, evident in the tic in his jaw and white knuckles as he gripped the steering wheel.

The luxury car practically drove itself, so it couldn't be the winding roads back to her house. She waited until they pulled up to her drive to ask.

"Hey, you," she said, turning toward him. The corner of his mouth quirked up, but he didn't answer. "You doing okay?"

"Of course. Why do you ask?"

She put a hand on his, felt the tension brewing. What made them both good emergency doctors was the same thing that made them good friends. They had the unique ability to see beyond words and read what was wrong below the surface.

"Because I can see confusion in the muscles of your jaw." She traced them with her thumb. "And feel concern in your hand." She squeezed it. "And your brow looks like it does when you're faced with a problem you can't solve in surgery."

He didn't turn to her, but his lips drew into a flat smile devoid of humor.

"Just a lot on my mind. I'm sorry. I'm not sure I'm good company tonight. I should go."

She pulled his hand until his gaze followed. "No. We don't get to pull that with one another. You don't have to stay here tonight—I'm not holding you here. But you do have to talk to me."

Ares bit his bottom lip, his eyes lined with moisture. His jaw could have cut steel, and though he looked like he wanted to say something, in the end he only shook his head.

Ruby's hands trembled. She'd never seen him so worked up. Not since that night they'd first become friends. He'd never told her what happened when he went back to Greece that only time, but on a tough night in the A&E, he'd said something about "not losing another one." They'd earned the tough win in the A&E, and their gentle teasing had started as her way of lightening his mood.

Once or twice, he'd get emotional at work right after surgery again, but he'd never been up for talking about it. If there was any wedge in their friendship, it was whatever had occurred that evening all those years ago. Or what had happened before they'd met.

"Is this about that night we had in the A&E?" She didn't need to say which night. His shoulders corded. "Or whatever that triggered from before you came here?"

"Not directly."

Ruby was rudderless, adrift after what seemed to be a great night at the rehearsal dinner. Small pings of awareness steered her thoughts, though.

His texts from the other day that made him frustrated and closed off. The shadows when she'd mentioned Ariadne. That night and any reference to it since.

They were all connected somehow.

"Then is it your family, or something I did?"

He squeezed her hands and leaned in until their foreheads met.

"Nothing you did. Never. You're…you're perfect, Ruby." His dismissal of the first part of her question—if this had to do with his family—spoke volumes.

She understood. It'd been awkward when her mom had pulled her aside and asked about an engagement of Ruby's own on the horizon. The thing was, she wanted one, and try as she might, she couldn't imagine anyone else but Ares at the end of the aisle from her.

Therein lay the problem.

She couldn't have that, but part of her had begun to *want* it, despite what both had said in so many words was off the table. No dating, just friendship and…damn good sex. That line was so thin, though, wasn't it? Before sex and deep friendship gave way to real feelings?

She'd crossed it, but had he? Asking was a risk, but saying nothing…this was the one time words actually mattered. She needed to know how he felt before she said anything.

Where words were failing him, she could read part of him at least.

His hands fisted in her hair and he inhaled deeply. She wrapped her arms around his neck and held him tight. He groaned into her neck, sending a ripple of want over her. His emotions were so potent, so distilled, they filled the space between them. She felt his hesitancy and a despondency that almost crippled her. Maybe he wanted to back off with her and regretted having her as a date to his family's party now that it was less than twenty-four hours away.

But there was something else, too. An urgency in the way he gripped her. A mutual need. She chose to answer that instead and tilted her head up to meet his lips with hers.

If he pulled away, she'd have her answer and she'd back off for good.

He didn't. Instead, his urgency turned to hunger, something feral and needy she'd never experienced. It acted like a match to a small flame she'd been carrying in her heart the past week, and a blaze ignited.

She pulled him on top of her at the same time he hit a button and her seat went back. Her gasp was swallowed by his growl of approval when their chests met. He rocked hips into hers, and any question he wanted the same thing as her evaporated.

He was hard as stone for her. It was fuel to her fire.

She wrapped her legs around him, fighting the cramped space for a way to get closer to this man, to let him fill her as only he'd been able to.

This inferno with Ares may not be anything she could have long-term, but she'd take every bit of what he made available to her until she was forced to excise her feelings like tumors.

His lips blazed a trail across her neck, and she arched her back to give access to all of her. His tongue and teeth played a game of teasing, something she and Ares had always been good at. But not like this. He was an expert at loving her into submission, at teasing out versions of herself she'd never known existed within her.

An untamed minx for one, a person who could love was another.

At that word—*love*—she exploded.

There was no dampening the blaze now that her feelings had been given a word to guide them. If he wasn't willing to talk, she'd use the unspoken language between them to show him.

She slid his jacket off his shoulders while he kneeled above her, back arched so she could pepper his chest with kisses as she unbuttoned his shirt, too. Her hands glided over his smooth, tan skin, memorizing his edges and ridges and ripples of corded muscle.

She cupped him over his trousers, palming his hard length and offering a promise of what was to come. He groaned, dipping his head to the deep-V of exposed flesh her jacket gave him.

"Can I come in?" His words were thick with desire.

She nodded. "Yes," she whispered, worried that saying too much would scare him back to where he'd been when they arrived at her house.

"Stay there." He stepped over her and was out of his door, his shirt open to the cold. Before she could comprehend what was happening, he tore open her door and pulled her into him with a fluid movement of a man possessed.

He tossed her over his shoulder and she squealed. Ares was tender and sensitive, a man shrouded in his past and the emotional fallout of some tough decisions Ruby could only guess at.

But he was all man, masculine and strong. She'd never been a slight woman at almost two meters tall, but he made her feel tiny in his arms, while at the same time making her feel like he'd protect her at all costs.

That was, by far, the sexiest thing about him.

"Keys," he demanded, tapping her bottom while she dug in her clutch. She gasped and handed them over. He had her door unlocked and her on her feet in front of him in less than her next breath.

Her backside tingled and craved more of that raw edge of desire he'd offered. Maybe then...maybe then she could burn off this desperate craving.

As soon as her feet touched the floor, Ares's arms were wrapped around her. His hands roved over her hips, which he squeezed and groped as if he were clinging to dear life.

She rocked into him, and he responded by tearing open the top of her jacket and shoving the shoulders down over her arms.

Since it was still buttoned, it acted like a brace, pinning her in place. Her breasts were exposed, and he bent to suck on each of them, his teeth grazing her tight nipples and sending her overboard.

"Ares," she moaned. "God, I want you."

Then she was moving backward, the feeling of falling and being out of control thrilling but not at all scary. Ares would protect her, she knew that.

Ruby's back hit the wall behind her, and she expected to feel the impact at least a little, but Ares's arms protected her head and shoulders. Pressed between his strength and the drywall, she melted into him.

She purred as his hands and lips made work over her breasts and top of her stomach. Without the use of her arms, all she could do to sate her need was hook her leg around his hips.

He groaned and moisture pooled in her panties. It was that easy between them. He so much as crooked a brow at her and she was wet and willing to take the man then and there. She had, too, in multiple on-call rooms between patients during slow nights when it was just them on shift. It was heady and dizzying how thick her desire for this man was.

It'd only increased seeing him with her mom at the rehearsal dinner. As calm as Ares was with patients, he'd pulled out all the stops with Ruby's mom. She'd opened up about her medical and anxiety issues, and Ares had brought her back down to the happiness of the event and how Eleanor had her whole family and set of friends under one roof.

He'd even danced with Ruby's mom, who Ruby hadn't

seen with that genuine a smile in years. A lock had clicked open in her heart, revealing how much of it beat for this man.

It was dangerous, the way every organ, cell and limb responded to Ares. It was as if they were designed from the same organic material and each part of her called out for him.

He undid her trousers and slid them off her hips. Then he lifted her up by her butt and sat her on his shoulders. His dress shirt fell off his arms in the process and he left it where it was.

This is so hot. She'd had some good lovers in the midst of the frogs she'd dated, but nothing like this, nothing close.

Here, her hands could grip his shoulders for purchase and thank goodness for that and the wall behind her. Ares's tongue slipped between the thin lace of her thong panties and into her folds. He sucked and pulled and her core tightened with lust. Gripping her back, he carried her off the wall and toward her bedroom, his mouth still on her sensitive core. He leaned her back on the bed, then, finally unbuttoned her jacket to free her hands.

They tangled in his locks as his tongue thrust inside her.

Ares kneeled in front of her, and held her hips in place while he drove her closer and closer to climax. She wasn't ready. She wanted to savor this moment with him, draw it out forever...

She gripped his hands and pulled away from his mouth, torn in half at the desire she felt and the simultaneous need to bottle this for later, when she wouldn't have him anymore.

"I want you, Ares. I want you to fill me."

He looked up, his lips wet with her. "That's what I'm

doing, my love." As if to prove it, he slipped two fingers inside her and kept thrusting while he held her gaze.

"No. You. I want *you*." She reached for his pants—how was this man still more than half-dressed? It was a crime. He shook his head slowly and deliberately and drew her hands behind her back so that her own weight pinned them to the bed again.

"Not yet. I'm not done here."

She could have said "no" and Ares would have stopped immediately, but it also would have ended their night. The part of her that wanted him in all ways, and didn't want him to stop what he was doing won out. She arched her back and inched closer to the edge of the bed, to his mouth.

He took that as a challenge and invitation, it seemed, to bring her to the most explosive orgasm of her life. She tightened around his fingers and bucked with the intensity of it, every cell charged and each of her nerves exposed.

Ares didn't remove his fingers from inside her, but used one hand to unbutton his trousers and let them fall to his ankles. He kicked off his loafers and left them in a pile as he found another condom in the same place as before and sheathed himself.

Ruby nodded. She still wasn't done, still needed him inside her. If only to know she still had this man in her life today. Tomorrow was a few hours off still, and she intended to stave it off as long as she could.

The next hour and a half passed in a hurricane of passion, winds of want and need hitting walls of fear and a ticking clock. Ares kissed every inch of her body, leaving marks on some, reminders of the storm raging inside him. She didn't care; she'd been laid to waste by him the first time they kissed and he'd proclaimed, "uh-oh."

She'd known, before he'd said the same thing a moment

later, that their union would be a problem. And now it was. Her nails dug into his skin, scraping along his scapula as if she was a surgeon trying to gain access to his rib cage.

She craved access to all of him, while knowing his thrusting against her was all she was going to get.

Ruby didn't feel the tears streaming down her cheeks or the orgasm until the second rocketed through her. Ares came right after her, a growl marking the moment. As he shuddered above her, Ruby lightened her touch to soft trails up and down his back, hopefully calming him. He kissed the top of her head, but wouldn't meet her gaze until she gently guided his cheek.

"You're crying," he said when he noticed. She nodded. "Oh no. Did I hurt you?"

No, but you're going to. She could feel that, even though the winds had calmed and the walls remained intact.

"I'm fine." He groaned and kissed her, biting rough on her bottom lip. She attempted to massage his arms to relax him, but he shook his head.

"I don't want to hurt you, Ruby."

Then don't.

"You can lay down. You won't hurt me," she urged. But that wasn't true, was it? She'd set them up to fail by agreeing to keep this physical aspect of their relationship while knowing it had an end date.

His face was a blend of postorgasmic bliss and something darker, more internally conflicted. Finally, he collapsed on top of Ruby, his chest on hers. They were bathed in sweat, but still, the only thing she noticed, felt, was the steady, fast beat of his heart.

His phone buzzed on the bed stand and they both twitched at the intrusion. He ignored it; however, it persisted.

"You can get that," she said. They weren't on shift until the next day, a short work stint since they both needed the evening off to attend Ares's family function, but it could be an emergency.

"It's not important."

"Are you sure? If Ryan or Angel—"

"It's not them. It's not about the hospital, not really."

Ares never brushed off work—almost to a fault, so she trusted that, at least. But there was still a wall up with no knowledge of what was behind it. Whatever it was—family she assumed—it was the real reason she and Ares wouldn't ever get a chance to see what this could be.

"Do you want to talk? I know we've dipped into unfamiliar territory, but I'm still your friend. You can tell me anything and I'll listen or give advice—whatever you need."

The phone rang this time, shrill and loud.

Ares finally swiped open his messages and frowned. He typed out a quick response and tossed it face down on the nightstand.

"I'm okay," he said. "Now, come here and hold me. I want to feel you next to me, Ruby."

She heard the words he didn't say louder than those he did.

While we can.

"Of course."

Ares's arms wrapped tight around her, and within minutes his breathing evened and a light snore told her he'd fallen asleep.

She traced his hairline with the back of her hand.

"I'm falling in love with you," she whispered. There. At least she'd been able to tell him how she felt before her world shifted and she'd be lucky to be left with a colleague and friend.

Time wasn't on her side, which meant, even in the safety of Ares's embrace, neither was sleep. How could she close her eyes when she'd wake up knowing her time with Ares was down to hours?

Surely, if she tried, only nightmares would follow.

Ruby settled in for what would be one of the longest nights of her life.

CHAPTER ELEVEN

IN HIS DREAM, he'd been at the edge of a cliff, peering over. He heard a voice calling behind him, a familiar one that felt like home. As the dustings of sleep wore off, he recognized it.

Ruby.

She'd been screaming at him to step back, that he was in a dangerous place and could fall at any minute. But when he'd turned back to face her in the dream, he'd seen what she couldn't.

There was a dust storm that was going to sweep them both off the edge. And that far away from her, there was nothing he could do about it.

He rubbed his chest, hoping to ease his pulse, his jagged breathing. The thing was, the dream felt so real, and in a way it was. They were about to be swept up, and if they weren't careful, they'd go right over the edge of something they couldn't come back from.

They could land safely, or never touch ground again.

Or they could crash and burn and take out everything in their path. When he thought of that eventuality, the people and important things in their impact zone, it made his skin itch with anxiety.

His career, for one. And he'd worked so hard to not make the mistakes from his past again. But it wasn't just about that anymore. There was more at stake.

His family, her mom and brother, their friends and colleagues at the Royal York, him.

Her. Ruby.

If he messed up down the line—as he surely would because there was no way he could balance the kind of love she deserved with what he needed—something would fall and he worried he knew exactly what would.

He cared too much about her to do that. If there was some way he could get out of the party tonight without alienating the same list of people he was trying to protect, he would. But maybe taking Ruby was a mistake. Before he could act on that, his phone buzzed on the table beside him.

She shifted in the bed, a soft moan parting her lips. His body craved hers, wanted to curl up against her. But he'd made up his mind.

Instead, he grabbed his phone, grateful for the distraction. If it was his family again, he'd have to lay down some boundaries, but at least it was better than having to tell Ruby he'd made a mistake, that he'd messed up with her in a way he wished he could take back.

That wasn't entirely true, but he couldn't afford for it to be a nuanced issue; he needed to take a step back to get out of this damning middle they were in.

Then he saw what was on his phone screen.

"Shit," Ares said.

Ruby shot up on her side of the bed. "What happened?"

"Our patient. I'm late." A small tear in the fabric tethering Ares between work and duty ripped. This wasn't near as bad as the event before, the one that shaped his work/life counterbalance, forcing him to choose between the two, but it was a slash on the path back there. By trying to be there for everyone, he was failing himself and the people counting on him.

Something had to give.

"We aren't due in for an hour," she said, checking her own phone. "Which patient?"

"Mr. Ramish," he told her.

"The driver?" The flat line of her lips made sense. She hadn't completely let the guy off the hook for the way he'd driven while drunk, injuring two others in his accident. That wasn't Ares's problem to fix. All he wanted to do was make sure the man got what he needed to heal with his family's support. Everyone should be so lucky to have that resource.

"I told the family I'd be there to talk them through what happened and make a treatment plan with Psych."

She nodded and got out of bed, finding underwear and an outfit in record time.

"What are you doing?"

"I'll come in. We were due in an hour anyway."

Being a doctor on call all the time meant they lived their lives making quick transitions. That didn't mean he felt it was okay to rouse her from what looked like much more peaceful sleep than he'd gotten.

"You don't have to do that, Ruby—"

"I want to. I wanted to talk to you anyway."

Ares tensed. "About?"

Maybe this was a good opportunity to find out whether she still wanted to join him for the party tonight, though as soon as he posed the question to himself, he knew she had to. Facing his family without her was worse than the fallout of explaining to them that they'd "split up." One problem at a time. He'd fix this issue with his family, use the party as a way to set up an annual visit of some kind, and then work on how to start to pull back from Ruby.

Getting them back to friends was the goal, but as he

watched her, his desire welling up inside him to let go, to allow him to let loose with her because who knew, they might make it…

He didn't think the genie could be put back in the bottle.

They got in his car, and drove in silence until they were over the bridge by the hospital.

"What were those pages and texts about super early this morning?" she asked, turning in her seat to look at him. "There were some the other day, too. I know it's not really any of my business, but we've never had secrets."

We've never slept together before this week either. He wasn't sure why that made a difference, only that it did.

"Like I said then, I don't want to bother you with it. It's just family stuff."

"And we're meeting them tonight, right? Don't you think I should know what I'm getting into? I mean, I like how we spent the evening, but it didn't exactly give me any insight into what you're going through or what to expect."

His frown returned. That was true. Last night, he'd made sure he focused on the one thing he wanted—to see Ruby's smile on her face while that was still within his control. To hear her calling out his name while he helped bring her to climax. It was such a pure joy on her face that he couldn't believe he'd been without it all these years.

Or that it was one of the last times they'd have it.

It doesn't have to be.

Dammit, his heart was persistent, wasn't it? But he had to ignore it. Between the distraction of his attraction to Ruby and his family's invasive presence, he'd almost blown it at work.

"I dunno," he said, mildly desperate to send the conversation back to fun, benign territory. "I think we had fun before bed doing other things."

They pulled up to the hospital car park and all he wanted was to put the car in Park and run from his feelings.

But that would mean running from her, and he'd never survive that. They just needed to go back to how things were before Christmas.

"Not that I mind how we spent the evening," she added, taking his hand and putting it to her chest. Her heart was beating so fast. "But I'd like to *talk* to you, too. There was something…off last night. Or at least, that's how it seemed to me. And sure, maybe it's family, but if it's me, will you please tell me? I can handle anything you need to say—we've been through too much to keep things from one another that impacts the other."

She knew him so well. God, how easy would it be to just ride this out, let their physical intimacy match the years of friendship they'd built into something solid and sturdy. But he knew from experience that it didn't work out in the end. And if he had to choose? He'd pick Ruby in his life at any cost—even if it meant taking a couple backward steps to the safety of their friendship.

Which meant…

Maybe he needed to come clean and tell her his reservations—that they'd crossed a line and he needed them to go back to the other side.

She'd understand, right?

When he met her gaze, saw the hope in her eyes—he knew her that well, too—he couldn't do that. He'd get through tonight, then be her date to the wedding like he'd promised, and then they could talk once the holiday was over.

Between Christmas, the events and the Kyle Windgate disaster, things had seemed to spin out of control for a while now.

"It's just my family." That was true. "They want me to

come to more dinners and cocktail hours while I'm here, but I work. They've never understood that I have to do this, which is part of how they made their way out here from Greece for a damned party."

Ruby smiled up at him, a gift he didn't deserve. But her eyes were serious.

"They're not here for a party, Ares. They're coming for you." He closed his eyes, the pull to go inside and just work through these emotions almost drowning him. "Moreover, the hospital will be fine if you leave it for a while. We can pick up the holiday slack and care for the patients that come in. In case you've forgotten, we're all on the same staff with the same training. Trusting us to do that is how you show you personally can't save them all. There will be other losses and patients who go to other physicians. You can't control everything."

He knew that, academically, at least.

"I know. It's not just that, though."

"What is it, then?"

Ares ran a hand along Ruby's shoulder. The angles of her anatomy would make physiology instructors blush. She was perfect. She would make someone so happy, and in another world, he'd send up a prayer different from all his others that he could be that man to her.

"Believe me, I know loss is coming. But the loss is about more than just medicine and patients." He sighed. He was getting dangerously close to a truth he'd kept close to his chest for a while now.

But mixing it with their friendship and physical connection was a cocktail that would land Ares and Ruby in the morgue this time.

It wasn't that their physical intimacy was the problem, not in the conventional sense. No, he craved every cell of her body as close to his as possible. All the time, no breaks, not even at work. How many times had he pulled her into an on-call room since they'd slept together? A dozen?

He recalled what he'd told her after their kiss on her porch. "Uh-oh," he'd whispered, unsure if it was meant for her or his own heart. "This is going to be a problem."

And it was. Because now he had to say goodbye.

"Then what happened? Talk to me, Ares. Please."

"It wasn't about the case, though they tried to get me to leave work, too. It was about you and I. They're…expecting us to be together."

She laughed and while he normally lived for the sound, it meant she hadn't picked up on the subtext.

"Well, yeah. It's why we're doing this whole fake dating thing, right?"

It was, but what he hadn't shown her was how she'd now become the center of the party, that every text was another question for what Ruby wanted, or what she thought about something they'd planned. Thankfully, he could reply on her behalf, the benefit of knowing the woman as well as he did.

But the implications were heavy. His family was pulling out all the stops for her, for *them*. And there was no real "them" to speak of.

"Sure. Hey, listen. I have to get in there. I'm sorry."

"No, sure. Of course." God, it was awful and awkward keeping anything from Ruby. He hated it. "We'll talk about this later? So I know how to show up for you?" she asked.

Was she asking as his friend, or his date? Because as her friend, he'd never been able to deny her anything, but their physical relationship had started to feel more real every day. And diving into his complicated family with her would only confuse that more. The best he could hope for was extricating himself without too much collateral damage.

"I'm hoping there isn't much talking at all at lunch. You forget our routine, Dr. Phillips?" he asked. They'd been meeting every lunch this week for a "nap," which consisted of some of the best sex of his life. Hell, every minute with Ruby in that way had far surpassed all his expectations. Their passion had worked last night to keep his feelings at bay and let him focus on the manifestation of them. Loving her body kept him from loving...

Her. Period. And he was too damn close to falling off that ledge. He needed to stay where things were comfortable. Normal.

He kissed her goodbye and made his way to the lobby, where his patient's family sat huddled together.

"Dr. Petrides, thank you for coming in. We're sorry to have you do this on your time off."

"I'm so grateful," Mr. Ramish added. "You easily could have let me rot—or worse."

Ares shook the man's hand, noting how steady it was now. He must have stopped drinking, or at least eased his intake dramatically in the past few days. The man reminded him of the patient he'd lost all those years ago. This was his second chance, and he'd almost blown it again.

"It's my pleasure," he said. As he did, Ruby walked by and gave him a nod and tentative smile. Work was sure to be impacted by their "breakup," which meant their friendship and gentle teasing certainly would be, too. But that couldn't matter more than this moment, now.

Ares talked the family through what they'd seen on intake at the A&E, then how he thought they should proceed to get the right kind of long-term care. Therapy and maybe grief counseling was the top order of business, and even Ares's eyes misted when they all hugged at the end.

He might be a bit of a workaholic, might take too long

with patients, but he made a positive difference in his patients' lives more often than he didn't.

They said goodbye just as Ruby passed by again, this time escorting a man through the lobby, her hand firmly on his elbow. He knew the look on her face. Frustration edging toward anger rippled over her features.

Her gray eyes were dark, and she didn't seem to notice Ares as she spoke low enough that he couldn't hear what she was saying from his place on the other side of the lobby.

"Excuse me," he said, giving his leave to the family. He followed behind Ruby, curious if she'd need his assistance. Where was security?

"This is completely unacceptable," Ruby said when he got close enough to hear. She still didn't see Ares, but he wanted to stick close enough that he could intervene if she needed to.

"All I'm looking for is a quote. Give me that, and I'll leave you alone."

She crossed her arms and scowled at the man. "Leave me alone, and I won't call the police on you for trespassing."

Ares had seen her focused but quick with patients—efficient, as she called it—and even curt if the situation demanded it. But never had he seen her so livid.

He wouldn't want to be on her bad side.

You might be, come Byron's wedding day...

"You know, the public has a right to the information about what happened to one of its citizens. Which means I have the right to ask questions to get them answers. It's the job, Doc."

He recognized the man now.

It was a reporter who'd been diligent and insistent that Ruby speak to him about Kyle's case and she'd banned him from the hospital after he'd harassed a patient. He'd come in twice asking for an interview with Ares, who hadn't had to say anything. He'd never been so grateful for his strong, broad frame and his more than two meters in height. His appearance did a lot of explaining for him.

So the guy had been bugging Ruby now?

A surge of protectiveness bowled Ares over. He took a step toward the reporter—Amos, if Ares recalled—but stopped. Taking care of Ruby wasn't his job. He wasn't her boss at work, her security guard, or even her boyfriend.

He'd relegated himself to no-man's-land and had no one to blame but himself for the helplessness that replaced his desire to protect her.

"I've told you repeatedly that your need for information doesn't trump my patients' need for safety, privacy and healing. And while we're at it, the kind of information you claim to be seeking is bogus since you work for a hack paper with a hack reputation whose fans are hacks and only read your garbage because they wouldn't know good journalism if it slapped them upside the head with a tape recorder. So, in case I was too subtle… *Get. Out.*"

Go, Ruby. He was consistently proud of this woman, and somehow, even after all these years, surprised by her.

Ares walked away, knowing she had the conversation under control. But this wasn't the last time Ruby would be faced with a man or a problem she might need help with. As her friend, hopefully he'd be able to be there for her some, if not most, of the time. But someone else would take his place when he stepped down from this temporary role, and that man would make her his world, and be there for whatever she needed.

Then step the hell up and be that for her.

He'd been thinking that since they'd first kissed. But it always came back to the same argument. He could help her, be there for her, or help hundreds. He'd tried the in-between and getting caught in the middle had made him crappy at both.

God, today was dragging, and thinking about the myriad ways he'd screwed up by catching feelings for his best friend when he knew he couldn't be with her wasn't helping.

To make matters worse, work was slow, which in their business was normally a good thing. At least it meant he didn't have to go to his parents' party for a couple hours yet. He couldn't believe how quickly the week had gone; it was time for the party already, which meant it was also the last night of the year.

Ares used the break in patients to head out front of the hospital with a cup of gold tea and an apple—and a lot on his mind. It wasn't half the breakfast his body needed after the exertions of the night before, but it would have to do.

The cool air helped aid the second part of his dilemma—thinking through what weighed him down so he could give his focus to his patients when he needed to. Otherwise, what was the point?

"Halfpenny for your thoughts?"

Ares swallowed his bite of apple and smiled.

"Hey, Ryan. More like half a gold brick."

Ryan, his friend and the head of midwifery, was the closest thing to a confidant that Ares had outside Ruby. The guys, along with two others from the hospital's medical staff, played pickup rugby games on the rare summer evenings they had off, and in the winter, that parlayed into cigars and whisky at Ares's house since he had the most space and best bar.

"That bad, huh?"

"Just got myself into a jam and can't quite seem to think my way out of it."

Ares could go for a whisky and cigar now, if only to calm his frayed nerves.

"I'm here to talk if you want. Or beat you at cards. I might need to take a few quid off you to make up for my poor performance last week."

"Name the day," Ares answered. At least he still had the guys. Though it wasn't the same when they laughed, smiled, or even shot him a glance. It didn't unlock a part of his heart and make his day just that much better.

They sat in silence for a moment, punctuated only by Ares's bites into his lame breakfast.

"So, you and Ruby," Ryan finally said.

Ares laughed, choking on his food. "Subtle. Nice."

"What's going on there? I mean, you two have always flirted, but it's never been like this. And you've never avoided my questions about her, either."

"I dunno," Ares admitted. The night before had been amazing and yet… It'd also shown him what was at risk if he kept it up. They would both be hurt beyond repair.

"Are you two together?"

"It's more complicated than a simple yes or no. But were we that obvious?"

Ryan shrugged. "Were? So, it's over then? Bummer. I liked you two. Anyway, it wasn't really anything anyone else would have picked up on, but I could tell. You okay, man?"

"Hmm," Ares offered. "I will be." He didn't know what to say that wouldn't sound like a piss-poor excuse for his behavior. He'd known there was no chance he'd be willing to change his life and invite someone into it, and still, he'd done just that with his best friend.

"Well, I maintain if you need to talk, I'm here. I know we mostly bullshit, but the guys have all got serious sides. We can hang."

"Thanks, Ry. I'll be okay and I'll talk to you about it later. Right now, I have to get ready for my parents' New Year's Eve party."

"That's right. Happy New Year, buddy. I hope it's a good one and you get the fresh start you need."

That term—fresh start—bugged Ares. What did that look like for him? Was it going back to how things used to be, or forging a whole new path? The latter scared the hell out of him.

"You, too." He downed his tea and tossed the apple core in the rubbish bin before slapping his friend on the back and walking inside.

His hands, feet—hell, all of him—wanted to go in search of Ruby and ask what she wanted out of a fresh start, but that would be counterproductive. On the other hand, it might give him some insight into her thoughts. Maybe she was just as eager to go back to their easy friendship as he was and he'd worked himself up for nothing.

But as he thought through the past week, how her gazes had lingered and her lips had sought his with more and more urgency, he wasn't sure that was the case at all.

Dammit. Looking back on the week, it was obvious to him just how much he'd egged things on, from dragging her into on-call rooms, to being the one to instigate the kiss, to making love to her every time actual feelings came up.

He was a worldclass jerk, and she'd see that soon enough. The thing was, she made him want to change, to be better for everyone in his life.

What that looked like was anyone's guess, but it didn't matter then, anyway. He had a party to get ready for and he'd never felt less festive.

CHAPTER TWELVE

RUBY WALKED OUT to the lobby of the Royal York Hospital at five on the dot. She and Ares were driving to his parents' hotel together, in the hopes of showing a united front. The problem was coordinating their schedules since their day had gone down different paths.

She'd spent a bulk of hers getting the damned reporter to lay off both her and the other hospital staff, then had two minor injuries that came in at the same time. Two teen girls working on a tumbling routine for their dance team, which apparently didn't take holiday breaks, had sprains when a third had landed on them during a stunt.

As New Year's Eve emergency room visits went, it certainly wasn't expected.

She'd changed for the party in the private on-call room with a shower suite attached since no one was using it late afternoon on the last night of the year.

While she'd felt confident in her outfit choice a couple days earlier, now she wasn't sure. She wore a deep blue strapless gown adorned with a black-and-gold shawl. It was intended to be a tribute to the Greek eye, but now she felt like it was too on the nose. She'd texted Ares to ask him, but he hadn't responded.

She checked her phone, replied to two messages from her mother, who seemed very interested in how Ares was doing. If only Ruby knew. He'd been distant all day, even longer if Ruby was honest with herself.

Tonight would be a big deal for Ares; hopefully when it was over, he'd be able to relax and Ruby could talk to him. She'd made some decisions over the past few days that differed pretty significantly from their talk at Christmas.

Namely, that she wanted to see if he'd be up for—slowly—inching forward from friendship to something... more. Something that let them keep the best parts of their friendship but also explore the physical connection and deeper intimacy they'd shared.

During the fifteen minutes she waited, an ambulance came in and she attempted to ignore the case. Other doctors were there to cover the shift.

Once thirty more minutes had passed—well after when they were already supposed to be at the party—Ruby still couldn't get in touch with Ares.

"Hey, have you seen Dr. Petrides?" she asked the nurses gathered at the station.

"Last I did, he was heading into a triage room with the inbound."

Ruby's fists balled at her sides and she struggled to maintain her calm.

"The inbound from forty-five minutes ago?"

"Yeah. Apparently, it was some patient he knew. The guy from Christmas, he said. Like that narrows it down." The nurse laughed, but Ruby didn't see anything funny about this. Ares was supposed to be off shift an hour ago, and with a drink already in hand by now. And he'd taken on another case?

Of course he did. He'd been telling her all along that work would always come first and somehow, *somehow,* she'd talked herself into believing maybe she'd be the one to break through.

"What room?" she asked through clenched teeth.

The three of them all pointed to the end of the hall, in triage one.

Ruby's four-inch heels clacked on the tile floor, sounding out of place in this austere space usually reserved for loss and pain.

Well, it was par for the course, then, that she was in search of her missing date who'd stood her up for his own party.

She masked up and washed her hands before going in, but left the rest of the PPE behind. Either way, she wouldn't be staying.

Ruby walked into the triage space, careful to stay out of the way. She expected to see him standing over an unresponsive body, but no.

Ares stood beside the bed, finishing up a suture on the driver's hand from Christmas Day. The two of them were chuckling about something Ruby had missed. However, she was pretty sure even if she'd been there, she wouldn't be laughing.

"Dr. Petrides, a minute, please."

Ares glanced up from his work and his gaze traveled over her, taking her in. Something registered in his eyes, but she couldn't read what with his mouth covered by the mask.

"Let me finish this stitch and I'll be out." To his patient, he said, "Sorry. I'll finish this up shortly and we'll make sure the tests come back clear. Then you'll be on your way to your granddaughter's birthday."

Ruby heard the start of the patient's reply, but the door shut behind her and she relished the quiet so she could calm her racing heart. If she had to speak to Ares immediately, she'd say something they both regretted.

She counted to five, breathed in through her nose, out through her mouth, and by the time Ares stepped into the hall, she'd regulated her shaking hands at least.

"I'm sorry," he said.

"You're not coming?" she asked. She had no need for his apologies anymore. She wanted a man she could rely on, and he wasn't that guy. Maybe he never had been, and Ruby had just seen the man she wanted to see.

The snack cakes, the teasing, even the incredible sex. None of them meant Ares saw *her*, wanted *her*. Was ready to do anything other than what he wanted, when he wanted.

"I'll be there, but late. Why don't you—" She raised her brows and crossed her arms over her chest, curious how he'd finish this sentence.

"Why don't I…?"

"Go ahead without me. You know where it's at, and I'll be there as soon as I'm done."

Ruby fumed. This wasn't the plan. He was sending her into the hornet's nest with nothing to defend herself with except an outfit that might or might not be patronizing. But what could she say that would change the circumstances?

"I'm leaving at eight if you're not there. I have no intention of ringing in the new year alone, Ares, but if I'm meant to, I'll be doing it in my sweatpants with a mug of Barry's."

"Okay. Fair. I'll be there before then, I promise." She didn't interrupt and tell him his word wasn't worth the weight of a hospital gown. She wasn't a patient at the Royal York, so she didn't matter. End of story. "You look amazing, by the way. That dress is incredible."

Her bottom lip quivered at the compliment. Was she so easily swayed by a kind word from him? The bare minimum wasn't enough, but it still wormed its way into her heart and took root.

"Thanks. I'll see you there."

With that, she turned around and walked back down the hall, refusing her body's desire to turn around to see if he'd cared enough to watch her walk away.

Twenty minutes and a thirty-pound cab ride later, she was at the hotel. It was posh, ornately decorated for the holiday, and his parents' party in the penthouse was no exception. Somehow, she'd gotten the color scheme of her outfit dead-on, as the whole space was delicately given those accents in a way that also enhanced the gold and paler blue of the suite.

Guests mingling were also in various shades of the four colors, and Ruby sighed with relief. There, at least, she wasn't an outsider.

Though, as more and more people walked by her, appraising her with soft smiles, she noticed how they all focused longer on her hair or seemed to lean in to look at her eyes closer. Since a majority of the guests were cultural clones of Ares with dark features and skin, it was safe to say she stood out.

"You must be Ruby," a kind voice said. Ruby turned and was met with what could only be described as a Greek goddess. She was shorter than Ruby, but still statuesque and regal in a glittering gold gown with blue and black bangles. Her hair was long with a gentle wave, and though she was a spitting image of Ares, her features were feminine through and through. "I'm Ares's mother, Athena."

Ruby shook her hand, not surprised at the woman's strength. She carried herself as if she had the weight of a company and family on her shoulders, which likely made the rest of her formidable as well.

"It's so nice to meet you. I'm sorry, but Ares got pulled by a last-minute case that couldn't be helped," Ruby said, parroting his words. They felt slick on her tongue. "He'll be here soon."

At that last part, she mentally crossed her fingers. The only thing more mortifying than showing up alone to your fake boyfriend's family's party was leaving alone, too.

"Hmm. Same Ares, I see. I'd rather hoped after we made the trip most of the way, he'd make the last three miles. But he sent you, which says a lot about his growth. I wasn't sure you existed at all, dear."

In the ways that mattered, Ruby didn't. She swallowed hard, desperate for a drink—anything at all—to make this less awkward.

"Well, let's not let that man get in the way of us getting to know one another." Ruby exhaled as Athena took her by the elbow and paraded them both toward the open bar. "Unfortunately, without him here to act as a buffer, you'll have to meet his YaYa alone." At Ruby's raised brows, Athena laughed. It was such a light, airy sound, Ruby had trouble reconciling the woman Ares mentioned from time to time with the genuine, caring one in front of her. "It's okay. I'll be your—how do you kids say it these days—your wingman?"

"Something like that," Ruby laughed, feeling better than when she'd driven over. She just had to get through this night, and she'd be able to put her focus on the wedding. Then, they'd be back to normal. Her stomach flipped. She wasn't sure she wanted that, either. But it was clear that wasn't being solved tonight. "I can handle my own, though."

Athena squeezed her arm and then asked the bartender for two whiskies. "I think you can, which I admire. I wish my son was here to share how you two came to be, but I'm glad he met you. I can see, aside from his workaholic tendencies, you're good for him."

Ruby wasn't sure about that, but she smiled and took the glass of whisky.

"Yamas," Ruby said. Athena grinned broadly and was even more stunning when she smiled.

"Yamas." They sipped and Athena exhaled softly. "I love visiting the UK for this alone. I get so sick of ouzo. Give me a fourteen-year-old Scotch or Irish whisky any day of the week."

Ruby laughed and nodded. "I knew I liked you," she said.

"Oh, darling, we're just getting started. If you like me, just wait until you meet Ares's cousin Thea. Perhaps it's better my son isn't here so he can't taint your views of us before you really get to know our family."

Athena spoke in jest, but there was an undercurrent of hurt in her words. The ladies met up with Thea and her husband Stasi, another Greek heir. Though the pair had been made for business reasons from what Ares had told her when he'd given her the—very—brief overview of who she'd be meeting, Ruby could plainly see how much the couple loved one another.

Stasi's arm never left Thea's waist unless it was to fetch her a drink or pull her face in for a kiss that made Ruby blush. That kind of open adoration unnerved her, but at the same time, sent a thrill through her veins.

She wanted that, too. Too bad the Greek man she'd fallen in love with would never be able to give that to her.

"So, you're the one who finally tamed my cousin? I have *so* many questions."

"Thea, go easy on her. At least let her have some food."

"Please. If Ares hasn't scared her away, none of us will."

Ruby laughed. "Food sounds amazing, but I'm happy to answer any questions about your cousin that you have." Why not, when he'd left her alone with his family?

As if she'd ordered before she walked through the door, a plate of food appeared before her. A small Greek salad with what looked like lamb, fresh pita that smelled amazing and some small chocolatey desserts was enough to make her mouth water.

"These all look amazing. Thank you."

"No olives," Thea said. "Ares said you won't eat them."

Ruby's chest constricted, and she had to sip her whisky to loosen it. "He—he did?"

"Yeah, didn't you know?" Ruby could fill a crash cart with what she didn't know about Ares Petrides and his family. "We've been asking him all week what you like and don't like so we get it right."

Ruby tried on a smile, but it felt as forced as it was. "I've been so busy," she lied, hating that she'd known these people for a matter of minutes and had already hidden so much truth from them. "He probably took that on himself so I could concentrate on work. What kinds of things did he say?"

Thea listed things on her hand. "Olives for one." That was true. But not for the taste. Ares had been there one lunch when Ruby cracked a tooth on one that still had a pit, and she'd sworn never to eat the infernal things again. She warmed, knowing he'd recalled that from years ago.

What he hadn't known was that she ate olives every chance she got, but chopped them at her own house, where she could be sure to catch the pits herself.

"You have to eat often or you get—" Thea continued.

"Like Ares on a normal day. Testy." Stasi finished for her. Everyone laughed. It explained why food just appeared at her side. It also explained the whisky in her hands the moment she arrived.

"Oh, and he said if we ply you with chocolate, you'll love us forever, so expect a steady string of sweets. We're not above bribing in this family," Thea said.

"Sometimes the bribes land you the love of your life, so it isn't all bad," Stasi added, kissing Thea deeply.

Hmm. What was the story there? she wondered.

"Careful," Athena said. Ruby waved her off.

"It's fine. I love chocolates, yes, but I don't think I'd need them to like you guys. Really, thank you for rolling out the red carpet, but I'm easier going than your son would have you believe. Just treat me how you'd treat the rest of your guests and that'll be great."

Thea smiled and kissed her husband's cheek. "Yeah, but you're the guest of honor, so good luck with being treated as anything other than a Greek heiress."

"Okay," Athena said. "I'm going to take you to meet some better behaved members of my family. You two behave yourselves. Don't think I won't fly you back to Greece before midnight."

They all wore smiles, diluting the threat. "Apologies. We don't mean to make you uncomfortable, but they're right. How much did Ares tell you about tonight?"

"Not much, I'll admit." A truth among the pile of rubble.

"Well, when he broke it off with Ariadne—our pick for him and a poor one, I'll admit—we weren't sure he'd ever open up to anyone again. Not just romantically, but around the same time as the breakup, he came home to finalize things with his severance from the business and something happened. He wasn't the same afterward. He hasn't been home since and we got tired of waiting for him, so we came here instead."

Ruby knew the day his mother was talking about. It was before Ares had worked for Royal York and they'd met right afterward. She'd thought him tough and unfeeling, but he'd turned out to be the more sensitive of the two of them after they got to know one another.

That was the same moment Ruby knew he had shifted his drive to work nonstop. He always mentioned being "forced" to stop dating, but Ruby still didn't know the story. Odd that his mother didn't, either.

"I'm glad you made the trip. Ares really does love you all. I think he's just so focused on work that it's hard for him to see that there can be more to life. It's all or nothing with him, but I'm sure he's glad you're here."

"I hope the latter is true," Athena said, stopping before they reached another group of women that made Ruby's heart stop. His aunts and cousins were all equally beautiful, though of various heights and builds than his immediate family, who all looked like Ares—tall, regal and as if they ran daily. "But make sure you don't let him treat you like the second option at the end of a day. You, dear Ruby, should be a priority. I know this much so far."

"Thank you for saying as much. Your son is amazing, and I know he cares about me in the best way he can."

Was it enough for Ruby, though, or would she always want just a little more than Ares was able to give?

Athena opened her mouth as if she had a reply at the ready, but then her face changed. Even though Ruby couldn't see who or what was behind her that made Athena smile so wide, her eyes light up as if she'd been given the keys to eternal happiness, she'd know just what made that possible.

Partly because she felt his presence the moment he walked in. It was as if the fans above them existed only to carry his scent to Ruby, that the air got heavier, stiller, with him breathing it.

Ares.

He strode over to them, giving Ruby a quick glance she couldn't read, then focused on his mother. He kissed Athena on each cheek, then put an arm around Ruby's waist, giving her a perfunctory kiss on her cheek as well.

To an onlooker who hadn't spent the past bunch of years watching the two of them tease one another, getting closer each day, it would look like a couple greeting each other after a short absence. But it was a lie on so many fronts. Starting with how rigid Ares's posture was. It was like leaning against stone. She glanced up at him, hoping to catch something that would tell her what he was thinking.

But he wouldn't look at her. Even his jaw looked as carved from marble as the rest of him. The irony that she thought of the Greek statues in the British Museum wasn't lost on her. He was as cold and unfeeling as she'd imagined him to be the year they'd met.

What happened? She wanted to know.

"Hello, dear. We were, as I'm sure you expected, just talking about you."

"I'd expect nothing less. How was the trip?"

How was the trip? Ruby wanted to scream. What about how much he missed them, wondered what they'd been up to since he saw them years ago? This wasn't the Ares she knew, not at all.

"Lovely, dear. Why don't you grab a drink and some food and we can chat? Your cousins have a little bet going about who will find the *flouri*. I believe the wager is up to ten."

"I've read about this tradition," Ruby said. "Whoever finds the gold coin is said to have luck for the whole of the new year."

"That's the game. The cousins add to it each year by placing side bets, which I don't necessarily approve of—I don't think luck starts with gambling one's hard earned money away, but what do I know? I'm as they say a 'boomer.'"

Ruby laughed. "I don't know. I think I might want to throw ten quid down on some luck. I could use it."

Ares squeezed her side as if she'd said something wrong. "It's ten thousand pounds." Ruby choked on the bite of cake she'd just ingested. "My family never have had any propriety about betting or the money they throw around."

"Oh. Well, good luck to you all, then."

"Enough talk about money. Let's get you to your YaYa before she hunts me down for keeping you so long."

"Whatever you think is best," Ares said. Ruby stiffened as his arm fell and he took her hand. It was rigid as the rest of him, and as he dragged her behind him—not beside him as he'd done the past week—she almost pulled back and demanded he tell her what was going on.

But this wasn't her party, no matter what his mother and cousin said. This was for Ares to show off his life, and she was only an accessory. A temporary one, at that.

The evening continued in the same way Thea had anticipated. Ruby was plied with sweets, and not only chocolate. There was homemade baklava from Ares's aunt and vasilopita—without a coin for her, go figure. She was also inundated with questions, jokes, and stories about her "boyfriend" that all made her feel as happy and comfortable as she'd ever been.

His YaYa was the sweetest woman she'd ever met, with a wicked sense of humor and so much sass it was a wonder she didn't run all of Greece herself. But she doted on her family and never, despite what Ruby knew to be true about Greek culture, made Ruby feel less welcome because of her British heritage.

It was amazing, except for the wet blanket masquerading as her date.

Despite Ares's cool demeanor, she laughed harder than she had in some time. Each time she did, though, she felt him tense beside her.

Too bad.

She refused to bow down to his poor attitude despite the fact that he'd invited her, then left her alone with his family. After all, this was the last day of the year and she was surrounded by fun people, incredible food and a stunning venue. It could be a lot worse, and likely was for anyone in the A&E at that moment.

That reminded her...

"How did your patient fare?" she asked Ares when his family seemed to be occupied by something going on at the other end of the palatial room.

Ares deigned to give her a glance, but it was clinical and brief.

"Fine. He'll heal, no thanks to me having to leave him there." He sipped on the same drink he'd been nursing the past hour and a half. Ruby's hackles went up without his family there to curb her reaction to Ares's temperament. So much for enjoying this no matter what. Ares seemed hell-bent on making that impossible.

"Sorry, but did I do or say something wrong?" she hissed. "I mean, you asked me to be your date for this party and you're treating me like I'm the one to blame for you being here."

"Not here," he growled.

Ruby crossed her arms over her chest to calm her shaking hands. *Fine.*

"Then point me to where, because we're doing this now." He walked away, expecting her to follow, which she did. He took her to an enclosed balcony with a door, which at least meant they could talk without his family overhearing. Why did that make her as nervous as it did?

"Okay, Ruby." He gazed out over York where the beginnings of fireworks were picking up even though they had almost ninety minutes to midnight. "Go for it. Tell me all the ways I've let you down."

She felt like she'd been punched.

"That's not fair. I've not done anything other than show up for you, and you're treating me like a contagious patient, or worse, someone you can't stand to be around."

At this, Ares finally looked at her. His eyes were conflicted, and his mouth moved as if he wanted to say something. But nothing came out.

"Ares. Talk to me. Something happened, and whatever it is, it's fine. We can get through it. But this is untenable."

"I don't want to talk about it. I'm sorry I'm late, but it couldn't be helped. I had a patient."

"It's not just about being late, though, sure. Let's start there. Because you weren't supposed to be working and you chose to."

"Are you telling me I should let my patients suffer so I get to a dinner party on time?"

His frustration was palpable. She'd never seen him so on edge.

"I've never once asked you to give up work for me, not once. But remember, *you* asked *me* to be your date to this party. This wasn't my event, nor was it my family who had to be appeased. I didn't even get introduced to them by you. I had to make do and pretend that you and I were this happy couple and that I knew what you were up to, even though you couldn't even send me a text to say you weren't coming."

"I'm sorry. It couldn't be helped." His voice was resigned, soft, but Ruby didn't care. He was wrong and she was tired of covering for him when he seemed uninterested in fixing the mess he made.

"I don't believe that, but fine. Let's pretend that's the case. What about the rest of it?"

He was back to gazing out over the fireworks, as if he were a million miles away.

"Ares," she said. "Ares, look at me."

He did, and she saw the end of whatever had been happening between them in his eyes. But damn if she was going to let him off without saying it. Not when she'd been there in every way he'd asked of her.

"Ruby—"

"No. My turn. Ares, I know I'm throwing inoculations at a situation that's terminal, but you need to hear this. I love you. Don't ask me how or when or even why. But I do. Maybe that's what happens when you start kissing and sleeping with your best friend."

"I told you I couldn't do more than that."

She held her ground. She was owed that, at least. "Do more than what?"

Ares gestured between them, his hands as shaky as her whole body felt.

"This. You and I. Me and anybody. I—" He paused, but for the first time in a long time, she felt more on the other end of his silence, so she gave him space. "I was in Liverpool before I came to the Royal York."

"I remember. It took us a bit to become friends, but I saw you the minute you walked in our doors."

"You did?"

She nodded. "It was the only time I ever saw your hair disheveled and a two-day stubble on your cheeks." She might as well be honest. "You were the most beautiful thing I'd ever seen. I knew I wanted to know you, but I never thought I'd get a chance to be your friend. To be honest, I didn't think you were in the market for friends back then, you were in so much pain. What happened?"

Ares's gaze landed on his feet. "I lost a patient." His

voice was a whisper almost lost to the whipping wind outside. "My parents kept bugging me to go back to Greece and fix things with Ariadne. I had no damn desire to fix something with a woman I didn't want to marry, and who clearly didn't want to marry Ares the physician. All she'd signed on for was Ares the business mogul."

Ruby, on the other hand, having seen a version of the latter tonight, was so grateful she had met Ares just as she had.

"You went back, though." It wasn't a question. He'd shared that much with her before, albeit with so many fewer details.

"I had to. I had to tell them to let me live my life, that I'd visit more if they'd stop pressuring me into a life that wasn't meant for me."

"Romance and love and all that?" Ruby asked. He'd never been what her friends would call sappy or lovey-dovey, even if he was caring.

Ares looked wounded.

"No. Not at all. Back then, I loved that stuff." *Back then.* So, it was a matter of timing, then. She'd met the wrong version of Ares after all, it seemed. For how she felt about him at least. "But they finally forced my hand, and I went back to Greece. Just before I left, I got a patient who needed some serious attention. His wife brought him in with their infant, and he was in bad shape. I promised her I'd do everything in my power to save him."

Ares's gaze shifted to the ceiling as if he was holding back a torrent of emotion. She put a hand on his arm, but he flinched. God, had they really fallen so far that she couldn't comfort her best friend when he was in so much pain?

"I knew how bad he was, even after triage and he was moved to intensive care. And I still—"

Ruby closed her eyes and nodded. She knew the end to this story without him having to say a word.

"I still went to Greece even though I knew I shouldn't have left him in the state he was in. I trusted the on-call doc to do what he needed to do to follow-through on a promise I made. And…" His voice broke, and he ran his hands through his hair. "And he was dead before I even landed in Greece. Had I stayed—"

She took his hand, no longer caring what it meant or didn't mean.

"You might have lost him anyway. That's medicine, Ares. You know from a logical perspective there was the same chance he fatally suffered from his injuries under your watch. Then what?"

Ares shook his head and removed his hand from hers.

"But I didn't. I left and he died."

"So you decided not to let anyone in close enough to drag you away from work so you never had to experience that kind of loss again?"

He met her gaze, finally, and Ruby recognized shock in his wide eyes.

"Yes. That's exactly it."

Ruby's smile was devoid of any humor. "And in doing so have lost out on so many other things that make life worth living."

Ares's sardonic laugh was almost cruel.

"Ha! Isn't that rich? You gave up dating and dove into work, too. And don't tell me it's because you haven't found a prince in the frogs. You don't want to find anything, do you? Your parents screwed up your idea of what love looks like, and you're cashing in your chips."

She laughed, but it was devoid of any humor.

"At least I was *trying*, Ares. Yes, my father abandoned

me and Matt, yes, my mom might as well have. Sure, Byron added onto that pile, but I got the apps and went out on dates and no, I didn't give up. Not even when I found myself falling for my best friend. I know it's scary to trust in something you can't know the outcome of, but being open to it is at least *something*."

The party went on inside, and Ruby couldn't be sure of the exact time, but judging by the festivities, they were inside the last hour of the year. Her new year wasn't going to start remotely close to how she'd hoped.

"Ruby, I can't."

"Won't, you mean."

He nodded, then shook his head, as if he didn't know what he was agreeing to.

"I shouldn't have even let it get this far. I told you—" His voice lodged in his throat. "I don't want anything more. I was honest."

"You did. And I told you how I felt at the moment as well. But I need you to look me in the eyes now and tell me things didn't change for you, too. That you didn't fall for me, too."

He wouldn't look at her, his gaze focused on his friends and family inside. He'd made himself an outsider in every aspect of his life except for work. Of course he threw himself into that; it was safe.

"You know, you can change your mind at any time and it doesn't mean your life is any less amazing or fulfilling." She was over trying to make him want her. That had flatlined. But she could remind him what life could be if he, at some point, decided to give in to his emotions. "I can choose to love you and work hard at what I do. I can have both, but it means I'm going to have to be vulnerable. And yeah, it's scary and I'll never know until I talk to you if

I'm doing it wrong, but I'm willing to try and learn how to love you and show up for you. I am not giving up on my life, Ares, and I hope you don't, either."

Ares backed closer to the sliding glass door that would take him back to his family. She wanted that for him, but knew, when he left, it was over for them.

"I can't. I won't." He opened the door. "What we did was a mistake, Ruby, and I'm so damn sorry."

As long as Ruby lived, she didn't think she'd ever forget the look on Ares's face. It was twisted in pain, his lips and eyes moist with tears. She'd never seen him cry. Knowing it was because of her, broke her.

She fell against the railing, grateful for the strength it provided her when she didn't think she could stand on her own two feet.

"Okay," she said. What else was there but to let him go? How ironic that the moment she realized how much she truly loved him, he was asking her to leave. And when she was so willing to give him what he wanted at such great personal cost. "I hear you. And I'm sorry it got so convoluted, Ares. You're off the hook for Byron's wedding—I'll tell them you had a shift come up."

He ran his hands through his hair again. Damn him that when his perfect style was tousled it was that much more seductive. Made worse was how it reminded her of waking in his arms after a night of lovemaking.

"I can honor that, Ruby. I made you a promise." His voice broke at the same time her heart did.

She shook her head, a pressure headache brewing behind her eyes. At least it staved off the tears she felt brewing.

"You didn't. You made me an offer, and it was a good one, at the time. But it was only as good as the circumstances, and they've changed. I've changed."

"Ruby—" he choked out, and she held out a hand.

"No. Don't. Please don't try to make this better. You told me what this was from the start, and I think in the beginning, I agreed. But when I realized how I felt, I didn't want to believe you didn't feel it, too." Her voice cracked and she looked up at the night sky, thick with dark gray clouds and moisture. A storm was coming. "I'm sorry for that. If I were stronger, I'd never have let myself fall this hard and put you in this position. The least I can do is let you out of being my date to the wedding."

The date that had catapulted this whole charade had brought them there, to this moment. Was it irony, or the universe's messed up sense of humor? Either way, it sucked, plain and simple.

When Ares didn't move to her, she stood. It would fall to her to close this door, once and for all. And she'd known it was coming. Damn her stupid hope that maybe—just maybe—she'd be met with a man ready to love her back.

"Goodbye, Ares. Please thank your family for having me."

At the door, she turned back to face him, tears already falling on her cheeks and smudging her makeup.

"Happy New Year. I hope you find whatever it is you are looking for."

Her exit was punctuated by fireworks and celebratory shouts and screams from both inside the party and the street below. At least everyone was distracted enough by the revelry they didn't see her slip out and flag a taxi to take her home—alone.

It might be the start of a new year, but it certainly wasn't a happy one. How could it be when she'd lost the one thing she knew without a doubt she didn't want to live without?

CHAPTER THIRTEEN

GOD, WHAT HAD he done? Why had he said what he had? Every damn morning after his mother's new year's party, he'd gone to work to find Ruby paired with another doctor. He was grateful on one hand that she'd thought far enough ahead to know how awkward it would be to work side by side for a while.

But he was also angry and sad that it was necessary at all. Not that he had anyone else to blame aside from himself. Well, more specifically his dumb, overthinking brain that had overridden the rest of his organs.

His heart screamed that it wasn't too late, that if Ares could just get a chance to talk to Ruby alone again they could repair this rift in their friendship at least, but his head won the argument and his heart, finally silenced, shriveled back behind its wall.

At the least, he'd seen his family more, had started to build back a relationship with them. He'd gotten together with them each evening, in the beginning to stave off the loneliness from the hole Ruby made when she wasn't there, and then because…he liked spending time with them.

They'd stopped asking about Ruby, sensing he wasn't up for sharing what had happened.

It didn't ease the ache Ruby's absence made, but it gave him something else he'd missed. As for Ruby…

Maybe it was best his heart had all but vanished. Because sure, it was her friendship he missed. The easy way she laughed and how it warmed his heart to be the one responsible for it. He also missed dropping off cakes for her before a long shift. He'd tried to put one outside her locker their first day back, but had found it in the giveaway bin before lunch. He missed teasing her and being on the receiving end of her sharp wit. Working with her and learning from her way of doing things in the A&E. Watching her grow as she learned from him as well.

Yet… It was also so much more than that.

He missed *her*. Missed her lips, missed her hands on his body, her embrace that felt like home and safety and all the things he'd run from.

He missed waking up next to her and starting his day in the best way possible.

But he'd gone and messed it up, so maybe he didn't deserve any of those things, especially with how much he'd hurt her.

Ruby's face had contorted into the same anguish he'd seen on the widow's face when he got back from Greece to make amends. Was Ruby right, that loss was loss, no matter what kind it was?

If that was true, maybe the mistakes of his past weren't as simple as he'd thought. Maybe he'd misread the outcome last time and had spent the past number of years righting the wrong error. Because right now, the lesson seemed to be that family would be there no matter what, and that he didn't have the kind of control he thought he did when it came to his career.

Medicine would always be there, but it didn't comfort him, didn't wrap him in the safety he needed when things were hard and seemingly impossible. It didn't make him laugh, kiss him and make him forget his worries, help him plan for the future. It didn't jump on a plane to new adventures with him or hold his hand while he faced the possibility of losing someone of grave importance.

Ruby did all of that, and more. And he'd brushed her off for something that was a calling, yes, but really was a paycheck in the end. He could lose the job tomorrow and find another one to pay the bills and feel like he was giving back.

But he'd blown Ruby off when it mattered most and—he glanced at the note in his calendar he hadn't had the courage to silence—he was about to do it again.

The wedding was tonight. He'd texted her, but as he'd expected, still hadn't received a reply.

I hope you have a great night, Ruby. I wish I could be there.

Ruby had the day off and missing her only intensified, knowing she wasn't even in the building. He wouldn't even get the chance to run into her in the halls, if only for an excuse to see those gray eyes on him. Sans laughter and joviality, but it was still…

Something.

He pulled up the invitation Ruby had forwarded to him. *Go*, his subconscious nudged. *Go to the wedding.* He could still make it if he left now, got ready fast and put that overpriced car of his to use. His skin rippled with anticipation. He waited a beat to see if his brain or heart had anything to say about the idea, but the only part of him that spoke up was quieter. More distant.

Be sure before you go. Know what you want and what you're willing to give up to get it, because she deserves better.

"Dr. Petrides?" a nurse asked. He glanced up. If he didn't get a grip, it wouldn't matter if he was physically present at work or not; someone would get hurt if he wasn't paying attention.

"What's up?"

"We've got an incoming. Can you stay? We're short-staffed without Dr. Phillips or the other two docs that called in sick today."

Ares, for the first time, was conflicted. His knee-jerk answer was "no." He was off shift and he had somewhere to be. Somewhere that he could finally admit was more important. He couldn't guarantee what kind of future he and Ruby would have if he showed up at the wedding, only that he owed her that at least, and if he was being honest, he owed himself that, too.

At a minimum, they could rebuild their friendship knowing Ares would do the work it took to maintain it.

That's not what I mean when I say do better. That's the same effort you've always given.

Maybe that was true, but wasn't it enough that he wanted to try for something other than work? He had to start somewhere, and Ruby was the only person—the only *anything*—that made him want to.

"I can't. I'm sorry. Dr. Phillips is at a wedding this afternoon, and I'm supposed to be her date."

The nurse smiled. "I love that. Well, good luck to you guys. I've always been rooting for you."

The first smile he'd made in days blossomed on his face. People were rooting for them? Maybe it was time he joined them. The voice from before was louder now.

Good for you. Putting yourself first isn't easy.

He knew that much to be true. He was also painfully aware this wasn't an overnight shift. He was terrified, not sure if he'd made the right decision to say goodbye to Ruby the other night, or if he was making the right decision now to find out if there was an in-between they could have.

Some scenario where he didn't have to give up everything he loved.

That's not going to work, the voice said. *Putting her first will be harder. But you'll have to. Don't go to the wedding if you're not willing to give up your old life.*

Was he? He didn't know. But he couldn't just let her go, either. She mattered so damn much to him. More than almost anything. He didn't know what that meant, or what to do about it, just that he needed to see her.

Be careful.

He'd go home, shower and think about it before he made a decision either way.

The medics rushed in just as he was turning in his tablet. "Unconscious female, late sixties and thready breath sounds. Collapsed in her hotel room, called in by her daughter, Athena, who's inbound behind the rig. Sounds like a vasovagal response but she hit her head."

Ares stopped. His ears rang as he processed the stats of the inbound patient.

Sixties. Hotel. Athena.

His YaYa.

"We'll get her started with a CT once she's stable," the nurse said. "I've got Dr. Johnson on his way in, but we can run triage until he arrives."

"No," Ares barked out. He'd already put his lab coat back on and signed into the tablet. "I'll stay. Give me the vitals."

The nurse looked at him, then down at the patient's name. "She's family."

"Do you have anyone else here? I'll cover until Johnson gets here."

She shook her head. "We don't, but I want you to give up the case when Johnson comes."

Ares nodded. Technically, the nurse had no power over his cases or treatment plans. But this was different. Treating family was tricky and a conflict of interest.

Before he was too deep in the thick of it, he shot Ruby a text. She wouldn't want to hear excuses from him, but she had to know he'd wanted to come to the wedding.

Ruby, I was on my way to see you, to talk to you and be there for you on what's probably a hard day. Believe me, I wanted to be there. I know you'll take this as another excuse with me bailing on you for work, but ask the nurses. I'd turned in my tablet and was out the door. But my YaYa fell and is on her way here. I have to see how she's doing. I hope you'll understand this isn't about work, but family. I'll find you as soon as I'm able. Please tell me that we can talk.-Ares

He met the gurney at the entrance and even though he'd known what to expect, it was still a gut punch to see her laid out like that. His YaYa was a formidable woman—she had to be to keep the Petrides clan in check—but lifeless and pale, she looked...

Fragile.

His pulse raced as he put the nurse on tests that needed to be run, IVs that needed to be placed and did his initial work-up alongside her.

"Her pupils are reactive," he said, and just saying the words relieved pressure in his chest. "No broken bones we can see, though we'll confirm that with further tests. Get her moved up the list for a CT stat."

"Dr. Petrides, there's two patients ahead—"

"Move them out of the queue." He didn't mean to sound so gruff, but his emotions were all over the place. Even he recognized that he'd need to step back when Johnson arrived. But between Ruby and his own ineptitude and now his grandmother...

He wasn't doing well.

The irony of deciding to put himself and Ruby first, only to miss the wedding for work—and not just any work, but his family that had caused him to spiral last time he'd chosen them over something—wasn't lost on him.

"Dr. Petrides—"

"No, I know." He groaned. "But get her on that list. Now."

She nodded. "I will." Ares bagged her with an oxygen mask while he waited for the CT to open up and the oxygen improved his YaYa's stats. He was hesitant to intubate at her age since depending on her CT results, she may not wake up out of the coma they'd have to keep her in.

"Please," he said, his prayer at the tip of his tongue. "Please let her be okay."

He'd been so selfish lately—caring only for what made him happy in the moment and would set him up for a future he'd thought he wanted. And in doing so, he'd put every person who loved him out in the cold to freeze.

He increased the IV fluids and his grandmother's medications and watched for any change. That CT would tell them so much more than just waiting and testing theories would do.

"Come on," he muttered. "Open up, already." He'd give anything for Ruby to be there, to talk this through with her, even if it came with another—earned—verbal lashing. Even mad at him, she was the balm to his wounded heart.

More of the prayer came to him, but he was terrified to speak the words aloud. He needed time to think, and he'd just been rushed from one emergency to another this whole week, either at work, or with the events he and Ruby had been going to.

I'll be better—with them, for them, for her.

His YaYa was, of course, included in the "them" part of the prayer, but it was Ruby who came to his mind when he'd thought of "her."

She was his best friend, but also someone who challenged and supported him, someone who he'd come to care for more than any friend he'd ever had. And if he was still being selfish—and stupid—he'd fight to keep that friendship what it was, but he wasn't so sure that was in anyone's best interest.

A sputtering from the bed roused him from his sats watch.

"YaYa," he said, tears brimming in his eyes as hers opened. "You're in the Royal York Hospital and I'm Ares, your grandson. You've suffered a fall."

Her delicate hand with paper-thin skin and midnight blue veins pushed the oxygen bag away from her mouth.

"I know who you are, Ares. *Theos*, I was there when your mother pushed you into this world. And I'll be around for a bit yet, thank you very much. A tiny little fall isn't going to change that."

He laughed, swiping at the tears on his face. The nurse looked at him with a mixture of confusion and concern. No one but Ruby had ever seen him cry, and that was only once. But damn if he couldn't help it.

"I'm glad to hear it. We've got some tests to run to make sure you're okay to release when Mom gets here, but yeah, I'd say it was probably just a small spill that rattled you. I'm so glad, too."

She tried to sit up but winced. "I'm a little sore, but

okay. Now, where's that doctor who ran out of our room the other night without so much as a goodbye? I've got a thing or two to tell her about our family and how we show up for each other."

"This isn't the time for that. You should rest."

"Hogwash. I'm going to take this chance while I have it. Now, send her in."

He sighed, feeling incredibly exhausted all of a sudden. The door opened and he heard Dr. Johnson talking to the nurse, then addressing him.

"Dr. Petrides, they sent me in to take over since this is family if I'm not mistaken."

Ares shook his head. "No, they were right. I'll hand over care, but if it's okay, I'd like to stay with her." Ares didn't want to have this conversation about Ruby with another man who was interested in her, but he couldn't stay quiet, either.

"Of course."

Ares addressed his grandmother. "She's not here today. She's at a wedding, and I'm supposed to be there with her."

His grandmother appraised him.

"And you're not because—" She waved him on.

"Because we had a disagreement. I've not been the best... friend to her lately."

Her eyes narrowed, telling him she saw right through him. He was the reason why Ruby had run out the other night and might not be back, especially since he'd already missed most of the ceremony of the wedding he was supposed to take her to.

"You hurt her," she said. It wasn't a question and thank goodness since Ares had no excuse.

"I did. Deeply. I had my priorities out of whack, and she paid the price."

"Then fix it, you daft idiot. This family didn't raise cowardly men, so don't go starting a new tradition. Fix your mistakes and be accountable for those you hurt."

His YaYa shrugged as if she'd suggested the simplest tweak to a recipe to make it better, not a vague statement that he'd been coming to on his own. He needed to know *how* to fix it with Ruby, and how to make sure he never put her in this position again.

As if she'd read his mind, she smiled and shook her head.

"Only you can figure that out, my love." He laughed. Of course she'd read his mind. "Because only you know her heart."

"I do? I don't know that I know anyone's heart. I thought I knew Ariadne's, but the way she handled our breakup... And how disappointed Mom was when I didn't choose who she chose for me. How am I supposed to buck years of tradition for something I want? Does that make me selfish?"

"You need to put that down. You and Ariadne were arranged, yes, but you cared for one another. She may not have handled things well, but my love, neither did you." Ares winced. No, he hadn't. It was part of why he'd been going home that fateful trip. But had he really changed? Could he be counted on when times got tough? "And you need to forgive yourself. You were young and even my old eyes can see how you've grown and changed."

"You keep reading my mind and we're going to commit you to the psychiatric ward for studying."

He laughed but she only shook her head. "I just know you, Ares. But do you know yourself? You've been burying everything that matters to you beneath old hurts, and the only thing that does is suffocate the good and allow the grief growing in the shadows to blossom." She squeezed his hand. "Did you know that your grandfather wasn't the man my family chose for me?"

"What? No, I—" He shook his head. So much of what he knew about his grandmother was changing in a matter of moments. "I didn't know any of that. Tell me more, please."

It was suddenly the most important studying he'd done in his life, since the knowledge might shape the course of his future.

"I'm going to check on the CT, but I'll be back for her in a moment. You should wrap up here," Johnson said. Ares nodded.

"I loved your grandfather the minute I met him at the fish market. He was a commercial fisherman, obviously not the man my parents would even want me glancing at, let alone building a life with." Her smile grew wistful. "I used to sneak out and meet him for a walk along the shore, or take a boat trip to this little island we found near his hometown. Zakynthos."

"That's where I grew up."

His YaYa nodded and smiled. "We ran away together and were married in secret, which only some of the family forgave us for, but you know what, Ares?" He fought back tears. He'd always known his grandmother was brave, but she was a rock unlike he'd ever imagined. "I did what was meant for me and never looked back. Along the way, what was meant for me included what was meant for my family to live wonderful, full lives."

He let the full understanding of what she was telling him simmer.

"Do you have a tuxedo?" He laughed at her non sequitur. "I do."

She nodded curtly as if some universal truth had been decided. "Then it's settled."

"I think I know where you're going with this, YaYa, but I'm going to need you to spell it out this time. I have a feeling I only get one more shot at this."

The nurse came in to wheel his grandmother out.

"Know your mind and heart, *Egonos*. Then follow them no matter what. You love her, yes?" Ares nodded. He always had, he realized. "Then think of how to tell her that in a way only she can hear. And then come see me with her. I miss the laughter of that *xenos*."

He might know Ruby, but his YaYa knew her Petrides family.

"Me, too, YaYa. Now, get better and I'll check on you soon. I'll send Mom in while I'm gone."

She nodded, and though he worried about leaving her, he needed to let go of what he was able to. It was the first stop toward letting someone in.

Ruby was his future, and the rest was just gravy. Now, how to find her and show her that every day for the rest of their lives.

Ares was late. Like, way beyond fashionably so. The ceremony and dinner were done, and the reception was in full swing.

Please let her still be here. He knew where she lived, but somehow, it seemed important to meet her there, at the event that had begun their fake-dating scheme. Who knew it would lead to real feelings on both ends?

But none of that mattered if he couldn't find her to express those feelings.

And then, he caught a glimpse of a silhouette he'd know anywhere.

Ruby Phillips.

God, she was stunning. Her hair was curled at the ends,

giving her a starlet appearance, especially sheathed in a gray dress that matched her eyes. Goddamn, that *dress*... It reached the floor but left nothing to the imagination. Curves he knew by sight and touch were on display in the gown, from the slit most of the way up her thigh—a slit that also showed off a black garter—to the formfitting satin and lace.

He swallowed hard, desperate for a drink to take the edge off his lust. But then he'd drown out the more important things he needed to feel in that moment.

Namely, *love*.

Watching Ruby press a hand to her chest in earnest as she listened to an elderly woman tell a story, he'd never been more certain of his feelings. The woman he'd once teased for being too efficient, too curt with patients had captured ahold of his heart and squeezed it, bringing it back to life.

He loved her, through and through, and no amount of reasoning through it, or chasing the feeling away with more work was going to make it fade. He loved Ruby Phillips enough to change his life. And the thing of it was, even if she denied him, which would be well within her rights, he'd keep trying to be the kind of man she'd be proud to know.

That's how he knew it was love—it wasn't precluded by her feelings for him, but merely what she brought out in him.

Even if he wasn't confident that he'd made as lasting an impact on her, she was different. She wasn't cold or unfeeling. No, she'd been hurt, and together they'd made one another stronger. Now, look at her, talking to a woman about who knew what when the Ruby he'd known would have found an excuse to head to the bar or hide from the conflict a family event posed.

Pride surged in his chest. It hadn't been all bad.

Until I became a coward and ruined it all.

He inhaled, the snug breast of the tuxedo tight on his

chest, constricting his air. Or maybe that was the ten-ton weight sitting upon it, waiting to see if, indeed, he'd effed everything up by slinking away when things got hard.

Only one way to find out. He headed toward the woman, the magnetic draw from his heart to her body as strong as ever. His gaze didn't leave her for a moment.

Ruby's face was exactly as he'd always imagined it at her happiest—her head was thrown back in laughter, her cheeks tinted pink with joy. And Ares had nothing to do with it. The knowledge stung like he'd been pricked with an IV needle, but he pressed forward. She deserved happiness no matter who helped her achieve it, though he wanted it to be him as much as possible.

As he approached, a man dressed in a sharp gray suit that complemented Ruby's gown beat him to it. He leaned down and whispered something in Ruby's ear, and the red that replaced the pink on her cheeks from earlier stopped Ares in his tracks.

He held his breath, waiting to see how she responded.

When she took the man's hand and let him lead her onto the dance floor, jealousy rippled over Ares's skin, turning it clammy. His throat, once dry, now felt thick with words unsaid. He had no right to feel anything other than happy for Ruby, though. Any jealousy he felt was his fault and his fault alone.

The envy turned to regret, which was somehow worse.

He'd lost his chance. Maybe this was what he deserved after the way he treated her. For him to feel the love and desire for this woman and let her go.

As he spun on his heel, his YaYa's words came back to him as clearly as if she was there with him.

Know your mind and heart, Egonos. *Then follow them no matter what.*

His mind and heart were centered around one person and they weren't at the exit of the reception hall, or back in Greece, or even in the Royal York A&E department.

They were wherever Ruby Phillips was. She was the center of his thoughts and the reason his heart felt as if it might explode out of his chest.

She was his home.

So, he listened to his grandmother and followed his heart and mind back to comfort and safety. To Ruby. As he did, he reaffirmed that he'd never let his fear get in the way of doing the right thing again. If Ruby chose another path, at least she'd done so knowing how he felt and what her choices were.

Risk and fear aside, he held out his hand. "May I cut in?" he asked. Then he awaited an answer that would shape the course of his life no matter what.

A new prayer emerged from the depths of his chest.

Please let it be an answer that lets me have one more chance with this woman.

CHAPTER FOURTEEN

RUBY WAS HAVING a good time, all things considered. The wedding, like the rest of the events leading up to it, was inordinately decorated to Byron's posh tastes. Dinner was delicious, if not overly fancy with four courses of delicacies. She was dancing with a good-looking man who in another life she might find attractive, if only she hadn't met a certain someone first. Ares really had ruined her for all other men, hadn't he?

But this wasn't about her. It was nice to see Byron so content, and his stunning bride looked...happy.

That's all Ruby hoped for, that her own pain at the breakup all those years ago led these two to what was truly meant for them. It wasn't her, even if she had backed off at work. No, even looking at the wedding these two had designed told her she and Byron never would have lasted with their disparate tastes.

Another thing the wedding made clear was how badly Ruby wanted a version of this for herself. The commitment, the friendship, the love...

Too bad only one person's face materialized when she thought of that.

Ares.

But he'd made his position on Ruby crystal clear.

So why did her body have the damn audacity to still feel

him as if he were right there next to her? She'd need to do a major Ares detox after the wedding and its shenanigans were through.

She inhaled deeply and was hit with a wave of spicy cologne that was so decidedly Ares she wished the man she was dancing with would spin her far away from whomever had the gall to smell like the man she loved and couldn't have.

He did spin her, right into someone else. They stopped as the other person held out his hand.

"May I cut in?"

It sounded like Ares's voice, too. Except… She glanced over and gasped.

"Ares," she said, disbelief mingling with something more hopeful.

Relief. He was there at the wedding. And as if the mere presence of him wasn't enough, he was dressed in a jet-black tuxedo that seemed to shimmer of its own accord. His hair was styled in a fashionable taper with a wave that reminded her of European wealth and royalty. Sometimes it was so easy to imagine him in the life he might have led had he stayed on in the family business.

And like each of those previous times she'd thought the same thing, she was so glad he hadn't chosen that path. Sure, they may not have worked out romantically, but to know him at all had been such a gift the past few years. If it weren't for him and his friendship, she'd never have found the peace she lacked after her breakup with Byron.

"Can't you wait until we've finished dancing?" her partner, Liam, asked. She shook her head and stepped away.

Only one man had ever made her feel more seen in his embrace, and he was still at arm's length away from her. She ached for him, even if it wasn't healthy to do so. Liam, on the other hand, was one of Byron's buddies from uni and apparently the least socially aware person at the wedding. To make matters worse, he'd just flown in from Abu Dhabi and had missed the previous two wedding events where Ares and Ruby had flaunted their new relationship.

Sure, the guy was handsome, probably the type of man who would show up on her apps when she braved getting back on them, but he was also a shadow of what she wanted.

Who she wanted.

Emergency medicine was about reading the signs and like he did at the hospital, Ares seemed to read her mind and her every movement.

"I understand. Honey, I'll call the babysitter and see what she wants to do about the rugrats and let you finish this dance. We can talk on the way home."

Ruby bit back a smile and turned toward her dance partner. "My husband gave me permission to keep dancing, but we should hurry. Our youngest is sick and last we talked to the babysitter, she had such bad diarrhea—"

That was all it took. "I didn't know you… I think I should…" he stuttered, backing up with each word.

Ruby waved.

"Take care, Liam. It was nice to meet you," she called. Turning to Ares, she couldn't fight the grin that fought its way to her lips. Loving this man was as natural as breathing. Teasing had always been part of their friendship, and she had hope they'd get that back someday.

"Thanks for that. He wasn't the sharpest tool in the shed, was he?"

"You know how to pick 'em, Ruby," Ares said. She opened her mouth to reply but then he was there, in her space, taking it up. She didn't mind at all. "I'm teasing, of course. That was more a jab at your choice in fake boy-friends than anything else."

She smiled, careful to breathe through her mouth so she didn't inhale the spicy wooded scent of Ares's cologne. God, this man was going to make forgetting him as difficult as possible, wasn't he?

"Yeah, he's a tough one. Might take longer than the others to get over."

Ares stepped closer to her, took her hand in his. Why did it have to feel so damn good?

"I'm hoping you take your time on that last part. Do you want to step out and talk?"

She shook her head. "I think I'd rather do this here so I don't let myself do something I'll regret."

He nodded, extending his other hand as if he was asking her to dance. She accepted it, but her chest ached as if she'd just undergone an angiogram.

"What are you doing here?" Ares swept her into a waltz that had her head and heart spinning.

"Remember me teaching you this back in the hospital lobby two Christmases ago?"

"Of course I do. You saved my backside before the hospital benefit." How could she forget? This man was responsible for so much of who she was, now that she thought of it. The way she slowed down with patients, a gift that only enhanced her role in that space. Then there was the way she looked at her career and her future with emergency medicine, another gift from Ares. She didn't want to hide behind work as if it were a shield from real life. She wanted work and life to intermingle so she could suck the joy from both. She had a sneaking suspicion after her week with Ares sharing her bed, that both would be magnified by the other.

And this man, this beautiful man who she'd thought had

ended things with her was there, gazing down at her with the same look he'd worn each time they made love.

Speaking of love…her heart was the only organ louder than her libido at that moment. She loved Ares, had told him as much, and he'd rebuffed her. But it didn't change her feelings. Wasn't that the truth about love? That it existed whether it was met in kind or not? It was sort of like medical care in a way.

The physicians and staff would be there no matter what, even if no one else showed up. Memories of how she'd persisted with the little boy who fell in the River Ouse a few days ago surfaced. She'd been driven by love even then. How couldn't she see that the undercurrent to all she did was the same feeling she overwhelmingly felt for Ares now?

Love was part of all she did, and she could no more hide from it than she could her own shadow in summer.

That didn't mean she shouldn't be a 100 percent sure where she put her energy, though.

"But you didn't answer me. What are you doing here?"

"I'm sorry I'm late, Ruby. I was going to say it couldn't be helped, but I put the wrong things first and then that thing with my grandmother—"

He'd texted Ruby about her collapse at the hotel and how he'd need to stay and care for her. She hadn't minded that, of course not. Which is why seeing him here was a shock; she wasn't sure he'd even want to share another shift with her after she'd admitted how she felt for him.

"Ares," she repeated. "It doesn't matter. You're here. But I thought—"

"I know what you thought and why you thought it. And Ruby, I'm so sorry. For missing the wedding, the dinner, half the reception and for…for everything else. I don't deserve it, but I'd like a chance to explain myself."

She ignored the bubble of hope that floated above her hurt feelings after their last interaction. She'd been here before with Ares.

"How is your grandmother?" she asked instead.

His smile was like the sun in spring. She'd missed it. "She's stubborn as usual. Medically, she'll recover fully. Hopefully soon, so she gets back to the hotel to tell my family what she and I talked about before I came here tonight. It might be nice for them to have a heads-up."

"About what?"

"How much I messed up with you. How I'm trying to make things right."

Ruby opened and shut her mouth twice before answering. His arms around her waist were making it hard to concentrate on anything else, and now more than ever, she needed clarity.

"Thank you, but it doesn't change the words you shared. You were pretty clear about how you felt." She was curious when he only nodded, but didn't shy away. Had he heard her when she'd said she needed someone brave, someone who wouldn't shy away when hard conversations needed to happen?

The hope fluttered back, as persistent as an arrhythmia.

"I said a lot that night, and all of it was true." Ruby's mouth opened in surprise. The upbeat tune that had everyone around them dancing to a different beat felt incongruous to the deep hurt she still felt. "But it was only half the story. Can I tell you the rest?"

She nodded.

Ruby was only mildly aware of the stares of others. She didn't care—she and Ares had done what they set out to do and more. No one talked to Ruby about Byron or how she worked too much. Aside from her mother's comment in the other direction, that she couldn't wait for Ruby and Ares to marry and give her grandbabies, the ruse had been a success.

The lingering hangover wasn't from it as much as the way they'd given into the perks of pretending to date. Their physical attraction wasn't surprising but her reaction to it was. Their friendship as the bedrock for their new intimacy had led her to fall fast and hard.

And she'd landed with a thud, in need of her own medical care. No matter. Tomorrow she could start fresh with all their fake-dating events behind them.

They swayed to the slow song, something new from a pop singer. He pulled her tight against him and she could no longer hide from his cologne, his strength, his power over her.

"I was scared, Ruby, and the things I said after you shared your heart with me—that I couldn't do this, well, that wasn't exactly true."

"Wait, but you said every word was—"

"I know. But it wasn't true because it was missing the other half. I said I wasn't sure I should stay or that I wasn't sure what loving you would mean. I never once said I didn't, though."

Her gaze shot up.

"I'm confused," Ruby admitted. But her heart pounded against her chest. Could he feel it?

"Ruby, I love you so completely it hurts to imagine life without you."

She gasped, and her feet stopped moving. He paused dancing, too, and sent her a look of pure love. It shot straight to her heart.

"You *love* me?"

He nodded. "More than I could have ever imagined possible. Enough that my mom might just get the one thing she's always wanted. If you can forgive me, that is."

"I just… I don't understand what changed."

Every cell in her body wanted to cry out that it didn't matter, that he'd professed his love and that was enough. But it wasn't. Love was only the beginning; she knew that now. What came next—the trust and vulnerability and laughter and friendship—that was the tough stuff. And it mattered so very much.

"Nothing changed, actually. It was just me waking up to what really mattered. For so long, that was work, and then I realized that was only part of what made life worth living. What was I working for, if not a life with someone? So, I realized it was time to make different priorities—free of my parents, my old ways of doing things, of people's expectations of me at work."

She still didn't understand how she fit into that.

"I don't want to be the pause or distraction to the different life you're making for yourself, Ares."

He cupped her face in his hands, traced her lips with his thumbs.

"You're not the distraction to the different life, Ruby. You *are* the different life."

Then it all sunk in. He wanted *her*.

"You're not scared still?" she asked.

He laughed, a lovely ringing sound she wished she could carry around with her.

"Oh, don't get me wrong, babe. I'm terrified. But not like you think. I'm scared I've missed my chance to show you how much I love you and want you to be the center of everything. Hell, you already are, Ruby. I'm always scared I'll make you frown instead of that lip-biting smile you have that I think is the most beautiful thing I've ever seen."

He leaned down and kissed her and she let him. It felt right, good.

"I'm scared I'll lose you, that our kids will be stubborn like me, and that my mom will try and convince us to live part time in Greece."

"Kids?" Ruby asked. Her heart might not survive this night the way it went tachycardic at each new line from Ares. "You want kids with me?" She'd only just admitted to herself that she'd miss it if she never got the chance, but with Ares out of the picture until now, who would she ever build a life with in time to hope for children?

"Hell yes, I want kids with you. Not right away. First, I want to take you home and strip you out of that dress." She swallowed, finding it difficult. "Then I want to kneel in front of you and ask you to be my wife. We'll have a short engagement because, come on Phillips—we've been building toward this for years now."

"We have," she whispered. It was no longer a question.

"So, we'll get married. Here, for your family to all be able to come. I kinda like the idea of drawing it out a little so we can have some fun with all of them." She agreed, but couldn't say as much, not with tears burning her eyes. "We've already determined that my family can travel, even my grandmother, who was cleared to leave after a clean CT. So, Ruby, will you?"

"Will I?" The wedding in the background drowned out as she focused on the man rubbing her ring finger.

"Will you marry me and let me tease and love you the rest of our lives?"

She laughed, unable to stop nodding.

Her heart was his the moment she'd met him; it just took her six years to figure that out.

"I do. I will, I mean."

"I like both those answers, but save the first for next month." It was Ruby's turn to laugh. "Ah," Ares said, kissing her again. "There's that sound I love so much. I want to make it so you always feel like you do when you laugh like that, Ruby."

She shook her head, leaning against his strong, solid chest. "That won't be possible. Life will throw us curveballs, but we'll get through it together," she said. He inhaled deeply.

"We will. We'll face everything together."

She leaned back, noticing that they'd somehow started swaying to the music again.

"Promise?"

Ares nodded and kissed her forehead. "I promise, and Ruby? I know you're right. There will be challenging times, but I'll never let you go again, okay?"

She couldn't have felt more like this new year was a gift if she'd unwrapped the man himself. Though, she did have plans for that later.

"Okay. I'll hold you to that and two more things."

"Name them," he said.

She leaned on her toes and kissed him deeply, the promise of a future between them.

"First, take me home and make good on that list you started," she said.

He growled with lust and her stomach roared with heat and something else. *Peace.*

"Yes, ma'am. And the second?" he asked.

"Promise me we'll take next year off for the whole Christmas and New Year holiday? I'm kinda thinking I'd like to travel somewhere with my family instead."

Ares cupped her cheeks and kissed her, pulling back only to whisper against her lips.

"You've got it, Ruby. And I'll even be the one to pack the snacks. We can't have my new wife getting hungry. Speaking of," he said, pulling back his jacket to reach his trouser pocket. "I brought you this, figuring you probably were too busy talking to eat."

In his hand was a snack cake that was smashed and still the most beautiful thing she'd ever seen.

"I love you, Ares Petrides," she said, tearing into the sweet treat that was only the second thing she wanted most in that moment. The first was in her arms, promising her the future she'd always dreamed about.

"I love you, Ruby Phillips. And I can't wait to show you just how much every day for the rest of our lives."

She smiled, sure there was probably chocolate on her lips, but not caring. The man who held her knew her inside and out and loved her just as she was.

That was a gift worth waiting thirty-odd Christmases for.

* * * * *

Look out for the next story in the
Royal York Hospital Christmas collection,
New Year to Nine-Month Surprise *by Louisa Heaton.*

And if you enjoyed this story, check out these other great reads from Kristine Lynn.

How to Resist Your Enemy
Nine Months to Marry the Princess
A Kiss with the Irish Surgeon

All available now!

NEW YEAR TO NINE-MONTH SURPRISE

LOUISA HEATON

MILLS & BOON

For Nick, with love xxx

PROLOGUE

New Year's Eve

'SERENA! YOU MADE IT!' Colleen Murphy, orthopaedic nurse and one of Serena's friends, pulled her into her arms in a warm welcome and gave her an effusive hug. Colleen was dressed as a 1940s gangster. Pinstripe suit. Hat. Fake machine gun looped around her neck.

Serena laughed and forced a smile, hoping her friend wouldn't take her to task for coming up with the lamest fancy dress costume ever—a doctor.

It had been a last-minute thing, though, to be fair. Serena had told herself she would not go to the party and that she'd stay in on New Year's Eve instead and just have a quiet one. In the *New Year*, she'd start her New Year's resolution of being more social. But she'd spent a *long* day at work today, and the idea of going home to her empty and no doubt cold flat depressed her. In an attempt to prove to herself that she did have a thriving social life, she'd grabbed some scrubs from work, draped a stethoscope around her neck, put her shoulder-length hair up into a twisty, messy updo and figured that would have to suffice. Her friends would forgive her.

Hopefully.

Especially since she only had a small circle of friends. She couldn't afford to lose any.

From inside the fancy wine bar that Colleen had booked months in advance, the party sounded like it was in full swing. Music pounded from some unseen speakers, disco lights flashed, and the noise of conversation and good cheer was practically oozing from the walls. This wasn't Serena's thing at all. She'd much prefer to stay at home, in the quiet, with a good book and a mug of hot chocolate. Maybe the last of the Christmas tunes playing quietly in the background on the lowest of the low settings. But she'd already spent Christmas alone. Did she want to spend New Year's Eve alone, too?

'Come on in! Everyone's here. My advice, sweetie?' Colleen leaned in to be heard. 'Grab some champers, neck as much of it as possible, and find someone to snog with when the countdown goes that you won't have regrets about in the morning!' She laughed, already clearly three sheets to the wind. 'I've got my sights set on that new porter, Giacomo.'

'Wait! Aren't you going out with Dupinder?' she yelled to be heard.

'Oh, that ended, sweetie! We move on, and we take our chances!' and her gangster-clad friend disappeared back into the crowd.

Serena laughed, wondering what happened between Colleen and Dupinder. They'd seemed sweet together. Her friend's ability to move on swiftly, seemingly without care, amazed her. Was that what it was like to pursue a relationship and believe that everything would turn out fine? To allow yourself to want someone and hope that maybe this was the one?

Serena began to make her way through the crowd. There were a lot of people here that she didn't know, though she recognized a few faces from the hospital. There might have been more she knew, but beneath their costumes or behind masks, it was hard to tell. She figured it was probably best to get herself a drink and maybe something to eat and then try to find a quiet corner to put her feet up and rest. Maybe no one would notice she was there.

Go me. What a rock star. I really need to perk up and get a life.

Jostled, she managed to grab a large glass of champagne from a circling waiter, because why not follow her friend's advice? Enjoy a little fun and let her hair down for once! It would be much more fun than sitting at home alone, feeling sorry for herself, which is what she'd been doing a lot of lately. She downed the first glass in one go, for bravery more than for any other reason, and then grabbed herself another glass. She'd go slower with this one. The drink was sweet. Crisp. The bubbles tickled her nose and tongue as she edged her way through the thronging mass and found a darkish corner from which she could observe everyone and see if there was anyone she liked. If there just might be someone she could kiss at midnight, as Colleen suggested? And not just a polite kiss, but a kiss that had the potential to be electrifying.

She missed the intimacy of being with someone. To feel important and wanted, if only for a short while. It had been a long time since she'd actually slept with anyone, though. Those dalliances had been very few and far between. Her last encounter had been...back in May?

Wow. Maybe too long.

But who to go for? One-night stands were great in theory, but in practice? There was a saying about dipping your nib in the company ink, and hospitals were places ripe with gossip. She didn't need it to be with someone who she'd run into every day. It had to be someone whom she barely knew. Who wouldn't expect anything to come of it afterwards. Who would keep their distance and guard her respectability and make it easy to keep going to work without worrying about running into them daily and having a distinctly awkward encounter.

Way to make the choice easy.

She smiled, watching her friends and colleagues. Laughing at some guy dressed as a pirate who was doing a very quirky dance that seemed to be a mix of body popping and robot with everyone cheering him on. She saw a junior doctor dressed as an angel pressed up close to her amour, doing a slow dance, despite the rapid thump of the music. Beyond them all, she noticed Ash Dhillon, an orthopaedic surgeon, whom she knew by sight, but who was someone she hadn't really had an opportunity yet to work with. She'd heard from others that he was a great doctor.

And the reason she spotted him was that he, like Sahara, had quite lamely come dressed as a doctor, only his scrubs were a different colour to her own. She smiled at the casually draped stethoscope around his neck, a twin to her own, though he had decorated his with a bit of tinsel.

Damn! Tinsel! I could have pinched some from the tree in the hospital's grand reception, though she wouldn't have pulled the whole thing over onto her, the way Kyle Windgate, singing superstar, had in early December.

Ash was a handsome guy. Quietly handsome. Effortlessly handsome. Almost like he didn't know he was good-looking. He wasn't preening at this party, but was standing quietly, not even dancing or swaying to the music, but trying to talk to some guy she didn't recognize by leaning closer to shout in his ear. The guy nodded and shouted a response back. Friends, then. Colleagues? Ash smiled and cast his gaze across the room. She felt it sweep over her, move on and then…return? He frowned slightly and looked away, almost as if he was perturbed.

My outfit. It's because we're wearing the same thing. It's embarrassing. I wonder what his excuse is for not finding a real outfit for this New Year's Eve fancy dress party?

Probably the same as hers. A last-minute decision to come. But she'd liked the second glance. The way his eyes had widened slightly. The shift in his stance. It had been exciting. Alluring.

Would he make a good candidate?

He was hot. Mysterious. She knew almost nothing of him, except for his work. She had never worked with him and probably never likely would. Being a physiotherapist, she worked with post-surgical patients. She would hardly be up on the ward a lot, though she did sometimes have to go there. But she'd not run into him yet! So…

Serena allowed her glance to run over him. He was trim. Fit. At least six feet. Dark hair. Dark eyes. Intelligent, most likely highly skilled, being a surgeon. But was he single? He wasn't wearing a ring, but not a lot of men did these days.

I'm smiling. He can see me smiling at him. Uh-oh. He's coming over!

Nervously, she sipped at her second flute of champagne and tried to act like she hadn't seen him come over.

'Hello!' he said, with the most gorgeous smile she had ever witnessed. 'Looks like we both raided the same dressing-up box!'

Serena laughed and nodded. 'I think we did!'

'Would you like a drink?'

She knew she ought to keep a clear head. She was nervous, out of her comfort zone and at a party, and a handsome guy was talking to her. If this ended in a hookup, then maybe she needed to watch the alcohol. She showed him her flute, still almost three-quarters full. 'I'm good at the moment, thanks.'

'Excellent. Cheers!' He raised his glass to hers and clinked them.

She took another sip, examining his face more intently now he was closer. He had the most wonderful eyes. Dark. Devilish. With sickeningly full lashes. She would have killed to have lashes like his. 'I'm Serena.' She held out her hand for him to shake.

'Hello, Serena, I'm Ash.' He took her hand in his, sending trembles and goose bumps up her arm. He had a strong grip, but it was the way he looked so intently into her eyes when he said her name that gave her excited, anticipatory shivers. She could imagine him breathing out her name, whispering it into her neck, his lips brushing her skin.

She leaned in to be heard, inhaling his scent. 'You work at the hospital.'

'Yes. Ortho surgeon. You?'

'I work there too. Physio department.' She stumbled forward slightly as someone bumped into her from behind, her free hand pressing against his chest to stop her fall. He was solid. A wall of muscle.

He steadied her, smiling as his hand caught her bare arm, sending delicious shivers along it. 'Important work. You get everyone after I'm done with them.'

She was trying not to think about what it might feel like if he touched her elsewhere, so she tried to keep the conversation on an even keel. 'I think I've seen your name on some of my cases.' There was no *think* about it. She had done, and he'd pulled off some pretty impressive surgeries! 'Didn't you once rebuild a guy's hand from scratch?' She wanted him to know that she'd noticed.

He smiled. 'His basic structures were there—I just put his hand back together again after he shattered it.'

'I'm a big fan of your work,' she replied, blushing. Because she wanted to reach out and touch him again. To connect to him physically. Her gaze was drawn to his lips as he spoke, wondering how his mouth would feel upon hers. If he was a good kisser. His mouth looked delectable! All this leaning in they were having to do to be heard…she could smell him, and he smelled wonderful! Whatever cologne he was wearing was doing indescribable things to her insides.

'You're the true hero. I patch them up, but you guys

get them working again,' he said, his lips by her ear, his hot breath against her cheek.

Serena appreciated his compliment. It felt good to be acknowledged. She loved her job. Loved watching patients get stronger and more confident again after an injury.

'Thank you! You're very kind! And hot!' she said, her bravery boosted by the loud music and all the bodies around them. Everyone up close. The junior doctor dressed as an angel had her arms draped around her beau's neck, gazing into his eyes and laughing. Colleen was trailing a finger down Dupinder's chest. It seemed that New Year's Eve was a night for throwing caution to the wind. And why not?

'You too,' he replied, looking directly into her eyes. In his gaze, she could see that he was picturing them both together, and it was singularly one of the most arousing gazes she had ever experienced. His look told her that if they got together, for no matter how short an encounter, he would give her the time of her life. She would be left with pleasant memories and the warm afterglow of a scintillating and mind-blowing orgasm.

Serena swallowed, suddenly feeling dizzy and overwhelmed. She *deserved* to let go. To just *enjoy* herself with him. Hadn't she been alone enough lately?

'Want to go somewhere a little more private? Bring in the New Year with a bang?' he whispered.

Yes. She did. She nodded. He reached for her hand and pulled her away with him, through the throng, squeezing past people. She felt the strength of his hand in hers, leading her, turning to check that she was okay, making sure she wasn't lost to him, and finally guiding

her up the spiral staircase that led to the top level of the
wine bar, the VIP section. There was another door here
leading to a roof terrace, but he turned in the other direction, away from the blare of the music and the strob-
ing disco lights and into the quiet of what looked like
an old storage room, if an old storage room was allowed
to have such amazing things in it. Clearly these were
previous furnishings and decorations. Candelabras. An
old red velvet-lined booth. Drapes. Lanterns.

Serena closed the door behind them, turning the lock.
'This is just a one-night thing, okay?' she clarified.

'Absolutely. One night.'

'And we never speak of it again?'

He smiled and moved closer to release her hair down
around her shoulders. 'Never.'

'And if we meet at work, we won't make it awkward?'

'We won't.'

He was up close against her now.

'Because we're responsible, sensible adults?'

He nodded. 'I'm going to kiss you now. After I'm
done kissing you, I'm going to do lots of other unspeak-
able but delightfully wonderful things to you. Is that all
right?' he whispered seductively.

She swallowed, aroused. And nodded. 'Ditto.'

And suddenly his mouth captured hers, and time
stood still.

Ash just wanted to lose himself in her. To take away the
darker thoughts that always plagued him at this time
of year.

He used to love Christmas and the new year, but a
couple of years ago, his life had fallen apart on New

Year's Eve. Instead of it being a time of reflection and resolutions, it had become a dark period in his life that he'd rather just forget. He'd even offered to work the New Year's Eve shift at the hospital, but his boss had told him that no, he'd done that for the last two years. It was someone else's turn.

'Besides, Ash, it would do you good to have a break. You've worked non-stop for the past month, not a single day off. For health and safety reasons, I need you to take some time away.' Jack English, the chief of orthopaedic surgery, had informed him that he was giving him a whole week off. Ash's protests had fallen on deaf ears. Jack was determined. 'You worked Christmas Eve, Christmas Day, Boxing Day and all the days in between. I mean it, Ash.' His boss had sighed then. He was one of only two people who knew about Laila here. The other was Ryan Carlton, a friend he'd worked with before at a previous hospital, and who now worked here as the head of midwifery. 'Look, I know it's difficult for you, but I think it's time you found a new coping mechanism.'

And instead he'd found Serena.

He'd not meant to go to the party, but the idea of sitting at home didn't appeal, nor did the idea of glumly staring into a drink at a pub. And that was when he remembered Colleen, a nurse on his ward, was throwing a New Year's Eve fancy dress party at some posh central York wine bar. In a moment of madness, he decided that he would go there, have a drink or two, enjoy the company of colleagues and friends and maybe sleep on someone's couch afterwards.

Then he'd seen a woman. Someone vaguely familiar, but whom he couldn't place. Dressed in scrubs like him, and he'd wondered what her excuse was for not having a proper costume. But it was the way she stood apart that intrigued him. For all intents and purposes, she should have looked like she belonged there, but he could sense that she felt isolated from them all, as if coming here tonight had been a last-minute decision. Maybe it was a strange attraction between two hurt, lonely souls, but he felt pulled in by her and couldn't resist going over to say hello.

Now he was caressing her soft, smooth skin, gazing past her shoulder into the reflection in a mirror, loving the way when he licked her neck, she dropped her head back and her caramel hair cascaded down her back. The way her back narrowed into her waist and then the swell of her curvaceous hips, his hands running over them, exploring, touching, squeezing...

He'd not slept with a woman since his marriage fell apart. There'd been dates. Polite dinners. Someone to share a conversation with, or a glass of wine when he'd missed female company. And each time, he had walked them home, or shared a taxi with them and bid them good-night at their door with a peck on the cheek. He'd been invited in once or twice, but he'd never stepped over the threshold. That seemed like going too far. Something he'd not been ready for.

But now he was in what seemed to be an old staging room with this goddess. He barely knew anything about her. They'd not stared at each other over a restaurant table and played the game of being interested in the other person's life, asking about parents and family and work, what she was like as a child and what she'd always wanted to grow up to be. They'd not clinked glasses and stared into each other's eyes and laughed at feeble jokes to be polite. They'd not put on their best front, their masks that kept them protected.

Protection...

'Wait,' he said, pausing, breathless. He'd been able to stop himself. It had been so long. After years of not having sex, it was a wonder he hadn't exploded at her first caress of him.

'What is it?' she asked, her eyes dark with desire, her lips swollen from their frantic kissing.

'Do you have protection?'

She blinked at him, reality slamming down onto the both of them. 'No, I don't!'

It was a moment that should have sobered them both up immediately. A moment where they put on the brakes and got re-dressed and muttered embarrassing apologies and slipped from the room to avoid each other for the rest of the night.

But that wasn't what happened. Ash didn't want to leave the room. Not yet. He used to carry a condom in his wallet. 'Hold on,' he said, rummaging in the back pocket of his scrubs, finding his wallet and delving in the depths. Yes! He had one, and he looked down at her with mischief in mind.

Serena bit her bottom lip, drawing his eye. 'Now, where were we?'

And he smiled back at her devilish face.

Full steam ahead once again as he lowered her into the velvet booth.

For once in his life, he just let loose and allowed himself to not think at all.

CHAPTER ONE

SIX WEEKS LATER, a heavy snowfall in mid-February surprised everyone. The weathermen had forecast chilly temperatures and had mentioned that there might be a risk of black ice and sleet, but snow? When Serena woke up that morning, she'd gazed at the snow that was almost a foot deep outside her kitchen window and felt her inner child want to dash out there and make a snowman, whereas the adult that she was told her to calm down, make herself a coffee and something for breakfast and maybe, just maybe, she could stop herself from feeling so unwell.

There was a bug going around work. To be fair, there always was in winter. Rhinoviruses, influenza, norovirus, and now, of course, Covid—there was always something going around in the colder months, filling up A&E and acute medical wards, but it hit staffing levels, too. One particular virus had been making a few of the staff feel sick and exhausted and bunged up, and that was what Serena figured she had. The last few days, she'd not been feeling her best. Fatigued, even though she'd been getting a good eight hours of sleep per night. Fatigued and achy, like she had the flu. Her nose was bunged up, she had a headache, and everything tasted like metal. Ugh. It was horrible. But everyone else at work had powered through, so she figured that she would have to do the same. Especially today. She'd been assigned a new patient to treat—Kyle Windgate, the singer who had been injured in Royal York Hospital's Great Christmas Tree Disaster. Her supervisor, Cole, had cornered her yesterday. Told her about it so she'd be prepared.

Kyle had been putting on a Christmas concert in the hospital's grand foyer at the beginning of December. A young man who'd won a televised singing contest to find the next hot singer of the moment, he'd captured the hearts of the nation with his clean-cut looks, handsome face and earnest, honest vibes. The hospital, learning that he was a local, had contacted his manager and asked him to start off the hospital's Christmas celebrations with a Christmas carol or two whilst he placed the giant golden star on the top of the tree.

Unfortunately, the crew that had put together the platform for Kyle to get to the top of the tree had not installed it correctly. It had collapsed. Kyle, reaching for anything to keep himself steady, had fallen and pulled the tree down upon himself, breaking his leg and injuring his hand.

Reviewing his file notes yesterday, Serena had felt herself go all hot under the collar when she'd realized that the surgeon who had operated on Kyle was none other than Ash Dhillon, the man she'd had an uncharacteristically quick one-night stand with six weeks ago.

She'd had one-night stands before, of course. But usually it was with someone she'd gotten to know first over the course of a few hours. At a dinner maybe, or, like her last one, at a physiotherapy convention where she'd been spending the night. It just seemed safer to feel like she knew that person if she was going to be vulnerable with them, even though, technically, could you ever actually know someone properly after a couple of hours?

She'd picked her consorts with care, making sure it was never anyone she would have the chance of running into again. At least, not for a long time, anyway. But with Ash, it had been impulsive and risky, yet fun, and it had certainly been a fascinating way to ring in the New Year. She would have liked to be able to tell herself that her orgasm had chimed with the New Year ringing in, but that wouldn't have been the truth. In actual fact, their mutual orgasms had occurred about ten minutes prior. By the time Big Ben chimed midnight, she and Ash had managed to get back into their scrubs and made it downstairs to share in the cheering and the singing of 'Auld Lang Syne'—albeit gazing at each other from across the room with secret smiles.

She blushed at the memory, still not quite believing that she had done such a thing! In the weeks that had followed, she had not run into him again, even though they both worked in the same hospital. She'd been working in the main physiotherapy department with her outpatients and had avoided any need to be called up to the ward, which had suited her perfectly.

Gazing at the snow, she realized that it would probably take her longer than normal to get to work. The traffic would be going slower, and there'd be more of it on the roads. There could be accidents…who knew? But she didn't live far. She figured that this morning, it just might be better for her to walk to the bus stop and catch a bus. She had no energy to be clearing her car of snow and sitting in its freezing cold interior as she waited for the windscreen to defrost. Her ancient car took ages to warm up these days, and she didn't trust the battery, either.

Better to clomp up the road twenty-five metres and catch a warm, overheated bus that would drop her right outside the hospital. Probably safer, too. Serena had seen enough people come through her doors suffering from the after-effects of having broken something after slipping on ice.

She poured hot water into her coffee mug, then a splash of milk, and stirred it before taking a sip. She winced. It was too hot and too…what? She couldn't quite describe it. She loved her coffee and her hot teas, but lately? With this bug going around? Things just tasted weird, but she'd checked herself to see if it was Covid. Her test had been negative, so that was a relief. This was something she was going to have to push through. Everyone else had had it for about two weeks, so maybe just another week to go, if she was lucky, then she'd feel right as rain. She hoped so. It was hard to help other people and keep up a smiling face when she felt weird and groggy and ever so slightly sick, no doubt from all the mucus draining from her nose.

Serena poured her coffee down the sink, rinsed the mug and then grabbed her winter coat and Wellington boots. Her work trainers she kept in her locker at the hospital, so she didn't need to pack those, but she did want to take a healthy lunch to try and tackle this bug with as many vitamins as she could. She grabbed a small bottle of orange juice and a pre-made salad she'd bought from the shop yesterday on her way home. The salad she'd meant to eat last night, but she'd instead craved a cheesy pizza with mushrooms for that umami kick and had ordered in instead. Indulging herself, telling herself it was okay. That one indulgence didn't matter. Moderation and balance, as she often told her patients when some of them went overboard with their physio and began working out *too* hard. Or too little, or not at all. It was like some didn't want to get better.

Well, she did.

It took ten minutes for the bus to come. In that time, her toes began to freeze in her Wellington boots, even though she had on thick boot socks. But on the bus, the heating was on full. Though the windows were steamed, she sat and looked out at her neighbourhood as they drove through it and thought about Kyle Windgate. He was her first patient of the day, and she wondered if he was coming in via taxi. Or was he so much of a celebrity these days he had a car, with a driver, provided by his record label? It had been ten weeks since his surgery with Ash to repair and plate his tibia and fibula. Weeks of being in a cast. His leg muscles would be weak. Unaccustomed to bearing his weight or allowing movement.

I'll get him back on his feet no problem, she thought to herself.

As she ambled through the hospital foyer, the scene of Kyle's accident, it all looked back to normal. No more tree. No more Christmas lights. The ladies on reception still had all those paper hearts draped around their desks in celebration of Valentine's Day, which had just passed. No doubt they'd change it soon for eggs or chicks in preparation for Easter. She gave her friend Yvonne a wave and walked on past the bank of elevators and down the corridor to the physiotherapy department. It was one of the newer parts of the hospital, only recently renovated in the last year, and they were all very proud of it. First in, she filled the kettle and switched it on to boil whilst she went to her locker to rid herself of her slushy boots and hang up her winter coat.

It was nice and warm in the hospital, so her uniform of white polo shirt and navy trousers and trainers was perfect. She put her hair up in a clip to keep it away from her face and returned to the kettle to make herself another coffee. Maybe this one would taste better?

It didn't. But she forced it down and sat in the staff room waiting for everyone else to arrive.

Cole arrived next. He was her boss and head of the musculoskeletal team. Then Vanessa and Tricia arrived together, and then Paolo.

'Hey guys, kettle's boiled,' she said.

'You're a star.' Nessa smiled, rubbing her cold hands together after taking off her coat. 'That snow's crazy, huh? Guess we're going to get an influx of new patients soon, if that black ice they keep talking about is under all of it.'

Tricia opened up her backpack and pulled out a plastic tub. 'I brought everyone breakfast muffins!' She began to pass them around, and when the tub passed under Serena's nose, a wave of nausea rolled through her.

She pulled a face and waved a pass, hoping not to offend. But the idea of eating one of them truly turned her stomach.

'You still got that bug?' Tricia asked.

'Yeah.'

'You do look a little green with it.'

'Thanks.'

'Are you sure you don't want one? It might help.' Tricia persisted, still holding the tub out to her.

Serena gazed down at the muffins. Under normal circumstances, she would have agreed that they looked lovely and would have taken one. They were large, and she could see cranberries and white chocolate chips, all delicious things, but honestly? If Tricia didn't remove them, they were going to get a new, bilious topping...

'No, thank you.' Just speaking made her feel like she might throw up.

'Serena? Could I have a quick word?' Cole asked, coming out of his office.

Delighted to be rescued from the muffins, she nodded, got up and followed him into his office. Cole closed the door behind her. 'Take a seat.'

'Uh-oh. You sound serious.' She smiled to show him that whatever it was, she would help anyway.

Cole laughed. 'Not really. Just dotting some *i*'s and crossing some *t*'s. The hospital lawyers are apparently quite freaked out still since our local boy done good had his accident here with the Great Christmas Tree Disaster.'

'I bet.'

'Anyway, as you know, I've asked you to take on Kyle Windgate for his physiotherapy, which starts this morning.'

'Yep.'

'Well, there are a lot of eyes on this, as you'd may expect. I've just had a phone call from the esteemed lords of the hospital's boardroom. As Kyle's a local celebrity and he hurt himself here at the hospital, was operated on by one of ours and is now getting his physio here, the powers that be think it would be a good thing, in light of the media interest, that his surgeon also be involved in his aftercare and keep an eye on his recovery.'

'His surgeon?' He meant Ash.

'Yes. Ash Dhillon. You might know him?'

Flashes of their night in the glitzy wine bar storeroom flooded her memory then. His lips against her flesh. The way he'd pressed her arms above her head with her back against the velvet booth as he'd finally slid into her and made her gasp out loud. The way she'd been grateful for the thumping music outside the room so no one could hear all the noise *they* were making. 'I've, er…seen him around, I think.' She blushed, hoping Cole would just think that she was having a hot flush from this bug she had.

'Well, the hospital board have been getting a lot of pressure from outside sources to make sure that Kyle's recovery is done absolutely correctly and that he emerges from this with a good outcome. They think it pertinent that Ash be seen working with you to ensure Kyle gains full mobility and is able to get to his tour beginning in the late summer months. We all think that with you and Ash working *together* on Kyle, we can achieve this. No one will be able to say that we didn't give Kyle our absolute best.'

'I don't need Ash to help me,' she said, not happy about the idea. 'I'm a good physio! And since when did surgeons get a say in that? I am a professional, and I will treat Kyle how I treat all my patients—the same!'

'I'm with you, but you know what things are like

when lawyers get twitchy. We all have to go that extra mile, and to be honest? I tried to say the same thing as you, but I've just had a call and been told in no uncertain terms that Ash is in the room, whether we like it or not.'

Serena shook her head in disbelief. 'Well…what sort of input am I meant to give Dr Dhillon?'

'He's just *overseeing* Kyle's sessions. You'll be in charge of the physio—you know what you're doing. The lawyers and the board just want Ash in the room, that's all.'

'It's a waste of his time.'

Cole nodded. 'Agreed. I've heard that Ash isn't happy about it either.'

I bet.

'It's not for long. Just until this blows over and the media gets interested in something else.'

'Fine. But I want it on the record that I disagree with this. I should be allowed to do my job whether lawyers or the board are twitchy or not. And I don't need his surgeon there, watching me whilst I work.'

'Noted.'

This was ridiculous! He should not be feeling this way! It was just another department in the hospital. He was a doctor—a surgeon, for crying out loud—and he should feel comfortable going anywhere in this place. The hospital was like home for him. It was his saving grace. His soft place to fall. Here at Royal York Hospital, he was useful. He changed and saved lives! And after the surgeries he performed, a lot of his patients ended up in physio afterwards.

So why was he standing here with one hand against the door, ready to push it open but hesitating?

Serena Fleming.

He'd like to say he'd forgotten all about it and had only recognized her name when the powers that be had marched into his theatre yesterday and told him he was expected to oversee Kyle Windgate's recovery and work with his physiotherapist to ensure an optimal outcome. For appearances' sake. Make the media and the world feel that local boy done good, Kyle, was getting the best treatment ever. Working with Serena would make everyone happy.

But this last month or so since New Year's Eve... he'd kept thinking about her. He put it down to the fact that she was the first woman he'd slept with since his marriage breakdown and divorce. It was bound to have felt strange, but even though it had just been a one-night stand, he'd felt something that night. Something he couldn't quite grasp. Or describe. And as elusive as it was, he'd tried not to examine it too closely.

Until now.

But, he reasoned, they were both grown-ups. Both adults. She probably wasn't too happy with him butting in on her turf, either, but they would both have to deal with it.

He sighed and pushed the door open, striding into the department with his head held high and hoping beyond hope that this would all go well. Especially Kyle's recovery. He was a young man, in his prime. If he did what Serena told him to, there was no reason he shouldn't recover and regain full use and strength in his leg. The surgery had been good. He'd performed his best work despite the fact that his boss and his boss's boss and his boss's boss's *lawyer* had watched through the viewing window, all of them no doubt panicking about an imminent lawsuit that was about to befall them all.

There'd been no lawsuit. Not against the hospital. The company that had put up the platform were the ones at fault. Now that the hospital wasn't going to be sued for millions, everybody in the boardrooms had begun to relax. This was just the powers that be making sure Kyle got treated perfectly, just in case. But as far as Ash was concerned, all his patients should be treated the same, whether they were a famous singer, a cleaner, a president or even, yes, a lawyer.

His eyes scanned the corridor, looking for Serena, and then he saw her. Sat behind the reception desk on the phone, talking to someone. She seemed to notice him at the same time he saw her, and he watched as a blush warmed her face. She looked away, continuing her conversation.

Clearly she remembered their night, which was good. It wasn't like he'd had any practice with crazy one-night stands, but he'd hoped their sexual encounter had been just as much fun for her as it had been for him. And seeing her again? Brought it all rushing back. Most importantly, he wanted to seem gentlemanly and adult about this. He didn't want it to be awkward for either of them, even if it would be difficult to look her in the eyes, after all the things they'd done to one another.

He slowed as he approached the desk, glancing around for Kyle, but clearly their young star had not arrived.

Serena finished her call and put down the phone. She looked up at him. 'Dr Dhillon.'

He smiled. 'Miss Fleming.' Now that the blush was fading, he could see she looked a little pale. Almost tired.

'How are you?' she asked.

'I'm good. How are you?'

'Perfect! I'm great! You?' and then she frowned, realizing that she'd already asked him how he was and he'd answered and that maybe perhaps she was babbling? He saw this and a whole lot more wash over her expression. She tried to cover it by gathering up some paperwork.

So he gave her an easy out. 'I take it our esteemed pop star is not here yet?'

'No.' She began walking down the corridor. He followed her, rushing to catch up until he fell in step alongside her. She walked fast. Almost as if she wanted to escape the situation they found themselves in. Him, here in her territory.

'If it makes you feel any better, I'm not here to tread on your toes or cause you any embarrassment,' he said quietly.

Serena stopped abruptly and turned to face him, squaring her shoulders and sounding surprised he would even think that. 'I have no reason to be embarrassed.'

He smiled. 'Good.'

'You should know, though, that I'm not entirely happy about this situation.'

She really was as beautiful as he remembered. 'Me overseeing Kyle's physio? Or just me being here in general?'

'Both.'

'Ah. Well, I agree with you. I'm missing early morning rounds, which my registrar is having to do. I happen to think my time is more valuable up on the orthopaedic ward, but we are all mere puppets for the powers that be, so I'm going to try to make this work.'

'This is my department, Dr Dhillon. My expertise. I'm in charge.'

He liked that. 'Call me Ash.'

She blinked at him, slightly blindsided by his kind and almost submissive attitude. He wasn't submissive in the least, but he was willing to let her call the shots here, because she was right. This was her turf. He'd played his part, and though it would be good to see Kyle again, he was more than happy to accept that Serena would guide Kyle through the next stages, not him.

'Fine. You can wait here.'

Her stomach felt like a washing machine on its fastest spin cycle. The second she saw him stroll into her department, it had gotten even worse. Now she stood in the bathroom, splashing water onto her face and staring at her pale reflection, before she had to go back out there and pretend everything was normal.

It *wasn't* normal. It would *never* be normal. She'd fallen for his scintillating good looks with him dressed in scrubs, but seeing him this morning dressed in dark trousers and an open-necked white shirt, his sleeves halfway rolled up revealing his beautiful forearms, with lovely dark skin and muscles that spoke of a man who worked with his hands?

Because she knew what his hands could do. What his mouth could do. His lips. His tongue! *Dear God, his tongue...* There'd been a moment in that storeroom when he'd trailed his mouth down her body, when he'd knelt between her legs. It had been like he was worshipping at her altar as she'd gasped and writhed and arched above him, her fingers caught in his raven hair. She'd pulsed and ground herself against his tongue, crying out.

How was she supposed to work with him when all she could think of was *that*? Hence the cold water on her face. A slap of cold reality. *Focus.* One hour. That was how long she had to get through with him watching her. She could do that, right? If she focused on Kyle and not him?

She dabbed at her face with a paper towel and grimaced at her reflection. She looked ill. Dark circles beneath her eyes, pale skin with a greenish tinge. Maybe she should have a lemon and ginger tea to settle her rolling stomach?

Yes. Good. A plan.

She left the bathroom and headed to the staff room to make herself a hot drink to put in her insulated travel mug. Taking a sip, she winced at the heat but was grateful for the soothing lemon and ginger flavor. As she marched back to her room, she noticed her celebrity patient on his way in.

Kyle was using his crutches. His injured leg, now out of its cast, was not yet weight-bearing.

'Mr Windgate?'

He stopped, turned to see who had called his name and smiled at her. He was a handsome young man. She could understand how he would have appealed to a lot of young teenage girls. 'Hi.'

'I'm Serena Fleming, and I'm going to be your physio. It's very nice to meet you at last.'

He propped himself on his crutch to free his hand to

shake hers. 'Likewise. I'm looking forward to throwing these out and getting back to full strength.'

'We'll have you on your feet soon enough, don't you worry. If you'd like to follow me?'

'Lead the way.'

She smiled and began walking back to her room, where Ash was waiting. Her stomach rolled again at the sight of him—damn the way he made her feel!—and she felt a little acid burn the back of her throat. At her desk, she sipped at her tea, figuring that the more she could get down her, the quicker the ginger would start working.

'You know Dr Dhillon, of course,' she said as Ash got to his feet to greet Kyle.

'Doc! Yes, great to see you. I wasn't expecting you today,' Kyle said.

'Thought I'd oversee the recovery of my most famous patient ever,' Ash said, shaking the younger guy's hand.

'Wow. Going above and beyond.'

'No problem. How's the leg been treating you?'

'It aches a lot still, but I guess that's to be expected?' Ash nodded.

'Take a seat, Mr Windgate.' Serena pointed to a chair next to her computer station, determined to take control of this consult.

'Kyle, please.' He settled down into the chair, placing his crutches up against the wall next to him.

Serena sat in her seat and tried to ignore the sensation of Ash sitting behind her as she began her workup with Kyle, asking him about his current health situation, his exercise regimen if he had one, if he smoked, vaped or drank alcohol. 'And the cast has been off for how long now?'

'Two days.'

'Okay, great.' She smiled at him. 'Can I get you up on this bed over here so I can have a look?'

'Sure thing.'

She got up from her chair and glanced at Ash. She couldn't help it, and she started when he stood too. Of course he'd want to look at how well Kyle had healed, what scarring was left, but his proximity to her was alarming as they stood side by side, whilst Kyle pulled up his loose joggers to reveal his leg.

It looked pale from being in a cast. Comparing it to his other lower leg, you could see the difference. There'd been some mild atrophy of the muscles. A manipulation of all his joints—hip, knee and ankle—showed that he still had movement, even if it was stiff and pained him somewhat.

'Can you flex your foot for me and point your toes up to the ceiling?'

Kyle grimaced as he did so. 'What do you think, doc?'

'You've healed really well. This scarring should become invisible eventually,' Ash said.

Serena bristled. This was her consultation. He was only meant to be overseeing. So why didn't he just go and sit in the corner? Why did he have to stand right next to her, looking so amazing and smelling so delicious?

Her stomach rolled again. She held her hand to her mouth as she swallowed down bile and cleared her throat. 'Okay, erm... Kyle. What I want you to do first for me, is we need to work on your stability. I'm going to ask you to just try, if you can, to gently rotate your ankle clockwise for me.'

Kyle's face scrunched up as he concentrated on turning his ankle.

'Any pain or discomfort?' she asked, trying not to think of *her own* discomfort. This bug she had was really beginning to affect her stomach. She wished she'd been able to eat a proper breakfast, because that might have helped mop up whatever mucus she swallowed overnight as she slept. But the idea of eating had made her feel even more nauseous, even though, weirdly, she'd also felt hungry at the same time. She'd thought about having toast, and she'd wanted the toast, imagining it sitting on her plate with butter and maybe jam or honey, but then the idea of having to put it in her mouth to take a bite?

Ugh.

But she was strongly beginning to think that missing breakfast had been a mistake, especially when she had such a physical job, helping patients.

She grabbed a yellow resistance band, a long loop of latex that was often used in physio and sent home with patients. 'Right. Okay. I want you to loop this under your foot like a stirrup, and then if you can hold each end? Perfect. Now, point your toes at the ceiling. Holding on to this band, I want you to slowly point your toes away from you. Like a ballerina. That's it. Keep doing that for me, nice and slowly, though.'

'What does this do?'

'It helps build up your strength and stability. Don't worry about remembering all of these exercises that

I'm going to show you, by the way. I'm going to email you an exercise sheet for you to work on at home. How does that stretch feel?'

'Weird, but good to be moving again.'

'Good.' She glanced at Ash, feeling his eyes on her. He was looking at her quizzically, then glanced away as if embarrassed to be caught watching her.

Her cheeks flushed, and she had to force back those images of that night they'd spent together. Why was she tingling? And why, oh why, did she have to deal with him on a day in which she felt so sick?

'Stand up for me now,' she instructed Kyle. 'Good. At home you can do this and support yourself by holding on to the back of a chair, or with your hand against the wall, but I want you to practice laying your foot flat on the floor. You don't have to put too much weight on it, but I need you to be stretching out those tendons to get them used to bearing weight again.'

'Okay.'

'How does that feel?'

'Like it's pulling everything.'

'It'll feel that way for a while. Now, keeping all your weight on your good leg, I want you to practice lifting up the heel on your left leg and then placing it down again.'

'I can feel that.'

'You will. When you're stronger, we can do this with the resistance bands, too. For now, I want you doing this exercise without.'

She led Kyle through a variety of strengthening exercises. After about an hour, she bade him goodbye, promising to email him with a sheet of exercises he could do and how many reps he needed to do each day before he came back again. As she waved goodbye with a smile, she waited for him to go out of eyesight, and then she turned back to Ash. 'Shouldn't you be going, too?' She really could do with him gone. She needed to breathe. Needed to think. Needed to gather herself to be able to type up notes without that feeling of him watching her.

'Yes, I should get going. It was impressive to watch you work.'

'Thank you.' She would accept the compliment, even though she figured watching *him* at work would probably be even more impressive.

'You should come up to the ward sometime. Take a peek in theatres. Watch a surgery or two. I often find these interdepartmental crossovers can be quite beneficial to both parties. We should have done it sooner.'

'Maybe I will.' She said, knowing that she would not, under any circumstances, find herself *voluntarily* going up to the ortho ward to seek him out. No matter how delicious he was.

She must have looked quite green then, or uncertain, because he smiled as if amused. 'Unless you get squeamish about seeing raw blood and tissue?'

No, she wasn't squeamish. But she was incredibly nauseous, and the bilious burps she'd been holding back for Kyle's appointment could be held back no longer.

Serena suddenly accepted that she was going to be sick. 'Excuse me...' she mumbled, pushing past him and hurrying for one of the staff bathrooms in the department, but they were both in use. Instead, hand over her mouth, hoping beyond hope that she wasn't going to be sick in the corridor, she rushed out onto the concourse next to the physiotherapy centre and found the closest public restroom, banged into a cubicle and bent double over a toilet as all that had been threatening to emerge since she woke this morning decided to make its appearance after all.

Serena groaned, feeling a close sweat dotting her brow as she stood and wiped her mouth with tissue. Someone in the cubicle next to her flushed the toilet. Their door opened, and she heard someone at the sink turn on the taps.

Embarrassed, but feeling slightly better, she flushed her own toilet and took a deep breath. Thank goodness she'd not been sick in front of Kyle or Ash! That would have been mortifying!

Stepping out of the cubicle to go wash her hands, she paused when she recognized her friend stood at the sink.

Ginger Ashby. She was a midwife here at the hospital. Since the last time Serena had seen her, she looked like she'd gotten a few more grey streaks in those beautiful red curls of hers. She glanced at Serena with one eyebrow raised. 'You okay?'

'Fine.' Serena went to the sinks and washed her hands before splashing cold water on her face. It made her feel a little bit better. But not by much. Had anyone else actually been sick with this damned bug?

'Sounded it. Heavy night last night?'

'No. I've just got this bug that's been going around.' She grabbed a paper towel and dabbed at her face, wondering how on earth she was going to explain this to Ash. Hopefully he would have returned to his own department and wouldn't darken the doors of her own until Kyle's next appointment.

'I've not heard of it actually making people throw up.'

'Maybe it's a different bug? There's plenty about.'

Ginger was looking at her funny. 'Or maybe it's not a bug at all.'

'What?' Serena was confused. What could it be, then? What was Ginger implying? There was a tone to her voice that suggested she knew exactly what it was, but how could that be?

'Do you think you might be pregnant?'

Serena laughed. 'You're a midwife! Of course that's what you're going to think it is! But if you were a gastroenterologist, you'd think it a bug. A neurologist would suggest migraine. It's what you see all the time. It's what you'd expect. It's called confirmation bias.'

Ginger smiled. 'You trying to convince yourself there? Or me? What I see is a young woman in her prime. Being ill mid-morning. Pale. Exhausted-looking. And excuse me for stepping over the line here, but I don't remember your boobs straining against your top like that the last time I saw you. Now either they've got bigger or your uniform has shrunk in the wash.'

Serena looked down at herself. Were they bigger? They had felt sore lately, but everything about her body had been feeling off. 'My boobs are just fine, thanks.'

Ginger held up her hands in apology. 'Okay. Well, I hope you feel better, then. Usually it happens around the thirteen-week mark!' she said with laughter as she left the bathroom.

Serena stared after her. It was ridiculous what Ginger had suggested. Pregnant! Ha! Not possible. The only man she'd slept with recently was Ash, and that was weeks ago. Six weeks ago! And...*and I've not had a period since then.*

She felt her heart thud in her chest, but she calmed herself quickly, reminding herself that she had endometriosis. That often meant that her periods weren't regular anyway. She'd been told by a specialist years ago that it was so bad, she would struggle to conceive. People who struggled to conceive did not get pregnant after a one-night stand!

It was the whole reason she didn't get involved in a relationship. She'd have always felt that she was less than. Unable to give her partner a child, even though having a family was the one thing she'd always wanted. Her diagnosis of endometriosis years ago had separated her from her family. Her mother. Her sisters, who had all produced many children. Serena had twelve nephews and nieces! And though she was happy for them, it made them sad for her. So she'd just begun to stay away lately. It had seemed easier. Like one-night stands had seemed easier. No pressures. No expectations.

No disappointments further down the line.

No. She couldn't be pregnant. It wasn't possible.

She looked up at the mirror, and her gaze dropped to her breasts. Were they bigger? She'd felt like her bras hadn't been fitting right but had put that down to the fact that none of them were new. Maybe they'd just lost some elasticity, or something?

Her gaze dropped to her abdomen. Did that look rounder, too?

No. You're just looking for things now. What had she said to Ginger? Confirmation bias? Looking for evidence to prove a theory? Forcing information and evidence to fit?

Ginger *had to be* wrong.

Serena left the bathroom and then remembered she still had Ash to deal with.

What if he was waiting for her in her workroom?

What explanation could she give?

I'll just tell him I had a late night.

After all, it's none of his business.

Okay, so that had been awkward. Clearly Serena was not dealing with the fact that they'd had a one-night stand very well at all. She most definitely had not liked him standing near her and had appeared incredibly uncomfortable. And then to rush off like that? Like she was going to be sick?

Maybe it wasn't him. Maybe she was just ill. There was a bug going around. He wanted to get back to his own department, see his own patients, but as a gentleman, he needed to stay. Make sure she was all right. Tell her he felt no embarrassment that they'd been intimate together.

In fact, she'd not just changed him. She'd been the first person since his wife he'd felt attracted to like that. She'd helped him take a huge step forward. One he'd thought he'd never take again.

Get close to someone? No. No way. That complication was never going to be for him again, not after losing Laila. He'd been torn in two. Torn asunder. His heart ripped into shreds and left to rot. He'd felt dead inside. For a long time. His only passion in life had been for his work. His patients. Surgery. Where he could win the battle sometimes for life over death. Or at least quality of life. He'd not looked out of himself for a connection with anyone in ages. Serena had been his first, and he felt strangely attuned to her.

He'd wanted to come say hello before in the weeks since their one-night stand. It had felt strange, though, and so he'd avoided it. Knowing that she was in the same building as him but never actually meeting. When physios had come up to the ward to work with some of the inpatients, he'd always wondered if she would come up. But she never had, and when he'd asked one of them about it, he'd learned that she generally worked with the outpatients. He'd thought about coming down to visit.

But they'd made a pact. One night only. To save on awkwardness at work. Him coming down to see her? Despite her being on his mind an awful lot since that night? Well. She might think he was hoping for more, and he wasn't. Not like that. Romantically, anyway.

He saw her coming back down the corridor, and he instantly perked up. She looked a little flushed, a little awkward, glancing at him briefly before sitting down at her desk. 'I thought you'd be gone by now,' she said, as if irritated.

'Just wanted to make sure you were okay. You left in a bit of a hurry.'

'Did I?' she asked, trying to pretend she hadn't just run out of here like she was being chased by a swarm of bees.

Serena Fleming was a puzzle to him. Why would she pretend that she hadn't just rushed out of her department for some unknown reason? 'Heavy night last night?'

She shook her head. 'No. Why do people keep say-

ing that to me? I'm fine,' she snapped, tapping away at
her keyboard. He came to stand behind her and watched
her input her notes in Kyle Windgate's file.

'Right. Okay. Forget I said anything. Well. I guess
I'll see you for his next appointment?'

'Yes. Bye then.' She briefly gave him a polite smile,
then turned back to her screen.

He smiled. 'Goodbye, Serena Fleming.' And he
walked away, amused and confused by her reaction to
him. Clearly the one-night stand thing had made her
extremely uncomfortable.

Maybe the next time they met, things would go a lot
easier?

CHAPTER TWO

THE RIDICULOUS SUGGESTION by Ginger that Serena might be pregnant haunted her thoughts all morning. It couldn't be true, and she would prove it. She had endometriosis. Severe endometriosis, a diagnosis that had devastated her dreams for one day having a family of her own. It couldn't be possible. Not from a one-night stand during which they'd used a condom. So, determined to take a test and show the negative result to her friend Ginger, she waited for her morning break and then rushed to the pharmacy a little way down the street.

She knew she could have asked the pharmacy in the hospital for a test, but one, she didn't want to be seen queueing and have someone ask her what was wrong, and two, she didn't want gossip spreading from a pharmacy tech that Serena Fleming, physiotherapist, had bought a pregnancy testing kit, because people would leap to conclusions.

Pretty spot-on conclusions, but still. Better to go down the high street, so her coat would cover her uniform and hospital ID lanyard and no one would know her. It would be the perfect anonymous purchase. Then she could get back to the hospital, pee on a stick and prove to herself that Ginger's suggestion was totally and utterly ridiculous!

And yet…

There was a small, very weird part of her that kind of wanted it to be true. Though she didn't want to admit to that, she couldn't help but wonder and hope. She'd always wanted to have a child of her own. A family of her own. She'd always wanted to carry a baby and be pregnant and experience what so many other women got to experience. To be glowing, to sit and stroke her growing bump, to shop for baby clothes. She'd spent so long being alone since her depressing endometriosis diagnosis. The idea that she might not be alone after all was dizzying and hypnotic. And tempting! Oh so tempting!

But she didn't want to hope because she knew, logically, that her endometriosis most definitely meant she'd pee on this stick, the result would be negative, and her hopes would be dashed, even if this wasn't the most perfect situation in which to conceive a child. She'd dreamt of marriage and family. Of having a husband that adored her, whom she adored in turn. Why was life teasing her like this? Tempting her with what could be? But she felt strongly that the result would be negative and would be heaps more awful on top of how ill she already felt, and it would truly ruin the rest of her week. Yet another reminder that things like that would never happen for her and that she'd been a fool to think otherwise. Even if it did give her the satisfaction of seeing Ginger's response.

It didn't matter that she would be a single parent if it were positive, or that she'd somehow have to negotiate a relationship with Ash, as he was the only person she'd slept with in months, so he would be the father. *He'd only wanted a one-night stand, remember! Not a family!* That was a complication of a positive result that she chose not to think about, because she knew there really wasn't any point anyway. It simply couldn't happen.

The pharmacy was quiet, probably because not many people were out and about in the snow. A few people browsed the shelves. Serena cast her gaze over who was in the store to make sure there was no one there she knew, but everyone appeared to be total strangers. She went to the shelf, pulled a testing kit off it, and took it to the till to pay for it, stashing the box into her pocket as quickly as possible so that she could get it back to the hospital without being seen.

With five minutes left of her morning break to go before her next patient arrived, she locked herself away in the bathroom stall of the staff toilet. Sweating like crazy and still feeling sick, she completed the steps as laid out in the leaflet, reading the instructions properly to make sure she did it right. She didn't want to get a weird result and then worry that she'd not done it correctly.

She tried to calm her breathing. What was the point in getting worked up? It was going to be negative. It had to be negative! So she'd been sick. So what? There was a bug going round. Maybe her boobs looked bigger because she'd put some weight on this Christmas? There'd been plenty of nights she'd sat in alone, gorging on mince pies and chocolates and watching her favourite Christmas movies, sobbing at the happy endings that seemed promised to everyone else but her. It had seemed a better choice than going out and faking festive fun. Christmas was for families and surrounding yourself with loved ones. Though she had a family and had spent Christmas Day with them, she'd felt very much aware that, at the age of thirty-five, she ought to be celebrating with her own family by now. With a husband and happy brood of children. Yet because of the endometriosis, her inability to conceive, her ex had left her, abandoning her for someone who could give him the children he wanted. She'd spent years staying in either because of pain and bleeding and discomfort, or the fact that she just didn't feel worthy to be with anyone! She'd enter her forties single and alone. Her fifties the same. Her sixties. Seventies. However long she lasted. She'd become the perfect cat lady instead.

Serena checked her watch. Three minutes. Long enough, right?

She reached for the test and stared at it.

Two lines.

Two lines was…she grabbed for the packet and double checked, her heart thudding in her chest so hard she thought it might break a rib or two in its bid to escape. She even dropped the packet and rushed to pick it up again, her nausea abating briefly so that her body could deal with the shock of what she was seeing.

I'm pregnant?

There it was on the box. And in the instructions. Two lines meant a positive test. Two lines meant that she was pregnant! From a one-night stand with a stranger! She couldn't believe it! How was it possible? When she'd been in that long-term relationship with Ralph a few years ago, before the endometriosis had been diagnosed, they'd had unprotected sex because they'd *wanted* to have a baby, and nothing had ever happened. He'd left her after they'd found out she would have incredible trouble conceiving. He wanted to start a family as he was much older than her and didn't want to wait anymore.

And yet she had once-in-a-lifetime mad, crazy sex with Ash, *once*, using protection, on New Year's Eve and *suddenly I'm up the duff*?

She laughed. In shock. Not quite believing it. There was a second test in the box, and she figured she would run a few minutes late getting back from her break to do the second one, but that one showed a positive result too.

Oh my god.

I'm going to be a mum!

Now all her symptoms made sense! She didn't have a bug. This was *morning sickness*. The nausea, the exhaustion, the slight weight gain... She was two months pregnant! And though she'd not planned on this happening, she knew instantly that no matter what, she was going to keep this baby, and she would raise him or her with or without Ash's involvement.

Oh god. I'm going to have to tell Ash.

Ash was in theatre, working on reducing a butterfly fragment in a forearm fracture, but his mind kept going back to his puzzling morning spent with Serena. He couldn't get her out of his thoughts. From the New Year's Eve party and how she'd looked to the way she'd been with him earlier with their patient, Kyle.

She'd clearly been uncomfortable with his presence. Not only uncomfortable but ill, too. Nor had she wanted him involved with her consultation. She thought he had no place being in her workspace. Or maybe she was just upset at seeing him again after their one crazy night on New Year's Eve? It had affected him, too. Either way, her reaction had been a bucket of cold water to his libido, which had been stirred by her body and her touch. He'd been in hibernation for a long time, yet with Serena, that had changed. All he could do was think about her, so when he got asked to keep an eye on Kyle's recovery? He'd been happy at the idea of seeing Serena again, even if she had not felt the same way about him.

After placing the plate, he put in the first screw at the proximal end and then a second at the distal end before filling in the others. His patient, who had come up from A&E, had managed to break their forearm after a rugby tackle in school had gone incredibly wrong. They would certainly have a nice scar and a nice cast for friends to sign.

With the fracture secure and stable, he began to close up.

As he sutured, he began to think about how he'd approach their next joint consult with Kyle. He'd be professional, polite, but keep his distance. Let her know that her message had been received loud and clear. That he could be a grown-up about it and that what they'd had, what they'd shared, had simply been a brief and incredibly delightful interlude, but that was all it was. Nothing would come of it, and it most definitely would not be repeated, even though he did feel sexually attracted to her still. Maybe he would consider intimacy again with someone else if the opportunity ever presented itself?

'Thank you everyone. Let's get Reuben up to recovery, please,' he said, pulling off his mask, gloves and gown and discarding them in the bin before heading to the scrub room.

At the sinks, he replayed the surgery in his head. It had been a smooth repair. The next part was down to Reuben, regarding recovery. And then maybe, if he needed it, someone like Serena to make him strong again.

He thought of her smile. The wicked delight in her eyes that New Year's Eve. Her soft moans, the way her body had felt pressed against his...

Ash sighed and dried his hands with paper towels.

He really ought to stop thinking of her that way.

She wouldn't appreciate it. She really wouldn't appreciate it at all!

As he stepped out of the scrub room, he got waved over by a nurse. 'Call for you, Dr Dhillon.'

'Who is it?' he asked.

'A Miss Fleming from physio?'

Serena? He felt his heart flutter wildly and surprisingly in his chest, but quelled the sensations. She was probably just calling to clarify a few points about Mr Windgate's therapy. 'Serena?'

'Hi. Erm, are you busy?'

'Always, but I have time for you,' he said, wincing, hoping that hadn't come across as too much and wondering how he'd even managed to rustle up the charm that New Year's Eve. Maybe it had been the alcohol, though he'd not had too much to drink at all.

'Do you have a free moment today in which I could meet with you?'

Meet with him? Voluntarily? This had to be about Kyle. It couldn't be about anything else, as they had nothing else to talk about. 'Let me check.' He pulled his mobile phone free and checked his calendar for today. He had an outpatient clinic this afternoon that he knew was full. 'I could meet you for lunch, or anytime this evening?' Lunch would probably be better. He didn't imagine she'd want to use up her spare time this evening to meet with him. But he was wrong.

'Tonight would be good. There's a coffee house that stays open late just down from the hospital. Do you know Donnie's Café?'

He tried to think. 'Is it that place next to the pharmacy on the main road?'

A pause. 'Yes, that's the place. Can you meet me there?'

'Sure. About six-ish? My clinic should be done by then.'

'Perfect. I'll see you then.'

'All right.'

She didn't say goodbye. The call terminated, and he tried to draw clues from the tone of her voice. She'd seemed a little distracted. A little…discombobulated. Breathy, yet businesslike, too. Was she feeling better? Perhaps she wanted to apologise for their meeting earlier? It had been difficult for them both.

But if it wasn't that and it was Kyle, he wondered what it was about his case that she wanted to discuss with him. Or maybe she wanted to ask him to *not* sit in during Kyle's appointments anymore? Maybe she wanted them to both lie to the hospital board that he was there each time, even though he wasn't?

There was a lot of media interest in Kyle's accident, though. The Great Christmas Tree Disaster had been in the local news for weeks, and Kyle's management team had certainly made sure his picture was in the papers a lot. His social media had gone into overdrive as he streamed from home, showing his cast and how he got about since the accident. His followers had soared in recent weeks, and there was even talk of a new number one single.

And if she didn't want to talk about Kyle?

Hmm.

She'd not wanted him there that morning. He'd made her uncomfortable. He could see that. Sense that. It exuded from her very being. And let's face it, if it was about work, surely she would meet him *in* work? Not out of it.

So maybe what he needed to do here was just make it clear to her where he stood. He wasn't in the market for any kind of relationship, so she was completely safe in that regard. He wasn't about to become a thorn in her side, or some stalker that was about to ruin her life. Yes, he was attracted to her, and the night they'd shared had been amazing.

But he'd been married, and it had failed. He was a divorcee. He'd not been the best husband, and he'd never been there for his wife when she'd needed him. He owned that now. He would not be good for *anyone*, and he'd sworn off relationships anyhow. One night did not a relationship make, no matter how hot it was.

He would make that clear to her, just in case she was worried about having to keep up contact with her one-night stand. He wasn't about to go all *Fatal Attraction* on her.

She'd be relieved to hear it, no doubt.

* * *

It was raining heavily now, washing away the snow and turning it to slush by the time he arrived at Donnie's Café. He'd left his car at the hospital, figuring it would only be a short walk to the café and back again, but halfway there, the heavens opened. By the time he reached the steamed-up windows of the café, he was as sodden as a drowned rat.

He shook his jacket of excess water and ran his hand through his hair as he stepped up to the door with a sign that read Dogs Welcome, People Tolerated. A little bell tinkled above his head as he stepped inside. A wall of heat met him as he scanned the room, looking for Serena.

She was sat at the back, both hands around a big mug of something hot. She raised a hand in acknowledgement.

He smiled back and indicated that he would quickly order a drink and then he'd be with her. His clinic had not overrun, but he felt like he'd talked himself dry, and he was badly in need of something hot. He ordered a decaf latte and went to sit opposite her.

Serena looked just as she had this morning. Slightly green, slightly pale and extremely uncomfortable at his presence.

He didn't like making her feel that way, so he decided to reassure her right away. 'I take it this isn't about Kyle?'

She looked down at her mug and shook her head. No.

'Okay, well, before you have to say anything, let me just tell you, I know we had our crazy night, and for me it was amazing, but I understand what it was. Just one night. Neither of us was expecting to have to work together like today.' He laughed briefly. 'I mean, we both know it's awkward as hell, but I'm perfectly capable of working with you without wanting to keep tearing your clothes off, and I'm sure you feel the same way too.' He smiled, trying to gauge how his little speech was going down. 'I mean, as in, we can work together, not that you want to tear my clothes off.' He frowned, wondering why he'd just said all of that. What if she now thought he was crazy? 'Sorry. I'm not good at this. Just to say that I'm not looking for a repeat of before, even though it was great. We can carry on like two normal people who have to work together. I respect you *immensely*, but I'm just not relationship material, so we can relax, yes?'

The waitress arrived with his latte and placed it down in front of him.

Ash thanked her, feeling quite proud of his speech. He looked up at Serena, expecting to see relief on her face, only it wasn't there. So he decided to soldier on with his attempt to make her feel better. 'We can be professionals! Just because you and I are being forced to work together to oversee Kyle doesn't mean that we shouldn't take the opportunity to be at peace with that, knowing it's just professional courtesy. Then we can carry on with our jobs despite what happened between us,' he added. Smiling, to show that there was no harm done. Even if it did make his heart beat a little faster to be sat opposite her like this. The paleness of her face made her eyes look large and dark. And her lips, though pale, were still full and soft. He'd kissed those lips. Made those eyes close in ecstasy. But for the sake of a good working relationship with a colleague, he would put those memories and those urges to experience them again to one side.

'That's great,' she said, even though she didn't sound like it was great.

'Okay. So there isn't a problem here?' he asked.

'I'm afraid there is.'

Ash was confused. Hadn't he made himself clear? He sighed and leaned in. 'I'm not looking for a repeat, Serena. I never will. I'm a bad choice, not a good partner relationship-wise, and I would never inflict myself on you,' he said, trying to make her laugh. Her mood was confusing and puzzling. He hoped that by being self-deprecating, he would make her feel reassured.

'I'm pregnant, Ash. With your baby.'

He sat and gaped at her, his latte halfway to his mouth.

Surely he'd misheard? He put the mug down. 'Say that again.' His own tone serious now.

'I'm pregnant. With *your* baby.'

Ash went still and simply stared.

CHAPTER THREE

HE WASN'T SURE how long he actually just sat there, staring at her, as the words sank in. Five seconds? A minute? More? But he did understand the panic response that his body went through. Terrifyingly, his mind presented him with a mad rush of memories of what happened with his wife, Nina, and their daughter, Laila.

That pregnancy had been a surprise, too. They'd not been trying to get pregnant. Their relationship had been faltering for some time. In fact, it had been a miracle that they'd gotten pregnant at all, as they'd been like ships in the night for weeks! Of course there'd been moments of reconnection. Yes, maybe they had been forgetful about protection once that time on Nina's birthday, when they'd both gotten more than a little tipsy to make the evening flow better, but…the pregnancy had shocked him, making him see that they would both have to be better partners with one another if they were going to be parents, too.

And he'd tried. But had he tried hard enough? If he was honest with himself? No, he hadn't tried hard enough, and then, when Nina went into labour…

'*Pregnant?*'

'Yes. When I saw you this morning, I didn't know. I

thought I had this bug that's been going around. That's what I put all the symptoms down to. But then someone suggested that I might be…and anyway, I went and got a test afterwards, and it was positive. Both of them.'

He nodded, but it was all still sinking in. A baby? A *baby*!

Serena leaned in. 'I didn't think I could! Get pregnant, I mean. I have *severe* endometriosis, and we used a condom, and…god knows how long you'd had it in your wallet. We should have checked it, but I guess when you're in the throes of…' She stopped and blushed, two pink circles of colour in her pale cheeks. 'Anyway, I thought we'd been careful.'

'You can be as careful as you like, and things can still go wrong,' he said, thinking about Laila. Most days, he tried not to think of her, because every time he allowed himself to do so, he'd get so maudlin. It just wasn't good for him to keep reminding himself of his biggest loss and his biggest failure. Nina and Laila were the past, and he didn't want to repeat the mistakes of the past, so he chose to look forward. To live his life alone so that he didn't disappoint someone else. And he'd been doing just fine at that. Until New Year's Eve.

And now Serena was telling him that she was pregnant? 'Are you…keeping it?' He had no idea of her personal situation, or anything about her at all, really!

'I am.' She stared at him as if daring him to challenge her decision. She raised her cup to her lips, and he could see that her hand was trembling.

Was she afraid? She had to be. This was just as unexpected for her as it was for him. He wanted to rage. To shout. This wasn't how it was supposed to happen!

And that was when he realized that he would need to step up and step out of the world he'd been living in and into one in which he was *better*. He'd lived for years accepting that he'd let someone down, and he'd simply been adrift through life since. Yes, he was a damned fine surgeon, a brilliant doctor and all of that, but what else was he? He couldn't let her down! Not in the way he'd let Nina down. He couldn't allow himself to fail again. If there was a chance that he could be a father... If this pregnancy went well... A glimmer of hope presented itself. Maybe this was his second chance? To get it right?

'You need to understand something, Ash. I didn't think I would ever get to be a mother. I have endometriosis, like I said. I was told that I would probably *never conceive* without intervention. It was that severe. So to discover this, as terrifying as it may be, as unexpected and surprising it may be, I am going to go through with it as it could be my only chance to have a child. For as long as I am able and for as long as this pregnancy stays viable. I just thought you ought to know, in case you wanted to be involved.'

'Of course I'm going to be involved,' he said, a tinge of unexpected anger poisoning his voice. 'Did you think you were going to tell me this and I'd walk away?'

'After the speech you just gave me when you sat down? Perhaps. I am prepared to do this alone if necessary. Not every guy would want to step up when his one-night stand gets pregnant. I mean, it's not like we know one another very well.'

'Well enough, it would seem,' he replied, thinking about the embryo nestling in her womb right now. Growing with every second. His child.

'Yes, well, I just thought you ought to know.'

He nodded. He felt sick. From the shock. From the idea that he could be about to go through the most emotional thing in his life once again. 'And you need to know that I am not stepping away. I am *going to be involved*. I am going to be a father.' He felt his throat constrict on the painful words, because he'd nearly been a father once. No, that was wrong. He *had* been a father. Only his daughter hadn't lived long enough. But how to tell Serena about this? Right now, whilst she seemed so terrified as it was? How to tell her that his one and only daughter had been stillborn? It was probably best, right now, to keep that little bombshell to himself, even if was a burden that he carried alone. He would carry that burden forever, even if it killed him.

'Right. Okay. Well… I'm glad to hear it.'

'Are you okay?'

Serena gave a short laugh. 'I'm terrified! You?'

'Same. I don't know how we're going to do this, but I guess we will work out a way. Somehow.'

'I guess so.'

She didn't seemed thrilled with his lack of confidence. Had she been expecting someone to take charge? To set down the rules and tell her how it was going to be? Because he wasn't like that. That wasn't the kind of guy he was. What they were about to embark upon would take consideration and discussion and equal views. He wasn't going to barge his way through this and insist they get married or something stupid like that! Even if he had always believed that he would be married to the woman he would make a family with. The way he had with Nina. But that marriage had failed badly, and he wasn't sure that he could even imagine a second one. His parents had been so sad when he'd gotten divorced after they'd lost baby Laila. Like he'd let his whole family down. No one in his family had ever divorced before, and he couldn't imagine how they were going to react to this—a baby out of wedlock, with someone he barely knew!

'Have you made an appointment to see your GP?'

She shook her head. 'Not yet. I wanted to tell you first. I'm going to ring them in the morning. Make an appointment.'

'Okay. Have you told anyone else about this?' He didn't want to become an object of gossip.

'No. My friend Ginger guessed. She's a midwife. She's the one who suggested that I might be pregnant after she caught me vomiting this morning.'

'So you did rush off to be sick?'

Serena managed a weak smile.

He downed the dregs of his latte and wished he had something stronger. 'Serena, I need to say that...'

'Yes?'

The way she was looking at him! No. He couldn't say it. She needed assurances from him right now. Not a horror story.

'Nothing. It's fine.'

Serena had prepared herself for telling Ash about the baby. She was expecting him to want nothing to do with her. To make it quite clear this was something she would have to face alone if she was going to choose to keep the baby.

The fact that he didn't do that had her in shock. Especially after his little speech he'd given when he'd arrived at the café. All that stuff about not looking for a relationship, that he wasn't the best partner, and what had he even meant by that? Why wasn't he good? Had he done something? Had he been cruel? Or absent? And if so, did his promises mean anything? That speech had been a warning as much as it had been information. What was she meant to think when he'd said he wasn't a good partner? He was going to say something, then changed his mind. What was that about? He was indecisive, clearly, and she needed to be strong.

She knew that she would appear optimistic with him, but inwardly? Secretly? She would hold on to her independence. Her own strength, knowing that until he could prove it to her, she would not depend on him for anything. She would be brave and stoic and enter this new phase of her life with her own courage. If Ash managed to stay the course alongside her? Then that would be a bonus. But she would not count on him, because Ralph, her ex, had taught her that you couldn't count on anybody.

'Serena Fleming?'

Serena looked up at the doctor and smiled, then followed them down the corridor towards the GP's consulting room. Closing the door behind her, she settled into a seat.

'Good morning. What can I do for you today?' the doctor asked.

It wasn't her usual GP. Hers was away on holiday, so she was seeing the locum, Dr Hamilton.

'I'm pregnant. About two months, I think.'

'You've taken a test?'

She nodded, revealing the story of how her last sexual encounter had been on New Year's Eve and that even though they'd used protection, the test results had been positive.

'It can happen. Prophylactics do have a two percent failure rate.'

But they'd used it correctly. Hadn't they? It was all such a blur. The panic at suddenly remembering they both needed protection, Ash finding that condom in his wallet, the hurry to put it on and…had they put it on properly? Had it slipped, or split? She couldn't remember the after part. Only the frantic dressing and her giggling as she'd been overcome with realization at what she'd just done with a stranger in a storeroom, of all places! Returning to the party afterwards and pretending that she'd not just had such amazing sex that it had left her legs all quivery.

'Two percent? That's higher than you'd think.'

Dr Hamilton smiled. 'May I ask your situation and plans?'

'I'm single, but I'm going ahead with the pregnancy, if I can. I have severe endometriosis. I got told I'd struggle to conceive, so to actually be pregnant…' There was no need for her to say any more. Dr Hamilton would understand.

She nodded and began typing on her keyboard.

'Am I at risk, doctor? Will the endometriosis mean I might miscarry?'

'Not a lot of studies have been done on it, but there is some evidence that having your condition can result in a bit of a higher risk for you, due to the scarring and adhesions that might restrict the uterine growth or the site where the embryo implanted.'

'I see. That just makes it even more certain in my mind that I want to try and keep the baby. Are there any other complications I should be aware of?'

Dr Hamilton called up some research on her computer. 'It says here that you may be more at risk for a premature birth, or need a caesarean or experience placenta praevia—where the placenta attaches itself low in the uterus and causes bleeding right before birth.'

It all sounded so terrifying. 'Right. I guess I don't have control over any of those things. All I can do is watch over myself and be hyperaware of any bad signs?'

'Knowing your own body is important, but you have to remember that these are just *statistics*. There's no saying that this will actually happen to you.'

'But it's a possibility?'

'Yes. It's something to be aware of. So let's get you referred to the midwifery team, and they will get in touch with you to arrange a scan. What job do you do?'

'I'm a physiotherapist at the hospital.'

'So you're quite fit? Do you drink? Smoke?'

'I drink on occasion. Mostly socially, but I don't smoke.'

'I'm going to ask you to *not* drink if you can, and I'm going to recommend you take 5mg of folic acid every day. We'll get you booked in for a blood test to check you for anaemia and a general checkup, okay?'

'Okay. Is there anything that I can do to ensure this pregnancy stays safe?'

Dr Hamilton gave her a sympathetic look. 'I know you're worried. Every woman is, but if you look after yourself, eat well and get plenty of rest and fluids, then that's all you can do. It's out of your hands, I'm afraid.'

'What will be, will be,' she said, nodding. 'Thanks. I'd better get back to work.'

'All right. Well, best of luck, and remember the folic acid. It's important for baby's spine and brain development.'

'Thank you.'

Serena left the GP surgery and drove the short distance to the hospital. The snows had gone, but it was still freezing, and she was wrapped up tight like a bug in a cocoon. Now it was official, she figured she would have to tell her family, but only after she'd made it through the first trimester. What was the point in getting them all excited that she was finally going to be having her own little one, only for her to lose it so soon after? She'd accepted that her severe endometriosis would stop her from being able to get pregnant. Now she had to accept that it might just end it, too. She felt tears prick her eyes. Why was life so cruel and uncertain?

How did others live with it? Dr Hamilton had told her that all she could do was look after herself and basically that it was out of her hands. That lack of control was scary when it was about something so important.

I guess all I can do is try to enjoy every day and cherish every moment that I'm pregnant, in case it ends soon or it never happens again.

At work, her first two patients both suffered from the same ailment—plantar fasciitis. This was pain felt in the plantar fascia, the fibrous tissue that connected the heel to the toes. It was mostly experienced in the heel and underside of the foot. It was often worse in the morning, or after a period of being sedentary. Once inflamed, the fascia could take up to a couple of years to fully heal. Her first patient was a middle-aged woman who had spent a lifetime squeezing her feet into heels for work. Alongside her plantar fasciitis, she also had bunions on both feet—bony lumps that most often formed on the joint below the big toe, causing her toes to point out-wards. Her second patient was a younger man, used to ultra-marathons and being an athlete. Plantar fasciitis did not discriminate! And it was a painful condition that could be wearing. Serena gave them both exercises they could do at home and arranged to see them both again in a month's time. Her third patient was an elderly gent who was recovering from having a hip replacement in his late seventies.

Clark Davies ambled into her room with his walk-ing stick.

'Morning, Mr Davies, how are you?'

'Not bad,' he said, settling into his chair with a bit of a groan. 'You know how it is.'

She smiled at him but noticed he had some pallor to his skin, and he also looked clammy. 'Feeling all right today?'

'Think I've got this bug that's been going around. That cold thing, you know?'

She did. But she also knew how thinking you'd got that bug thing going around could actually be masking something else! Serena reached for his wrist and laid her fingers on his pulse point. His pulse felt rapid and a little irregular. 'Any pain anywhere, apart from the hip?'

'Achy all over.'

Frowning now, she grabbed for her stethoscope that lay on the desk and began to listen to his chest. His lungs sounded clear, but she felt instinctively that something else was going on.

'Eating all right?'

'I'm a bit off my food, to be fair.'

'Going to the toilet?'

'I think so. I actually had a good night's sleep. Normally I wake up two or three times to wee, but I didn't have to last night.'

'And this morning? Have you passed urine?'

'I tried, but no. Is something wrong?' Clark looked worried.

Maybe. His surgery was recent. 'When did you last have your wound checked?'

'Couple of days ago.'

'And it was all right?'

'Yes. A little red, but the nurse wasn't unduly concerned.'

'Do you mind if I look at it now?' She didn't normally examine wounds, but she was concerned about Clark's condition. He could have an infection, or worse, sepsis. Lack of urination and temperature were signs.

'Of course, dear.' Clark ambled painfully over to the examination bed, groaning as he lowered himself with a sigh and undoing his trousers.

Serena pulled on gloves to examine the wound. It did look red and worse still, it did look infected. 'Stay there.' She went back to her computer and looked at the surgeon's name who had performed the operation—Dr Gideon. She knew she couldn't send Clark home like this. He needed to be seen and preferably by his surgeon. She dialed through to orthopaedics, and the phone was answered on the eighth ring.

'Ortho ward, Nurse Murphy speaking.'

'Colleen? It's Serena in physio.'

'Oh, hi! How are you?'

'Great. Listen, is Dr Gideon around?'

'He's in theatre. Why?'

'I've got one of his patients with me, Clark Davies, date of birth tenth of May, 1948. He had a hip replacement surgery, but he's come in today not feeling well, high resp rate, temperature, with a lack or urination, and his wound looks purulent. I think he needs to be admitted or at least seen.'

She heard Colleen speak to someone on the ward, relaying the information to a guy in the background. 'Serena? I'm passing you over to Dr Dhillon.'

Ash. Her heart skipped wildly, and she gripped the receiver.

'What is the patient's temperature?' he asked, his voice on the line amplifying her nerves.

Of course he had to sound businesslike in front of Colleen. 'I haven't actually taken it. But he's clammy and pale, and both he and his wound feel hot to the touch.'

'I'll come right down.'

'Thank you.'

Ash replaced her phone handset, noting her hand was trembling, and went back to her patient. 'I've got an ortho doctor, a Dr Dhillon, coming to examine you. See if you need to be admitted.'

'Why? Can't you just give me some antibiotics and send me home? My dog will need feeding.'

'I understand, Mr Davies, but as a practitioner, we have to put you first and not your dog. You have signs of an infection that need tending to, and I can't do that. Is there someone you can call to take care of your dog?'

He nodded and pulled out his mobile phone.

She gave him some water to sip as they waited for Ash. When he arrived, Serena smiled at him and introduced him to Clark.

Ash was friendly and kind as he examined Mr Davies and concluded that there was a very real possibility Mr Davies was developing sepsis. 'See this mottling to the skin here?' he pointed out to Serena.

She could have sworn that it wasn't there before, but she nodded.

'Don't worry, Mr Clark. We'll get you sorted.' He turned to Serena. 'Can you organize some porters to transport him to the acute medicine ward?'

'Of course.' She did so, and they both waited for the porters to arrive, which they did within five minutes. As Mr Davies was wheeled away, Ash turned to her.

'You could have just saved his life. Good spot.' He smiled at her, and it did strange things to her insides. Their relationship was different now. Not just colleagues that had shared an incredible night together, but now people who were about to embark on a new adventure in life, with *one another*.

'I just did my job.'

Ash checked to make sure no one was within earshot. 'How did it go at the doctor's?'

She nodded. 'Fine. I've been referred to the maternity team, and she said they'll get in touch about a scan soon.'

'You'll let me know when it is? I'd like to attend.'

'Of course.' He seemed subdued. Was he having second thoughts already about being involved? Maybe she could reassure him. Let him know that this might not happen. 'She did warn me, though.'

He frowned. 'About?'

'About my endometriosis. That because of the scarring from the tissue, I have a higher risk of miscarrying.'

His eyes seemed to widen, and he gazed down at the floor as he thought to himself. 'Right.' He seemed to go still, as if contemplating something. 'I guess we can't do anything about that.'

Tears welled up then in her eyes, and she struggled to stop herself from bursting into tears. It was like an underlying shock that she had been controlling since the chat with her GP had finally broken through to the surface. Maybe it was because he hadn't comforted her after she'd just shared that terrifying notion with him, but she just felt overwhelmed and suddenly alone, despite him telling her previously that he would be involved.

'Hey, are you all right?' he asked as she sniffed and wiped at her nose, stepping back from him, grabbing for a tissue from the box she kept on her workstation.

'Fine! Just this cold thing, that's all,' she lied, sniffing again and desperately trying to regain control of her emotions. Maybe it was hormones? And if it was, then maybe she should see that as a good thing? If she was awash with pregnancy hormones, then didn't that mean everything was all right? But her embarrassment at crying in front of him like this made her finally have an outburst. 'Aren't you a doctor?' she finally exclaimed.

'Er, yes...' He looked awkward. Unsure what to do.

'Then shouldn't you have better bedside manner or something? I've just told you that I might miscarry, and clearly that's frightening, and all you say is, *I guess we can't do anything about that*?' The situation took her right back to her ex. When she'd been told the extent of her diagnosis. How he'd just sat there and done nothing to soothe her as she felt the weight of the world upon her. All the responsibility. That it was her fault this was happening to them. He'd sat there and said nothing, and now it felt the same with Ash.

He looked at her, stupefied. Glanced around them. Seeing that the room was clear of other staff, he pulled her quickly against his chest, wrapping his arms around her, and began to make soothing noises into her hair as his hands rubbed her back. 'I'm sorry.'

Serena allowed herself to be held, resting her head against his chest. She could hear his heart thumping inside. Fast. She knew that maybe she'd scared him, but she was scared, too. 'This is just what you want, I guess. It would certainly help get rid of this nightmare I've dragged you into.'

'It's not a nightmare,' he said, his voice low and calm. 'Not yet.'

'No?' Irrational with rage, she pushed away from him and dabbed at her eyes with tissue. Though it had felt more than good to be held by him, comforted by him, she had wanted to fight against it. Maybe because she wasn't used to relying on others. She'd always got through stuff alone.

'I mean, it's not *ideal*, but…we're handling it. Aren't we? Best we can?'

'Is this your best, Ash?'

He paled then. Saw the muscle in his jaw clench and unclench. Ash sighed, hands on hips now. 'I'm just trying to navigate this, as you are. I'm not good at this, Serena, but I'm trying. I am. Look, it's out of our hands. Things can go wrong in pregnancy at any point, and no one can do a damned thing about it! I wish it were different—I do. You have *no idea* how much.'

He opened his mouth like he had something else to say, but then clamped his lips shut. He sighed instead. 'I have to go and admit Mr Davies. Can we speak about this again later?'

Is this your best, Ash?

Nina, his wife, had asked him that question right before she'd told him she was going to leave and file for divorce.

Is this your best, Ash?

No. He'd not given Nina his best, and right now he felt like he wasn't giving Serena his best, either. He was still reeling from the idea that he could be a father again after the devastating loss of baby Laila. Now Serena was telling him she might lose the baby because of her endometriosis? That was scary, too! Because if she did, how would he look after her when she was grief-stricken and came to him for comfort? He'd not been capable with Nina when Laila was stillborn. He'd turned away from her, withdrawn into himself and thrown himself into work. His only way of dealing with trauma and grief himself was to hide from it and pretend it wasn't there. If he allowed himself to be subsumed by work, he wouldn't have time to think about how awful he felt, or how he'd been failing his wife.

And it wasn't like he and Serena were in a relationship! She'd been his one-night stand and gotten pregnant—something that was already a miracle, considering her condition.

Holding her had felt…good. With her back in his arms, however briefly it had been, he had felt his body respond. He'd been afraid to reach out and hold her, but when he did? His desire to soothe her had been strong. Maybe he'd simply not known whether he *could* hold her? Whether it was allowed? Like he needed permission. He'd felt so uncertain, not sure where they stood with one another, except from the fact that they would share a child.

'I'm sorry I'm not good at this!' he continued. Feeling the same way he had when Nina had cried.

She blew her nose into a tissue and wiped her eyes. 'I need you to be better. To talk to me.'

'Yes.' He couldn't agree more, but how? This was scary, what they were doing. Bringing a new life into the world? If they were lucky? The chances that anyone was on this planet in the first place was miraculous, and there were so many dangers, so many ways in which it could be screwed up. If she wanted him to talk, then maybe he should? 'I faced something difficult in my last relationship. Something neither of us could stop from happening.' How best to word this? He didn't want to say it outright. Be blunt. What he had to say needed to be approached delicately. But she'd asked for openness, and openness she would get.

He'd been innocent in his marriage to Nina. Believing that everything would be fine with their pregnancy. Why wouldn't it be? Nina was young, healthy, strong. For nine months she'd not had a single thing make them think something could go wrong. All the scans were perfect. Nina bloomed and was beautiful. They painted a nursery and filled it with clothes and picked out a name when they discovered they were having a girl. They dreamed of all the things they would do together, and Ash fell in love with his daughter through her kicks and seeing her on scans and wondering about the little girl that was about to come into their world and how she'd wrap him around her little finger.

And then she'd died.

That day in which he'd had to sit by Nina's bedside as she was induced to give birth was the most horrific and devastating event that he had ever gone through, and there was no way he wanted to go through that again. Or see Nina go through it. No one deserved that. No one. So to hear not only that Serena was pregnant but also that she could also lose the pregnancy due to her endometriosis? He was right back in the kind of situation that terrified him. So sue him if he'd hesitated to hold her.

How to tell Serena all of that? She was already scared about her prospects of carrying this baby to term.

'You're telling me life is terrible. I get it,' Serena said, interrupting him. 'But I have enough horrible stuff in my life right now. I don't need any more.'

He nodded. She wasn't ready for it. She didn't need it. Hearing about Laila wouldn't help her at all! It would just scare her even more. His first instincts were right. He had to keep this to himself.

'I've got to go, but… I'll try harder,' he said instead, determined that this time he would be better.

Is this your best, Ash?

'Thank you.' She turned away from him. He sighed heavily before following the porters and going back up to his own department.

CHAPTER FOUR

SERENA BRUSHED OFF her upset to get through her afternoon patients and eventually came to the conclusion that no matter what Ash said, she had to accept that maybe she was going to be alone for this. Hopefully, it was just an uncertain start. After all, this was a situation he'd never been in before, and he didn't know how to handle it. Neither did she, but she was the one going through the physical changes. She was the one carrying the baby. Ultimately, if this child was born and survived to term, she would be its mother. He, maybe, would be on the periphery as they weren't actually in a relationship together. Though being in his arms, however briefly, had felt so good, even if she had pushed herself out of them, almost like she was punishing herself. Why had she done that? Got so angry with him when he was simply trying?

The idea that she might end up in a relationship where the father of her child saw his kid on weekends, or once a month, dismayed her, because she'd dreamed once of having it all. A nice house with a large back garden for kids to play in. A loving husband who remembered to treat her as his wife and not just as a mother. She would have a proper family of her own. They would go on holidays together and make memories, and maybe she and her husband would have a second kid, or a third?

But she wasn't going to get that, so she needed to adjust her expectations. Ash was not going to be perfect. Ash was not going to become a loving husband, and she didn't have a magic lamp she could rub to make her wishes come true. Which was a shame, because Ash, on the face of things, seemed nice. She could imagine him as a husband and a father, settling down and being... well, being her partner.

But that wasn't going to happen, was it? All she was getting was the chance at having a baby and a baby alone. Something she thought she wouldn't get, so maybe she should just accept that, and maybe the rest might come later? She'd believed that getting pregnant wasn't ever going to happen, and yet here she was. So... who knew?

She felt a strange pang down low. Like a period cramp. It came and it went in an instant. She rubbed at her abdomen, instantly concerned, but it had gone, and she still had patients to see.

Her phone rang on her desk, and she picked it up. 'Physio department. Serena speaking.'

'Hi, this is orthopaedics. We've got a patient that's just been admitted as s transfer from another hospital. C1 fracture and damage to the spinal cord. Wondered if we could get them booked in for some bed physio?'

'Patient's name?'

'Gareth Jones. Date of birth, the second of March, 1991.'

Serena tapped in the details and gazed at the information on her screen. Looks like Gareth had dived head-first into some shallow water a week ago. 'I could get someone to see him tomorrow? Mid-afternoon?'

'Okay. No chance we could get someone up today? He's feeling pretty low as he's quite a physical guy. I think if we could get someone up to chat with him about what he could be doing, how there's hope, it might help improve his mood.'

'Okay. Erm, I'll pop up, then, at the end of my shift.'

'Great, thank you.'

'No problem.' She put the phone down and added Gareth to her patient list. She didn't often go up to the ward as she mostly worked with outpatients, but in situations such as this, she didn't mind helping.

Another strange feeling in her abdomen came and went.

Nervous, she searched on the internet to see if abdominal pains were normal in the first trimester. She read that they were and not usually a cause for concern. They could be caused by uterine expansion, or the body's ligaments stretching, or even simply hormones, or gas.

But these feel like I do before a period.

Serena was used to cramps. To pain. There had been days she had spent curled up in her bed, wrapped around a hot water bottle pressed to her abdomen, doped up on painkillers, and still she felt pain. It wasn't a stranger to her, and these cramps seemed so minor in comparison.

She tried to push the worry aside as she saw her next patient—a woman who had been suffering badly with tennis elbow, or lateral epicondylitis, an inflammation of the tendons.

Gayle Fischer was struggling to do even the simplest

things at home without being in pain. Serena demonstrated some extra exercises she could do to strengthen
her grip and keep her elbow mobile, which included
weighted wrist flexion, ball squeezes and towel twists.

'I read somewhere that I could have ultrasound treatment for this,' Gayle said.

'It's a possibility, but I'd like you to continue with the
exercises first. If, after six weeks, you've not noticed
any improvements, then I'd be happy to refer you for
ultrasound treatment.'

'And how does the ultrasound work exactly?'

'It uses high-frequency sound waves that help increase blood flow to the area and accelerate the healing process.'

'And people have seen good improvement with that?'

'Some have, yes, but it would never be used alone.
The exercises I have given you are important, too.'

When Gayle left, Serena finished her outpatient
clinic. Once she'd written up her notes, she went up
to outpatients to see Gareth. None of the other physios
were available, and besides, she hoped to see Ash. To
maybe apologise for her outburst of emotions when she'd
simply felt scared.

She instantly gauged that her patient was severely depressed due to losing feelings below his neck, but he did
seem to be able to slightly wriggle his right thumb and
forefinger. She told him that was good. That was something they could work with. She spent some time with
him. Explained why even tiny movements now could
be improved upon. Strengthened. Expanded as he got
stronger. That trying to remain focused and positive was

a good thing. She hoped she was able to boost his morale before she said goodbye and left him for the night.

'Serena.'

She turned and saw Ash. He looked good. He always looked good. And that was beginning to be a problem. Because the more she saw him, the more she found her attraction to him increasing.

'You're taking Gareth's case?'

'No, I just agreed to come and see him. Cole will come up tomorrow afternoon. He's his patient. I came up as a favour to try to help boost his mood. The nurses were worried about him. Maybe he needs referring to the mental health team.'

Ash nodded. He was about to say something when she felt another pang in her abdomen, and her hand went to her belly. Something wasn't right.

'Are you okay?'

She blinked, thinking. She didn't want to panic. 'I, er...need the bathroom.'

'Just down there.' He pointed, and she rushed away from him, already fearing the worst.

She couldn't be losing this baby, could she? Not yet. Not just as she was beginning to accept that she was going to be a mother after all. To have her hope taken from her so soon and so cruelly would be unthinkable!

Inside the toilet stall, she pulled down her bottoms and saw the bright red blood in her underwear. Instantly she went into shock. Trembling, feeling sick, she cleaned herself up and washed her hands, and then she stumbled outside the stall.

She must have looked awful, because Ash was by her side instantly. 'What's wrong?'

She almost couldn't say the words. Almost felt like if she told him, then it would be real. But as she looked into his eyes, he must have seen her fear. There was no way she could ignore this and hope that it wasn't happening. 'I'm bleeding!'

'Oh my god…are you sure?'

'Of course I'm sure! What do we do?'

'Okay…okay, sit down here. Let me call maternity and see if they can do a scan. That's the only way we'll know for sure.' He got her settled into a chair.

She nodded and watched him rush off and grab the phone at the nearest desk and punch in an extension number. She heard him give details. Two months pregnant. Bleeding. It didn't seem real! That he was actually talking about *them*. That this was the situation she had found herself in.

Serena was used to seeing blood. Her endometriosis had always given her irregular periods, but every time they had come, the pain had been unbearable and the bleeding incredibly heavy. She was used to this. But seeing blood like this? Knowing that she was pregnant…it was scarier than all the pains, all the clots, all the bleeding she had ever had before. This bleeding meant something *different*. The possible loss of a little life. A little life she had begun to love. Begun to *want*.

Ash put down the phone. 'I've got an ultrasound tech waiting for us on the third floor. Can you walk there, or should I get you a wheelchair?' He looked anxious. His hair mussed up from how many times he'd run his hands through it whilst on the phone. He was scared. She could see he was truly scared.

'I can walk.'

He shook his head. 'No, I'm getting you a wheel-chair—just in case.'

Serena wasn't sure whether or not walking would stop her from losing this baby, but she gave in to it. Her heart was thumping out of her chest, and she felt hot and clammy. Sick to her stomach at the idea that she might lose this precious miracle baby so soon.

When Ash returned with the chair, he helped her gently into it and then began wheeling her to the bank of lifts. It seemed to take an age for one to arrive, and with every second that passed, she wondered about her baby. Whether it was already gone. If this was already too late. Should she have responded at the first twinge she'd felt earlier this afternoon? And if she had men-tioned it, would she have saved this pregnancy from failure? If she lost this baby, would she ever forgive herself for not getting herself properly checked out im-mediately?

Ash's hand rested on her shoulder, stroking her slightly. She reached for it with her own, squeezing his fingers tightly, taking her strength from him.

Yet tears fell from her face as Ash pushed her through the hospital towards maternity and the scanning room.

'Serena?' A sonographer stood in a doorway. A young brunette with kind eyes and gentle smile.

She nodded through her tears as Ash pushed her into the darkened room.

'I'm Skye. Tell me what's been happening.'

And so it came out in a rush of words, a rush of fear, her words tumbling over each other in Serena's need to explain everything in the hope that somehow, her explanation would cause Skye to say that it was okay.

That this often happened. That it would be all right. She caught Ash flinching when she mentioned she'd been having twinges all afternoon.

'Why didn't you say anything?' he asked.

She didn't answer him. She already felt guilty enough about it. How she would never forgive herself if she'd waited too long. She just needed to see the screen. To find out if the baby was still in there or not. She was too busy steeling herself for the worst news ever.

If this baby was gone, lost before it had even had chance to thrive…

'Okay, lie down on the bed for me, and we'll take a look.'

Serena shifted herself from the chair to the bed, aided by Ash, who held her arm like she was a fragile old woman. Then she was lying down, pulling her bottoms down a bit, so that Skye could tuck in a piece of blue paper to protect her clothes from the cold gel that was now being squirted onto her abdomen.

Serena almost didn't want to look. Believing somehow that if she didn't look, then she wouldn't see an empty womb. That if she just averted her eyes for a moment longer, then the baby would still somehow be alive. She squeezed her eyes shut and prayed as she felt the transducer wand being moved over her abdomen.

'Serena? Open your eyes.' Skye said softly.

So she did, her gaze falling to the screen. There, miraculously, was her baby, its heart fluttering in its chest! Still there. Still very much alive! 'Oh my god! It's okay?'

Skye smiled at her. 'Baby's okay.' She began to point at the screen. 'This is your cervix, and can you see this here?' She pointed at something on the screen.

Serena wasn't sure what she was looking at. 'Yes?'

'It's endometrial tissue attached to your cervix. I think that's what's bleeding.'

'But baby's fine?'

'He or she is fine. Want to hear the heartbeat?'

'We can do that?' she asked in surprise.

'Of course.' Skye pressed a button. Suddenly the loud thumping of their baby's regular and fast heartbeat filled the room. Serena laughed, elated, relieved that the worst had not happened.

She looked to Ash, saw his face lit up by the glow from the screen. Was that relief she saw on his face, too? And happiness?

In that moment, she realized that they were holding each other's hand. Almost like they were a proper couple. And she liked it. Was glad of it. Knowing that he'd been just as scared as she was. Maybe she wasn't alone, as she'd once thought?

'So we're okay for now?'

'You're okay for now. But I'd recommend that maybe you go home and take it easy, Serena. Rest up, and if the bleeding gets worse or you pass clots or experience any kind of worsening pain or cramps, you come find me, okay? I'll always fit you in.'

'That's very kind of you. Thank you.'

'We look out for one another here, right?'

Screna nodded, sitting up and wiping off the gel. Then Skye handed her a couple of pictures she'd printed out. 'One for each of you.'

She watched as Ash took his and studied it, a smile creeping across his face. She realized, suddenly, that this life they'd made already meant so much to him.

Despite the shock of it. Despite the surprise. And they were in this together. But if they were going to do this, then maybe she needed to know more about this man who'd once warned her he didn't make a good partner. Oh, she knew he was a doctor, but beyond that, what did she truly know about him? This man with whom she would one day, hopefully, raise a child?

They couldn't blindly stumble through this, reacting crazily like she had today.

There had to be more to it. More stability. Surety.

She wanted to know the father of her baby. She wanted to know if he would always be there to hold her hand.

Ash decided to drive Serena home. He wanted to make sure she got in safely. A light snow was drifting down again, and though it wasn't really settling, the roads were covered in black ice. He didn't want her to be in any kind of danger. He felt like they'd already avoided a potential threat today, and he didn't want to experience another one.

It had been terrifying to sit in that room and watch the scan, catapulting him right back to that day in maternity when he'd sat by Nina's hospital bed as they'd strapped on the CTG machine and the midwife had not been able to find their daughter's heartbeat.

He and Nina had gone in because Nina had said she'd not felt the baby move for a while. The hospital had told them to come in to be monitored, a midwife telling them over the phone that they often found that babies would suddenly start moving and kicking again the second their moms got monitored.

In the room, they'd waited with bated breath as the midwife had first struggled to get the belts around Nina's abdomen and then struggled to find the heartbeat with the transducer plates. *Maybe baby is in a strange position?* the midwife had said at first. There'd been a student midwife with her, and Ash had watched both their faces as the room remained stubbornly silent. Then the awful words. *I think we'd better ask one of the doctors to come in.*

Ash had known then that something was wrong. But so many people these days had babies with no problem. He'd still clung to the belief they would be the same and the midwife had just struggled, that was all. Maybe she was newly qualified? Maybe their daughter *was* in a strange position! It happened.

But the doctor only confirmed what the midwife had already begun to suspect. A scan showed no heartbeat.

So sitting in that room today with Serena, waiting to hear the dreaded silence once again, only for the room to fill with that delightful thrumming of a vibrant, beating heart, he'd never felt so much elation in his entire life! He'd reached for Serena's hand without even being conscious of it, squeezing it, stroking it, letting her know that they were in this together. When they'd realized, he felt he'd not wanted to let go. Aware of how much they each needed the other. Heat suffusing his cheeks, glad of the darkness in the room so she wouldn't know just how much he'd needed to hold her hand.

'This is it,' Serena said, pointing to a small house with a red door in a row of terraced homes.

'You should just rest tonight. Put your feet up. Maybe order in so you don't have to stand and cook.'

'Maybe. Or…would you like to come in? For coffee?'

He thought about it. He would like that, even if it just meant he could keep a watchful eye on her for a little bit longer. Ensure that she stayed okay. 'All right. But I'll make it. You're meant to be resting.'

'I have the whole weekend to rest.'

'There's Friday to get through yet.'

'I'm not rostered tomorrow. It's my day off. I only work four days, Monday to Thursday.'

'A long weekend every week, huh? That must be nice.'

'It is, but… I'm kind of scared of spending it alone. What if the bleeding gets worse?'

Of course. She'd be terrified. So would he. He so desperately wanted to help. He'd promised to be better. To speak up more. 'Have you got anyone who can be with you?'

She shook her head. 'My family aren't close, and the friends I have are working at the hospital.'

Could he ask? Should he ask?

'How about… I come in and stay for a bit, then? At least until you go to bed, and then I'll go home? I'll call you tomorrow to check on you, make sure you're okay?' This way, they could learn more about one another. He wanted to know her.

She nodded. 'I'd like that. We need to spend more time with one another if we're going to have a baby together.'

She was right. They should know each other better than they already did. And nor did he want to make the mistakes of the past and *not* be there for her. It would be hard for him to watch over her when he'd be worrying about her and the baby non-stop, but he thought he could do it. He'd power through his fears somehow. 'I agree.'

'Good.' She reached into her bag, pulled out a small bunch of keys and passed them to him. 'Lead the way.'

He smiled. 'I'll try.'

It felt strange to stand behind Ash as he unlocked her front door and stood back to let her in. Not since her ex had she ever brought a guy to her home—certainly not a one-night stand! And yet here she stood beside the man who'd held her hand as they'd stared at their baby on the screen. A man she had feelings for whether she wanted them or not. And he was unlocking her home and letting her in!

A strange situation to say the least.

Did he look at her place and see a mess? She admitted to herself she wasn't the most fastidious of cleaners, but she hoped that he saw cosy and homey rather than cluttered. Her living room space was occupied by a large sofa filled with a mishmash of decorated cushions. Over the back were not one but two separate throws— an old crocheted thing of granny squares that her mum had made for her when she'd gone off to university, and a fleecy one that she'd bought on impulse one day, suckered in by how soft and cuddly it was. A low coffee table was covered in books and a mug of peppermint tea from the night before that she'd not picked up. Around the base of it, she spied some biscuit crumbs. Lamps lit the room rather than an overhead light, and her bookcase was stuffed to overflowing with fiction that she treasured. Piles of books sat on the floor near it. On the walls hung an eclectic mix of art that she loved, including one terrible piece that she'd painted herself when she'd impulsively joined an art class a couple of years ago. It was meant to be a pot of flowers, but she'd been going through an abstract phase. It looked more like a cacophony of colour and weird angles exploding in the centre of the canvas.

'Take a seat,' she said, standing there, feeling nervous. Not used to having a man in her haven. Not knowing how she should behave when logic screamed she should be wary, but her body cried out for more contact.

He turned and looked at her. 'No. You take a seat. Go on, sit down.'

Oh right. Yeah. He's here to take care of me.

She wasn't sure in what form this taking care of her would arrive. He'd already admitted once that he wasn't a good partner, so maybe he was learning about himself, too?

She stepped around the couch and settled into it, pulling the fleecy throw over her legs.

'How are you feeling?' he asked, settling into a chair opposite her, keeping his distance. She'd noticed how he'd very deliberately made sure not to touch her after the scanning room moment. Did he think it a mistake? 'All right, I think.'

'Are you still bleeding?'

'I've not felt much since the scan.'

He nodded. 'That was a very scary moment there.'

'It was.'

He nodded some more, clearly building the courage to say something that was on his mind. 'Serena—'

'Ash—'

They both spoke at the same time and laughed.

'After you,' she said.

'I'm upset that you didn't tell me you'd been having pains all afternoon.'

She nodded. Understanding. 'I'm sorry. At first I thought they were nothing. Ligaments stretching, you know?'

'I do. But I want you to be able to come to me. To tell me how you are feeling. Good or bad.'

That seemed reasonable. 'I will,' she promised.

'We could have got you scanned sooner, could have prevented something bad from happening.'

'You're right. I was scared, though. Told myself it was normal after looking up the symptoms.'

'You can never be sure doing things like that. From now on, I'd like to request that you contact me, and we can decide together whether we need to be panicking or not.'

Serena nodded. 'I am sorry. It's just that I'm used to taking care of myself and not sharing that burden with anyone else.'

'I understand, but…it's different now. I'm part of this. That's my baby, too.' And he reached out and took her hand in his, sending thrills through her body at his touch.

She stroked the back of his hand.

She liked that he was insisting on this.

He *cared*.

For the baby, maybe, but at least he cared.

Nina hadn't said anything. About the baby not moving. They'd both been extremely busy. Ash was working hard, getting that precious overtime in for some extra cash for when the baby arrived, providing money even if he couldn't provide for her emotionally as they'd both grown so far apart. Nina, at home on maternity leave, had been busy nesting. Prepping the nursery mostly, trying to hold their home together, even as they felt it breaking. Both of them doing their part to pretend that everything was fine because they were having a baby. They were still good friends, if nothing else. When they'd sat down that fateful night together after he'd finished work, he'd laid a hand on her belly and asked her how their little bean was doing.

Er...yeah, fine.

You don't sound sure.

She's probably sleeping right now—I have been on the go all day.

Oh, right.

So they'd eaten their evening meal. Ash had showered and laid out his clothes for the next day as he had an early start and didn't want to wake Nina by rummaging in his wardrobe. But by the time they went to bed, he noticed her frowns.

What's up?

She still hasn't moved.

She's probably sleeping like you said.

She's never slept this long. She's always kicking me as I lie down to go to sleep.

Try moving about. Or eat something sweet.

So she'd tried, and nothing worked. Ash had rubbed her bump and spoken to it. Usually when he laid his head against Nina's bump and talked to his daughter, she got active, but not that night.

I'm worried, Ash. I can't feel anything.

He didn't have his stethoscope at home. It was in his locker at work, and they didn't have any home tech they could use to listen in to the baby. So he suggested she ring in to maternity and ask their advice. See if they ought to be worried. They were told to come in for monitoring.

Ash had always wondered if by noticing earlier, whether Laila would have been born alive or not? The doubts, the what-ifs, were terrible! And it had happened again today, with Serena not saying anything. Keeping her fears to herself, and that scared him. So when he saw their baby on screen, its little heart thumping away, nothing could have prepared him for how overwhelmed with relief and joy he would feel in that moment!

'What would you like to drink? To eat?' he asked her, realizing that he couldn't remember if he'd ever pampered Nina in such a way. Their pregnancy had been unexpected. A surprise, just like this one. He'd simply gone into work mode, working all the hours that were possible, double shifts, overtime, staying late. Nina had been so independent and strong, and she'd never been good at letting people take care of her, so he'd done what he thought he could do to help—earn more money. But had he ever just stopped and made her a drink? Or tried to pamper her in any way? Or cook a meal? Or had he just accepted that she was an independent woman who liked her own space? That they'd been living like roommates rather than as lovers? Occasionally they'd eaten out, but had he ever cooked her a meal?

'Tea, I think. Coffee isn't great for me right now.'

'And to eat?'

'You don't have to make me anything.'

'I do. You're resting.' He really wanted to take care of her. In fact, he was surprised by how intently he wanted it.

'I don't know what I've got in the fridge.'

'I'll go look.' He entered the kitchen, raising his eyebrows at her extensive and eclectic mug collection, the jungle of herbs growing in the windowsill, two whole shelves of cookbooks and all the magnets on her fridge. Everything looked mismatched and yet somehow seemed to belong. He filled the kettle and switched it on, then pulled open her fridge. He saw stuffed olives, cheese, some specialist sausages. A box of twelve eggs that only had two in. A tub of butter. Condiments filled the door, alongside a carton of milk and one of juice. Orange juice. With bits.

He began opening cupboards, looking for her pantry items, but apart from about fifteen different types of herbal teas and a couple of cans of beans or tomatoes, there wasn't much. Her freezer had some frozen vegetables and some sad-looking fish fingers at the bottom.

'How about I do you a hearty fry up, without the fry?' he asked when he headed back to the living room. 'I'll poach it and bake it so it will be healthy.'

'Are you sure you want to do this? You can go, and I can just order in.'

'I don't think so. Besides, those sausages will go out of date if you don't eat them today.'

Serena smiled and sighed, slightly shaking her head. 'Fine. Fry up without the fry. Sounds delicious.'

He smiled and returned to the kitchen.

* * *

'You're not a bad cook. I guess that's something else I know about you now. Good doctor, good surgeon, good cook. You're three for three.' Serena smiled as she pushed her plate away, feeling full. It was the first proper meal she'd eaten in ages, and it probably helped that he'd prepared it and cooked it. The aromas from the kitchen had been a little nauseating for her stomach, but when the food arrived, she'd been starving. She'd begun to learn that eating something was better than not eating at all. And Ash had looked good in her apron! Tying it about his waist like a professional chef and tossing a cloth over his shoulder as he'd busied himself. She could get used to this!

Ash had poached two eggs, cooked sausages in the oven, baked beans and tomatoes in pans on the hob and served it all up on two slices of sourdough bread that he'd toasted. He'd put black pepper over the top of it all and served it up with a *voilà!* 'Thank you. I'd like to think I know my way around a kitchen.'

And around a woman, she thought, but didn't say. She didn't feel brave enough to compliment him on his sexual techniques, even if she was pregnant with his baby!

'Let's see how long it stays down for.'

'You've been having lots of issues with the morning sickness?'

'Some. It comes out of nowhere sometimes.'

'Ginger is meant to help. And have a packet of biscuits by the side of your bed so you can eat before getting up and moving about.'

'Oh. Right. I'll try that.'

He smiled and looked at his watch, his face falling at realizing the time. 'Well, I guess I'd better get going. I'd hate to overstay my welcome. You'll be all right for the evening? You have everything you need?'

She nodded. 'You could never, you know.'

He frowned. 'Never what?'

'Outstay your welcome.'

He smiled, and she enjoyed very much the way he was looking at her. She was tempted, oh so tempted, to have more of his company. And not just his company. Strong physical urges kept washing over her in waves, making her feel hot and uncomfortable, gazing at his strong hands, his forearms. The way his hair fell over his forehead, making her want to reach out and smooth it back.

'And I think it would be good for us—if you could stay, I mean. We need to get to know one another a little better. I hardly know anything about you. Yet here you are in my home, cooking for me, with your baby in my belly, and I don't even know your favourite colour, or who your last pet was, or if you have any family,' she said, when really all she could think of was what he would look like in her bed.

Ash smiled and returned to the couch opposite. Sitting down. 'My favourite colour is blue. But dark blue, like a navy, more than anything else. My last pet was a dog that belonged to my parents, and he was a Labrador cross. Mostly black with a white blaze down his chest, and he lived until he was thirteen years old. His name was Max. And I do have family. They live in London, mostly. It's where I'm from, where I worked originally.

Then I got a posting here, and I've been in York ever since. You?'

She smiled at him. Okay. Details. She could give him some details. 'I like red, which goes well with navy, so that's nice. Let's see, er, my last pet was a goldfish called Princess that I somehow managed to kill after one week of owning her, and my family are now living in Scotland. Glasgow, to be specific.'

Ash listened and nodded. 'You couldn't keep a fish alive for more than one week?'

She laughed. 'No. Doesn't bode well, does it?'

'But you're better with plants! Those herbs out there are thriving!' he laughed, pointing towards her kitchen.

She laughed too, enjoying his laughter, his smile. He hadn't laughed or smiled much since discovering the pregnancy. She liked the way it made his eyes gleam and crinkle in the corners. She looked forward to more opportunities to make him smile and laugh. 'Let's hope I'm better with babies.'

The light in his eyes faltered briefly before returning. 'Yes. Let's hope so.'

Serena smiled at him, thinking over the last few hours at the hospital. The fear. The panic, and then the relief at discovering that she was still pregnant, despite everything. It had been a rollercoaster of a day. Now Ash had cooked for her and made her tea, and he was ready to go home and rest. And selfishly? She suddenly didn't want him to leave at all. She wanted him to stay.

'I should go,' he said, standing. 'We can find out more about each other at the weekend. How about I pop round and take you out somewhere for coffee, or lunch?'

That sounded good, though she was upset that he

couldn't stay. But she didn't want to be selfish. He'd had a long day too, and he'd come here and cooked. Perhaps all he wanted to do was kick back at his place and rest? 'Sure.'

'I'll call you tomorrow. Rest up. Don't do anything, and if there are any problems or you have any concerns, you call me, okay?'

'Okay,' she agreed.

'Don't walk me to the door. I'll see myself out.'

'Okay.' She sat there looking up at him, feeling awkward. Normally she would walk someone to the door. It felt the polite thing to do. Instead he stood there looking down at her, and she wondered if he was thinking of dropping a peck onto her cheek to kiss her goodbye. It would be nice if he did.

The indecision in his eyes was plain for her to see, and part of her wanted to reach out and take his hand and tell him to stay. But in the end, he just gave a small, embarrassed laugh and left the room.

She felt herself deflate. She'd hoped for a kiss. Was that wrong? Or was it just the hormones?

She heard the front door open and then close again. Her shoulders dropped, and she hugged herself tighter beneath the fleecy blanket. They'd taken small steps today. Tiny steps in getting to know one another a bit more. But she knew it wasn't enough. Not yet.

She turned on the television and began watching a program, when suddenly there was a knock at her door. Frowning, she got up to see who it was, putting on the safety chain and cracking the door open to peer outside.

Ash stood there smiling, and her heart soared. He'd changed his mind! Visions of them spending the night together flooded her, and she wondered if he'd lean in and kiss her softly on the neck and purr into her ear about staying the night.

Instead, his frozen breath billowed around his face as he handed her a packet of ginger biscuits. 'For your bedside table,' he said. 'So you don't get sick in the morning.'

Serena laughed and undid the chain, opening the door wide to accept them. What a sweet thing to do! 'Thank you.' Her fingers brushed his as she accepted his thoughtful gift and their eyes met. Both of them seemingly uncertain about what should happen next.

'You'd, er…better go and put your feet back up.'

'I will.'

He turned to go, and she watched him sadly, about to close the door when he spoke once again. 'And Serena?'

'Yes?'

'We can do this. You and I. I really think we can do this.'

She smiled, realizing that he was going to be a complete gentleman about this. Besides, what could they actually do? He wasn't going to come in and ravish her after she'd bled today! He was doing the right thing. Even if it still might have been nice for him to have just lain with her and actually slept with her, his arm around her, so she didn't feel alone tonight. 'I hope so. Good night, Ash.'

'Good night.' He turned to go again, and she watched him leave, standing in the cold night air, her arms wrapped tight about herself, watching the father of her baby get into his car, start the engine and give her a wave as he drove away.

He liked navy blue. And he'd had a dog called Max. And his family lived in London. But he was more than that. He was a doctor and kind and caring, and though he might not be her romantic partner or spouse or husband-to-be, he was showing her more consideration and care than any man ever had. Despite his earlier warnings.

So maybe she wouldn't have to go through this alone at all?

CHAPTER FIVE

That Saturday, Ash arrived back at her house. Her bleeding had thankfully stopped, and they'd arranged to spend some time together. It was imperative really. They needed to build a bond and get to know one another more, and Ash suggested that maybe they could go to the cinema together and watch a movie? That way it wasn't anything strenuous whilst she was still taking it easy.

Ash looked gorgeous when she opened up her door and saw him.

He stood there smiling and hesitantly handed over a bunch of flowers that he must have bought from a florist's. It felt like she was being courted, and she liked it.

'They're beautiful, thank you.' She put them in a vase in the kitchen and grabbed her jacket, and they headed out in Ash's car.

'It's still cold, isn't it?' she asked.

Ash turned up the heating in his vehicle and smiled. 'It won't be when you're in the latter stages of your pregnancy. It can be hard to carry through the summer months.'

He must have heard that from somewhere. Ginger, her midwife friend, who had called her yesterday to check on her, had pretty much said the same thing. It was very reassuring to have Ginger as a close friend, especially when Serena was worrying so much about her pregnancy.

'I hope I get that far.'

'I do too.' He turned to look at her and smiled, and she felt it was the most genuine smile she had ever seen. He really wanted this! Which was crazy, because when she'd met him in that café, Donnie's Café, to tell him about the pregnancy, he'd initially given that huge speech about not wanting a relationship.

She watched him as he drove, stealing glances when he was busy observing traffic at intersections. It still felt odd to know that she'd gotten herself stuck in a situation such as this with Ash. Both of them loners, both of them brought together by a surprise pregnancy. Both of them trying to navigate their way through a difficult and emotional situation. And yet it was more than that. She could feel herself developing feelings for him, which was crazy, but it must have something to do with her hormones. But she enjoyed spending time with him. Enjoyed seeing him smile and laugh and look at her in the way that he did. It made her wonder if he was thinking about more, too.

At the cinema, they perused the boards. She learned that Ash liked watching science fiction movies, which was something she enjoyed as well, so they picked an epic space saga they'd both heard about, bought a bucket of sweet popcorn and some drinks, and headed in to watch the film. They picked good seats—the cinema wasn't very busy at this time in the afternoon—and settled down to wait for the trailers to start.

'What are your thoughts on trailers?' he asked.

'I like them! I like knowing what's about to come out.'

'You like previews?'

She smiled. 'I do.'

'Then I have a question for you about previews.'

'Okay.'

He paused. 'When we get to the anomaly scan, are you going to want to find out the sex of the baby?'

Serena sucked in a deep breath as she contemplated the question that had come completely out of left field. The scan seemed so far away! If she could make it to twenty weeks. Was it possible? But…yes, she thought she'd want to know, even if part of her was like, *if you find out the sex, you'll get more attached, start thinking of names, start planning and what if it all goes wrong? You'll be devastated.* But she knew in her heart, that she'd be devastated to lose this baby either way, so why not get to know it? Get to know it and enjoy it as much as she could! *Choose* names. *Plan* a life. Wasn't that the privilege of all new parents-to-be? 'Yes. I'd like to. Why? Wouldn't you?'

'I would.' He gave her a quick smile and then ate some popcorn, clearly not willing to embellish further.

She instinctively felt like he had more to say on the matter, but that he'd chosen to keep it in, stuffing the words down with the food. She was going to ask him more, but then the room went dark and the screen came to life and she forgot all about it as the trailers began.

Ash was terrified of finding out the sex of the baby. He wanted to, but also knew that if they did and he found it was a girl, then he would be even more scared of history repeating itself.

Would he ever relax?

Or would he only breathe out a sigh of relief when the baby was born, healthy and happy? Just lately, since finding out about the baby, he often felt like he couldn't breathe. Like there was a tight band around him, and it was made of fear. Every time he thought about the baby in Serena's belly, it squeezed him ever tighter. Made him feel like he wanted to be with her always, so that he could be there instantly the second she thought anything might be wrong.

It was worse when he was at home, or at work, *away* from her. Because he didn't know if she was all right. He tried his hardest to stay away, to give her space, because it wasn't like she was his girlfriend or his wife. He had no claim on her at all. They were just friends at this juncture. Even that was hard, because he really liked her, and he did find her very attractive. Even more so now that she was pregnant with his child. It stirred protective feelings in him, feelings he had to rein in, because, again, she wasn't his. He had no right to claim her as his, and he wasn't even sure if he was capable of doing so. He'd sworn to never get romantically involved again after the failure of his marriage. His relationship with Nina had shown him that he wasn't good enough to be a husband. He'd gotten it so wrong before, and no woman needed his failings.

And yet…

Something felt very different here. Serena made him feel…well, lots of things that he kept trying to capture and examine properly, but they felt elusive, like they didn't want to be examined. They just wanted to be. What it meant to him to share space with her. To be in her company was wonderful. Talking to her, finding out about her, intrigued him. Admiring the way her hair fell softly across her shoulders. Her beautiful smile and the brief moments in which they touched were electrifying. Like now. Close together in the dark of the cinema…

He tried to concentrate on the movie. It was good! Fast-paced, interesting. Very atmospheric and claustrophobic, but he was just so terribly aware of the woman at his side. The way their hands kept brushing each other's accidentally when they both reached for popcorn at the same time. The way she yelped and then laughed at a jump scare, her eyes gleaming with amusement in the dark. The way she looked at him in general… He liked the way she looked at him sometimes. Made him feel special.

Afterwards, they came out, and Serena was blown away by the film. 'That was amazing! The part at the end? When Stacy found out that the comms officer had been the saboteur, and she lured him into a trap of her own? That was pretty impressive, and clever, too, don't you think?'

'Yeah! It was good!' But for Ash, the best bit had not been the film. For him, the best bit had been sitting next to Serena for two and a half hours. Having her close. Knowing she was safe and well and happy. Feeling a part of something.

It was something he'd like to experience a bit more often.

And it terrified him slightly as to what this all meant.

* * *

'Kyle! Good morning! How have things been going with your exercises I set you?'

Kyle looked at her. 'Not bad. I tried to use that stretchy band thing you gave me, but it really makes my hand ache.'

'You had a small, stable fracture in your left hand didn't you?'

He nodded.

'Well, maybe I could give you some hand exercises, too?'

'I've been trying to play my guitar. Does that count as hand exercise?'

Serena smiled at him. 'I'm sure it helps your dexterity, but I can certainly forward you some exercises you can do at home to help strengthen the hand.'

'Good. I'm going on tour in a few months, and I need to be able to play through my set.'

'How many months is a few months?'

'Three.'

'Then let's get you stronger! Are you managing to do all of your exercises every day?'

He shrugged. 'Not every day.'

She was going to mildly berate him. If he wanted to be fit for touring in three months, then he ought to practice every day. Instead, before she could say anything, Ash piped up from behind her. 'It needs to be every day, Kyle, if you want to be pounding that stage in front of thousands of fans.'

Serena looked at Ash before turning her gaze back to Kyle. 'Okay, show me how you've been doing the exercises.'

They went through each of them step by step, Serena examining his form, making adjustments if necessary. Making him stand straighter. Focusing on his core and hip. 'How does that one feel? You had tightness before.'

'It's better. Still feels a little stiff in the morning.'

'That will pass. Are you taking painkillers?'

'No.'

'That's excellent.'

Kyle was a good patient. She knew that when she set exercises for homework for her patients, not all of them stuck to them. Oftentimes, they'd start off with good intentions, and then the exercises would fall by the wayside. That was up to them, but it often meant it took them longer to heal or they suffered stiffness for longer periods of time.

But at least she still could offer a variety of exercises they could do to help themselves. The pregnancy was just something that was happening. She was taking folic acid and trying to eat right, but what else could she do? There were no exercises she could practice every day to strengthen her womb or keep the baby where it needed to be. The success of her pregnancy actually had nothing to do with her, and that made it quite frustrating. So when patients ignored her advice when all she was trying to do was help them, it made her frustrated at times. Like they took their health for granted. Someone wise had once told her that if a person did not find the time to look after themselves, then they would, at some point, be forced to *make time* to take care of themselves when they became sick, or broken.

Every month since puberty, Serena had been forced to deal with the pains and problems of her reproductive cycle. Taking the contraceptive pill had not helped regulate her or lessen the pain or the bleeding when she had it. A coil had been impossible to insert, the pain too much, and she'd had to ask the doctor to stop. Once, she'd been prescribed tranexamic acid for the heavy bleeding, but it had made her so nauseous, she'd been unable to do anything. Serena had become accustomed to riding the waves of her severe endometriosis and trying not to drown in the pain and exhaustion of it all. Missing days from work. Missing family occasions. Missing out on life in general. And so she'd withdrawn.

No one else in her family seemed to suffer, so she'd felt very alone with it all. Facing a fight alone, feeling that no one else could truly understand what she was going through. *And to think I once asked my doctor for a hysterectomy.*

Once she'd talked Kyle through some weight-bearing exercises for his bad leg, she insisted he did them at home 'I'm sure you're aware that the hospital has got eyes on us all here and well…if you don't recover well enough for your tour, I don't want anyone suggesting I didn't do my job.'

'I'll do them. I promise.'

'You will?'

He shrugged. 'I'll try my best.'

'You need to do more than your best, Kyle,' Ash said. 'In fact, I have a suggestion.'

'Okay.' Kyle looked intrigued.

'What about if I give you the number of a freelance physio who could come to your house every day and make sure that you do. Like a personal trainer? Someone to spot you.'

'I already have a personal trainer. Mind you, I've not seen him since before Christmas.'

'Okay, so what if I gave them a ring? Tell them how important this is and to incorporate your physio into your everyday? But they'd have to come round *every day*.'

Kyle nodded. 'It'll cost me, but… I'll give you Craig's number.'

'That's great. I'll call him later on. Talk him through it.'

It was a good suggestion. Serena was annoyed that she hadn't thought of it herself. Kyle was different to her other patients. He was a celebrity, so *of course* he had a team around him! 'Okay. So I want you doing the original exercises I posted you, and now these newer weight-bearing ones, which I'll also email, along with the ones for your hand.'

'Great.'

When Kyle left the department, Serena turned to Ash. 'Good thinking about the personal trainer.'

'I didn't think he'd mind me suggesting it. There was no way I was going to let your reputation be tarnished because he didn't put in the work himself.'

'Thank you.' That was nice of him. Showed he cared.

Serena smiled awkwardly at him. Since the movie, since spending time with Ash in a non-professional setting, seeing him outside of work in a social way with him tending to her every need, she'd begun to feel a bit weird when she thought of him. What were they to each other? Were they more than friends? She had all these feelings inside! And every time she saw him, it was a struggle to contain them.

It didn't help that he was good-looking, and her body was flooding with a rush of hormones that made her feel all the feelings. How could she not think of what it might be like if they had an actual, real-life romantic relationship? They'd already slept together, and dammit, she liked him a lot!

'Well, I'd better get back to my own patients,' he said, as if he had been thinking the same thing.

She smiled and nodded, turning away to her computer so they didn't have a moment like they'd had on Saturday after the movies.

Because that hadn't been awkward at all!

He took her home after the movie. It had been really nice to just hang out with her and chill. No patients, no one they knew around them. They'd been anonymous in the dark of the cinema, and they must have looked like any other couple out and about that day. But it wasn't a date. Not at all. And when he'd driven her back home, he walked her to her front door.

'Well, that was lovely, thank you,' she said, reaching for her key from her pocket.

He smiled and nodded, realizing that if this *had* been a date, he'd be thinking about kissing her goodbye now. Problem was, he *was* thinking about kissing her goodbye. On the cheek was probably the polite thing to do, seeing as this *wasn't* a romantic interlude. But he yearned to do so much more. To take her face gently in his hands and tilt it to his and brush his lips against hers and... 'You doing anything nice the rest of this weekend?'

She shook her head. 'No. Just resting. Trying to keep

food down will be my main occupation, I think.' She smiled.

'Well, the popcorn stayed down, for which I'm grateful.'

Serena laughed. 'Baby seems to prefer unhealthy things. I will have to break them of that habit if I'm to raise a healthy kid.'

Ash hadn't been thinking beyond the baby age. He'd never passed that age with Laila, and all his focus had been on Serena getting to the end of the pregnancy and giving birth. But yes, if this kid made it, they would grow up, go to school, become an actual person that he would have responsibility for and be a role model to. What would they be like? More like their mum, Serena? Or him? The thought had made him smile.

'What?' She looked at him strangely.

'Just thinking of what it might feel like to be an actual dad.'

'Mmm.' Her gaze went into the distance, as if she was imagining being a mum.

'Think we'll screw them up?'

'Oh, one hundred percent.' As she laughed, the afternoon sun glinted in her hair, making it look like threads of gold were entwined within the caramel strands.

It made her hair look soft and inviting, and he resisted the urge to reach up and touch it. Instead, he'd taken a step back, away from her, overwhelmed by the urge to get closer, fighting the impulses that made his fingers twitch in anticipation of touching her. Afraid that if he did reach out to touch her hair, she might not like it, and the idea of her rejecting him? Was not one he wished to contemplate. Better for him to endure this strange in-between world that he was in.

'Well, I guess I'd better let you go?' she said.

'Yes.' He nodded. 'I've got a lot on.' He hadn't, but he thought it best to say.

'Of course.' She smiled at him as if waiting for him to peck her on the cheek, or just say goodbye, or walk away.

'I'll, er…see you Monday?'

'You will.'

This lingering was helping neither of them, and he knew he needed to do something! So he stepped forward to kiss her goodbye. Just a friendly one. On the cheek. Nothing more. His hands on her shoulders as he leaned in. His lips brushing her skin ever so lightly, almost as if there were no contact at all, and yet he felt a rush of something. Of desire? Of nerves? Of want? Electricity. He felt it. Did she? Up close, his lips on her skin, his nose in her hair above the ear, he could inhale her perfume. It was a heady scent—the same scent she'd worn the night they'd met. Sense of smell was a strange thing, and it could remind you, so clearly, of the past. In his mind's eye, he saw, in one mad rush, that New Year's Eve and how he'd explored her body, his tongue licking her, tasting her, claiming her every secret place, and how she'd groaned against him, how she'd ground against him, her gasps, her breathing, her moans of pleasure. The images came in such a rush, so sudden and unexpected, his brain hit Pause so that he could enjoy them. He just stood there holding her, his eyes closed, with his lips still against her cheek. She turned to look at him, uncertain as to why he'd stopped moving. He opened his eyes and gazed at her with what must have been lust, and…

Panic filled her face, and she stepped away from him, jingling her keys, bringing him back to the present, to reality. He laughed, nervously, raised a hand and walked away, back to his car, his body jangling at the abrupt nature of the change that had been suddenly thrown over him. A dash of cold water.

He sat in his car, turned on the engine and immediately drove away, glad that at least one of them had had some sense.

They were not in a relationship! She would not have welcomed a less tentative kiss. Because where would it have ended up? Where would it have led?

They could not complicate what they had with feelings like those!

It was imperative to Serena, despite her physical feelings for Ash that she wasn't sure she could trust right now, that everything between her and Ash remain platonic to avoid the risk of anything going wrong, like a relationship that would crash and die having been built on a moment of lust. Lust was not a solid foundation upon which to build something that would have to endure for decades, because lust was fleeting. That was all she and Ash had had. One moment. And since then? Everything she was feeling for him was just hormones. It had to be. She'd heard other women speak of this—the pregnancy hormones, making you act and feel in ways you wouldn't normally—and the feeling that she couldn't truly trust herself was dizzying and tormenting. Hormones were wrong and false, a mirage, only there because of the baby she carried in her belly. To be honest, that was the only reason he was still involved with her.

The baby. Not her. He'd told her, right at the beginning, that he wasn't the type of guy looking for a relationship, and nor did she want one either.

Well, maybe she did, but she'd resigned herself to being alone and had become so good at isolating herself and cutting people off, it was difficult to let anyone in that she felt she could trust. That she felt would understand her, or put up with the endless months of pains and difficulties she sometimes faced because of her condition. Ralph had left because of it. Why wouldn't Ash? Even she'd leave if she could.

There'd once been a time that she hadn't been able to leave the house, and it had taken months to get her pain levels under control. Who would want to put up with that? Even she didn't! Never mind someone else. And Ash seemed so sweet—why burden him with that? Ash who was so kind, warm and funny. Ash who was so sweet and who looked at her like she was his favourite person on the planet right now. She wanted to keep the innocence of that. The purity of that. Why ruin it?

'How is Gareth getting on?' she asked Cole as they sat together in his office, eating their lunch. Gareth was the inpatient on the ortho ward who'd become quadraplegic.

'Not bad. He's seen the mental health team now, and I'm going up there every day to check on him and give him some bed physio. It's going to take him some time to adapt to his new restrictions. How's our celebrity, Kyle?'

She smiled. 'He's doing well. He should be good for his tour in a few months. Ash has contacted his personal trainer and sent him a list of all his recommended exercises to make sure he works on them every day.'

'That's good. He's lucky he can do that.'

'The perks of being a star.' She smiled.

'And how are you?' He raised an eyebrow.

'I'm good.'

'You, er…have anything you want to tell me?'

She looked at him, blushing with the guilt of hiding something. 'Like what?'

Cole smiled. 'You know…any kind of news…'

'Like…?'

He leaned in. 'I saw you this weekend. Coming out of the cinema with Dr Dhillon?'

She flushed. 'Oh! Right, well, we're just getting to know one another a bit, that's all. Because we're working together so much.'

'It's not that often! And besides, I didn't really mean that. I'm talking about the way you laid your hands on your belly as you walked out.'

She shrugged, avoiding meeting his eye. 'I had a pain.'

'Oh. Is the baby okay?'

'The b-baby?'

Cole smiled. 'I notice things about the human body, and it was the *way* you did it. Like you were *cradling* it. The way a woman might if she were pregnant? And before you say anything, don't think I haven't noticed the morning sickness.'

Serena closed her eyes. She hadn't even told her family. Neither she nor Ash had told them, and they weren't going to until they got past the first trimester. She opened her eyes again to look at Cole. 'Fine. Yes, but don't tell anyone.'

'I knew it! Dr Dhillon's the father?'

She nodded.

'I didn't know you guys were dating!'

'We're not. It's complicated.'

'But you must be thrilled?'

Serena smiled. Cole knew of her monthly struggles with her health. More than once he'd found her doubled over at work. 'I am. It's just a scary time at the moment, what with my endometriosis. It puts me at higher risk of miscarriage.'

'Oh. Well, if you need me to adapt anything for you at work here, then you just let me know, okay?'

'I will. And you won't say a word to anyone else?'

'Not until you tell me I can.'

'Thanks.'

'Serena?'

'Yes?'

He smiled. 'Congratulations!'

'I'm struggling sometimes to get the chords.' Kyle said, sitting in front of them both.

This time, he'd brought his guitar with him, and he got it out of its travelling case.

'Can I show you?'

'Sure,' Serena said.

Ash watched as Kyle lifted the guitar onto his lap and began to play. It wasn't a tune he was familiar with, but it seemed quite the haunting ballad, and he didn't know what Kyle was talking about! It sounded perfect to him. He almost forgot that they were there to work with him as he sat, his mind a million miles away, just absorbed in the music.

Nina had always liked to listen to sad songs. She'd said that she liked the stories they told, the emotions they evoked, and how a good cry could always make you feel better—whatever you needed. But this music reminded him of something in his past that he'd not wanted to remember. A moment in time, in which his heart had been broken. A moment in which he'd felt empty. Powerless. Hopeless. *Useless.*

'Did you hear it?' Kyle said, sounding frustrated, a furrow between his brow.

'No,' Ash said, brought back abruptly into the present.

'Nor me.' Serena said, looking and sounding confused. 'It sounded beautiful.'

Kyle sighed. 'My hand tires, and I struggle to get that Cadd9 chord.'

'Is guitar the only instrument you play?' Serena asked.

'I play a bit of piano.'

'Then might I suggest you play more? The piano will allow for that finger placement, the stretch of your metacarpals, and will exercise and strengthen those tendons you need to move to reach the chord. It'll probably be better for you than squeezing balls or using grip strengtheners. At least for you, anyway.'

'I could give it a try.'

'Don't give up, Kyle,' Ash said, trying to pull his thoughts from that dark episode in his past. 'Lots of people think having surgery is the hard part, but it's not. It's this moment right here, where the struggle shows. Where people try to regain strength, where they try to regain what they had once before. It's scary when you have to put in all the work again on something you could once do flawlessly. But you'll get there if you just stick with it and find the courage to walk the path again.'

'I guess.' Kyle made a fist, then stretched out his fingers, looking at his hand.

Serena gazed at Ash. He looked away, uncomfortable under her scrutinizing gaze. 'If you'll both excuse me, I've got to go. A scheduled surgery. I'll see you next time?'

Kyle nodded. 'Thanks.'

'Serena? I'll see you later?'

'Okay.'

And then he was gone, walking away from the department, worrying that he might have said too much. It was that sad song Kyle had played. It had taken Ash back into the past, sitting with Nina as she'd sobbed silently and held Laila. There'd been music playing, not in their room but someone else's. He'd not thought about it for all this time, until he heard Kyle playing, but it had been guitar music. Soft. Melodic. Haunting. The guitar had simply reminded him of how he'd felt, his world ending in the unnatural silence of a stillborn baby, and it had become too much. He'd sat there, feeling tears sting the backs of his eyes. It startled him because he'd not cried about Laila for so long now, refusing to let himself do so in case he could never stop. Nina had sat there in her hospital bed holding their daughter, and though he was in the same room with her, sharing the same grief, he'd felt alone. Knew that Nina felt alone, too, and he'd wanted to reach out to comfort her, but he just couldn't move. His grief had paralysed him and that was why he didn't want to allow himself to think of his daughter. He couldn't be paralysed again.

And he couldn't let Serena know. Not yet. She had enough worries about the pregnancy. He couldn't tell her about his daughter! She knew he'd had a failed relationship, but not what had happened. It had been best to just let her know what a bad partner he was, because that was his defence mechanism. His wall. His plaster cast that kept him safe from anyone else wanting to get close. The plaster cast stopped him from getting hurt again. Protected his wound.

In the corridor, away from prying eyes, he wiped his eyes and took in a steadying breath. He could not let anyone see him like this.

Would not let anyone see him like this.

Serena wasn't a fool. She'd seen how Kyle's guitar playing had brought forward some emotion in Ash that she didn't understand. Had it been the piece of music played? Was it something Ash recognized, and it tied to some upsetting memory?

It intrigued her, making her want to go after him and ask him if he was all right. Comfort him the way he'd comforted her that time. His obvious vulnerability pulled at her, but she couldn't go after him! She was still in a consult, and she had to treat Kyle and advise him. But when he'd gone and she'd finished her morning's clinic, she decided to see if she could find Ash. Check on him. Make sure he was okay.

But, she told herself, *I'm only doing this as a friend would.*

Her care for him, her concern, it was just friendly. Nothing else. Fuelled by hormones to have natural worry for the father of her child. Something that had to go back to caveman times, perhaps? Needing the male figure to be okay enough to stick around to protect its child.

I'm doing this for my unborn baby.

That was all, she told herself. Hoping if she told it to herself often enough, she'd begin to believe it. She wanted her baby to have its father. She needed good communication with the father, and if that meant showing she cared, then so be it. And she'd promised to tell him if something was wrong. Surely that went both ways? There was nothing wrong in checking up on him. It wasn't like she was trying to pursue a romantic relationship with him, and why would she? He'd already told her once before that he was no good in relationships. Why would she even want to get involved with a guy who had already warned her he could be flaky?

She checked the ortho ward. Spoke to Colleen and discovered that Ash wasn't in a surgery anymore. Something had gone wrong. He had in fact gone for a break, and that he had to be in the hospital somewhere.

Well, that narrows it down!

She checked the cafeteria, the concourse, the shops on the ground floor, but there was no sign of him. She was just about to give up when she spotted a lone figure sat outside in the frost-rimmed memorial garden. All wrapped up and sipping out of some thermal mug. Serena wasn't dressed for the outside, but her overriding concern for Ash pushed that to one side. She headed outside, shivering through her polo shirt and cursing herself for not thinking to bring her jacket.

'Hey,' she said, standing beside him as he gazed down at some bush that still had its leaves. She had no idea what it was. She'd never been green-fingered. Those herbs in her kitchen window that were thriving? Were some sort of fluke.

He looked up. 'Oh. Hey. Wait, aren't you cold?'

'I'm fine,' she said, trying to stop her teeth from chattering.

'Here, take this.' And he began to remove his own jacket, unzipping it and draping it around her shoulders. She was encased in his residual warmth and the aroma of him, and her insides practically swooned with ecstasy.

'Thanks. Won't you get cold?'

'I'm fine. I have a hot drink. It's coffee. Want some?'

She shook her head. Coffee was often a no-go lately. 'Needed some peace and quiet?'

'I didn't have the best surgery. Just needed a breather.'

'What happened?'

'Oh, you know, complications with the anaesthetic. Nearly lost them due to a reaction, and they were only there for a shoulder repair.'

'Are they okay?'

'They are now, but it was a close call for a moment. Malignant hyperthermia. It comes out of nowhere. Luckily we caught it fast, administered dantrolene to reverse it and applied cooling packs.'

'Cooling packs?'

'The condition makes the body's temperature soar. But he's okay now. We'll just have to find another way to fix his shoulder.'

'And you? Are you okay?' she asked, glad of the increasing heat of her own body enveloped in his jacket.

He nodded and smiled. 'How's your morning been? Hopefully not as dramatic as mine.'

'Oh, you know. I was worried about you.'

'Me?'

'You left so abruptly after Kyle played his guitar.'

'I had a surgery.'

'So you said.' There was something he wasn't telling her, and she had no idea what it could be. But if there were things he was keeping to himself—important things—then could she really trust him? She wanted to. Wanted to implicitly, but it wasn't like she knew him well enough to discern if she could yet. And all this uncertainty, all the not knowing simply reminded her that Ash was only there because of the baby. Not her. She didn't want to be abandoned again. Needed him to know that he could lean on her the way she was leaning on him. 'You can talk to me, you know,' she said.

'What about?'

Serena shrugged, trying to seem casual as she looked out at the garden. 'About anything. About what worries you. About what scares you. I may look like a simple physiotherapist, but let me tell you, this is where other people's confessions come to die!' She tried to make a joke of it. To seem maybe less threatening. Safe.

'I don't have anything to confess.'

Why did she not believe him? Maybe he wasn't saying anything because he felt that *he* couldn't trust *her*! How to show him that she was someone he could feel safe with? 'You know, when I was eighteen years old, my brother told me something. Something secret. That he liked guys. He came out to me and asked me to not say anything until he was ready to tell Mum. I kept his secret. Kept my word. When people confide in me, their stories go no further than me. I can be trusted. It means something to me. And *them*.'

'Is this your way of trying to make me spill the beans?'

'Only if there are beans to spill.' She smiled, giving him a playful nudge with her elbow.

He looked at her for the longest time, almost like he was trying to weigh her up. Then he shook his head, smiling. 'There are no beans.'

She deflated, feeling like she'd failed him in some way. She wasn't sure she believed him, though, and it hurt that he was keeping something from her. She had to tell him when something was wrong, but *he* didn't have to? 'Just remember that I offered, and the offer will forever stand.' She glanced at her watch, saw it was time she ought to be heading back for her clinic. She stood up and began to remove his jacket, reluctantly handing it back. 'Thank you. I'll catch you later, then.'

As she began to walk away, he called after her. 'Is your brother okay?'

She stopped and turned to him. Smiling. 'He's married to Jack, the love of his life. And yes, Mum went to the wedding.'

Scott Larkin was in surgery to have an amputation of his lower leg. He'd been fighting bone cancer for some time, and the tumour that had grown through his tibia and encroached into his fibula was no longer reacting to treatment. The bones and the leg had to go to save Scott's life and stop the cancer metastasizing someplace else.

He was a young man, only twenty-three, and had always been athletic. To lose his leg had been their last resort treatment, and here they were facing it, but Ash and Scott's oncological team had all agreed that it was now the way forward. He would heal and be fitted for a prosthetic, and he would have a much better chance at recovery.

'You ready?' he asked Scott before the anaesthetist, Jacob, could administer Scott's drugs.

'As I'll ever be. We cut away the old so that I can have a fresh start, right?' Scott's teeth chattered with nerves.

'That's right. That leg has served you well for many years, but all it's doing now is holding you back and endangering your future.'

'So let's make it vamoose.' Scott chuckled.

'I've got you, okay?'

'Okay.'

Ash nodded to Jacob, who administered the drugs to make Scott lose consciousness for the surgery.

'Count back from ten for me.'

'Ten…nine…eight…sev…'

Jacob smiled as he inserted the breathing tube. He listened to Scott's lungs to double-check position and watched the machine to ensure Scott's oxygen saturations were all at normal, expected levels. 'Out like a light.'

'Okay, let's begin. Scalpel?'

An amputation could be a relatively quick surgery. In Scott's case, it took Ash just over an hour to complete, and it went smoothly, including the skin flap he'd created to cover the stump for healing. When it was over, he sent Scott up to the recovery ward, knowing that this time tomorrow, Scott would probably be going home. On crutches, with a bag of tablets, starting his road to recovery. At some point, he would see Serena or one of her team and then the prosthetics team. Scott had already told him that he was going to try out for the Paralympics, wanting to run before he could walk, so to speak.

He admired Scott. His optimistic attitude. So much of physical healing was down to a positive mental outlook. Maybe it was an approach that he himself ought to take? Just because his past with Nina and Laila had been heartbreaking, perhaps he ought to go into this new adventure with Serena with a more optimistic attitude. Perhaps if he believed in a great outcome for the pregnancy, then they would have one.

And yet...

He wanted to so badly, and yet he feared doing so. Because what if he allowed himself to feel for either of them and was assured that this would go fine, and then it didn't? Could he withstand having his heart ripped in two again? It was hard enough fighting his feelings for Serena without having to work his way through that trauma.

Scott had had the bad part of his body cut away. The part that was hurting him. But you couldn't do that if the part that hurt you was your feelings. Your thoughts. Your emotions. Those were the things poisoning his body, so how was he supposed to deal with those? In some ways, he envied Scott, which he knew was ridiculous. Wasn't he getting a second chance with Serena and this baby?

She seemed to care for him. He'd felt her trying to reach out when they were in the memorial garden. He so desperately wanted to let her in, to let down his barriers keeping her out of his heart, but it was so difficult. He didn't want to hurt her the way he'd hurt Nina by not being there enough. His mind kept telling him to hold himself back. *Don't get involved. That way, if you fail, you're only hurting yourself and not her.*

But I'd be letting down my baby, wouldn't I?

No. He couldn't imagine doing that. If fate was good enough to let his child live, then no, he would *never* let them down. To be given a second chance like this? How many people got second chances? Not many. Though this was unexpected and rare and miraculous, he wanted to hold on to the hope that this baby represented. He or she could be a new beginning for him. For Serena, too.

That was a part of him that he would never cut out. Or cut off. And the best thing? If this baby did survive, the lovely Serena would be in his life forever more, even if it was just as a friend and colleague.

Because Serena was beautiful inside and out. She was amazing, and he was beginning to see that more and more. To have her with him through this journey was more than he could ask for.

He just had to make sure he didn't screw it up.

'When your family know about the baby, I think I'd like to meet them,' Serena said as they sat together in her house.

Ash had brought around breakfast bagels first thing, surprising her. Now they sat in her kitchen, eating them.

He paused mid-chew and smiled. 'Why?'

Why? That wasn't a question she'd been expecting. She'd just assumed that when he did tell his family, *they* would want to meet *her*! Surely that would be natural?

To want to meet the woman carrying their future grand-child? 'Because they'd want to meet me, wouldn't they? Get to know me?'

'Possibly. I'm just not sure I'm going to tell them until much later.' Ash looked uncomfortable.

Now it was her turn to ask. 'Why? You think I'm still going to miscarry?'

'No! It's just…you know, I don't want them thinking that we're in some sort of a relationship. This is going to be difficult enough for them as it is.'

'Well, we are in some kind of a relationship, aren't we? We're going to be parents, and they're going to be *grand*parents, and I'm going to let them be in the baby's life. I'm telling my parents once I get past this first trimester, and I know they'll want to meet you.'

'Really?'

'Yes! Do you not want me to meet them?' She felt a little hurt. Was this what he'd meant by being a bad partner? That he didn't let anyone meet his family or his friends? That he kept them out?

'I do. It's just…complicated.'

Serena wondered briefly if it was anything to do with his background? Ash had told her before that he had mixed-race parentage. His mother was white and his father, Indian. Surely they wouldn't have a problem with her? 'I don't understand how.' Again, she was beginning to feel like he didn't trust her enough to tell her his concerns. The hurt that came from that ruined her appetite for her bagel. She got up, threw the rest of it in the bin and placed her plate in the dishwasher.

'Not hungry?'

'Not anymore.' She sighed and began wiping down

surfaces that didn't actually need it. She was frustrated. Angry that she couldn't fully understand his concerns. She really wanted to know him better! He was going to be the father of her child! And he was keeping her out. It was so important that she know him and trust him. If he was going to keep putting up barriers, then…well. It would cause her to put up barriers of her own.

She was used to navigating her way through this life alone. She could easily do the same for this, if need be.

'It's not you. It's just…they have a lot on their plate right now, and I don't want to tell them about you or the baby until we both know that everything is going to be all right. I don't want to hurt them if there's still risk.'

He looked down, sounding worried, and suddenly she understood. This wasn't just about her. It was about him, too, *and* his parents and maybe they *were* going through some things personally and didn't need the added worry of her at-risk pregnancy. Maybe it was safer to let them know about it when she got closer to delivery.

'Fine. But you'll come with me in a few weeks to meet my parents?'

He smiled at her, nodding happily, feeling better on safer ground. 'Of course. I'd love to meet them.'

'Great. I think they're going to like you a lot.'

'Have you already told them about me?'

'No. They know nothing about you.'

'How will you explain our…situation?'

'I'll just tell them the truth. That's all anyone deserves, right?'

CHAPTER SIX

ASH ASKED SERENA if she'd like to go for a walk, and they headed out into the cold, crisp morning. He found himself wanting to put an arm around her or hold her hand. To avoid that, he kept his hands firmly protected in his jacket pockets. They found themselves walking down a high street filled with cafés and little boutique stores. One of these stores was called Bundle of Joy. Serena stopped to look in the window, her face lighting up with delight.

The window display was filled with a mix of white, cream or very light taupe-coloured Babygros and romper suits with teddy bears and building blocks, and he couldn't help but notice the smile that was growing on Serena's face.

'Aren't these cute?'

He looked and had to admit that they were. 'Yeah.'

'So small! Our baby could wear something like this.'

Ash smiled. Maybe. One day. If they were lucky. 'I think I'd prefer something with a bit more colour.'

'These muted colours are all the rage right now,' she said.

'I'm not sure a baby cares about fashion.'

'No. Just as long as they're healthy, fed and dry,' she agreed. 'Would you mind if we went in?'

Of course he didn't mind. He wanted her to be happy.

He'd not been in a baby store since that one time he'd gone in with Nina. A week or two before their lives were turned upside down, they'd spent a fortune on things because Nina had panicked that she didn't have enough clothes, or muslin squares, or bottles, just in case she couldn't breastfeed. And then she'd spotted this cute baby bath she had to have and some feeding bras. They'd bought a new mobile for the crib even though they already had one. She thought it would be more interesting for their daughter when she was born if these things rotated, played music and also played white noise. It had cost a lot. Nina had spent hours nesting in the nursery, making sure it was just so and perfect for the arrival of their own little bundle of joy.

And then baby Laila had died in utero, and Nina had still had to go through labour and delivery. And afterwards? Unable to do nothing, Ash had come home and stared at the walls of his home, wondering how they were going to continue without Laila. He couldn't fathom it. In his own confused and grief-stricken state, he'd believed that it would be wrong for Nina to come home from the hospital and see all of that stuff. He'd packed up the nursery into boxes. Taken down the crib and put it all in the attic. Taken the letters that spelled his daughter's name off the walls. He'd done it for his wife, believing he was helping. But he'd been wrong. She'd hated that he'd taken it all away. The anger in her eyes? The beginning of the end.

Seeing all these baby things here, the padded letters on the wall behind the till spelling the word *baby*? Well…it brought it all back.

'Don't you think it's still a little early for us to be in here? We're not in the clear yet. Maybe we never will be. Not until he or she is born.'

She turned to look at him, surprised. 'But with that reasoning, I'll never buy a thing! Let's just go in, and I promise I'll only buy something small. How can you resist?'

The joy and light in her eyes were impossible to ignore. Of course he wanted her to be happy and look forward to this! The pregnancy might be her only one. Who knew? So shouldn't he let her enjoy it? But at the same time, he didn't want to pack up another nursery. He didn't want to have to shove into a box whatever thing she decided to buy today. He wouldn't be able to bear it!

But he could say none of that to her. He had to pretend that everything would be fine. And maybe it would be? She'd had no more bleeding since that first time. Despite the nausea, Serena seemed to be doing okay.

As they stepped inside the shop, a little bell rang above their heads. He was instantly overwhelmed by the sight of all the baby clothes hanging on racks. The images of happy, healthy babies on the walls. Soft toys. Natural wood. A wall of monitors and gadgets. He headed over to these as they seemed a lot less emotional to look at than baby clothes.

Behind him, he could hear Serena oohing and aahing over various things as he focused on video monitors and even breathing alarms. He felt his anxiety rise as he realized that he'd never relax! What if their baby was born fine? What of it? Because the fear would never end! There'd be the risk of sudden infant death syndrome. Of diseases. Of accidents. Illness. What if the baby had something wrong with it genetically? What if it choked on something? What then? All these gadgets were meant to reassure an anxious parent, to give them some feeling of being in control, but none of them could. Not really. And here he was, stuck in the exact type of situation he'd never wanted to be in again!

'Ash! Look at this one!'

He turned to see her holding up a pure white Baby-gro with a cute embroidery of a mother duck sheltering all her baby ducklings under its wings. It was beautiful and heartwarming and absolutely terrifying. 'Cute.' He tried to sound enthusiastic and smile, too, but it was getting increasingly difficult in this world of blue and pink and neutral colours.

'You just want to buy it all, don't you, but I guess we shouldn't tempt fate.'

He felt relieved. She was seeing sense. 'No.'

'Maybe just a teddy, then? Something that will sit in the corner of the crib?'

A teddy? He could deal with a teddy. 'That sounds a sensible idea. How about that one?' Trying to seem enthusiastic, he pointed at a teddy that looked the least babylike. It was soft, fluffy and dark brown, with a red bow around its neck.

'Hmm. Or this one?' Serena picked up a teddy that looked like it was made out of patchwork. Blue, pink, peppermint green, butter yellow. It was a mix of colours and had a cute face and wide, sewn-in smile.

'Mmm-hmm.'

'Oh! Look at that one!' She reached for a very fluffy teddy in the palest of pinks. It was beautiful and looked very much like the one that he and Nina had bought for their daughter's crib. That teddy was with Nina now. She'd taken all of their daughter's things after the divorce. He wondered if she still had it.

'Not sure we should get pink. It might be a boy,' he said, managing to force out the words, hoping that it would be a boy. Having another daughter, finding out their baby was a girl, would terrify him.

'You're right. Maybe something neutral, then?'

In the end, Serena selected a pale beige teddy that wore a pair of orange overalls and had a hat, like it worked in a hay barn or something. Her eyes gleamed with her purchase. Ash left the store with a huge sigh of relief, exhausted at trying to keep it together in a store that had only brought back bad memories. He needed a quick diversion. 'Should we stop for a pastry?' He needed a hit of sugar, something to take his mind off the fact that they'd started buying for the baby and they weren't even out of the first trimester. This felt silly. Tempting fate. Dangerous to do. Making plans. Thinking of the future when it wasn't promised. He knew all too well how it felt when those plans crashed and burned and took your heart with them.

'You're annoyed,' she said, pouting slightly.

'No. I'm not.'

'You think we shouldn't be buying this early, that it's still a risk.'

'Well, now that you've said it, yes. I think so.'

'But I want to be able to enjoy this, Ash! I don't know how long I have with this baby, and I want to feel like any other new mother-to-be, getting giddy over silly things like baby clothes.'

He softened. 'I know. I do.'

'But you'd prefer us to wait until after the first trimester?'

He sighed, long and heavy, feeling a headache twisting tight behind his eyes. He was in an impossible situation. He so desperately wanted to just pull her in and hold her and say sorry and tell her to buy whatever she wanted. Because he could not offload all his fear onto her. She'd just said it. She wanted to enjoy this, and she had every right to! He would not make this worse. 'Just…don't buy anything else. Please?'

'Fine.'

The mood was tense when they entered the café. A mood not made better by tea and cake. They sat mostly in silence, the tension in the air thick, punctuated only by the occasional sip of their drinks or a mouthful of Victoria sponge.

'I'm sorry. I don't mean to ruin this for you,' he said, meaning it. He hated that he'd upset her. He'd not meant to.

'It's fine. I know you don't really want this baby.'

Her words shocked him and went straight to his heart like a knife. He leaned in close. 'That's not true! It's *absolutely* not true!' Laila had not been planned. She'd been a surprise pregnancy. Maybe he'd not been ready for that responsibility, but by the time they'd lost her? He was more than ready to be a father. But he was a father with painfully empty arms! 'We may not have planned this, but I am *totally ready* to be the father that this baby needs. I want him or her *so badly* that it *hurts* me. So don't *ever* say that to me. Ever!'

She looked at him in surprise. 'That's the first time you've said that. That you want this baby.'

'I'm sure I've said it before.'

'Not to me. But I'm glad to hear it.' She smiled. 'Thank you for saying so. I apologise if I misread the situation. It's not ideal, all of this. I always imagined I would be married to the man I would have a baby with, if I'd ever gotten married at all. I'd always kind of assumed that wouldn't be for me. I'd tried to make my peace with it. Then I met you, and we did this crazy thing on New Year's Eve. Now we find ourselves having to deal with an unexpected pregnancy. I mean, how are we going to do this, Ash? The co-parenting thing, if we get that far?'

'I don't know.'

'We need to work it out.'

He nodded. 'We will. Let's just get past the twelve-week mark first.'

'Does she know about Laila?' Ryan asked.

Ryan was newly engaged to Ginger Ashby.

'No. I can't. I want to, but I can't! She's already terrified. I can't burden her with the knowledge. That's my load to carry.' Serena already had too much to worry about. Her endometriosis put their pregnancy at some risk already. He saw how that tore her apart, but how she kept trying to be brave despite it. He wished he had her courage.

'But?' Ryan raised an eyebrow. His mate always knew when there was something else that was bothering him.

'But I think she knows I'm holding something back. She doesn't trust me because she knows I'm not being completely honest with her. Sometimes I can feel her pull away, and that scares me.'

'Perhaps you should just bite the bullet, then? Face the fear and do it anyway. Maybe it's a burden that is best carried by the both of you.'

'I face the fear every day. Let me tell you, it's not a good thing to feel. I want to protect her from that.'

Ryan nodded. 'I get it. But… I lost Ginger once, all those years ago, because I was too afraid to tell her the truth of my feelings. And just recently, when I found her again, I still tried to hold pieces of myself back. That hurt her, too. Sometimes I think women would just prefer to hear the truth and not be left wondering if the silence is somehow their fault.'

Ash listened intently. Was he hurting Serena? He somehow felt his truth would hurt her more. Perhaps if he could just show her that he cared for her and that he was trying to make her happy, that would be enough until it was safe to tell her everything. All he needed was to keep this to himself for a few more months, but in the meantime, he would make an extra effort to show her how much she meant to him. How special she was. How much he needed her.

Because she meant a great deal. She was always in his thoughts. He missed her when she was gone, his heart brightening when they were together. And he'd not felt that for a long time. It was nice to feel it again. Being alone and independent and not looking for a relationship had been great, but it had also been lonely. He'd not realized just how much he'd missed having someone to talk to. And when he went home to his empty flat, he'd find himself thinking of her and wanting to be with her. Just to sit on the same sofa and chat with her was enough. To gaze upon her. Watch her lips as she spoke and listen to her laughter and feel all warm and gooey inside when she absently laid a hand on her belly.

These feelings for her scared him half to death.

But he didn't want to be rid of them.

If anything, he embraced them.

And dreamed of something more.

Serena knew that she and Ash needed to work harder on communicating with one another. Yes, he was withholding something, but perhaps he was doing so because *she* was holding back, too? Trying to keep things platonic when her body and soul yearned for more from him.

Was she being fully open with him? Open to *his* thoughts, *his* feelings? Allowing him to be who he needed to be? She was so wrapped up in her fears that sometimes she withheld and only thought of her own needs. But they were in this together. This pregnancy was a shock to both of them, and no, it wasn't ideal, but it was happening. Now she knew that he very much wanted this baby, and he'd been appalled that she'd thought he didn't want it. She'd assumed, in the same way she'd assumed no one would want to be with her because of her severe endometriosis. The same way she'd assumed this would never happen for her.

Yet here she was. Pregnant.

She had a chance for happiness here, and maybe she needed to let him in more? Not be so standoffish, because wouldn't this situation be better if she and Ash were closer? If he felt like he could come to her about anything and she, in turn, to him?

So today, she was making an effort to be warmer. More welcoming. More relaxed, as much as she could be. In her morning break, she decided to go up to the ortho ward with a peace offering.

The ward looked busy. She spotted Colleen doing the drugs round and gave her a smile and a wave, but left her be as you weren't supposed to interrupt the nurses when they were doing such an important job. Heading to the reception desk, she leaned over and smiled at the nurse who was on duty. 'Hi. Is Dr Dhillon around?'

'Erm… I think he's with a new paediatric admission. Actually, I'm glad you're here, because he asked me to notify physio about her. Could you stop by?'

'Er, sure. Which bed and bay?'

'Acorn Ward. Bed two. I'll buzz you through security.' Acorn Ward was the small paediatric orthopaedic ward that was situated alongside the adult department.

'No problem.'

Curious, she headed down to Acorn Ward, the double doors opening for her thanks to the nurse, and instantly spotted Ash sat on the end of the bed of a young girl.

Here in Acorn, the walls were painted brightly. The hospital had had some young artist come in and paint a woodland mural filled with rabbits and squirrels and deer. The trees held birds, and the painted sky was blue and cloudless.

She came to stand behind Ash. The little girl in the bed looked up at her, causing Ash to turn around to see whom she was looking at.

'Hey! Lenore? This is my good friend, Serena.'

'Hi,' said Lenore.

'Hello! Who's this?' asked Serena, pointing at the bear Lenore was holding.

'Sooty.'

'He's a very handsome bear!' she said.

Ash turned to her. 'Lenore is in hospital today because we are hoping to make her back all better.'

'Fabulous!'

'Her mum was able to drop her off, but she couldn't take any time off work, so I'm hoping to fix her back. I've told Lenore that someone from physio would help her to get strong again afterwards.'

The little girl looked so small in the bed and so alone, clutching Sooty like he was her lifeline. Looking up at Serena with fear and apprehension.

Serena stepped forward, crouching down at the side of the bed. 'How old are you, sweetheart?'

'Five.'

'Five? You're being very brave, you know.'

Lenore nodded. 'Sooty helps me.'

'He does? That's good. Well, we are all here to make you better. If you need anything, everyone here will do whatever they can to help you. Do you like ice cream?'

Lenore nodded.

Serena smiled. 'Well, when Ash has fixed your back, you make sure you ask for ice cream, okay? You deserve it!'

Lenore nodded and smiled shyly.

She and Ash left Lenore with a nurse who began to read her a story, and they headed out into the corridor.

'What surgery is she going to have?' she asked.

'She has scoliosis. It's begun to restrict her breathing, so we're going to be using titanium rods to straighten and fix her vertebrae.'

'Oh, okay. Big surgery for a little girl. And her mum had to leave?'

'Her work were threatening to fire her if she didn't turn up. Apparently they've not been the best employers when she's taken time off to look after her daughter.'

'Surely she could make an official complaint?'

'I think it's the only work she could get, and she doesn't want to do anything to annoy them. She needs the money.'

'Poor thing. She must have felt awful leaving Lenore behind.'

'She did, but I promised that we would look after her.' He glanced at her. 'I know you don't usually work up on the ward, but I'd like to ask you to make an exception here. You'd be perfect for her physio, especially as you've both met and made a connection. I've told her mum we can keep her in for longer and get her physio done here, as there's no way her mum will be able to take her to appointments and miss work.'

'Of course! I'd love to help her, bless her. Poor little thing, all on her own. When does she go up to surgery?'

'In an hour.'

She checked her watch. 'When will her surgery be over?'

'Mid-afternoon?'

'Okay. I have patients only till three. I'll pop up afterwards and see if you're both out of theatre.'

'Thanks. I appreciate that.'

She loved his smile. It was so much better than his frown, which he wore a lot lately, and she knew she'd been responsible for that frown. She much preferred making him smile. It warmed her heart. 'By the way, I brought you something.'

'Oh?'

She pulled the teddy they'd bought at the baby store from the small bag she'd been holding and passed it to him. 'A good luck charm. I thought you could take care of it until it was needed. I want their daddy to give it to them, whoever they may be.'

He took the bear from her and held it to his chest. 'I'll guard it with my heart.'

Serena smiled. And she would try to guard him with hers.

CHAPTER SEVEN

ASH LOVED WORKING on paediatric patients, but Lenore, at five, with her long, dark hair and large brown eyes, simply reminded him that Laila, if she'd lived, would be her age now and maybe even look a little like her.

It made him sad, this visible reminder of what he had lost. Of what Laila could have been. A little girl now, going to school, making friends, learning about the world and away from her parents for the first time.

He should have art on his fridge right now. Stuck in pride of place with fridge magnets. He should be reading bedtime stories and arguing over bath-time and listening to her chuckles as she splashed too much. Should be tucking his daughter into bed and passing her a favourite teddy and telling her he loved her and would see her in the morning.

I shouldn't be torturing myself with these thoughts.

Perhaps he and Nina should never have named their child. Because giving her a name had made her into a proper person. A person whom he had never met and yet loved deeply. He'd dreamed of a future for her but would never get to hear her laugh or see her smile or feel her arms around his necks. And she'd never had the chance to know his love for her. Maybe that was why he kept his love so tightly wrapped up inside and hidden behind barriers of protection?

And yet…they'd needed a name for their hope.

Laila.

Laila Sahana Dhillon.

She'd been beautiful. Perfect. Which was probably why it was so hard to accept that she'd died. He'd held his daughter briefly, his heart swelling with love for her, even though her eyes would never open and see him. Never know that it was her daddy holding her. He'd kissed her forehead. Once. Twice. Cradling her, soaking in every aspect of her face.

She'd felt so fragile. So small. So precious. And had simply looked like she was sleeping. He'd been able to pretend, for just a short while, that that was all she was doing. But she would never wake. He would never hear her cry. Never hear her voice.

He'd passed her back to Nina. Eventually the midwives had come to take her away, and that moment had been the ultimate death knell for his marriage. Nina had sobbed desperately as Laila was taken from her arms. He'd been so grief-stricken himself, he'd simply slid down the wall and crouched in a corner and cried.

Laila had been their hope to pull together two people who had begun to grow apart. Without her there, he'd felt unable to reach his wife and comfort her. Nina's walls went up. When he did try to be there for her much too late, she simply pushed him away. After that whole reaction to him packing up the nursery so she didn't have to deal with it, he'd returned to work with a fervor, trying to fill the hole that was in his heart. Why try to love when it was always taken away from you?

The divorce had simply been a mercy for both of them. He'd needed a new start, and he'd come to York, leaving his old life behind.

But there were times like these with Lenore that reminded him of what could have been.

He held the teddy that Serena and he had bought and stared at it.

Would they ever get to put it in a crib?

Would their child one day hold it and cradle it like a loved one?

Would she refuse to be separated from it or be unable to sleep without it? Cry if she didn't have it?

He hoped so.

He would give anything to experience a difficult night getting his child to sleep. He would give anything to feel them bounce onto his bed in the morning looking for morning snuggles.

He would give anything to get his second chance at happiness.

He held Lenore's hand as she went under anaesthetic as he didn't want her to be scared and felt it slacken and release as the medication took her under. The anaesthetist did her job in getting her hooked up to the ventilator and ensuring she was stable before he went to scrub. When he was done, he double-checked her ID and had one last final look at her X-rays and scans, showing the way the scoliosis had curved Lenore's spine in an unnatural S shape, creating constriction on her lungs' ability to inflate properly. The poor little girl had had years of wearing a cast and had caught chest infections. She had once been admitted for pneumonia and Covid.

'Thank you, everyone. Let's begin,' he said. 'Scalpel.'

He was going to use growing rods, which only required small incisions in the back. They were the best bet for a child under the age of ten whose scoliosis was severe and preventing their natural growth. First he needed to place two rods either side of the spine, attaching them both above and below the curvature. These rods would be lengthened at periodic time intervals to keep up with Lenore's natural growth. The hope was that in time, when Lenore's spine stopped growing, she could have them removed or replaced with longer rods.

He'd gone through the risks with Lenore's mum. Making sure she understood the implications of the surgery. Risk of infection from the surgery itself. Risk of damage to the spinal cord, which could cause all sorts of complications. Also, of course, the risk that the surgery itself might not be successful.

'How many of these surgeries haven't worked?' she'd asked.

'I've seen one in which the spine curvature was stronger than the rods,' he'd admitted. 'But I've done hundreds of these surgeries, so please bear that in mind.'

Lenore's mum had taken some time to think about it and decided to take the risk. He'd admired her bravery. Making a decision like that to put your own child under the knife was not one that was taken lightly. And as he sliced into Lenore's skin with his sharp blade, he hoped and prayed that if this baby he was having with Serena ever needed surgery, he would have the strength to give the doctors permission to do the same.

Lenore had a right thoracic curve and a left lumbar curve. He began to place the rods along the vertebrae.

It was a minimally invasive surgery, and when he was done, they did post-surgical X-rays to check that everything looked good. The paediatric team checked her lung fields and was happy, and so Lenore was eventually sent to recovery with a paedriatric nurse to sit by her side as she came round from the anaesthetic. When he came out of theatre, Serena was waiting for him. 'How did it go?'

'As well as could be expected,' he said with relief. Any surgery was risky, but operating on a child came with its own set of emotions, and he was always greatly relieved when these surgeries went well.

'That's great! Congratulations.'

He sighed. 'All the hard work is on her now. If you could work on strengthening her core and giving her post-surgical exercises, then she should do great. I'm going to call her mum, give her the good news.'

'Okay. Wanna meet for a drink in the café after to celebrate?'

He wanted to pull her towards him. To hold her. To feel his stress dissipate with her touch. 'I'd love that.'

She bought him a coffee and a pastry in case he was hungry. When he slid into the booth opposite her, looking tired yet happy, she had to resist the urge to lean forward and cradle his face in her hand.

He was a good man. And he cared, deeply, about his patients. She could see that. The way he'd been with Lenore?

'You're going to be a great father, you know?'

He looked at her and smiled. 'I hope so.'

'Is it more difficult to operate on children?'

'Oh, yes! I mean, you try, as a surgeon, to treat every

patient on your table the same way, but when you know that it's a child, there's just that extra fear. That need to go the extra mile.'

'I get that. I feel it too. Wanting to make sure you fix them properly so that their lives are pain-free as much as they can be. Giving them the tools to live a healthy life.'

'Do you think parents ever stop worrying about their kids? Even when they're grown up?'

She laughed. 'No! My mum doesn't. She's always ringing to check on me. What about yours?'

'Mine are the same. My dad is very much focused on me doing well in my career, and my mum is always asking if I'm eating properly and getting enough rest.'

'They sound lovely.'

'They are.'

'Well, hopefully, one day I'll get to meet them.'

He nodded.

She doubted then. Was he *really* going to let her meet them? He didn't seem sure whenever she mentioned it. Did they really have a lot going on in their lives, like he'd said? Or was it more to do with the fact that she and Ash were not in a proper, established, legal relationship? Sometimes the older generation had different ideas. Perhaps Ash was trying to protect her from that.

'How are you feeling, anyway?' he asked.

'Good. Some of the nausea is getting easier to cope with. I was able to eat my lunch today without worrying it was going to come back up.'

He smiled. 'Good. And there's been no more bleeding?'

'No. Listen, I'd like to cook you dinner. Treat you, look after you, the way you've been taking care of me.

What do you think?' And maybe they could have another heart-to-heart?

'You don't have to do that. You're meant to be resting when you can.'

'I'd have to cook for me anyway. Why not cook for two?'

He smiled at her warmly, his smile going right to her heart. 'I'd like that. Thank you.' She saw him glance at her hand on the table as if he wanted to reach out and take it. But didn't.

'Tonight?' she asked.

Ash nodded. 'Tonight. It's a date.'

She blushed. Suddenly feeling all excited.

The vegetables were in a steamer, two pieces of salmon were being cooked en croûte with spinach in a puff pastry casing, and she had a sauce on the go and wine chilling in the fridge. For him, of course. She was sipping at orange juice when there was a knock on her door.

He's here!

Serena hurried to the door, giving herself one last final look-over in the mirror. She'd decided to make a bit of an effort, after all, and since New Year's Eve, he'd not seen her dressed up, with her hair done and some make-up to make her feel special. She wanted to show him that she was trying here. That he was more to her than just the father of her baby. He was her friend, if nothing else, and maybe one day, if they were both brave enough, something more?

It is possible, isn't it? I mean, there has to be an attraction there. It's why we got together in the first place!

When she opened the door, Ash stood there in a dark

shirt and jeans, holding a bunch of flowers in a bouquet. 'For you.' He passed them towards her, and she accepted them as he stepped in and dropped a kiss upon her cheek.

Tingles of delight shivered across her skin at his lips upon her once again. She blushed, closing the door behind her.

'Something smells good.'

'I hope so. It's salmon. Is that okay?'

'It's perfect.'

'I'd better find a vase for these. Come with me into the kitchen.' She led the way, placing the flowers into water and then turning to offer him a drink. He accepted an orange juice, same as her.

'I'm not having wine until you can have wine,' he said.

That was sweet. 'Take a seat.'

'Is there nothing I can help you with?'

'Nope, it's all done.' She wanted him to be relaxed. She wanted to treat him. There were things she wanted to talk to him about, and she wanted to show him that she was making an effort with him. Not just taking him for granted.

She served up the salmon en croûte, and they enjoyed a pleasant evening just chatting about general things. Then, when she served up their dessert, a passion fruit soufflé, she decided that now was the time to talk about what was on her mind.

'I want to be honest with you, Ash. I did have an ulterior motive in asking you here tonight.' Her nerves tingled in her stomach. It had been difficult to eat, too, because of it.

'Oh, I get it. You want me to do the washing up, don't you?' He smiled.

She laughed. 'Well, that might be nice, but no. Not that.' She paused, taking a deep breath as she assembled her thoughts. 'It's about me and you. Specifically me and you and the future.'

'Okay.' He put down his spoon and listened, and that was what she liked about him. He never just listened to her as if he was only ever giving her half his attention. He fully focused, like she was important. Which was good, because she wanted to be important to him.

'I like you, and I know we're in this situation together because of the baby, but even if I weren't pregnant, I would still like you. Very much indeed.'

He smiled, eyes gleaming in the candlelight of the kitchen. 'I like you.'

She smiled. 'Good. It's just... I know we've talked a little bit about the baby and everything, but we haven't really spoken about what *we're* going to do if we make it through the full nine months and beyond the birth.'

'How do you mean?'

'Well, have you thought about it? How we'd actually parent this baby together?' Because she had. She'd thought about it quite a lot. Mostly when she was trying to get to sleep at night. When she allowed herself to be hopeful. She'd been trying to keep things platonic between them, but it was getting more and more difficult for her to ignore her needs and desires when it came to herself and Ash. She liked to think that they could one day be something more.

'Maybe a little.' He looked serious. 'I guess I'm more focused on just getting through the pregnancy right now. Taking it one step at a time.'

Serena nodded. 'I get that. It's just... I feel a little in

limbo here. The pregnancy is uncertain. The future is uncertain. You and I are uncertain.'

'I thought we were okay?'

'We are! I'd like to think of you as a very good friend now, as well as a colleague, but one day, hopefully, you're going to be dad and I'm going to be mum, and I don't want to feel alone doing that. Having you call me to book a time to come over and see your child.'

He tilted his head. 'You won't be alone. You'll have me.'

'But in what capacity?' She sighed and shook her head. 'Let me start again. I like you, and I have feelings for you. Strong feelings, like I say, that would still be there even if it weren't for the baby. I guess I just want to say that…' She blushed. 'I'd be happy for us to be *more than friends*, if that was what you wanted too.' It was scary to put it out there. To say what she wanted. What she needed.

But she'd said it. It was out there. Part of her hoped that the thing he'd been holding back from her was his feelings, too. That he'd been so entrenched in being this single guy who didn't date, he didn't know how to get himself out of the lane he'd carved for himself. That he didn't want to lose face by admitting his feelings for her and having her turn him down. So she'd said them instead. Even though she could have gotten this whole thing wrong.

'Wow.'

'If you don't feel the same way, then that's fine. We can carry on as friends, and I promise you I'll never try to rip your clothes off…' She laughed nervously. 'But I think honesty is important, and I just wanted you to know.'

It felt incredibly scary to make herself this vulnerable. To put this offer out there and not know how it might be received.

'I'd be lying if I said I haven't thought about it,' he said. 'What red-blooded guy wouldn't? You're intelligent and kind, warm and funny, and let's not forget, extraordinarily beautiful. There is an attraction between us, or this situation would never have happened.' He reached out and took her hand in his, stroking the back with his thumb.

She sensed a but.

'But it's such a risk, isn't it? I mean, what we have right now, we're both dedicated to doing right by this baby. We work together. We're friends... If we add *romance* to that equation, it might be perfect for a while, but what about when things get tough? What if we fall out? I'm committed to this baby and to you, and I don't want to lose either of you by taking a risk on trying for something more.'

Serena nodded. 'I guess that's a reasonable worry. But who's to say it would go badly?'

'Who's to say it would stay good? I really do like you, Serena, and god, yes, I have many flights of fantasy sometimes about what could potentially happen between us. But with the pregnancy so uncertain still and all the complications and upset that would go with it if things went wrong... I don't want to lose you over any of that by not being good enough.' He squeezed her fingers tightly then, stared down at their entwined hands and looking scared.

'You've said that before. That you weren't enough. That you weren't a good partner, and maybe you weren't with someone else. Maybe with that person, they weren't truly meant for you and it would never have worked, no matter what it was that broke you apart. But who's to say it wouldn't work with me?'

'I understand what you're saying, and you're probably right, but I was hurt so much by that relationship breakdown, and we never talk anymore. We're apart. Estranged. And I don't ever want to be in that situation with you. So if it's okay, for now at least, I'd just like to be your friend. Maybe, just maybe, if you still feel the same, then we can revisit this after the baby is born?'

She nodded, biting down on her bottom lip to try and stop the tears she could feel forming behind her eyes. She'd been stupid to even suggest it! Clearly everything hinged for him on this baby being born first. Everything else? He would make wait. Allowing himself to be closer to her. Allowing himself to have feelings for her. Meeting his parents. She tried to pull her spiraling thoughts back into line and remain strong. Keep face. 'Of course. That's sensible. I just thought I should raise it, you know?' But now she was fighting the urge to pull away. To regain face. To be nonchalant and pretend it wasn't all that important anyway and that she wasn't bothered. But she was.

'Of course. And I thank you for doing so. You're amazing.' He lifted her hand to his lips and kissed it.

She half laughed and hoped he didn't notice her glazed eyes. But he was still holding her hand. She pulled it free to push her spoon, with another embarrassed laugh, into her soufflé, so that she could try to eat her emotions.

Ash stood in Serena's bathroom and stared at himself in the mirror. He felt deflated. He felt...*horrible*. Turning her down like that? After all those times he'd dreamed of kissing her again? Of touching her skin? Imagining moments in which they might have shared their lives and been something more than what they already were? She'd been offering him everything he wanted and he'd said *no*? Asking her to wait? Was he crazy?

Hearing the words coming out of her mouth had been *everything*. To know that she thought more of him than he'd realized, to know that her feelings for him were growing too? He'd so desperately wanted to be brave and pull her to him and hold her and just say yes! A thousand times, yes!

But he knew that he couldn't. Because that would mean accepting his feelings for her were stronger than he wanted. If he allowed himself to be open and say yes, then he might fail her like he'd failed Nina. He'd not been there for her. He'd not worked at the relationship as he should have. And he didn't want to fail Serena at all right now, so maybe it was preferable that he think of what was best for the baby right now?

He needed to protect himself and his heart for this. He needed to keep up the barriers he'd established for just a little longer! He could wait. He was strong enough to do that, he knew. And he'd said that one day, they could both try for something more, on the understanding that if it didn't work out, they wouldn't cut the other person out of their lives. But would he risk that? Really? He had a shot at a second chance of fatherhood here, and he didn't want to lose it. Getting into a romantic relationship with Serena, even though it felt like something he wanted, was probably not going to be a good idea. Not yet, anyway. He couldn't risk it falling apart. He just couldn't. So to protect himself and her, he had said no. Not that she'd understand fully, but one day maybe she would. Hopefully, on that day, they would look back and laugh and say *do you remember that time I suggested we could be more than just friends?* And they'd laugh and laugh, and everything would be fine.

But if everything was fine, why was he hiding out in her bathroom, feeling terrible that he'd made a mistake?

'Stupid. Stupid,' he muttered before running the taps and washing his hands.

It had been a little awkward as they'd eaten dessert. And it had been an amazing soufflé, yet he'd not been able to fully enjoy it. He'd told her it tasted wonderful, and she'd smiled and thanked him, but then she'd gotten up and started rinsing plates. He'd helped her clean up the kitchen, but they'd mostly worked in silence until he'd noticed her surreptitiously checking the time. And so he'd said he'd go but asked to use the bathroom first, and here he was.

He didn't want the evening to end like this! It had started so well. He'd been blown away when she'd opened that front door and let him in. She'd been wearing a dress, a lovely wraparound blue dress that emphasized her shape and curves. When he'd leaned in to say hi and kiss her on the cheek? He'd almost pulled her in close to inhale her perfume and nuzzle her skin and just *hold* her.

But he'd stopped himself from doing that, too. Why was he torturing himself like this? Was he punishing himself for everything that happened with Nina by not letting himself have happiness with Serena?

She'd been so kind, so warm, in opening up to him

like that. She'd made herself vulnerable, and damn, if that didn't show him her strength, then what did? Serena had taken a chance in telling him how she felt, not knowing if he would reciprocate. And he'd blown it. Like a dummy.

Ash let out a breath, straightened his clothes and gave himself one last look in the mirror. He would put this right. Trepidation be damned.

With a bright smile, he headed out of the bathroom and down the stairs. He found her in the kitchen, wiping surfaces that were already clean. 'I'd better be off. Let you get some rest.'

'Oh. Okay.' She turned and smiled at him.

'Thank you for a wonderful evening.'

'My pleasure.'

'I mean it. I treasured every moment.' He took a step towards her until they were inches apart and then leaned in to place a soft kiss on her cheek. And whilst he was there, whilst he had his lips next to her ear, he said, 'You mean more to me than almost anything. Please just wait.'

He pulled back to look her in the eyes so she would be able to see the sincerity in his words. Because she did mean more to him than almost anything. She was everything. She'd been in his thoughts almost constantly since New Year's Eve. And he never wanted to hurt her. In no way did he ever want to be the reason for her pain.

But this close to her beautiful eyes? Her sensuous lips? Her perfume still making him dizzy with desire? He felt an urge and an irresistible pull that he simply could not resist. He'd coped before because they'd always kept a respectable distance, but this close again? After such high emotion? He wanted to comfort her. To make her feel better. And the need within him to feel her touch on his skin again?

Her lips parted as she gazed at his eyes and then his mouth.

She wanted his kiss. She wanted more. And hadn't he denied himself enough? Would it hurt *just to kiss her*? Would it muddy the message? Surely a simple kiss would be enough. A kiss to imply a *future promise*. A kiss to satisfy this deep, burning desire that was filling him.

And so he leaned in. Slowly. Tentatively.

And his lips met hers.

And once they did? All the self-control that he thought he had disappeared in an instant.

He's kissing me!

Serena was surprised. Startled, actually. They'd talked, and she'd thought there wasn't a hope of them having a relationship together, at least not yet. Not until after the baby was born, he'd said. Even then, it would be something to discuss.

It had felt like a brush-off, because who knew how either of them would feel by then? They could have met someone else in the meantime! Though obviously she'd thought that would apply to Ash and not her, because who would want to get involved with a woman who was already pregnant with another man's child? She'd felt like she was being left behind again. Like she was being abandoned again, even though she knew he wasn't actually doing that.

And he'd tried to be kind about it! That was what made it so heartbreaking. He'd not wanted to hurt her.

He'd said, plainly, that he'd thought about them being together but wanted to hold off from anything like that.

And yet…

With his body pressed against hers and his lips on hers…she felt dizzy. This was emotional whiplash and she was stunned, yet also hungry for him in a way that she'd never thought she could be. And she wanted to soak up every possible moment with him in case he suddenly changed his mind again. She wanted to devour him.

Maybe it was all hormones pulling her strings right now, but she wanted him. Wanted to wrap herself all around him, envelop him, absorb every inch of him and never let go.

'Ash? Are you certain?' she breathed. She didn't want him to regret this. She didn't want him to lose control and for this to go badly and then for work to be all weird after.

'God, yes!' he replied, his hot breath against her neck as his hands began to explore her. As much as she wanted this with him, she most certainly did not want it on a velvet booth in a bar's storeroom like it had been before. There was a much comfier and spacious bedroom upstairs.

'Then let's do this right,' she said, taking his hand and pulling him upstairs, her heart pounding, every inch of her skin tingling in anticipation and excitement.

She was going to give him a night to remember.

She was going to make him reconsider.

And when they got inside the bedroom, she kicked the door shut before they fell into bed, pulling and ripping at each other's clothes, desperate to find skin. To touch. Thrill.

Explore.

* * *

She woke to see Ash's head on the pillow next to hers, and she smiled contentedly. She'd hoped that he would stay. That he wouldn't wake at some point in the night and disappear because he felt guilty or whatever. The fact that he'd stayed was good, right?

Because it felt good to her. Last night had been incredible! Everything she could have dreamed it would be. New Year's Eve sex in that storeroom with Ash had been outstanding, but getting intimate with him in a soft, comfy bed, with no time limit and no worry about anyone walking in on them, had been so much better! They'd been able to get into their rhythms. Be playful. Take their time. Tease. Laugh. Gasp in delight.

Ash had been tender and also ravenous. There'd been moments in which it had seemed like he just couldn't get enough of her, marvelling at her new curves, cradling the gentle swell of her abdomen. In turn, she had had to make herself slow down. She'd wanted him so badly! But making herself explore his body to find out what he liked sexually had been a joy, and when they'd finally come together at the end? They had cuddled and spooned and talked. Around midnight they'd gone for round two and done it quickly, hungrily, before falling asleep in each other's arms.

But what did this all mean? Because yesterday at dinner, he'd said he didn't think they should get into a romantic relationship. She knew sex wasn't a relationship, but it had to mean something, right?

She hoped that it meant he'd changed his mind. That from this point onwards, they could move forwards together as a proper couple and give it a try. Why shouldn't they? Her whole reason for not dating was her severe endometriosis. She'd thought that no one would want to be with her because she wouldn't be able to give them a child. Yet here she was, pregnant with his baby, so her entire reason was out of the window!

Ash was amazing. She knew in her heart they could be amazing together. Last night had shown they were compatible.

He stirred briefly, and she admired the musculature of his chest, his beautiful dark skin against the white of her sheets. His hair black, like a crow.

She couldn't wait to be wrapped in his arms again, so she moved forward, lifting the duvet to shuffle closer to him. His brown eyes opened, blinking softly as he realized he wasn't at home, and then they landed upon her. 'I must have fallen asleep. I'm sorry,' he said, pulling himself into a sitting position and ruffling his hair. 'What time is it?' He glanced over at the bedside clock. 'We'll be late for work.' And he swung his legs out of bed and pulled on his boxers that were within reach. He turned to look at her. 'Mind if I use your bathroom?'

'No.' She watched him disappear from her room, and then she heard the shower turn on.

Was he not going to say anything about what an amazing night it had been? Perhaps he just wasn't a morning person? That had to be it. Not everyone was. He would no doubt say something when he got out of the shower.

She turned and nibbled on a ginger biscuit, as was her morning habit now, and then she got out of bed herself and decided to go and put the kettle on and make some toast and eggs. They had to have something to eat before work, especially after all the energy they'd expended last night.

Serena briefly considered joining him in the shower, because she needed to wash up, too, but figured she'd give him some space just in case. Joining him in the shower could be viewed as pushy, and he might not like it. Maybe she could get the chance again another time when she knew that he liked it.

So she made them both tea, buttered some toast for him, and put his boiled eggs in egg cups. She needed to wash up, too, but she nibbled at her toast first, taking small sips of tea as she listened to the strange noises that indicated someone else was in her home with her. The shower turning off, the shower door sliding open and closing again. The bathroom door opening and his footsteps heading towards her bedroom and pausing, no doubt to gather his discarded clothes from the night before. He cleared his throat and was quiet for a while before she started to hear his footsteps come down the stairs.

Her stomach felt nervous, the butterflies flying in full formation as he appeared in the doorway to the kitchen, dressed and ready for work.

She gave him her best smile. 'Hi. I've made you tea and toast, and there's some eggs there if you're hungry.' She wanted him to see that she cared for him. That though she still hungered for more of last night, she was able to take her time and show him she wanted to be there for him in other ways, too.

'Oh. That's very kind, thank you.' He settled into a seat opposite her, adding milk to his tea and stirring the cup before lifting his eyes to look at her. 'Last night was… amazing,' he said, shaking his head as if in disbelief.

She nodded and smiled. 'It was.' Last night had been the best night of her life so far, and she very much wanted it to continue.

He winked at her as he sipped at his tea, then took a huge bite of his toast. Clearly, he was hungry after last night! She felt wildly hungry, too. For the first time in ages, she actually wanted to eat breakfas, and didn't worry about it coming back up. And it was all to do with him. Lovely Ash.

'We should do it more often,' she said with a smile.

He smiled back. 'We certainly worked up an appetite! I'm starving.'

He hoped she didn't feel like he'd used her. He'd tried not to. Tried to put the brakes on when she'd asked about them being more than what they were. And he thought he'd managed that without hurting her feelings by being as honest as he could within his limits. Of course he'd not been able to tell her the real reason. He so desperately wanted to be with her! But if he was and then she lost this baby, and she found out about Laila after… she'd hate him for not telling her about it. For keeping something so monumental from her. This way, trying to keep her at arm's length, just as friends, had seemed the right thing to do.

Until he'd tried to kiss her goodbye, and then?

It had been so hard to not kiss her passionately. So difficult to hold back from doing what he'd so badly wanted to do for a long time. He'd just thrown caution to the wind, telling himself that the next day he'd clarify that it didn't mean anything, that it was just physical, that they'd both just scratched an itch. Maybe they'd scratch the itch on occasion, just to help them both get by until they could fully be together, but…

His words hadn't come out the way he'd planned them in the shower. Instead, he'd remained non-committal, afraid to say the words he knew might hurt her feelings.

Ash knew he could make this all go away by just saying, *screw it, let's be together.* Throw caution to the wind and roll with whatever happened to them.

But he was too scared to.

So instead, he voraciously ate his breakfast, filling his mouth with food and tea. There was never any time for her to ask him deeply personal questions. He cleared away the dishes and cleaned her kitchen whilst she went to shower so that they could just go to work together.

Start afresh. Start anew.

A brand new day.

They'd be adults about this.

She'd understand.

Eventually.

Right?

Kyle was doing great. He'd been working hard with his personal trainer at home, who'd been making sure that he stuck to his physio. This was the first time he'd come for his appointment beaming a smile, looking really happy and feeling much stronger and more confident as he showed her what he could do.

'My hand is so much better now, too. There's this really complicated guitar solo I have to do in the middle of my song "Lawless," and now I can do it. I can get the complicated chord changes, and it doesn't hurt. I've nailed the song the last three times in rehearsals, and I'm managing to play a two-hour set.'

'That's great, Kyle,' Serena said, really pleased with his progress. Sometimes all an outpatient needed was a clear goal, something to work towards. Then they would put in the time to get better.

'The leg's doing really well, too. It can still sometimes feel a little stiff to begin with, but once I get going, it's like I never had surgery at all.' He grinned at Ash behind her.

'Well, I think it's worth you continuing with your physio for a few more weeks, at least. Just to make sure you're fully limber and in good condition before your tour starts. Where's your first concert?'

'London. Then I go to Cardiff for a couple of nights. But about midway through the tour, I'm back here in York, and I'd like the two of you to have these. As sort of a thank-you.' And he passed her two VIP tickets to his concert.

'You don't have to give us these,' she said, passing one to Ash so he could see what they were. It felt good to imagine going to places with him. Like a proper couple. A couple with a hopeful future, after so long of being on her own.

'I do. In fact, I'd like to call you both on stage at the concert and thank you, if that's all right? I think my fans would love it. A couple of guys from the hospital board have been in touch, and they think it's a great idea, too! Getting to see the two people who got me back to fitness so I could complete my tour.'

On stage? She'd be heavily pregnant by then. She couldn't imagine standing on a stage in front of a roaring crowd, being cheered. Would she have to bow? 'Well, that's very kind. Thank you.'

'So, I'm good? Do I need to come back again?' he asked.

'I'm happy to say that this is our last session, as long as you continue with your physio at home. But if you feel you develop any issues, you can give us a ring, and we'll see you again. We keep your name on our books for six months after your last appointment, just in case.'

'Perfect. Well, it's been great knowing you guys.' He got up and gave her a tight hug before moving past her to hug Ash. 'Shame we had to meet at all, but that's showbiz.'

'Yes. You take care, Kyle.'

He gave them both a quick salute and strode away.

Serena turned to Ash, mock sad. 'That's it, then! You don't have to come down here anymore. We just have Lenore now, so I'll have to come up to you.'

He nodded. 'Will you be up later?'

'I'm coming to see her after lunch. How is she doing?'

'Not bad. She was feeling a little sick after the general anaesthetic, but we gave her something for that, and she seems a lot happier.'

That was good. 'Okay. I'll see you after lunch.' She smiled and watched him go before turning back to her computer with a happy sigh and typing in her notes for Kyle's appointment. Everything was looking rosy. For Kyle. For Lenore.

But most importantly, for her and Ash.

'Okay, Lenore, what we're going to do today is get you sitting up and moving from the bed to the chair. If you're feeling up to it, we'll go for a walk around the ward. How does that sound?'

Lenore looked up at Serena and Ash. 'Will it hurt?'

'Well, we've got you on painkillers, so hopefully not. But we'll go slowly and at your pace, okay?' Ash said, kneeling at the side of her bed.

Lenore had been lying flat since her surgery. She'd been too scared to move and had said she wouldn't try anything until Serena came. Her mother had visited late the previous night, but Lenore had still been feeling drowsy. The nurses were hoping to change Lenore's bed, so if they could get her up, it would be a win-win all around.

Lenore bit her lip, still holding her teddy, Sooty, in her arms.

Serena leaned in. 'Shall we show you how we're going to sit up with Sooty first?'

Ash thought that was a clever idea. He stayed quiet whilst Serena demonstrated the way they'd help Lenore sit, using the teddy as an example.

'Ready?'

Lenore nodded again.

'Okay, first you're going to roll onto your left side. Bend your right knee so your right foot is on the bed. That's it. What I'm going to do is take that leg and slowly roll you over onto your left. Ready?'

'I'm ready.'

Poor little Lenore was nervous, and Ash could perfectly understand why. But getting her up and moving after surgery was so beneficial to the patient.

'How was that?' Serena smiled.

'All right.'

'What we're going to do next is swing your legs over the side of the bed. At the same time, you're going to push yourself up on your arms and sit on the edge. We'll help you.'

'Okay.'

Serena was great with her. She would make a great mum. He could see that. And Lenore was such a sweet little thing. Tiny. Dainty. Like a strong wind would blow her over. But with her dark hair and large dark eyes, he couldn't help but see how his own daughter might have been, if she'd lived. His life would be so different. Maybe still married? If he wasn't, would he even have slept with Serena? Would she just be some physio he occasionally saw in the corridors? Would he be going home to Nina every night?

No. Probably not. Their marriage had been failing before Laila. They'd gotten married impulsively, without thinking it through, and maybe he'd just not been ready for a committed relationship like that. He'd failed her many times during their marriage, and she'd often felt second place to his job and his patients. It wasn't a sacrifice she'd been willing to put up with. Was that why he was doubting his ability to be fully committed to Serena?

'How's that feel? Any dizziness?' Serena asked now that Lenore was sat up on the edge of the bed.

He could see she looked better already. Her scoliosis had made her slump before, but now, in her back brace, she looked straighter, taller. Stronger.

'No.'

Ash passed her Sooty to hold, smiling at her as she

took it from him and gave the bear a cuddle. 'You're doing brilliantly,' he said, proud of her.

'We're going to stand now. I'll hold one hand, and Dr Dhillon will hold your other hand.'

Ash felt the little girl slip her tiny hand into his, and he was hit with a longing so strong for his own lost daughter that he had to fight back tears. If Laila had lived, how many times would he have taken her hand in his? To go for a walk? To go fly a kite? Collecting her from nursery? Such a simple thing, to just hold his daughter's hand and show her his love. He never got to show Laila how much he loved her. He never got to do the simple things with her. He'd imagined it. Reading to her at night-time from a favourite storybook. Having her sit on his lap or fall asleep on his chest. Pushing her on a swing and listening to her laughter. Would he get the chance with this baby in Serena's belly?

Lenore's hand seemed so small and fragile in his own larger one.

Hesitantly, she stood, and they both stood either side of her.

Ash looked across at Serena and smiled. Would this be what it might be like one day with their own child? Each holding their child's hand? Going for a walk, swinging their son or daughter between them?

We're going to be a family.

His yearning for a family was so strong now. His desire to fulfill that need within him that had died the day Laila died was back with a vengeance, and it was so overwhelming *he* was the one that felt dizzy, not Lenore.

'How do you feel?' Serena asked.

It's too much! he wanted to scream.

'Okay,' Lenore answered.

'Want to try and go for a little walk?'

Lenore nodded, and so they began to take steps. Small steps at first, slowing their own pace right down to match the small girl's.

She was doing so well! Ash felt a pride that he hadn't felt for a long time. He had done this for her. He had fixed her spine so that she could stand up straight again.

'Lift your head up. Don't look down at your feet. Try to imagine you're standing as tall as you can be,' Serena said.

Lenore straightened, lifting her head.

'Think we can make it to the nurse's desk and back?'

'Yes.'

And so they walked, all the time Serena coaching Lenore on her posture and not taking too large a step. They walked with her to the desk, waved a hello at Colleen, who sat behind it on the phone, and then turned and slowly made their way back to the chair beside Lenore's bed and settled her into it.

'Well done, Lenore! That was brilliant!' Ash said, feeling as proud as a father.

'I did it!'

'You did! Well done!' Serena beamed at her. 'That's enough for now, but I'm coming tomorrow morning, and we're going to do it again. If you're up for it, we'll walk a bit further?'

'Okay.' Lenore smiled, hugging Sooty.

Serena stood, and he went with her over to the nurse's desk.

'I'll email over some exercises the nurses can do with her whilst she's in bed if they want.'

'That's great. Thank you.' He appreciated the way they were dealing with their relationship. Serena seemed to understand the situation.

'Well, I'd better be going.'

'Sure. Erm, we're okay?' He needed to know. Needed that reassurance. Okay, so she didn't have all the facts, but he did, and one day she'd know and look back and realise.

Serena nodded. 'We're great, aren't we?'

He'd asked Nina once if they were okay when he knew that they weren't, and she'd said *fine*.

'Of course. Let me take you out to dinner.' There was no reason they shouldn't. It was just dinner.

'Are you looking to wine and dine me, Dr Dhillon?' she asked with a smile.

He laughed. 'We should spend time together. Know each other a bit more.'

She looked him up and down, smiling, nodding. 'Sounds great!'

'Tomorrow? I could book Lucio's?'

'Perfect.'

'About seven?'

'Sounds great. I'd better go before Cole wonders where I am.'

He watched her walk away. If only she knew how much he wanted to sweep her up into his arms! If only she knew how much he felt for her. How important it was that they kept their boundaries until after the baby was born.

That last night? Had just been physical.

CHAPTER EIGHT

LUCIO'S WAS A TINY yet perfect Italian restaurant, hidden away down a side street in the centre of York. Run by Lucio Rosetti himself, the restaurant prided itself on genuine Italian recipes that had been passed down the Rosetti line for decades.

Though small, the kitchen was open plan, so the diners could watch the chefs in the kitchen preparing their food as they chatted loudly in Italian or gestured passionately, discussing orders and who was doing what.

The round tables were covered in pure white linens and chrome salt and pepper shakers. Each table had a small glass bowl filled with water in which flower heads floated. Serena and Ash's table contained the head of a beautiful orange-yellow chrysanthemum that looked like the centre of the sun. The waiter pulled out her chair so she could sit down.

She glanced across the table at Ash. He looked tired, with darker circles beneath his eyes like he hadn't been sleeping. She knew the feeling. The last few nights, she'd lain awake wondering about their future. Imagining happy days for them both. Lying in bed together, maybe stroking her bump, waiting for kicks and then gasping with joy at each one. Him being by her side as she gave birth. The way he'd plant a kiss upon her lips afterwards and tell her how much he loved them both. Maybe one day planning a wedding? The possibilities for the two of them having such a deep connection were endless.

I mean, here we are, on this lovely date!

'This looks amazing.' Serena had not been here before, but Ash had, and he'd been the one to tell about the place. Apparently the food was really good, which was great because her appetite was beginning to thrive again. Her nausea was lessening, and she had begun to notice cravings—mostly for cheese. She was making sure to avoid any that were mould-ripened or unpasteurized.

'I'm glad you like it.'

It was an agony to sit opposite him when all she wanted to do was sit beside him. Maybe with her head upon his shoulder? Holding his hand? Pressing her lips to his? *Mmm. Maybe that will come later this evening!*

The waiter poured them both a water and presented them with menus to choose food and drinks. Serena chose a fruit juice and a pasta with a tomato and vegetable-based sauce, and Ash chose the Rosetti lasagna.

'It's good to get away from the hospital sometimes, isn't it?'

She nodded, noting that he seemed nervous.

'Lately, our personal lives seem to be just as entwined as our work lives. I think it's good to be away someplace different.'

'A break is always great,' she agreed.

The waiter arrived with their fruit juices.

She wondered why he was nervous. At how quickly their relationship had changed? Surely he could see that what they'd done had been a good thing, the way she did? That they'd created a firm foundation for themselves? Discovered that they were a good physical fit as well as an emotional one? They were having a baby together! They were going to be a family. They'd slept together! Why did he look like he had something to say?

'Are you okay?' she asked.

Surely he wasn't having second thoughts? They'd been so good together, and the other night had been the most wonderful night of her life!

'I am. But we, er…do need to talk.'

She felt a chill. A talk? 'What about? I thought we were good?'

Was he trying to keep her sweet? So that he could have the best of both worlds whilst she felt desperate for any scrap of affection he could give her? It wasn't a good feeling, being the person yearning for more. It made it feel like Ash had the power and the control, and her happiness was being yanked out of her own hands at the last minute.

She needed to take it back. Grab some self-respect. Barely containing her hurt, she decided to just ask. 'What do you want to talk about? This date?'

He frowned. 'It's not a date. It's just dinner between two friends.'

'Friends?' Her voice rose an octave higher than she'd meant it to. She leaned in. 'We had sex!' she hissed. 'Actually, no, it wasn't sex. We *made love*, and *friends* don't do that.'

'It was sex. Just a physical thing. An itch we both needed to scratch.'

She stared at him, horrified. Realised that all the hours she'd spent dreaming of a future with him were slowly spinning away down the drain. Clearly she'd read more into that night than he did. 'That's what you think we are? Friends?'

'Serena, I told you…that's all we can be. I've been consistent in telling you that I can't be in a relationship, and the other night was just an animal attraction. That's all.'

'All?' She felt sick. That was all she was to him?

Why was he always hiding? Putting up barriers? 'Why don't you trust me, Ash?'

He looked at her over his drink and settled it down upon the table. 'I do trust you.'

'You say you do, but you don't show it. I've exposed myself. I've told you how I want this relationship to be, but you hold yourself back and give nothing of your heart, despite the other night. Why is that? Why do I feel like I'm being left hanging? Given scraps to eat when you know I want more?'

He kept his voice low. 'It's never been my intention to make you feel that way. I want you to be happy.'

'I can't be if you're going to friend-zone me. What is it? Why won't you share your heart with me?' She could feel tears burning the backs of her eyes. Traitorous tears. She didn't want them showing right now. She didn't want her argument weakened by them. She didn't need him feeling sympathy or pity for her. She just wanted answers. Straight answers. That were given freely, not because he felt emotionally manipulated in any way. Which she wasn't doing. She just got that way when she had to be confrontational.

'We're having a baby. We've slept with each other more than once, and it has been amazing. We match. We're good. And I want to be with you, and you want to be with me, or so you say. Why wait until after the baby is born? What are we waiting for? Are we really so fragile that we'd fall apart if this baby didn't survive?'

Ash looked uncomfortable, but again, he was saved by the arrival of the waiter, this time with their food.

It looked delicious. Smelled divine. But Serena couldn't take a bite. She forced a polite smile for the waiter, who disappeared, then looked back at Ash.

She wanted an answer. A straight answer.

'I just think it would be better for both of us if we waited,' he said finally. Still not giving her what she wanted. *Needed.* It wasn't enough.

'Better for you, maybe.' She didn't want to sit here a moment longer. Not feeling the way she felt right then and there. What was the point of them spending this time together in a beautiful Italian restaurant if they weren't actually going out? It all just felt like a façade. Like they were acting. Pretending everything was all right when it wasn't!

So she got up, grabbed her coat and left.

It was frigid outside, and she could feel the tears on her cheeks freezing in the biting wind. But she raised her arm and hailed a taxi, and she was into its lovely warm interior before she knew it, glancing back at Lucio's as she drove away.

He never came out.

Maybe I'm just not worth chasing.

Ash sat in the restaurant, staring at Serena's empty seat. He'd hoped taking her out to dinner, to one of his favourite places, would show her that even though they needed to pull up on the reins, she was important to him. They'd have a nice dinner still. A nice evening. He'd hoped that they'd have pleasant conversations over the finest Italian pasta. Then he'd drive her home and share a sweet goodbye kiss with her on the doorstep, and that that would be enough for them both for a little while. But that was never going to happen now, either. Serena was not content with the tidbits of affection he was giving, hoping that she would wait for him to be ready.

How did protecting himself and his heart result in him getting hurt anyway? And her, too? He wanted to tell her about Laila and Nina, but how, without terrifying her completely? It scared the hell out of him, and what was it she'd said? *Are we really so fragile that we'd fall apart if this baby didn't survive?*

Yes. That was most definitely what he was afraid of. He'd been married, and his relationship had failed. He'd not been good enough for his wife. He and Serena were *not* married. There was nothing holding them together. They were not seriously committed to one another. They would be able to separate *so easily* if they lost this baby. Losing a baby *did* tear people apart. He'd been a victim of that already, and he couldn't go through it again. Holding himself apart was *protection*. Keeping her in the dark about it—*protection*. Already the ghosts of a pregnancy past were threatening to tear them apart.

He didn't want to lose her, though. Was that being selfish?

She was his everything.

And all he had to do was somehow make her realise that, whilst keeping them both safe from potential hurt.

She didn't want to see Ash. She was still angry. Still mad. Still frustrated with the situation between them, but Lenore was being discharged today, and she'd promised she would come and say goodbye. She told herself this would be the very last time she would come up to the ortho ward.

Serena hoped that Ash would be in surgery, or busy with a clinic, so that she could slip in and out without having to see him. But when she arrived in Acorn Ward, there he was by Lenore's bed, smiling at the little girl as she chuckled at something.

'Serena!' Lenore spotted her and waved happily. 'Mummy's here! I'm going home today!' There was a middle-aged woman sat next to Lenore's bed, holding her daughter's hand and smiling. She looked tired. Exhausted, but no doubt relieved that her daughter could go home.

She could find a smile and happiness for Lenore. The little girl was so sweet, incredibly cute, and if Serena were to have a daughter like Lenore? She'd be very happy indeed. 'I know! I've come up to say goodbye to you. Have you packed your things?'

'Mummy's going to do that in a minute, but Dr Ash has said we can go!'

She picked up the stuffed toy, trying not to even look at Ash, and wiggled the toy at the little girl. It hurt not to be able to speak to him. 'Don't forget Sooty.'

'I won't.'

'I have something for you, Lenore.' From behind his back, Ash produced a teddy bear that wore a T-shirt with the hospital's logo on it. 'This little guy is given to all girls and boys who come into hospital and are so brave, and I think he'd like to go home with you!'

Lenore's face lit up. She took the bear and gave it a

big squeeze before holding it back out in front of her to take a better look.

'What's his name going to be?' Ash asked.

'Cookie!'

'That's a great name!'

Serena could see that Ash was just so great with her. He was good with kids. If everything went well and they got back on good speaking terms, then maybe this could be them one day? Sitting with their child and talking to them about their toys and giving them names and playing with them? She hoped so. She so desperately hoped so!

Just looking at him, she could see he loved kids. He was down on Lenore's level and gazing at her like he was truly invested and interested in anything she had to say. Like her happiness was his utmost goal and *he* was happy because she was happy. He was most definitely going to make a great father to her baby.

'I'm glad that you're going home, but because I have a surgery soon, I won't be here when you go, so I have to say goodbye to you now. Is that okay?' Ash asked.

Lenore nodded and smiled. 'Thank you for looking after me and fixing my back.'

'You're very welcome.'

'Can I have a hug?'

Ash paused, glanced at Serena, then nodded. 'Of course.'

Lenore held out her arms, and Ash moved forward to give the little girl a hug as she'd requested. As Lenore's arms went around Ash's neck, Serena saw a strange look cross his face.

Lenore's mum must have spotted it too. 'You've been

so good with her. I knew I was leaving her in capable hands. You must be a father yourself?'

Ash let go of Lenore and stared at her mum. 'I, er...' He grimaced, turning it into a fake smile. But the other woman's words had truly affected him.

He stood and quickly made his excuses, looking pained. Serena watched, stunned, as Ash hurried away, and was he wiping his eyes? *What is that all about? There's something going on that I don't know. That he hasn't told me yet.* Why had that comment about being a father upset him so? He was *going to be* a father, if everything went well. Unless her words had upset him in another way. What had she said? *You must be a father yourself.* Was he? Did he perhaps have a secret family somewhere that she didn't know about? Surely he would have mentioned them?

'I'd better say goodbye too.' Serena gave Lenore a hug. 'You keep Cookie and Sooty safe, and remember to do your exercises at home, yes?'

Lenore nodded. 'I will.'

'I'll make sure she does,' her mother confirmed.

'You take care.'

Serena wanted to find Ash. See if he was all right. Seeing him upset like that had really torn at her own heart, and she needed to know that he was okay, despite the situation between them. Something wasn't right.

Maybe it's just kids? Maybe he has a soft spot for them? Maybe Lenore reminds him of someone? But who? Does he have a daughter that he doesn't see for some reason?

Serena had so many questions! And she wanted so many answers. But would she get satisfying explanations? Or would he brush off her concerns and keep those barriers up like he always did? Honestly, he was lucky that she was even bothering to check on him after Lucio's, but something about this told her it was important and might be the key to unlocking the truth about him. But if he brushed her off again, then that was it! There'd be no more between them.

She found him in his office, staring out of the window, looking out across York.

Serena had never been in his office before now, and she looked around it with wonder. Were there clues here to his reason for keeping her out? There was all the usual stuff you'd expect to find—a desk, computer, bookshelves, a replica of the human skeleton on a stand, various model joints. An ankle. An elbow. A shoulder. An entire spine. And a notice board with various health posters on it and some thank-you cards.

Some framed certificates. But no family pictures. If he had one somewhere, there'd be pictures. Surely?

'Are you all right?' she asked, frustrated by the lack of answers here, too.

Ash sighed and continued to look out of the window. 'Yeah.'

'Lenore…she's special to you, isn't she?'

'She's a great kid,' he said, non-committal.

'You were upset saying goodbye. You were upset at what her mother said. About you being a father already.'

He turned to look at her, and she could see that he'd fought hard to keep back the tears. 'Some patients affect you more than others.'

Yes. Yes they did. There were many patients over the years she had gotten to know. Gotten to see heal and grow better. Stronger. But you knew that you never got to see their whole story, or how it ended. You had to let them go.

Serena stepped forward into his office and walked over to the window so that she stood in front of him. 'Why won't you tell me how I can help you?' she asked softly. '*Let me in, Ash*. Don't make me beg.'

And he looked at her then, pain etched across his face with indecision. She could see in his dark brown eyes how he was weighing up what to say to her. Almost as if, even then, he was considering telling her only a partial truth and not the full extent of it.

She knew she had to make him see that she was serious. That this was their final chance to talk. After this, if she didn't get him to tell her what was bothering him, then it would all be over, because she couldn't carry on like this!

But the idea that it could all be over with him made her own tears appear. She didn't want to lose him! This could all be solved if he'd just talk to her! And so, without thinking, she stepped towards him and cradled his face in her hands and pulled him towards her for a kiss. She needed his kiss. Needed his touch, because if this was the last time she was going to experience it, she wanted it to be memorable.

And it had been too long since she'd felt him in her arms, too long since she'd felt that she truly mattered. She wanted to feel that way again. Like she was precious. Valued. Important.

Loved.

Did he love her? Would he ever love her? Because

she knew she felt that way about him, which was a cruel irony considering how their relationship was going!

Feeling him respond in her arms, hearing a small sob in his throat as he kissed her back was everything. It meant that she'd not been wrong. They did have something between them. She hadn't imagined every aspect of this or read too much into it. Ash wanted her too. The way he was kissing her back? Like she was the very air that he breathed? Like he couldn't get enough?

But then a thought entered her head. Insidiously, it crept quietly from the dark recesses of her logical brain and slowly began to make itself louder. It reminded her that the first time they'd slept together, they'd never intended it to be more than one night. The second time they'd slept together, after she'd given him her all and allowed herself to think that they would become a real committed relationship, Ash had told her it was nothing but scratching an itch. Both times, he'd stepped away after he got what he wanted, and wasn't she giving of herself again? Again he would step away, and she needed to be careful.

So she slowed the kiss. Ended it. Breathing hard, she stepped away from him. Defending herself by creating space before he could.

Ash gazed at her with glazed, hurt eyes and said, 'I was married.'

Serena frowned. Shocked. *Married?* Maybe she was on the right track then. There was a secret family.

'What?'

'I was married to a woman named Nina, and we had a child.'

A child! Serena took another step back. She knew it!

Perhaps she'd always known it. *Ash has a child?* 'In all this time of knowing me, you never thought to mention you had another family? How could you have kept this from me?' Serena cried, devastated that her growing, gnawing suspicion had actually been the truth.

This explained everything! Why he'd been holding back. He had a whole other family! Maybe that was why he didn't want her meeting his parents—in case they let it slip!

No wonder he'd kept a part of himself walled off. He'd been hiding a family. Now that whole scene with Lenore made sense. He'd said she reminded him of someone. It had to be his daughter. Maybe she was the same age? And he hadn't seen her in years, so she simply reminded him of all that he'd lost.

I've been such a fool!

She'd taken him at face value. Had assumed that Mr One Night Only was like that because he feared commitment. Boy was she right, but only in ways that she hadn't even begun to suspect.

He had a child, and he'd not thought to tell her that their own baby would have a half sibling? Why was life so damned complicated? Why couldn't she ever have simple happiness? She'd thought that maybe he was holding back something *small*. A molehill that he'd made a mountain of. That together, somehow, they would overcome it, and she would make him see everything was fine. But a daughter and a marriage weren't something small.

He tried to tell me, at the beginning, that he wasn't a good partner. I should have listened!

CHAPTER NINE

ASH TURNED TO his top drawer. He pulled it open, reached into the back and drew out a photograph. He stared at it for some time before looking up at her.

'I never intended to let anyone get close to me ever again. Not romantically. Not after what happened with my wife, Nina, and our daughter. Laila.' He passed the photo to her with a heavy sigh.

It was a picture of him holding his daughter, wrapped in a blanket. Ash was staring down hard at her. No, not *her*. Laila. Her name was Laila. A pretty name. Serena could imagine her, with dark hair and eyes like her father. She was beautiful, without a doubt. Was this why he was holding himself back? Because he could never love her the way he already loved his other family? The one he'd lost?

'I *was* married, like I said. I'm now divorced, and we're divorced because our daughter died, and…it was hard for us to connect after it. I wasn't there for her the way I should have been because I was so busy processing my own grief. I built walls around myself, keeping everyone out.'

Serena stared at him. His daughter had *died*? That was horrific! She shook her head in shock and dismay.

She'd gotten this wrong. So, so wrong! 'What happened?' Maybe she just needed to accept that his heart was damaged and would never be fixed? Maybe she should just accept that this was a journey she would be going on alone?

'She was stillborn.' He looked at her with fear in his eyes. 'And I didn't want to tell you about the loss because I didn't want to worry you. You were already at risk because of the endometriosis. I thought by withholding that truth, I'd stop you being even more scared. I could hold myself back so I wouldn't get too attached to you or the baby and therefore wouldn't get hurt again if this pregnancy didn't last.'

'That's why you wanted to wait,' she said softly, realizing her part in this. How she'd pushed for more. How she'd demanded more of him than he was able to give. Could he give it now? Now that she knew?

'I was so scared of going through that again. It's a pain like no other. There's no way to describe it. You can only feel it when it happens, and I wouldn't wish it on anyone. I barely survived it once. I felt like I let my wife down. Even now, I feel the guilt of it. Not being good enough. Or strong enough. She dealt with it alone, and I told myself not to do that to anyone else ever again.'

Serena had tears trickling down her cheeks, imagining his pain. The horror of it. That he'd had to go through it at all broke her heart. No wonder his face in the photo looked so distraught. 'You can't blame yourself, Ash. Working here in this hospital, we see families deal with loss all the time. How the families can break apart under the pressure of their grief. No one is to blame. Each person, each family will deal with it in their own unique way. Some pull together. Others are torn apart. It's no one's fault. Maybe one day, you and Nina will be able to talk about it, but…you can't keep living with the guilt or it will destroy you. You did your best. You did what you could, how you could, in that moment of time.' She slipped her hand into his. His skin was cold, but she felt him squeeze her hand back in gratitude. And the sadness that had been on his face, was it beginning to lift?

Now that she knew, she realized that she wanted to fight through this problem with him, *together*. He was too important for her or their baby to lose. They could be stronger together. Pulling together.

'You're amazing, you know?' he said. 'I don't deserve you.'

'You're wrong. I don't deserve *you*. I think you've been the strongest of the two of us, carrying this hurt alone. To think that you've been holding this pain inside all this time, and I never knew! I thought… I thought that you were trying to abandon me and… I kept telling you what *I* wanted and what *I* needed, and when I didn't get it, I immediately thought the worst of you.' She was appalled at herself. He'd simply been trying to protect her. Protect himself. She could see that now. And she? She'd been trying to not be left alone again.

'You've only ever asked to matter. There's nothing wrong in that.' He stroked her face, tenderness in every delicate touch.

'I could have been kinder. More considerate. More patient. I have faults. I'm not perfect, at all.'

'You're perfect for me.'

She felt her heart gladden. Swell with love for him.

'I'm not perfect, but we could both be imperfect together? No matter what happens with this baby? We could get through this together, you and I. Letting this moment unite us.'

Ash smiled and nodded. 'I'd like that very much.'

'Is it too early to tell you that I love you? Is that too scary? To let you know that I'd like to be loved in return?'

'No. That's not scary to me at all anymore. I love you, too.' He pulled her face towards his, and they kissed.

The sweetest kiss she'd ever had.

EPILOGUE

'MERRY CHRISTMAS!' SERENA WHISPERED into her husband's ear as they lay in bed together on Christmas morning.

She felt Ash stretch, and then he yawned and turned to face her, only to laugh and smile when he realized that their baby son, Aston, had made it into their bed during the night.

'Did he cry? I didn't hear him.'

'No.' Serena smiled, stroking her son's cherubic, sleeping face. 'I just wanted us all to wake up together on our very first Christmas morning.'

Ash leaned over to breathe his son in. 'Why do babies smell so good?'

'So that you make more?' She laughed.

'Well, it's never too early for that,' said Ash, raising a suggestive eyebrow.

'I agree, but your family are getting here in less than an hour, so I'm not sure we have the time.'

'Later then?'

'You can count on it.' She smiled, reluctantly getting out of bed and pulling on her gown.

It had been a whirlwind of a year. Ash had wanted them to be married before their baby's arrival, so they'd gotten married in a small ceremony mid-March. She'd given birth to Aston just a few months later. He'd come a little early at thirty-six weeks, but he'd been healthy and happy. He was such a good, easy baby, it had made Serena wonder if there were more of them in her and Ash's future. She hoped one day to give Aston a little sister or brother to play with.

They'd invited Nina to the wedding. It hadn't felt strange at all, and she was glad when Nina accepted, asking if she could bring her new husband. Serena and Ash offered to meet them both before the wedding. Serena thought Nina was great, and the best thing? Nina and her husband had had a child of their own, so both Ash and Nina had got their happy endings. Ash had spoken privately to Nina and apologized for how he'd withdrawn after Laila's death, but Nina had told him that he'd got nothing to apologise for. That everyone handled death differently, and that she'd withdrawn too. That she'd felt herself withdraw from Ash so much, he would never have been able to reach her if he had tried. It had been good for the two of them to finally talk. Afterwards, Serena had felt a huge weight had been lifted from Ash's shoulders.

As she brushed her teeth, got washed and dressed, Serena could not help but beam at how happy she was and how fantastic her life had become! She'd hoped for such happiness but had never thought herself capable of actually having it!

When the doorbell went, she carried the now awake Aston in her arms to the front door and welcomed in Ash's family. Hers were soon to arrive too. And as Christmas Day got busier and busier, louder and louder, as more guests and family arrived, she found herself sitting there with her son on her lap, marvelling at everyone, including her huge extended family, and how much everyone was loved.

It was chaos, with presents being unwrapped, Aston giggling and playing with wrapping paper rather than his toys, people talking and laughing and being full of Christmas cheer. Serena thought that one day, she and Ash just might get to add to their family.

In fact, she would suggest to him, much later that evening when they were alone again, that they start trying that very night.

Because she loved Ash and her son so much! They'd beaten the odds once. Why not try again?

Life was finally letting them both have the love and the family they'd been craving for far too long.

And Christmas was the perfect time for making wishes!

* * * * *

*If you missed the previous story in the
Royal York Hospital Christmas collection,
then check out*

Wedding Date with Dr. Petrides *by Kristine Lynn*

*And if you enjoyed this story, check out these other
great reads from Louisa Heaton*

One Night to Twin Miracle
The Surgeon's Relationship Ruse
Best Friend to Husband?

All available now!

MILLS & BOON®

Coming next month

A FAMILY MADE IN THE ER
Alison Roberts

Of course, that kiss shouldn't have happened.

The very last thing either Isla or Jake needed was another complication in their lives.

So, by tacit agreement, it seemed they were both going to choose to ignore it. They'd both been a bit stunned in its wake, so it was no surprise that they just left it hanging a little awkwardly in the air and had gone into their separate bedrooms and shut the doors. Arlo was awake early the next morning so they weren't going to say anything that he might overhear, and Jake got his wish to go and see the driftwood teepee before they drove back to town in time to go and look at houses for sale.

But now it was several days later and still nothing had been said. If Jake was still thinking about that kiss as much as Isla was, he was managing to hide it very well. Their interactions at work since then had been completely professional but now they were heading towards another weekend where Arlo wouldn't be at school, and he apparently wanted to stay with Isla and play on the beach with Ben and that would mean Jake would be there at least some of the time and...

… and maybe that was why Isla was becoming even more obsessed with that damn kiss.

Continue reading

A FAMILY MADE IN THE ER
Alison Roberts

Available next month
millsandboon.co.uk

COMING SOON!

We really hope you enjoyed reading this book.
If you're looking for more romance
be sure to head to the shops when
new books are available on

Thursday 15th January

To see which titles are coming soon, please visit
millsandboon.co.uk/nextmonth

MILLS & BOON

TWO BRAND NEW BOOKS FROM

Love Always

Be prepared to be swept away to incredible worldwide destinations along with our strong, relatable heroines and intensely desirable heroes.

OUT NOW

LET'S TALK

Romance

For exclusive extracts, competitions and special offers, find us online:

- **f** MillsandBoon
- **X** @MillsandBoon
- **O** @MillsandBoonUK
- **♪** @MillsandBoonUK

Get in touch on 01413 063 232